CW01424706

Published by Crai
Copyright © Crai

First published in 2021

Whilst place names, buildings and locations in this story may be real, the histories and facts may have been altered to suit the authors needs and should not be regarded as fact. All characters are a work of the author's imagination and any resemblance to persons living or dead is purely coincidental.

ISBN: 978-0-9557503-8-0
1st edition

Printed and bound by CPI Group (UK) Ltd, Croydon, CR0 4YY
Typeset by Lisa Jackson at Jackson Designs

All rights reserved. No part of this publication may be reproduced, stored in a retrieval system, or transmitted, in any form or by any means, electronic, mechanical, photocopying, recording or otherwise, without the prior permission of the author.

www.craigphoenix.co.uk

Cover photographs by Trudi Crumley
Cover artwork by Trudi Crumley

Acknowledgements

This book has taken a long time and a lot of research: especially understanding some of the aspects and history of cryonics. In my quest to write this book I have been lucky enough to be able to speak to many experts covering many technical subjects. If any of the facts are incorrect it is down to myself who may have manipulated them to the benefit of the story.

In no particular order I would like to thank the following people for their help.

Roger Breavington - A Detective who served in the force in the 60's

Nic - Who is a current serving Detective.

Dr Christian Hatt MBChB - Thank you for your anecdotes and time in answering my emails.

John G. Baust, PhD, FACC, FSC - UNESCO, Professor & Director, Institute of Biomedical Technology - Thank you taking time out to talk to me and point me in the right direction for further information.

Elaine Heckingbottom - Thank you for your valuable input, and spending many hours helping me edit this book. To be able to talk through passages.

Trudi Crumley - Once again thank you for your time and help.

There is also a bibliography of research books that I have bought, read and interpreted for my own needs.

Part 1

Chapter 1

1954 August

The *pinging* railway tracks warn of an oncoming train. It sends a rush of thoughts scurrying round my head; mixed up emotions of the tumultuous feelings I have for my twin sister, Sheila. *Our* Alsatian, Rex is another sign of the life I have been destined to live; one half of everything. I never seem to get something that is mine; solely mine.

"Come on, you pair, it's time to go." Father bellows.

He always shouts 'you pair'. Thirteen years I have been the left side of her right and I am sick of it. I want to be me! I want to be singular! I want the unshared attention. I want our friends to be my friends! I want it to be *my* dog! I've overheard them, many times, talking about me; me, discussing *my* bad behaviour – they believe I am to blame for the regular arguments we now have, I am the guilty one, I am the 'devil's child' (that's what they said). It just fuels the lies and the animosity I have towards my sister. They don't know what to do with me. *I* know! Get rid of her. Get rid of my bloody perfect shadow.

"You'd better not be playing near the railway tracks. I've told you a million bloody times before. Now get out here."

"I'm not." We say in unison.

I cringe as anger cascades through me.

Picking up a stick laying nearby, I throw it; then watch as in slow motion it arcs its way across the tracks beyond the flattened fence that once would have kept us out.

Caught in a strange euphoria I watch, helpless to the events I have set in motion. A heady mix of thoughts tumble through my mind as Rex bounds after the stick, pulling Sheila against her will. She doesn't have time to scream. I was always stronger, physically, and therefore told to hold the lead but I'd passed it to her. Was it on purpose? Did I pre-plan this?

Even with her agility she cannot stop what is happening.

Seconds pass like minutes as the moment comes with horrifying splendour: the *thwack,* as Sheila is struck by the train and sent flying; the yelps as Rex is dragged mercilessly along; the screeching of the train as it breaks; metal on metal.

My sister and Rex are now out of sight and in my head there is just silence. A joyous chorus of silence! My hands are shaking. I feel instant gratification before two strong arms sweep me up.

"Where's your sister?" comes the frantic question that drags me back into the real world. "Your sister?" This time the question is quieter as if he understands the horrifying reality.

Rex limps into view, whimpering, his tail between his legs, his collar and lead missing.

"Sheila?" Father's voice has lost its authority as he tentatively looks towards the railway tracks. I see the realisation strike him. He hugs me tighter and I feel for once that it is about me, just me.

Chapter 2

2002 July

"Speed dial office." Sam commanded, tapping the steering wheel, before continuing his duet with Sinatra.

"Simpson and Partners. How can I help?" The professional tones of Jasmine interlaced with Frank.

"Can I speak with Sam Talbot, if you please?" Sam tried his best Irish accent deciding to have a little fun. Jasmine usually fell for one of his routines; it was just a little banter to lighten the day.

"No, I am afraid he is out on business. Can I ask what it is regarding?"

"Well, I really needed to speak to him personally. Can you put me through?"

"Sorry, he is not in the …" Jasmine pauses. "Very funny. Hello, Sam. Your usual 0800 number busy?"

"No, just up to my credit limit. What can I say? It is lonely on the road." He smiled to himself. "You sound a bit tired; that husband of yours keeping you up?"

"No, just the little one. Started teething."

"I remember that." A memory of Edward, his son, snared him and he sighed. "It gets easier. How is Charlie finding it, having a little sister?"

"Jealous as hell. I hope that gets easier! Who can I put you through to?"

"Keith, please."

The naff interlude music kicked in as Sam reflected on his son; the sour memory never getting any easier; in fact the closer he got to retirement the more he lamented on never having grandchildren to kick around with. Turning sixty next year was frightening. Margaret and he had a few things planned, including their research project, but the thought of a grand-childless life bit at him – hard.

"Hi, Sam,"

3

"I have just been into Gardners Soft Drinks and they weren't ha ..."

"I know, I know. I have been trying to sort it out all day," Keith interrupted. "It seems Brazil got two containers mixed up, Gardners got the one destined for Tunstall drinks and ..." Beep. beep, beep.

"Keith? Keith? Bloody modern technology. Speed dial office." Sam arched his back, twisting it to ease the dull ache that settled at the base of his spine. He checked his mirrors.

"Simpson and ..."

"Hi, Jasmine. Can you put me through to Keith again I got cut ..." The phone cut out again.

Chapter 3

1954 October ⟨13⟩

The house has been strangely quiet this past month. I have been lavished with so much attention – even if their eyes show distrust; there is a kind of fear in them when they look at me. I wonder – do I need them? Could I despatch them as well? I haven't missed Sheila at all. I expected to. I expected to feel guilty; but I don't.

I have relived the moment of the impact again and again, the noise, the smell of the day, the way father hugged me so tight. The police had so many questions it was almost overwhelming, instead it added to playing my part perfectly – it came across as shock, I overheard them say it. Inside I am shocked, shocked that I'd carried it out. It makes me tingle inside, putting my teeth on edge, and nothing seems to satisfy that. I think back to other times over our, *my*, thirteen years when I had wished something bad to happen to Sheila, wishing that I had done it then.

At the funeral I watched her coffin being lowered into the ground. My older brother, believing it was his duty to comfort me, wouldn't stop trying to hug me; it felt suffocating. I couldn't stop imagining pushing him in the hole! I seem to have awoken something inside. A strange urge, that since then I find difficult to fight. I don't look at people the same way; I imagine them dying, watching their life expire before me, with me in control.

Chapter 4

2002 July

"Speed dial office."

Glancing in his mirror Sam eyed the white van, he'd just swept past, lurch erratically from behind a lorry. The driver was holding a can of drink in his left hand and trying to light a cigarette in the other ignoring the traffic around him. Now safely in front Sam smiled, contentedly, as he observed another car take evasive action.

A loud explosion brought Sam's attention rapidly to the road in front as a plume of thick grey smoke engulfed his car.

"Simpson and ..." Jasmine's sweet and sexy voice filled the car for the third time.

The smoke briefly cleared in time for Sam to see a mangle of cars stopped in front of him. Ramming the brake pedal down, he gritted his teeth as the car juddered as the anti-locking system kicked in. His grip tightened on the steering wheel, white knuckles showing, as the wall of broken vehicles loomed ever closer. Sam prepared for the impact only for it not to happen as the car stopped inches from the mess.

Sighing, he relaxed. Suddenly he heard an almighty screech of tyres, a quick glance in his mirror showed the lorry he'd not long passed jack-knife and within seconds his car was being swept along, its dark ominous shadow swallowing him as the car was forced towards the debris in front. The airbags exploded around him, his face feeling the full force as his thumbs broke. The thirty-ton trailer flipped and started to squash his car like a bug. Frozen in place, and with no time to react Sam heard the rear window shatter as the ear-splitting screech of metal filled the car, accompanying Frank's 'My Way'. The two rear passenger windows imploded. In slow motion the panels of the car crumpled like paper as the full weight of the trailer concertinaed Sam's car into the wall of metal in front, before landing on top, the trailers' load acting like ballast.

Sam, with little time to think, or even register any pain, mentally tried to fight the inevitable outcome. Death.

He expected his life to flash before him as the space around closed in but there was just excruciating pain and for the briefest nanosecond a feeling of light-headedness, although one memory flashed up like a beacon in his mind – his first encounter with Margaret.

Chapter 5

1960 February

Medical School Days
Student Union Bar

"I got you a couple of pints, Sam," Mike offered, slurring his words and pointing to an empty glass on the table, as Sam looked at him with envy, "but I drank them." He laughed at his own joke.

Nearly an hour late, Sam looked dejectedly at the empty glasses then around, the dreary wood-panelled open space of the student bar, which harked back to a gentleman's club, and didn't do anything to quell the grey half-light that was becoming the sludge of his college life. It was busy as usual, everyone looked as though they had no pressures. He slumped down on a seat.

"It's all right for you, you don't have to work to help pay for your education. I had this table of businessmen who wouldn't go. 'Another bottle of Champagne *my friend*.' They aren't trying to get an education. I'd bloody give'em Champagne laced with cyanide if I had it to hand. It's hard enough ..."

"Chill out, Sam. Sit down. I was about to get another round, just make sure you drink it this time." Mike stood up swaying uneasily before tripping over his chair. "I think I'm a bit bladdered." Sam steadied his friend, letting a long sigh massage his dampened spirits. He had been up late into the night for the last three nights trying to get his head round the nervous system, but the information would not stick. He loved the idea of a career in medicine, yet struggled to make any headway in understanding rudimentary subjects. If his results didn't improve, he knew he would get thrown out. His grades were dropping fast. It was surprising that he had survived the first year, with the amount they all had to take in swamping him. He put his head in his hands, trying to wipe away the mire that seemed to envelope him.

"Hello." The soft voice broke through the mêlée of the noisy student bar. He hadn't even noticed that Michael had been sitting with anyone. "I'm Margaret."

Sam perked up, bewitched. The deep-set hazel eyes glistened in the dim light giving her intense stare, enchantment; her straight waist-length free-flowing black hair and pale skin tone giving her a slightly ethereal appearance.

"You going to say hello or what?" her pleasant and unassuming voice was drawing him in already.

"Mmm, sorry, yes. Hello, I'm …"

"Sam." Margaret finished. "Mike said you and he are in the same class." Margaret drank in Sam's features; his mousy coloured hair and smaller than average ears; his brown effervescent eyes that shouted 'honesty'; his wispy top lip, softening his face, complimenting his small, almost petite frame.

"Yes. Although I don't know how long for?"

"Are you changing courses then? I didn't think they allowed that." Margaret crossed her legs and stared intently at Sam, confidently, putting him a little on edge.

"No. It's just that I don't think it will be long before I get asked to leave." He couldn't hide the depression from his voice as his dream of being a doctor faded.

"You been a bad boy then? Did you really poison someone? Tell us all the juicy goss'." She leant in, moving her Rum and Coke to one side, her interest obviously piqued.

He smirked at her sudden keenness.

"No, no murder, nothing so glamorous I'm afraid." Sam stopped, as immediately Margaret appeared to lose interest. She sat back and looked nonchalantly around the bar. "But maybe I should?" he added more exuberantly, knowing it sounded lame. There was something about Margaret that Sam could not resist, her lips enticing him to kiss them.

There was an awkward silence whilst Sam desperately tried to think of something to engage this young, attractive woman in conversation.

"So you studying medicine then?" Inside he cringed.

Margaret frowned. Sam wanted the world to swallow him; the day was going from bad to worse.

"Here we go." Mike placed three drinks on the table sloshing the contents around precariously as he fell into his seat. "Oh, yeah, Sam. I forgot to introduce you to one of the first years, Margaret, she's a friend of a friend, sort of."

"We've met," Sam answered wearily.

"You don't waste any time do you mate," Mike added playfully.

"Actually I think he fancies me. Whether he'll actually tell me or not … remains to be seen."

Sam flushed scarlet grabbing his pint for something to do, gulping at the contents trying to pretend that the conversation was not about his embarrassment.

"Go for it, Sam, I did."

Sam sprayed the contents of his drink over the table, making him even more embarrassed.

"Ask her out, I meant. It was those tits that did it for me. What do you think, mate?"

"He's a bit shy, your friend, Mike."

"I think he's having a bad day."

Margaret and Mike stared at Sam waiting for a response. After a moment or two, Sam found his confidence and jokingly added.

"Why don't we just forget the small talk; your place or mine?"

"I like him. Can I keep him?" Margaret clapped her hands together in mock gleefulness.

"He's all yours. Take him. Make him a man. This pussy cat is no good to me." Mike answered.

"Thanks." She smiled flirtingly at Sam as he looked from one to the other.

"Why do I feel that I've been party to something I know nothing about? Some preordained path."

"I don't know. Why do you? We can discuss it later if you want?" Margaret winked leaning into him and smiling demurely.

Sam laughed nervously. Margaret's sassiness and confidence was getting him unexpectedly aroused.

"Get a room you two. I came here to have pleasant conversation, not to play matchmaker."

"Obviously just your destiny, my dear." Margaret answered.

"What were you discussing before I arrived?" Sam sipped his pint, finding it even harder not to look at Margaret.

"We were discussing the likely success of transplanting organs from one person to another. There is a lot of research going into the field, and whilst history shows limited success, albeit of a primitive nature, with rejection being the big issue…" Margaret was interrupted by Sam.

"I would have thought that would be the least of the concerns." Margaret and Mike frowned profoundly. "Look…" Sam continued. "… unless you just happen to have another organ ready to be transplanted, the actual issue I foresee, is having a supply of useful organs on hand. It is all very well having the knowledge and expertise to do the operations, but think about the amount of useful organs that get buried every day. If they could be harvested and stored somewhere similar to what we do for research, yet keeping them in a useable state, then that would be an achievement which would make transplant surgery worth considering."

"Hello, is that human parts limited," Mike held his fingers up imitating a telephone. "I'd like to order two kidneys and liver please."

"Ha, ha, Mike. But the theory shows it could be just like your stepdad's spare car parts business."

"And do you have any theories on how suspending life can be achieved? After all that is what you are suggesting." Margaret leaned into Sam, her eyes studying his.

"Not yet, he can't tell his neurons from his synapses. Can you?"

Sam scowled at Mike. Whilst his knowledge was not the best, his physical surgical skills and ideas were sound. It was surprising to him that he couldn't grasp the rudimentaries.

"You're not funny, Mike." He turned towards Margaret. "I have ideas that have a little knowledge to back them up; however, at this stage I don't really have the time to look into it further." He paused. "What with my failing grades I am struggling to …"

"I'll help you. We'll soon get you whipped into shape." Margaret smiled suggestively.

"I would take that whipping if I were you." Mike added.

"Well, you're not me."

"No, you're right. I'm intelligent, good looking, suave, sophisticated, rich and funny." Mike bragged.

"Funny, definitely … not sure about the rest. I'll let you have rich as well." Margaret answered, then holding her breasts added "And these babies will never be yours, that's for sure."Then turning back to Sam. "So how about that whipping then?"

Sam's eyes widened in surprise unsure how to react.

Chapter 6

1955 February
Summerhouse

"So, you're the one that is using our summerhouse as your own!" I kneel down and extend my hand towards my neighbours' cat, backed up uneasily against the summerhouse wall; after being disturbed from his slumber. "Come here, Smudge; no need to be afraid."

Smudge is looking at me cautiously. With a little patience he eventually decides to re-settle on the box where he had been resident before I turned up, purring sweetly as I scratch his neck.

It has been a quiet few months and I still can't stop thinking about my sister and how perfect it all seems. They've put Rex down as Mother blamed him for it, we all had to say our goodbyes. His innocent eyes stared at everyone; questioning us. He must have sensed something was up as he was marched out of the house. He kept looking back, his tail between his legs.

I smiled: "Don't worry it will all be over soon." Father gave me a disdainful look.

If only he knew.

Inside there is a feeling that I want to know what it felt like as Sheila's life expired, feel that last breath in my bare hands. Stroking Smudge I can't help but wonder what it would be like to take his innocent life; feel his last heartbeat.

Smudge rolls over so I can stroke his belly. The purring is so loud for such a small cat; I can even feel his purr. My mind swims with how many ways I could kill him. I playfully look at the spade standing idly in the corner.

I have been looking at biology books recently in class and am fascinated by the internal workings of a body. It would have been nice to see Sheila's body … to see what a mess the train had made of her insides. She died instantly, apparently. Shame!

"Shall I take your life, Smudge? See what it feels like."

Chapter 7

2002 July

Sam's own screams filled his ears before abruptly stopping; aware that he was no longer being crushed, the road ahead clear, all pain – gone!

Confusion rallied his thoughts. Arms still outstretched as if gripping the steering wheel in desperation. He was no longer in the drivers' seat.

"Where am ...?" He suddenly noticed the driver. "Who are you? " confusion ransacking his thoughts. "What the hell? This is my car!" He pointed to the dent in the dashboard where a decking timber had shot forward under heavy breaking, once.

"Not quite." The driver broke his confusion.

Sam glared at him. Was this a dream? Had the whole day been a dream?

"What the hell is going on?" Sam flared, eyes fixed on the driver.

"Nice car this, I never got to drive one when I was alive."

Sam studied the car further, frowning in consternation. Frank was still playing on the stereo. His phone perched in its cradle.

"Who ... what? I ..."

"You're dead, Sam," the figure stated irreverently, staring ahead.

"No! No, I'm not. I was just ..."

"Yes. You were, but now you're not." The man turned to face him, his piercing blue eyes burning Sam. "I can put you back there if you want?" The man clicked his fingers.

Sam immediately felt searing pain rip through his body; every cracked bone screaming at him. He couldn't move. He couldn't breathe. He was dying.

A voice cut into his head. "Do you want to stay here?"

"No," he barely gasped.

Instantaneously he was back in the passenger seat. Panic surging through him as he tried to comprehend what was happening. Looking through the windscreen he could see they were travelling North instead of South on the M1, Sinatra crooning 'My Way.'

"I don't understand."

The man didn't answer.

Sam turned sharply in his seat and stared out of the rear window at the other carriageway; smoke billowing, creating a thick, black toxic fog around the scrap-yard of vehicles. As if on cue a clearing in the smoke exposed the flattened mess of a blue BMW; his blue BMW, squashed under the trailer that was about to be engulfed in flames.

"Who are you?"

Chapter 8

1955 July
Summerhouse

It has been a year since Sheila's death. Mother's still broken; Father is drinking more; neither speak to me much, they give me a wide birth – is that their distrust of me? My brother, James, is more interested in girls now so is hardly ever home. I am left to my own devices, thankfully.

I still can't placate the thoughts ... of death ... the image of my sister ... the satisfaction I felt. There is an irresistible pull to try it again, take another life. Would I get away with it? Twice? Or ... would it be too obvious? Do I care? The power!

The summerhouse has become my sanctuary – away from my parents' fighting. No one comes in here anymore, except Smudge and myself. I almost tried killing Smudge a couple of weeks ago; not sure why I didn't. Ian, next-door's son and owner of Smudge, had been quite nasty to me on the way home from school. I relented though ... again, not sure why – he deserves to find his beloved Smudge dead.

Talk of the devil.

"Hello, Smudge." He really has got a loud meow. He is quite comfortable with me picking him up now.

It is there again. That impulse. I've practised with my brother's old teds, grabbing their heads firmly and twisting sharply, one of the teds head came off in my hand as I had twisted with such force, perfection – I wanted there to be blood and that pulse of life, but there wasn't.

Smudge is purring away contentedly. I can feel it in our usual loving routine. Then almost as if I am playing with him I place my hand over his small head and twist sharply with all my might. I hear it clearly snap.

I relish the few seconds after as the body dies. That last heartbeat. There is a last twitch as though the body hasn't realised it is dead. It takes a few minutes but I feel the warmth dissipating. There is a whiff of bodily fluids as the muscles give up.

I am curious to see inside. The pictures in my biology books have only fuelled my imagination. I have my father's Stanley knife, bin bags and old newspapers.

Laying Smudge out on the paper with a bin bag underneath I cut along the stomach, there is blood as expected. Pulling the skin apart, I study the rib cage before delving in. The blood – my hands are covered in it; it is thick and silky to touch. I lose myself as my fingers drink in the details. It is a luxurious feeling and, biting my lip, I can feel a tingle growing inside. I wonder if Doctors feel the same thing when they operate, their hands in other people's bodies. Control. Power.

I have no idea how long I have been in here but suddenly I notice the sun has moved round and is now shining directly in to my eyes. Smudge has grown cold. I want to take a token prize, maybe an organ – but I have nowhere to store it, so resist the desire. I bag him up with little thought for what he was, my companion for a short while; only eager to dispose of the body, knowing Ian will miss poor Smudge. Serves him right for threatening to punch me if I didn't stop enticing his cat into my garden.

Chapter 9

2002 July

"Why don't you call me, Geoff, after all that is my name; well, the name of the person you knew who looked like this." He raised a hand. "Before you ask, and they normally do, don't worry about Margaret. She'll be more than taken care of … in time. It's you I'm here for." Geoff stated pointedly.

Sam sat restlessly trying to unravel his thoughts as the car gathered speed and the world whizzed past in a blur of merging colours. It was inconceivable to him that he was dead … and conscious of the fact.

The realisation that he wouldn't see his retirement and enjoy the chance to travel, prickled. Margaret and he had always said they would, explore fully the science of cryonics, continuing the project they had started at Medical School. Not that they had made any progress; even the science fraternity were still struggling with the conundrum of freezing then re-animating life.

That dream faded as Sam stared ahead consumed by desolation.

Chapter 10

1956 October

Summerhouse

"Hi, your dad said you were in here."

Turning sharply, I am shocked to see my friend Gary standing before me. He looks shocked; as I have my hand inside a rabbit. He used to be Sheila's and mine; now he is just my friend. Some friends have fallen by the wayside, favouring Sheila instead of me; they appeared to tolerate me for a while but quite frankly I found them childish and immature. Gary is more on my wavelength, sharing a fascination with anatomy – we have discussed becoming vets, or doctors, at some point.

"It's a rabbit. I found it in the woods." I indicate the back of the summerhouse where the woods lay. "He must have died recently and I was checking the accuracy of the books." I hear the nervousness in my voice, concerned what he might say. "They're not the same. The picture's are poor substitutes."

"Do your parents know?"

"No, stupid." My confidence is back.

"Wow, that is so cool!"

"Isn't it? Feel this, it's its kidney."

Gary takes the offered prize.

"It's still warm."

"I found it a few minutes ago, it must have just died."

We spend the next fifteen minutes, pulling organs this way and that before clearing up and heading out on our bikes to dump the body.

"That was awesome! I can't believe we just did that."

"I know."

"Where are we going to dump the body? Why didn't we just bury it?"

Racing along, we are high on the excitement and I am high that I have found someone to share it with.

"We can go to the wool mill on South Street. There's an old well there. That's where I put the last one."

"You've done it before!" Gary sounds incredulous.

Is he on my side?

"Yes, once. It was next doors cat. I killed it." As soon as the words are out I realise it is a mistake.

From then on his face shows shock and there is only silence as we ride. I cycle straight to the well and throw the bag down it; a few seconds later there is a splash. I turn and look at Gary who is staring at me as though I am a freak.

"Did you kill the rabbit?" The question is hard for him to ask.

I don't answer. I thought he understood that.

"You did, didn't you? How could you? You said a cat. You killed a cat as well?" He looks at me disgustedly. "You're sick. I'm telling my dad." He rides off slowly, leaving me standing flummoxed.

On impulse I cycle after him.

"Gary. Gary?"

"I'm not talking to you. You're twisted!" He has tears in his eyes.

I catch up to him and try to grab his arm. He twists, sending his handlebars in the same direction toppling him over. I fall the other way as his bikes crashes into mine.

"Gary, you can't tell! I won't let you!"

He doesn't respond. I get up and look at him. I had been unaware we ridden so close to the edge of a loading bay of the old disused factory; three feet below, Gary's body is pierced by two metal rods, blood is saturating his clothes. His eyes are staring up at me. He is alive.

I jump down beside him placing my hand on his torso. I feel his thick, warm blood on my hands, his faint heartbeat; suddenly I am lost in ecstasy. Slowly, I look at his face – his eyes are pleading with me but I can't help myself. I watch my friend fade away.

I feel his heart make its final beats, boom boom; boom … boom; boom … … boom; boom.

"Oi! What are you doing? You shouldn't be in here."

I can hear it but I am still wrapped up in my pleasure.

Chapter 11

2002 July

"You're not real. What are you?"

"I am called many things, Sam. How you want to refer to me is of no consequence. But know this, you *are* dead and must take this journey with me; there are things I need to show you." Sam opens his mouth as if to interrupt but Geoff raises his hand. "I do not judge and do not care which way you go. I have earned my place. You merely see me in a form that is acceptable to you. I am simply your … journeyman."

"No. No. This isn't possible. I have a wife. Look." Sam frantically pulls out his wallet, thrusting a photo of Margaret into the driver's face.

"You think I care about your family photos, they are just dust." Sam flinches as the photo crumbles to ash before his eyes; the cloud flying around the car like a mini tornado until it dissipates.

"Let me out!" He yanks the door catch frantically. "I've got to get back to Margaret." Stopping abruptly, his face contorts into a half-smile. "I've fallen asleep at the wheel haven't I? I am now unconscious in a ditch somewhere. It's my body's way of protecting me from the pain of the crash. I don't remember seeing it happen but my brain registered an impact and immediately disconnected my body to save the discomfort."

"Do you want to believe you are there, in that twisted wreck?"

Sam studied the driver who vaguely seemed familiar, unable to place him. An explosion of an image came to him.

"Mr Hatcher?" A maths teacher from school who had a temper like a hungry wolf, with a bite to match. One instance indelibly etched in his mind was when he'd asked a question after Mr Hatcher had enquired whether anyone had any questions; telling the class not to be afraid to ask, so he had. The next thing he knew was the blackboard rubber hurtling in his direction, catching him on his cheek.

Mr Hatcher bellowed. "Are you stupid boy? Do you not understand the English language? Do I speak in riddles?"

Almost knocked senseless by the missile Sam had struggled to find his voice, "But, Sir you aske…"

"Did I say you could speak?" Mr Hatcher stormed towards him, his large paces closing the distance in seconds.

"But, Si…" The slap round the head came as swiftly as the blackboard rubber had.

"Now does anyone else have any questions?" The class shook their heads. "Stupid idiot."

"I am whoever you see me as."

"Is he dead?"

"Yes."

Cascading thoughts turn to Margaret. Turning round in the seat he could still see the accident, a fading blot in the distance with a large, pitch-black funnel of smoke rising in to the sky; red brake lights flicked on as traffic slowed to a stop in the queue that was building behind.

Sam still couldn't equate it in his head. He didn't feel dead. Placing his hands in front of his mouth he breathed out heavily, expecting to feel his breath. There was nothing. No warmth, just nothing.

Chapter 12

1957 January

Gary's Inquest

I sit quietly on a hard wooden chair, with my father next to me. I am not sure why I have been brought here but there are all kinds of people around me: policeman, doctors and court officials.

I have almost been completely ignored since being brought home by the police after Gary's death. Father was hesitant and didn't drag me into a welcoming hug.

Was it suspicion I saw in his eyes that day?

Mother doesn't want to know, and James has moved out to live with a friend. It is like they are scared of me.

I think back to the day Gary died. It *was* an accident – really it was. Or maybe there is a darker side that takes over when needed. I am thankful as I am not sure what I could have done otherwise; he was going to tell on me ... I thought we shared something. He enjoyed the autopsy as much as I did, so why did he have to go and spoil it? It seems you can't trust anyone; I certainly can't.

The meeting is called to order and I shut off, until I'm shaken by the sound of Gary's full name. A little while later I am asked to recount my story; which I do, devoid of emotion as if in shock that I am being questioned. It fools everyone ... except my father.

He almost pushes me out of the hall in front of him, after a verdict of 'accidental death' is registered. I try to look at Gary's parents. His mother is in floods of tears; his father is merely stony-faced.

"I want to go to medical school." I announce on the way home.

Nothing.

Part 2

Chapter 13

1963 November
Liverpool

William's jubilant mood had him almost bouncing along to the Beatles new offering – She Loves Me – which he played on a loop in his head. He loved his beat; his first solo beat as a police constable. Liverpool! He'd always wanted to visit, never believing he would be working here, close to the Cavern Club – where The Beatles had been spotted by Brian Epstein before setting off on their epic journey. He joyfully took in the sight of the Liver Building – an evocative first of a kind to be made from reinforced concrete. He was amazed by the new forms of technology, which were making an impact on the world, comparing it to himself starting his first beat, this beat, and the impact he intended to make on the criminal world; a boyhood dream from which nothing had managed to sway him.

Strolling along, a sense of responsibility rested on his narrow shoulders; his stride purposeful yet relaxed, loving every minute. The solitude and the early morning silence echoing through the streets, the glistening frost on the ground adding to the magical overture of the Mersey meandering away to his left. Life couldn't get much better, except for that first big arrest. His mind wondered what it might be: a notorious burglar, an arsonist, a bank robber?

His reverie was broken by the sight of what looked like a rolled up bedspread or rug near the semi-circular portico of the Liver building – he couldn't tell.

"Great, my first big case. A load of rubbish!" he chuckled to himself. Nothing could break his joy. The frost twinkled like a sugar coating.

Peel House couldn't have prepared William for the sight that greeted him. In training it was always just that, training. Although always told to expect the unexpected, this was real life, and as ugly as real life could get. It was two months since he'd left his training at Peel House and the optimism that had buoyed his excitement evaporated rapidly leaving an empty hollow sickness stuck in his throat.

Seeing part of a head his good mood plummeted to the pit of his stomach. "Excuse me, you can't sle…"

He gulped, hoping his eyes deceived him; that it was just a hobo sleeping rough; fearing the dreaded truth.

Drawing closer William could see the figure wrapped cocoon like. The frost sparkled as his heart pounded like an artillery barrage and the realisation sunk in. Deep down he knew what he was looking at. A dead body!

In training it had been mooted that trusting ones senses and instincts could be an asset. Right now, he wanted to doubt them, protest they were wrong.

Standing above the bedspread the haunting face of a woman stared back; a vile acrid burning sensation rose ferociously. His training failed him as his breakfast lurched back up. Turning quickly he heaved violently, splattering the pavement with its remnants. He knew he'd get in trouble for contaminating the scene, as some remnants splashed on the bedspread.

William couldn't help but feel compelled to stare back at what was once a pair of vivid brown eyes, which now wore a misty hue as they bore an indelible mark into his memory.

Chapter 14

1960 October

Medical School Days
Hall of Residence

So this is medical school; a chance for me to investigate the human body for real, in the open. No more pet autopsies, or accidental deaths, although it did prove one thing: you can get away with murder, if it looks like an accident. Oh well Sheila, Gary, your deaths have not been in vain.

I hope my roommate is not annoying, or they may have to suffer a 'little accident' as well. This room is a bit pokey. It will do, I suppose.

Can't wait to get stuck into the physical part of my course, it makes me tingle all over.

I think my parents were glad to see the back of me. The look of false pleasure plastered on their faces as James borrowed dad's car to drive me here conveyed their feeling of good riddance. Mum looked half-cut already. I think they need to have a 'little accident' to end their sorry lives.

Maybe I should arrange that?

Still, I am free from them, and in *Med school*; it feels good.

Chapter 15

2002 July

Dead!

Bewildered, Sam stared at the road ahead, thoughts scurrying in to view and then disappearing until his brain fixed on one.

"I'm not religious."

Geoff half turned, quizzically looking at Sam.

"Random. Just like in class. How did you ever make it in the world?"

"You were narcissistic in class as I remember." Sam thundered, regaining his conviction.

"So would you be, faced with hundreds of innocent eyes staring at you, waiting for the imparting of my wonderful knowledge, knowing the class were probably more interested in playing with their pubescent dicks than actually learning." Adding as an afterthought. "Or swapping matchbox cars."

Taken aback, Sam tried to remember what it was he had thought – it was a blank picture board that he thought would become fuller as he got older, and closer to death. He did remember this teacher appearing like a colossal giant on that first day of senior school when everything had been so foreign, only the odd familiar face from junior school in the wilderness of new faces.

"If you felt like that then why did you do it?" Sam half smiled. "I'm having a conversation with my teacher and I am dead. Supposedly. Ironic. You would be the last person I would expect to see when I died. If I am dead." Resolutely, Sam faced the road ahead, playing the dutiful passenger.

"You are; dead that is, There is no question of that. As for the last person you expected to see. Maybe your parents, John and Debbie? What would you have to say to them? What would they say about you, eh?"

"Maybe. I don't know. I can't say I've given it much thought. I can't say I have lost a lot of sleep over them in all these years?"

"Are you sure?"

"I don't have family. They made their choices and I was left to pay the cost."

"I see, like that is it?" Geoff stared at Sam like a scientist studying a new specimen.

"Yes, it is like that. You can call me bitter, I don't care."

"Everything and everyone matters, Sam. Every decision. Every twist and turn you make in life. Every interaction causes a reaction, the butterfly effect. Without it, the great wave of life would flounder and we'd all fall by the way side and die like the waste of space that many are."

"It still doesn't matter now. Whatever happens from here on in, I cannot change; and whatever was, is in the past; and whatever should be, will be, whether I am there or not."

"You sound almost philosophical."

"No, just annoyed that I never got to enjoy the rest of my life, or maybe never accomplished some of the dreams and aspirations I – we had planned."

"Like solving the riddle to eternal life that you and your friends were trying to do?"

"I always thought … never mind." Sam glanced out of the side window, the world whizzing by. "What happens now? Are you going to take me somewhere? Is this purgatory?"

Geoff laughed. "Purgatory! Purgatory is just something dreamed up to convince the ignorant that there are consequences for not obeying the morals taught to you. There is no such thing as purgatory *per se*, unless you want to believe that this is it?"

"So what is this then?"

"Just a journey most will take in the afterlife."

"So purgatory then?"

"If it makes you feel better, giving it a name."

"It doesn't make me feel anything. You speak in riddles. Purgatory, afterlife, it's all the same. Semantics."

Geoff shrugged letting the silence get consumed by Frank still crooning away in the background.

Geoff
Fletcher
medical
plans

Chapter 16

1960 November
Medical School Days

Finally, we get down to some *bodywork*. I have been waiting for this ever since I arrived. The professors are pleased with my academic work, I am finding it a little tricky, but with perseverance the information sinks in. It feels perfect.

I have met some nice people, and the social side is wonderful, yet it has been a while since I have autopsied anything. I didn't realise how much I crave that power! Now, today it looks as though finally I get to satisfy that in class.

"Hi, Sarah, Carl. What's Prof Leasing like?"

Carl answered, "he is knowledgeable, a leader in the field of the nervous system, runs a department at Oxford Royal Infirmary."

"Is there anyone you don't know about, Carl?" Sarah asked rolling her eyes at me.

"No, I like to know whoever is teaching me is an expert. You shouldn't teach if you are not at the top of your profession; it is just wasting everyone's time."

"Stick that in your pipe and smoke it," Sarah added snidely.

"We will get to experiment on a body today, won't we?" I ask wanting confirmation. This is what I have been looking forward to.

"Absolutely, we'll be paired off and that is pretty much how the groups will run," Carl explained. "Two people to one cadaver, there is usually enough. They are usually homeless who have died and have no family, or people who have donated their bodies for scientific research."

"You really are a fount of knowledge, aren't you?" I take in Carl's angular features. He has the look of an owl, except tall and wiry.

Professor Leasing drones on for about an hour as I anxiously wait to be allowed to approach our corpses. I am partnering with Indyra, she is quiet and happy to let me lead. Our corpse stinks, but I can't believe

I am about to cut into a human body and be praised for it. I hesitate with the scalpel in my hands: however, the feverish anticipation is greater than the actual act as finally I make my cut. We are looking for the liver today.

The body is cold and, for a moment, I am called back to Gary's body as he lay there dying, his warm blood oozing over my hands, the faint beat of his heart as slowly he faded away. This cold body does not come close and suddenly ... I feel disappointed and let down.

Chapter 17

1963 November
Liverpool

After locating the nearest call box to report his findings, William was told to wait until a Doctor turned up. It was a long, cold hour standing sentry, trying to avoid glancing at the face as it taunted him. The sickness in the pit of his stomach made him question whether he was suited to police work.

Just when he thought he'd had control of his reflux, another wave of nausea swept through him and he dry retched, his empty stomach performing painful gymnastics. With nothing to drink to wash away the acrid taste in his mouth, it left him fighting the pursuing gagging feeling.

"PC Travis, I presume." A kindly voice broke his concentration. Turning, he saw a short man tightly wrapped in a large overcoat, his bushy beard trailing over his scarf, a green patterned trilby perched securely on his head. "It's a cold one isn't it?"

Travis swallowed. "Yes," tasting the aftershock of bile once again.

"I'm guessing, from the look of you, that this is your first dead body?"

William nodded, guiding the Doctor to his find; not that it was hard to miss.

"Ah, I see you didn't manage to refrain from expressing your thoughts."

William bowed his head in shame without answering.

"Not to worry, you aren't the first, and I'm sure you're not the last. I'm Doctor Harding by the way. Right, let's look at what we've got, see if we can't get an initial determination of death." he looked back at William. "You going to be alright, son?"

Trying to be strong William answered. "I think I'll be ..." he gulped as another reflex started. "... okay."

"Look, it's nothing to be ashamed off. I've seen many first-dayers lose their dinner when confronted with a dead body. I certainly don't

33

hold it against you. I would say you need to prepare yourself for a ribbing from your colleagues though, once I file my findings, as I will have to declare it. After all you did contaminate the scene." Dr Harding had a sympathetic voice and part of William's anxiety had been from an expected dressing down instead of the sympathy.

Dr Harding fished around in his coat, pulling out a hip flask "Here have a nip of this, help calm your nerves." He passed William the flask and, William gulped down the burning liquid, later to find out it was brandy.

"Has your duty officer, or Inspector not been out yet? Running a bit slow aren't they?" Dr Harding had a habit of not allowing William to answer, letting each question run into each other.

"They said they'd be here shortly, an hour ago, probably about the same time they rang you. I am guessing it must be a busy morning."

"How about the Laboratory Sergeant?"

"Don't know."

As if on cue two figures pulled into view.

Chapter 18

1961 January
Medical School Days
Hall of Residence

Alex, my roommate has not come back since Christmas break
– flew back home to Russia and then never returned – at least the
incessant talking in that annoying accent has ended and I can enjoy
the tranquillity of the room to myself. No one seems to know why, or
has even bothered to collect Alex's possessions, everything left where
it was discarded. I have never known anyone so messy and smelly –
except my older brother, he loved to wallow in a mess. I have already
spied stuff I might like, once washed, after spending an afternoon
tidying because I was fed up looking at the detritus left behind. I don't
think I will make it clear to our house captain, just yet, that I have
an empty bed. I like this time to myself; I even managed an animal
autopsy in here last night, which added to the thrill. It hadn't been
planned, but I couldn't resist when I saw a cat crawling away after it
had been run over. It beckoned to me, teasing my inner demon; it had
been a long time. I watched for a while; then picked it up. It wasn't
even crying out in pain – maybe it just knew its time was up. Maybe
it was a sign for me.

Locking my door, I was distanced from the halls of residence's
hustle and bustle of late night frolics; consumed by the thought of
the next few minutes. Unprepared, I had to scrabble around to find
a plastic bag, the cat was fading fast; I didn't need to put it out of its
misery. I was a little concerned as I made the first incision in case it
cried out, so I prepared to muffle it with one of Alex's jumpers.

Alex's bed was my makeshift table; again more of Alex's clothes
were used to mop up the blood. Once inside I let the blood ooze over
my fingers, its warm stickiness was a frisson of euphoria. I closed my
eyes, allowing the next minute to slow down to a crawl.

I was broken from my reverie by a loud knocking; panic shot
through me as I saw the mass of red soaked clothes.

"There's a party going on in the student bar. You coming?"

"No, I've got some … studying to do."

"Please yourself, don't be a square."

I remained frozen, as I listened to the footsteps fade on the wooden floor. A realisation struck me that I was doing this too close to home. The euphoria quickly evaporated and I set about clearing up, planning my escape to dump the evidence. I racked my mind for a place that was close by but out of sight, I couldn't recall anywhere like the well I used to use. It couldn't stay here.

Quickly I assembled the detritus in a black bag. It looked bulky and suspicious. There was little I could do about that. Plan. I needed to plan this in future.

I made it outside and the tension eased as I drew comfort from the night. I walked around the streets for nearly an hour before I found somewhere that acted as my disposal site. With no one looking I threw the bag down an embankment into some bushes, breathing a sigh of relief.

The walk back gave me time to think and relish in how much I needed to feel life beneath my fingers, and how med school just didn't quite deliver that feeling, that fervour.

Chapter 19

1963 November

Liverpool

Shock from the morning's discovery still rallied William's thoughts as he sat shaking in the lounge of his lodgings; a place regularly used by new recruits until they found their feet. It was run by Mrs Mason – a friendly old lady who had lost her husband in World War Two, whose own children had grown up and moved on. Now she liked nothing better than mothering the young officers.

William was close to tears. During training they had seen dead bodies in the morgue but, somehow seeing it on the street, like a discarded piece of rubbish tore him up inside. Dead bodies had even been a matter of joviality.

"There you go dear. A nice pot of tea and some biscuits." Mrs Mason offered.

"Thank you." William muttered, still shaken. He had still felt sick hours later in his shift. Giving in, the duty officer had sent him home.

"I don't know if I can ever go back," he spoke solemnly.

Mrs Mason stirred the teapot.

"Now don't talk so. You just need time to accept. A hot sweet cup of tea will help. I'll make you a nice casserole for your tea; good wholesome food, that's what you need. Keep your strength up. There are nasty people in the world and we need decent hard-working officers like yourself keeping the streets safe."

There was silence for a few minutes as William's head swam with images and the bile started to rise again.

"I think you need a good tot of whisky in that tea, that will help bolster you."

Before William had time to refuse, Mrs Mason was pouring a good measure of malt whisky in his tea.

"Now drink up. It will do you good."

They sat in silence. Mrs Mason holding her own counsel.

William hated the taste of the whisky, yet dutifully drank it all the same. The image of the woman's face flashed up in his mind again, and he felt the uncontrollable well of emotion that he'd fought all day building inside – from laughing with colleagues as they ribbed him about losing his breakfast to the dread of seeing those jaded brown eyes staring emptily at him.

Unexpectedly the first tears came. They were unstoppable. Mrs Mason placed a motherly arm around him for comfort.

"Let it all out pet, it does you no good to hold it in. Best it comes out."

He hugged her tight as the tears relentlessly rolled.

"There, there."

Chapter 20

1961 May

Medical School Days

"It is so nice to be outside for a change, Margaret."

"I know, Sarah. I was surprised by Mike's change of view the other night."

"What on suspended animation? So was I. Maybe he just felt left out, I suppose we have been dissecting it rather a lot."

"Do you really think we will discover anything that isn't already known?"

"Not by talking, that's for sure. Generally discoveries are only made by actual physical experiments."

"You mean on animals!"

"Why didn't you study to be a vet?"

"I did think about it; my parents kind of pushed me this way I suppose."

"You do realise animals are used for research, whether you like it or not. I have been reading some studies on rats, dogs and cats; to be honest some people don't put the value on them that you do. Considering them something to be utilized for the good of the world."

"Use the criminals, at least they could speak and answer questions."

"True."

"Would you want to be frozen?"

"I don't know. I have never given it that much thought."

"I mean what would be waiting for you decades from now? It could be so lonely. How about money? Family?"

"I guess you need an open mind about that. Couples could always be frozen together, at least there is some certainty you would not be on your own 'until death do us part' and all that – although, that might put some people off. I think Carl sums it up articulately in that it is an adventure, and therefore a journey you may want to take, if that way inclined.

Here they are." Margaret pointed to Mike and Sam. "You all right Sam?"

He sighed wearily. "My last paper, I got a 'D', that's the fourth in a row. Professor Adlington said I needed to buck my ideas up, if I am to succeed. " Margaret guided Sam down onto the bench next to her.

"We'll just have to put in some extra work with you that's all." Sarah said as Mike sat next to her.

"That's what I said but he's not listening." Mike sighed.

"Why? It is not really surprising is it, Mike? Firstly my surgical skills are not very good, nowhere near yours, my knowledge … I am struggling to take it all in. I know there are other disciplines but I just don't know if I am cut out for this."

"Cut out!" Mike laughed. "I like it!"

"It's not funny, Mike," Sarah admonished.

"Yeah, I think it is, me trying to be a doctor!"

"Don't give up, Sam. I don't always find it easy, but Roger helps from time to time. We'll all dig in."

Sam sighed again. "What else could I do? I've wanted this since, I don't know when. Dreamed of it."

Chapter 21

2002 July

Susan
Jones

Frank Sinatra faded and Geoff sighed. "Not really my cup of tea. You got anything more rocking."

"That is pretty irrelevant at this time."

"Yes, I suppose it is. It's just nice to listen to some good music whilst we take this journey, your journey. After all there are things you must see before you move on."

"I have dealt with buyers like you. Never get a straight answer. They talk round you and treat you like scum off the bottom of their shoes when all you're trying to do is your job; providing them with an all round package, service and quality. They sit smugly, believing they are better than you. Keep you waiting for the allotted meeting time as it drifts by, without a care for the schedule of your day. Offer them a price and they don't give any feedback; then after the deadline passes call you up and say 'We need the first shipment next week.' 'Oh certainly sir.' The product only has got to come from Brazil. A six to eight week lead-time! But you're expected to do it."

Sam sighed, letting the annoyance fade, not even sure why he was so annoyed, he was dead, supposedly. Nothing mattered anymore. Then he reflected a little on his career.

"I remember the very first contract I won. She was nice, fair, not even hardened by the fact that she had to make it in a man's world." His mind conjured a picture of Susan Jones, relishing that euphoric feeling of securing the deal, for it to almost fall to pieces as she disappeared after the dinner meeting never to be seen again. "There is no need for anyone to be any different, we're all just doing jobs."

"She's on our list." Geoff stated matter-of-factly.

Sam scowled at Geoff; bitten by the sharpness of those tumultuous times, thinking he might lose his job. After all, it had been a kind of make or break situation.

"You're thinking only of yourself now, aren't you?" Geoff eyed Sam questioningly. "Never considering that other people were affected by her death."

"I ..." Sam started but was cut short, as he found himself standing near the Liver building watching William and Dr Harding studying the body of Susan Jones.

Chapter 22

1961 October
Medical School Days
Student Union Bar

"So my boy, what is it you wanted to discuss?" Mike slapped Sam playfully on the back.

Margaret smiled acknowledging Mike as she sat down. "He wouldn't say, just dragged me out of the bedsit and said we were meeting you. Had some important news."

"He's not pregnant is he? Margaret have you been experimenting on him?"

"Never mind what I have been doing to him. You'll only get jealous. But I always said you're not my type." She patted Mike's hand with friendly admonishment.

"Sexy, good looking, mature." Mike replied.

"No, skinny as a rake and with a mind like a pubescent idiot."

"I should bash both your heads together. It's like being at infant school." Sam smiled.

"Yes, Dad!" Both giggled.

Sam let them settle down a little before continuing. "I've made a decision."

"You're going to buy a round. Fantastic, I was getting thirsty." Mike responded eagerly.

"Stop it, he's trying to be serious." Margaret defended. "Go on babe."

"I'm leaving my course."

For once both were silent, staring at him in astonishment.

"But why?" Margaret finally asked. "And why didn't you talk to me?"

"Because, I've only just made my mind up. Today that is. Not this second before you say anything, Mike. I wanted to tell you both together."

Mike shrugged "Me? I would never. I feel hurt that you would think I'd say something so flippant."

"Yes, right. The only thing that would offend you is if you didn't have a drink in front of you." Margaret chipped in.

"True. Yes, true! I am offended. Look no drink, you call me down to the pub and don't buy me a drink." He folded his arms in mock hurt.

"Seriously honey, why are you leaving? We've been helping you with the theory. Your grades have picked up haven't they? I know last year was hard but this year you seem to be coasting it." Seeing Sam's expression, "Okay, not quite coasting it, but certainly better

"I was, but they've started falling again and to be honest I'm not convinced anymore that I want to be a doctor. I've been looking around. You know after that guy came in and talked to us about research facilities and the dearth of people in certain fields, I think that maybe, with the knowledge I've got so far I can try that side. It will certainly be less pressure than dealing with living people, especially as I just don't feel I could. And at least my skills won't be totally wasted."

"What!" Mike exclaimed. "Skills, when did you acquire skills? Living people! I would hardly call working on cadavers living people. Unless you've found away to revive them! You've been experimenting haven't you?"

"Ha, bloody ha. You know what I mean. I enjoy learning but I struggle with retaining all that knowledge in my head and I'm not sure I can handle the pressure. It scares the shit out of me, the thought of going off to the placements and dealing with real people and real issues. At least this way I can continue my studies but at a pace that suits me. Well, that's the theory."

"Well, it's your decision. You know I'll support you whatever you do." Margaret placed a hand on Sam's. "I suppose I can't say I am surprised. You did seem a bit down with it all. Have you found a position that you like?"

Sam felt the great relief at announcing his decision and relaxed.

"You know I like it when you go on top." Sam looked for Mike's friendly smile of approval.

"It's the tits isn't it?" Mike replied, not letting him down.

"Too right." Sam placed his hands on Margaret's chest. She slapped them away.

"Sorry, access denied now. You're not a medical student anymore." Her face was a picture of sternness.

"Looks like it's your right hand then mate." Mike concluded.

"You're always so crass Mike." Margaret smiled. "He knows he has access whenever he likes." She paused as Sam beamed a smile at Mike. "And when it suits me."

"Crash and burn mate, crash and burn. Now you going to buy me that drink or have I got to dehydrate first."

"Ah, good point. That reminds me ..." Sam started.

"That you have to buy a round. Yes, I know I'm gasping." Mike placed his hands to his throat and made gasping noises.

"No, dehydration. I was ..."

"Ah man, I'm dying of thirst here and it's your round. As you say d-e-h-y-dra-tion."

"Oh, alright but I want to talk to you about dehydration." Sam said getting up.

"Don't worry. You'll see it first hand by the time you get back."

Sam slapped Mike lightly round the back of the head.

"Do you ever let up, Mike?" Margaret asked rhetorically.

"Sam knows what's important, and drink is very important to sustain life. Isn't it?"

"Yes, all right, you've made your point. I'm going."

-

A couple of minutes later Sam returned with the drinks and sat down.

"Cheers, mate."

"Cheers." Sam replied. "Margaret gone to the toilet?"

"If that's where you get intelligent conversation."

Sam looked at Mike quizzically.

"That's what she said she was going to do." Mike frowned.

Sam suddenly realised what Mike meant, it was a love/hate relationship Mike and Margaret had sometimes. Sam sipped his pint wondering whether he should go after her or not, knowing sometimes it was best to let her calm down first.

"So, Mike, what do you know about dehydration of cells? I've been looking at a theory Roger expounded on – preserving living tissue by removing the water part, then rehydrating at a later stage, after freezing." Mike look nonplussed. "Remember when you took the piss out of him for reading that comic, 'Startling Stories' from America." Mike still looked blank. "Well, I borrowed it. I was intrigued; it was fascinating, this Ettinger guy has got an imagination and it got me thinking about whether it would be possible to suspend life through dehydration."

"No." Mike turned away. "Look at her, she is gorgeous."

"Come on, Mike, why?"

"Won't work."

"Why not? This story talks about suspended animation by removing water and freezing." Mike faced Sam. "Then being frozen for hundreds of years like that Buck something comic that Roger reads."

"Buck Rogers."

"That's it. Surely it is plausible?"

"Sounds like a Roger question to me. He's the geek. You're not turning into a geek are you?"

Sam sighed, knowing it was futile to try and have normal conversation when Mike was in this kind of mood; it annoyed him because Mike rarely showed his intellect. It was like he regarded it as being a negative to his personality.

"No. And yes, she does have nice eyes."

"Eyes. Has she got eyes, cor, I haven't got that far up yet."

Sam looked on disillusioned at Mike. "I'll see you later mate. I'm going to find Margaret."

Chapter 23

2002 July

"See, Sam, death affects many people in different ways. How would you feel, first day on the job and being greeted by that gruesome sight?"

Sam was confused as the focus turned to the young PC who heaved his breakfast over the pavement.

"Yes, I can see that. And I, too, know what it is like." Sam stated pointedly.

"Yes, you do." Geoff brushed the comment away nonchalantly and we will come to that in time." Sam *harrumphed*. "You choose not to see, or understand?"

"See or understand what? You're right, I don't understand and I'm still not convinced this is real." As soon as he had said it he realised what was coming next.

"I can put you back there in a snap if you want?"

"No! I just want to understand what the point of all this is. If am to *atone* for my life then I presume there is relevance to this meandering. Whilst you were all right as a teacher, you are not someone I would choose to spend this time with, dead or alive. Why can't you be Frank Sinatra? I am sure he would have something interesting to talk about."

The scene fizzled out and they were back in the car.

"Yes, I am sure he would, having accomplished so much in life, even if it was possibly by dubious means, so the rumours go. However, this isn't for your pleasure."

"So you say." Sam snapped.

"Families need closure; answers need to be addressed and I will get there when I'm ready."

Sam added sarcastically. "Don't take too long, I might fall asleep. I normally do as a passenger in a car." He fidgeted. "Do I have to see my family again? Not sure I want to."

"Not today. Let's look at how one member of a family is dealing with it."

Instantly they were in Calderstone Park in front of William, sitting on a bench.

Chapter 24

1961 December

Medical School Days
Student Union Bar

"Drinks on me," Mike called out, already half cut, stumbling over to the table where Sam and Margaret were enjoying a quiet drink.

Sam looked up, and then they both drained their glasses simultaneously.

"Good idea." Sam wiped the back of his hand across his lips. "Wouldn't want to deprive you of the pleasure of buying me a drink."

"Like I never do?" Mike slurred.

"He never said that." Margaret placed her empty glass back on the table. "You look like you've been out celebrating. And, when did you start wearing a flatcap?"

"I am being different. Had it ages. I have, and I'll tell you about it in a minute. Roger, Sarah and Carl will be along soon, to help continue this party."

"Party eh? Must be a worthy celebration." Margaret nodded at Sam knowingly. "As long as it starts to take away the smell of formaldehyde! I thought I'd have got used to it by now but it just soaks into every pore."

Mike spun round to head to the bar, then realised he hadn't replied and spun back to face his friends. For a brief second, his eyes lost focus and he wobbled precariously. Margaret put out a hand to steady him.

"Thanks, and yes it is."

"Is what?" Sam added playfully winking at Margaret.

"What?" Mike's eyes were like ball bearings, rolling around two dark pits.

"What's '*what*'?" Sam stifled a smirk.

"What?" Mike eyes appeared to struggle to keep focus on his friend. Unsteadily, he turned round to walk away again, then stopped, and turned back.

"What?"

"Exactly." Sam stated.

"Eh?" Mike exclaimed. "What are you going on about?"

"I don't know; you started it." Sam jollied.

"Stop it, Sam. Just get us those drinks, Mike." Margaret slapped Sam's hand playfully.

"Drinks? Oh yes, who wants a drink?" But before either could answer, he had stumbled off in the direction of the bar.

"I can't say I miss the stench of formaldehyde anymore." Sam referred back to Margaret's earlier comment.

"Yes, rub it in why don't you. I'm running out of perfume, trying to cover it up. Anyway, as I was asking before Mike interrupted, are you going to take the job?"

"I don't really see I have a lot of options at the moment. Especially as they wouldn't even take me in the research sector; my qualifications so far, 'don't cut the mustard!'" Sam imitated one of the responses he had received to an enquiry. "If we are going to get a place together, then I need to be working. Okay it's not the ..."

"Hi, Sam and Marge." The booming voice of Roger broke into their conversation.

"It's Margaret, ROGG!" Margaret corrected, emphasising a 'ger' sound rather than a 'j' sound.

"Oooh, tetchy."

"Only when it comes to you. Why do you have to be so arrogant?"

"On form tonight Marge? Oh sorry, oh so proper, Margaret." Roger's upper class snobbery cut through as he ran a hand over his slicked-back hair.

"Give it a rest, Roger." Sarah intoned, annoyed. "I have had this for the last two hours, studying for next weeks' exam. Unfortunately, I have to admit Roger is the best source of information on almost any medical subject. Plus he's just delighted because he has got his ten-week placement at BRI with Professor Lee. Anyway, how you doing Margaret? How did you do on Dr Frampton's test?"

"Sit here, Sarah." Margaret indicated the stool she'd dragged over earlier from the adjoining table. "Top of the class as usual. Bristol Royal Infirmary, some gits get all the luck: Professor Lee?"

"Professor Lee is only the most toppest neurologist in the country. And yes, BRI, and I deserve it as well." Roger stated like a proud baboon.

"That would have sounded okay if you hadn't used the word 'toppest', Roger." Sarah added, before continuing to address Margaret. "You're so lucky, I am struggling. Roger has been giving me extra lessons but ..."

"Oh yeah, I've heard about his 'extra lessons'." Sam snidely commented.

"Come on, Sam, I am not that desperate." Sarah caught the look on Roger's face. "Don't give me that hurt look; you're ugly and I only like you for your brain, and you know it! Plus *you* like hanging around with gorgeous women." Sarah breezed, glancing at Margaret as if waiting for confirmation of the fact.

"And modest, you left that off, Sarah." Margaret smiled.

"It is difficult to maintain my modesty, but you're right of course."

"Well, I have to agree with one thing." Roger started, "I do like to hang around gorgeous women. But in the meantime you two'll have to do."

"Get you." Sarah sounded almost impressed with his quick wit. "With a nose that big I'm surprised I didn't get knocked out whilst we were studying."

"The size of one's nose gives a fine indication of what *good's* the owner has to offer."

"At least it's never dull when you two are together." Margaret laughed "You two ought to get married, you'd be perfect for each other."

"NO way!" they both exclaimed.

"You think I would let her handle my heavy artillery."

"Don't make me laugh ..." Sarah retaliated.

"Alright can we call a truce for at least two sentences?" Sam broke in. It was followed by silence within the group, only the half-full bar's ambient noise filling their ears.

"Obviously not. Carry on." Sam said, jokingly. "Ah, now, finally the drinks have arrived!"

Mike lurched unsteadily towards them, two pints and a rum and coke in hand, their contents slopping jerkily over the edge of the glasses, depositing a trail across the floor.

"'Ere we go!"

"What are we celebrating by the way, Mike?" Roger asked.

"You don't know either?" Sam interjected.

"Nope, was just told to get down to the bar for a celebratory drink or two."

"Be cool people, all will be explained in due course. Do you want a drink?" Mike asked Roger and Sarah.

"No, I would just like to sit and watch the consummation of alcoholic beverages, whilst not partaking myself." Roger retorted sarcastically.

"Excellent, Roger, I can save myself some money. It's a good job I actually like your sense of your humour mate. The usual?" Mike left without waiting for an answer.

"Yes." Roger gave in. "So what's it like not being a student anymore Sam? All that time on your hands."

Sam scowled at Roger. It was still a sore point. His failure in medical school had in some ways made him feel like the outsider within this group. "Well as it goes, Roger, I have been offered a job. I can start next week, so every down has its up." Sam tried to sound jovial.

"Sounds good, Sam. What will you be doing?" Sarah enthused.

"Sales for an ingredients trader. Well, I'll start in shipping and work my way through to sales in a couple of years or so, maybe quicker. They want me to get the groundwork done first."

"Sounds very ... mmm, exciting." Roger yawned.

"Well, I am looking forward to it. Some of us don't have the brain capacity of others. Plus the prospects are good, so it's not all bad."

"Yes, but it is not medicine is it?" Roger persisted.

"No, Roger, it's not. But not everyone who comes here to study makes it through, so it's all about adapting to what life throws at you. And I am proud of Sam. It takes a lot of courage to finally admit when you're not capable of achieving a dream." Margaret's thoughts trailed off, realising her faux pas. She grabbed his hand to reassure him and, although he acknowledged it, the gesture was a little less responsive than she was used to.

"Well, there is nothing to stop me indulging my fascination with medicine in my spare time. I just won't be able to do it as a profession, that's all. It's not always doctors that make the breakthroughs in science. I enjoy medicine, but am just not that good with exams, the fundamentals, or the pressure ..." Sam trailed off prickled. He noticed that everyone looked slightly awkward; even Roger had the decency to stop digging. More silence followed.

"At least I won't have to work all the hours God sends, or watch our lecturers throwing dismembered heads across the room like rugby balls. Besides those lecture theatres are bloody freezing; be nice to work in a warm office." Then wishing to change the focus of attention, added. "Margaret's been offered a job." His pride was still jaded from her defence of him.

"Really?" Sarah leaned. "Doing what? Are you going to be quitting college as well?" She glanced in Sam's direction. "Sorry, Sam, I didn't ..."

"I know, don't worry about it." Sam sighed trying to hide his dismay.

"Oh, it's all right for Sarah to mention it but when I ..." the slap sent Roger's glasses flying.

Everyone looked at Sarah as it was quite out of character.

"You can be a real bastard sometimes, Roger." Sarah looked taken aback by her own actions. Surprised, Roger retrieved his glasses from the floor holding his cheek.

"Good shot." Margaret complimented her, laughing.

"I feel remarkably better now," Sam smiled sincerely.

"No, I won't be leaving college. It is more a side role to start with, a research position, that could possibly help with our little project we've been discussing, if we ever start doing practical research on freezing people, I think that could be quite exciting." Margaret continued.

"It's not that role Professor Parks was saying existed at that animal research lab. Please say it isn't? Those poor animals, I can't stand thinking of the cruelty that goes on in those places. Barbarians the lot of them." Sarah seethed.

"Calm down, Sarah, it's not that role. However, with an attitude like that how on earth do you manage on the top floor, with the animals and the physiology we have to do?"

"I've managed to avoid that part of the course so far." Sarah pugnaciously screwed her face up in disgust. "Those poor defenceless animals!"

"But, let's face it, without them we wouldn't know half the information we know now, or have half the products we have now." Margaret placated.

"I don't care, we should use the scumbags and murderers; let them sacrifice themselves. They didn't think twice about their victims did they?" Sarah vented, vehemently.

"Don't sit on the fence, Sarah, say what you mean." Mike added, returning with the drinks.

"Well, why shouldn't they contribute to society in a more useful way than our tax money, paying for them? It's the homeless people I feel sorry for. I mean, it's nice that their death means something to us as cadavers, but I sometimes wonder about their families. Do they ever know what happened to them?"

"Some probably didn't have families as such, that's why they were homeless. And getting back to another point, since when do you pay tax?" Sam couldn't help but fuel the change of topic.

Slightly abashed, Sarah responded "Well, not yet, but when I do."

"You got my vote, when you're elected." Roger supped his pint.

"Elected to what?"

"Prime minister." Roger stated.

"In this sexist world." Margaret opined. "It's about time they did though. We could certainly do a better job than the male chauvinists that have tried and failed to date."

"What is the job you were offered then?" Mike asked Margaret.

"Oh. MOD. It's a sort of placement initially, just a couple of evenings a week and a few free periods when I have them. After I finish, it will become full time."

"And?" Mike stated encouragingly.

"And what?" Margaret answered innocently.

"What's it doing?" Mike persisted.

"Top secret. Can't say. What's yours?"

"My what?" Mike replied.

"The job you've been offered. It was a job wasn't it? That's why we are celebrating isn't it?"

For a moment Mike looked confused. "Oh yeah, I have been offered a job as a spy; I'm taking a job in my father's company as a cover and I'm telling you this to throw you off the scent."

"You're going to sell car parts, instead of medicine?" Roger condemned. "I'm mixing with wasters. All this good knowledge and everyone wants to get out. We can do so much good in the medical profession. The world needs us!"

"What are you on, Roger?" Mike exclaimed. "I don't think it will be too difficult to find someone to take my place."

"Are you kidding? Knowledge is one thing, but surgeon's skills that you have shown are rare. With your skills you will be able to specialise: brain, heart, anything. Why waste that talent on car parts?"

"Wow, I never knew you liked me so much?" He then added mockingly

"I don't want your children if that was your way of making a pass."

"You really don't get it, do you, Mike? Whilst I have superior knowledge, I do not have your skill with a scalpel and your technical capabilities. In amongst your childish banter, I've seen you work on a cadaver, and the admiration the junior doctors lavish on you is immense. Why waste it?" Roger stopped, clearly annoyed.

Sarah broke the deadlock. "I think that was a marriage proposal you know. He never waxes that lyrical about people. If he were that passionate with me I might have been able to get over the ugliness ..." Sarah paused "... for a second at least." she giggled.

Silence settled.

"Well, that killed off the celebrations, didn't it?" Margaret raised her glass.

The others reciprocated, mutely and sullenly.

Chapter 25

1963 November
Liverpool

It was a bitterly cold yet bright day as William sat in Calderstone Park, his sombre mood punctuated by his breath rising like wisps, dissipating a few feet above his head; snow was imminent. Two weeks had passed since discovering the body by the Liver building; the frost-laden image still haunted his dreams. Her jaded brown eyes still bored into him every night, insidiously taunting him as her life force danced in his dreams.

Evenings at the pub would not provide salvation; only dulling the memory temporarily. The fact that he had never mixed well socially only added to the torture he suffered, exacerbating the loneliness; the sensation that the only career he'd ever wanted was slipping away from him.

His station Sergeant had told him to get a grip before it destroyed him; 'man up' the underlying sentiment. So William had, by drinking alone and getting so slaughtered he had ended up in a cell after passing out on the street. Only then was the desk sergeant more sympathetic, advising him to take a couple of days to get his act together. If he didn't, it would be a slippery slope to getting sacked.

It was the wake-up call William needed, and a brisk walk around the park put some perspective back into his sights. The fresh cold air, a nectar of sobriety emphasising that he couldn't forget her; he needed to deal with her death in the only way that should have been obvious from the start; catch the bastard who'd killed her. Being just a beat copper, he wouldn't be allowed to investigate as such: though there was nothing stopping him asking around, speaking with CID, making enquiries on his beat.

Chapter 26

1962 February

Medical School

"You're late, Roger." Mike, quietly admonished. "Where have you been the last two days? Professor Adlington is not very happy with you." Mike was already busy performing a cholecystectomy (removal of the gallbladder) from the cadaver.

"There was some business I needed to attend." Roger looked unusually flustered. "Why are you so concerned; you're the one leaving to sell car parts," he finished cuttingly.

"It doesn't mean I don't want to finish my course. Can you grab those clamps?" Mike couldn't believe Roger had not let this drop since December. "So I don't want to be a Doctor or a surgeon, it is my choice. It serves my purpose. Nice boots by the way, very trendy, so why are you wearing them?"

Roger moved the clamp into position.

"Then why waste everyone's time here, if you have already decided? They're comfortable and I like them."

"Because I like cutting up people! It is fascinating," he added with a macabre smile. "And, this is the only way that I can legally do it. It would be nice to work on live specimens though! Sorry, Mate." Mike apologised to the cadaver.

"You're twisted."

"No, well, maybe. It is nice having you admire my surgical skills; kind of cool. Oh my word, look at that!" Mike exclaimed loudly.

"Alright, Mr Thompson. Keep your noise level down, you're not the only one here." Professor Adlington called from his observation point.

"Well, I didn't expect that." Mike whispered, staring intently at the now visible sac type organ.

"What didn't you expect?" Roger grabbed another clamp.

"For it to be bright green. It kind of looks like some alien living organism has attached itself like a limpet, out of those comics you read."

"So I like reading science fiction stories. I don't see what so strange about that. It is amazing how many stories start to mirror discoveries. I like understanding what other people believe might be possible in the future. As Sam has re-iterated it is not always the scientists that make the breakthrough. These storytellers sometimes actually kick start theories that then take on a life of their own."

"I have some strange friends! I suppose you and Sam have discussed his suspended animation theory?" Mike replied.

"Actually we have discussed it with Margaret, Sarah and Carl. The principles of dehydration are sound but the science for suspending animation is not there yet."

"But I suppose you're all coming up with theories."

"Yes, actually we are. All theoretical, of course."

"Where's the fun in that? Surely you need to work on a fresh body"

"Pass the C10 Scalpel, please. That's not legal, is it?"

"Would be good though? At least everything would be in the correct colour, instead of the washed out grey of formaldehyde."

"What do you expect? They are dead. They have to preserve them with something." Roger expounded, visibly annoyed at Mike.

"All right, easy tiger. What's eating you today?"

"Can we just get on?"

"Ooh, yes sir."

Chapter 27

2002 July

Geoff, clicked his fingers and they left Calderstone park and were back looking at Susan's body. Sam's stomach churned like a vat of boiling acid as he took in the grizzly image of her body; it jarred with the memory from the dinner meeting all those years ago that was crystal clear in his mind. Her voice had been an affirmation of firmness in order to maintain her position; the alcohol subsequently allowing that facade to slip gently away, exposing her true self as someone to aspire to; the way she handled herself without being overbearing and rude like so many buyers he met prior to her. Then he remembered admiring her car, a reward for working hard, and her praising of him for being nice. He shivered as the memory prickled.

It was upsetting seeing her as she had been found after two years; inconceivable in his mind that someone could do such a thing. The questioning by the police had caught him off guard, especially when he had been suspected of her abduction and murder.

"The ripples, Sam," Geoff interrupted his quiet reflection. "The ripples of our actions are far reaching. If the slightest misplaced comment in anger can cause a wave of reaction, what do you think the loss of one life would cause?"

Sam's jaw bounced as if on elastic as he searched for a response. Susan's marble like face juxtaposed with how fresh and exuberant it had looked at the dinner meeting. He remembered the news reports that linked her death to a string of other deaths; a serial killer; she was the first.

"The press dubbed him the 'The Medical Man' because of the samples and organs that were taken." Geoff added.

"And she was the first?"

"That they know off. But many followed ..."

"Oh my god! I have just realised who that policeman is. I knew he looked familiar."

"You never were the brightest spark."

"Excuse me for not having instant recall for every little detail in my life."

"It may be a little detail to you, but not to that officer. It was his first ever beat on his own. It tainted him. Luckily he was one of the strong ones but it took some courage and soul searching; it could so easily have gone the other way."

"Are you my own doing?" Sam changed the subject, questioningly.

"You were never clever enough for that."

Chapter 28

1962 March
Medical School Days
Easter Fancy Dress Ball

"Hi, Sarah. No costume?" Margaret asked above the noise of the band.
Sarah looked and felt uncomfortable, almost regretting her decision.

"You know I hate dressing up. In the end, I couldn't be bothered. I thought, what the hell. It's not compulsory is it?" At that Mike and Sam staggered up; already looking worse for wear as they bounced along to the music that the band spat out; loud power chords crackling through the small PA system that was too large for the Student bar.

Sarah's eyes widened in surprise as she gazed at her three friends.

"What?" Mike exclaimed.

"It's just that I'd never noticed before how similar you can all look. I would almost have put you and Sam as brothers if I didn't know better."

"We're identical triplets." Sam acknowledged.

"Err, yes, I got that, but even so I'm surprised how close you managed to get. That must have taken some doing, Margaret?" Sarah eyed the fact that Margaret had managed to somehow hide her voluptuous chest.

"Believe me, more make up than I care to use in one year, and hair colour. And it's not the most comfortable thing in the world to strap your bust down. Feels like I am being crushed alive."

Sarah looked around the room, the party was in full swing and she was the only one she could see that wasn't costumed up. Her heart sank even further.

"Well you do have ample to share around. I wish I had some of yours, these fried eggs look about as enticing as ... I don't know what."

"They look alright to me." Mike lasciviously ogled them.

"Anything with breasts looks alright to you. It doesn't even have to breathe." Sarah answered cuttingly.

Margaret pulled her to one side. "What's up? You seem very, mmm, pissed off?"

Sarah sighed, "I still can't believe Carl is dead," she took a gulp of her drink. "Plus I hate these things."

"I know. Why would he take his own life? If you feel like that, then why come? It's not compulsory, as you say."

Sarah recognised the imitation of herself from earlier.

"I didn't fancy staying in on my own. I keep thinking about Carl."

"Where's Roger?"

"That's the other thing. He said he wouldn't come with me if I wasn't going to dress up and get into the spirit of things. Plus, he was feeling a bit down because of Carl, and his uncle passed away as well, recently, and no one told him. Left him a bit of money though."

"So he's here? That's a shame. Were they close?"

"Somewhere. He said they were, although he has never mentioned him before; not that I suppose he would, but, you know."

"And we always said he was the square." Margaret smirked placing her hand in front of her mouth to cover it up; however, it was too late. Rather than Sarah being offended she saw the funny side. "At least that will help with school fees."

"Oh sod it, let's get pissed."

"That's more like it, girl.

Chapter 29

1963 December

Liverpool

Morgue

"Dr Bartlett, how's my patient?" Ron chirped cheerfully.

Dr Bartlett eyed DCI Chappell curiously, "I'd say, because she's with me, dead. That's how I normally see them," he dryly smiled.

"I'll bring you a live one someday!"

"That would make such a pleasant change. Then I could ask them how they were killed." Dr Bartlett raised an eyebrow over thick black-framed glasses that sat on his fat face as though they were being eaten by his chubby cheeks.

"Certainly make my job easier." Chappell walked over to the ceramic slab where the body lay covered up; his three-quarter length blue trench coat was still done up to keep him warm. He hated the morgue. He hated death. He hated violence. When he'd joined the force, twenty-six years ago, he'd wanted to prevent the atrocities he'd heard about. That hope had been tainted so quickly as he realised he couldn't necessarily prevent the outcome, only try to discover the circumstances surrounding them; now he despised his job. He felt he was fighting a losing battle. Even his team seemed to accept it as a *fait accompli* of the failing system and he hated the sometimes lack lustre effort this then brought forth. Then there were the deals that you sometimes needed to do to get the right result; it all added to the souring image. Yet it was all he knew and he would do his damndest to make sure the best was done. Without fail. The only real prevention was a crystal ball – now that would have been a blessing.

"So what killed her?" Chappell asked.

"Her heart being cut out," was Dr Bartlett's blunt answer.

"Would she have been alive at the time?"

"Evidence shows she was. No petechial haemorrhaging visible so definitely not strangled, plus hyoid bone is intact. She is frozen in places."

"I know it has been cold lately, but I didn't ..."

"No. She was frozen on purpose; this is not from exposure. There are parts of the organs, and muscle tissue still frozen. Going to take at least a few days for her to thaw out thoroughly, so I can find out if any other method was used, do the usual toxicological tests et cetera."

Chappell almost choked. "Seriously?" He was stunned. "Someone took out her heart then froze her for good measure?"

Bartlett stared sternly at him. "Yes, although I believe, looking at the incisions, and coagulated blood she would have been sedated when the heart was removed, probably moments from death. That would at least be a blessing. The liver and a kidney are also missing. The extractions look as though they have been carried out by a surgeon; clean, precise and methodical."

"Jesus what kind of sicko is this?"

"I don't know. I can only tell you what I know at this stage." Dr Bartlett said, dismissively. "I'll call you in a few days when she's thawed out fully and I know more. But I would say you are looking for someone with a medical background, judging by what I am seeing." Dr Bartlett looked harshly at Chappell. "I will add, the likelihood of finding anything useful is slim. Whilst ice can store evidence, it can also destroy it too. I will not be able to give an accurate determination of how long she has been dead; the indicators will be off because of the freezing cycle."

Chappell shook his head in dismay. "Could it be a botched operation? A black market doctor covering his tracks?"

"Difficult to say at this juncture and I will not surmise on what I do not know."

Chappell did find Bartlett a tad protective with information.

"If you had to offer an opinion?" Chappell encouraged.

"Possibly. Who knows what the human psyche is capable off?"

"There has been no identification of her?"

"Not that I am aware, her prints were taken and we will do any medical record checks where we can."

Chapter 30

1962 March
The Red Lion

"You feeling okay, Mike?" Sam pulled up a seat in what had become their regular table in the Red Lion, since smuggling Sam into the student union bar had got more difficult. It was a largish pub with a private snug bar to one side – members only. It harked back to a spit and sawdust place from the history books; low beams, everything at a crooked angle and no table sitting easily on the flagstone floor – instead rocking unevenly, spilling drinks, a self-perpetuating system – the more you drank the more you spilled; win-win for the pub. The only modern item was a jukebox and even that was broken most of the time, or at least 'out of order'. An open fire raged when it was cold outside, the flames glinting off the metal souvenirs that adorned the walls: bed warming pans, copper pots, brass horseshoes and so on.

Mike looked up and smiled, "Hi, Sam," came the solemn reply, before adding in response to Sam's curious gaze. "What?"

"Is that a Coke?" Sam said, astounded. "You must be ill! You've normally had a few pints by this time."

"Where's Margaret? Maybe I would have, but I am a changed man after an autopsy I attended at Gloucester Infirmary."

"Yeah, right! She's just getting the drinks in. What happened?"

"The guy died from alcohol poisoning. He was thirty-four. Thirty-four! I got to go to the post-mortem. My god you should have seen the liver, or what was left of it. I thought some of the cadavers we saw were bad. Enough to put you off drink for life." Mike tried to be jovial but it didn't quite reach his eyes.

"How long will it last this time?"

"What, me not drinking alcohol? Probably about …"

"Here you go, Mike, thought you'd be ready for another pint by now." Margaret stopped and stared at Mike and then at the Coke in front of him, then at Sam.

"It's a coke, hun. He's a changed man. Had a bad experience at the Gloucester Royal Infirmary; an alcoholic died." Sam answered, consolingly with a hint of sarcasm.

"Bollocks! And that stuff is probably worse for you; all that sugar and flavouring and god knows what other crap they put in it. They used to drink beer because it was better than water, then we invented crap like coke." Margaret stated authoritatively.

Mike's eyes suddenly brightened. "I like this woman, she has a way of putting clarity back into my life."

"No, I just told you what you *really* wanted to hear."

Mike thought about that for a millisecond. "Well, it's rude to argue with a woman. Cheers." He grabbed the pint heartily and took a large refreshing gulp.

"It's never stopped you before." Sam interjected.

"What?" Mike defended, sighing at the beautiful taste of his favourite Newcastle Brown.

"Arguing with a woman." Margaret stated matter-of-factly. "You're sadistic by nature, you love to lose. Anyway everything in moderation and you'll be okay."

Mike didn't answer, obviously relishing the smooth dark liquid, he pushed the coke vigorously aside, almost sending it off the table.

"Now normal service has resumed, where are Sarah and Roger?" Sam asked.

"Didn't Margaret tell you?" Mike replied.

"We've both been a bit busy recently. This is the first time we've seen each other for about two weeks." Margaret sipped her vodka and orange.

"You live together! Surely you speak to each other?"

"Margaret's research has been quite intense recently; she's been coming in quite late, sometimes when I go out to work, and I have been busy, away on business as well."

"It must be another man." Mike toyed seeing if any jealousy existed between them. As usual, they remained steadfastly level-headed in total trust of one another, regardless of the flirting they might do with other people.

"I have all the man I need right here." Margaret placed her hand on Sam's leg. Sam smiled appreciatively, wallowing in the praise and a little surprised by an instant reaction.

"Sorry, Mike, you've either got it or you haven't."

"You're right." He momentarily dipped his head in mock sorrow, before continuing. "Margaret must have low self esteem to be satisfied by that chipolata."

"It's not the size. It's how you use it." Sam retorted brightly.

"Yes, dear, it is. Best you get some practice!" Margaret retracted her hand and smiled reassuringly.

"Well, that's my manhood cut down to size."

"Easy, Sam, you'll be a eunuch if this carries on." Mike laughed.

"Why are we talking about my manhood, anyway?"

"We needed a good laugh."

Mike sprayed beer over the table as he tried to control his laughter at Margaret's comment.

"Alright, alright. Anyway, speaking of manhood what have I missed about Roger and Sarah?" He took a gulp of his own pint.

"They eloped to Gretna Green." Mike stated simply.

It was Sam's turn to almost choke on his beer, barely managing to return the glass to the table as it dribbled down his chin.

"This *is* the same Roger and Sarah who despise each other?" Mike and Margaret nodded their agreement. "How the hell did that happen? What have I missed?" Sam wiped his chin with his hand.

"Research." Mike replied with a hint of sarcasm.

"We all missed it, and Sarah didn't say." Margaret looked scorned.

Sam answered. "What! Sarah's researching how desperate you'd have to be to marry someone like Roger, or how long one could remain married to someone like that?"

"No. " Margaret started. "She actually realised she admired his intellect and his intelligence; the attitude was something she could put up with. She announced it last week."

Mike and Sam stared at her in disbelief. "You're joking?" they both said in unison.

"Yes! He actually made a pass at her! She was drunk and acquiesced, but somehow that changed her opinion of him. Maybe he knew how to use his chipolata." Margaret smiled demurely at Sam.

"Why is it my manhood ..."

"Boyhood." Mike interrupted.

"Ha-ha, very funny. Can we change the subject before my boyhood becomes babyhood!"

"Actually, yes," Mike beamed. "Research!"

Sam and Margaret looked on expectantly.

"You going to expand on that Mikey boy?" Sam asked

"Maybe!" Mike took another gulp of his pint to leave them wanting more.

"Oh, just get on with it, Mike." Margaret snapped impatiently.

"Alright, alright. I have been thinking about suspended animation," Mike stared at Margaret and Sam, "no need to look so shocked, sometimes I can get excited about a subject that is not girls or music. Anyway, will it be a doctor or scientist who makes the breakthrough. As you say, everyone wishfully thinks about eternal youth, and that story you mentioned touches upon it."

"You mean you read it?" Sam asked, surprised.

"Yes, I did and it got me thinking about the cell research you are doing, Margaret."

"Methods of freezing human cells?" Margaret spoke keenly.

"Yes."

"You know my work is confidential at this stage; you know that I shouldn't really have said that." Margaret added cautiously.

"No, I know. Maybe we should look at it in the context of freezing human cells and then trying to re-animate them." Mike continued excitedly, "the space race is happening, right? We have the Soviet Union and America putting people in space. But how big is our galaxy? It is huge. There can be no way we can travel and live for the time it takes to reach some of the planets, so what if we could suspend life and re-animate it near the destination"

"We have already been discussing it, and done some research into." Margaret confirmed.

"Oh."

"We did try and involve you at the beginning but you weren't interested."

"Well, that was then, this is now. I'm allowed to change my mind, aren't I?"

"Yes, suppose. So what are you proposing?"

"We form a club to do that very thing. My step dad's got an empty unit we could utilize as a lab, I'd quite like to see my name in the history books."

"Sounds like some grizzly experiment in those comic books of

Roger's." Sam finished half-heartedly.

"No, not really, but we are all studying medicine, or have studied medicine," Sam waved the comment away, "and we all like the technical side of it. Combining all our knowledge and ideas why don't we see if we can't solve the question 'How do you freeze and unfreeze a human so they can live again?'" Sam and Margaret looked agog at Mike. It was true; all five, including Roger, Sarah and the late Carl had enjoyed dissecting the subject matter at length. And, they all knew the kudos at stake if you could actually answer the question to eternal life; or at least discover a way to live beyond your own death, once a cure had been found for the ravages of time, or illness. Yet Mike suggesting it was a bolt from the blue, and … he was serious; which was even more unusual!

Sam was the first to respond. "So we leave college and continue to study. Sorry you lot leave college."

"Yes, Sam, except the 'leave college' part. We can do it as a sideline and also continue once we have. Also, three, sorry, five heads are better than one. We could go down in history. Why not?"

"How about, hmm, money, materials, how do we freeze human cells?"

"Don't be so negative, Sam. Mike has a point … in principle."

"Yes, but, Margaret, we don't have access to cadavers, so we can't conduct experiments. Research is all very well but, without physical experiments, it is just theory as we have already discussed, and, as we know, you need to conduct the physical side to garner some of that knowledge." Sam's protestations were being lost as the gleeful expressions on Margaret and Mike's faces showed their interest was piqued, and that meant they would find a way to gain the materials needed.

"We just use animals, they're expendable."

"Not if you're Sarah they're not." Margaret answered.

"I still reckon she and Roger will be up for it too. Roger's knowledge is immense, beats nearly all of us put together, hands down." Mike concluded.

"Especially on the technical side of things." Margaret sipped her drink, lost in the kudos of their possible great discovery.

Sam looked at both of them.

"Dimethyl Sulfoxide is a good starting point for preservation,

I think."

Mike and Sam both looked at Margaret but Mike answered. "What about it?"

"We've been looking at it as a preservative for cells. In high concentrations it is toxic but we are looking at fifteen or twenty percent mix with a glycerol."

"Worth investigating then. How about funding? Although I suppose we'll *all* be working soon, except me who already is; so we can have a membership fund of sorts to provide working capital."

"Get you, all, Mr Businessman." Mike laughed. "I have family money, anyway. Plus an inheritance I got recently. Oh no, that *is* family money!" Mike corrected himself smiling.

"Hey guys. We thought we'd find you in here."

All three turned to see Sarah and Roger standing there, beaming with joy.

"Well, if it isn't the happy couple," Margaret said, laced with sarcasm.

Sarah picked up on it straight away.

"I'm sorry we didn't invite you guys. It just kind happened so quickly and ..." Sarah said abashed.

"Congratulations, Roger, you finally drugged someone enough." Mike smiled. "Was it research you were conducting?"

"How very droll, Mike. Some people are lucky enough to find a spark that leads to something more."

"I'm glad you brought that up! We have just been discussing the spark of human life and a research project in respect of cryopreservation." Sam said.

"I think they have better things they want to talk about just now; they have just got married." Margaret stated bitterly, but Roger's interest had already piqued as he leaned in closer.

Sarah turned to see him. "Lost him already! More interested in science," she sighed, feeling deflated.

Margaret smiled. "Men have small attention spans. Don't worry about it."

Chapter 31

1962 March

Following Day

I feel so tired. I couldn't stop thinking about the research project last night in bed; it buzzed round my head all night like an annoying fly. Cryopreservation for re-animation – the future! It's brilliant! It is like the culmination of my life so far: my sister, Gary, the animals; it gives them a purpose, a reason, a justification that satisfies my inquisitive mind – med school has done that to a degree; but I like the feeling of life beneath my hands, feel the pulse of the human body as I perform operations – there's nothing like it. The cadavers don't quite cut it. It is pleasing, but lacks something that I got from my youthful experiments. Power? Control? A frisson of ecstatic energy, feeling life diminish beneath my hands? How had I let it be subdued for so long, playing the dutiful scholar doing everything properly – that has its rewards. But this! All of a sudden I feel fired up, bursting with enthusiasm: to do something that is not following what is already known; searching for new theories, new knowledge.

But *dear* Sarah won't allow live animals to be sacrificed; so that brings us back to the cadavers and organs we can legally get access to. Sometimes, though, you need to sacrifice life to expand and explore new horizons; make history – my name in histo... no, our names. Suddenly the luminosity doesn't seem so bright, as Sheila's memory flashes back at me; a childhood of being half of one. Now, here, I will be one of five.

Dulling the euphoria. I feel a sense of distaste inside.

I suppose I was lucky with Gary and Sheila; no consequences, mere convenient accidents. But I know what still rests within me, and today, it feels like it wants to be let out again. Up to now, whenever I see someone who has annoyed me, I want to imagine them under

71

my knife, feeling their life in my hands; feel it beating for as long as I decide. But I have not conceded to the impulse, instead suppressing it. How has it remained so controlled for so long? It feels like a baying wolf ready to pounce. It's intoxicating.

I want to get immersed in it now. Today!

Yet a small voice, maybe as close to a conscience as I have tells me to tread carefully. Locked up is not something I want. But I want to feel that power again.

Glorious.

Chapter 32

2002 July

"Are you just going to insult me any chance you get?" Sam crossed his arms.

"I am not insulting you. I am merely pointing out facts as they present themselves. It is not for me to cast aspersions. I am just a guide."

"That's as maybe, but most guides I'd expect to be a little respectful."

"Maybe you don't deserve it?"

Sam ignored the question. "Is this like some kind of 'This is your life'? Have I got to relive every moment again?"

"No, Sam, there is a reason. Not everyone goes through this. Most don't need to, but sometimes there is a need, a justification you might say." Geoff held up his hand seeing Sam about to interject. "You must do the journey. There are no shortcuts, like some think there are in life."

Chapter 33

1963 December
Liverpool CID

"Morning Ron. Did you see the footy last night? This is Liverpool's year; Shankly is going to take them all the way! 1-0 against Man U at Anfield," Detective Mark Harris called as Ron entered their offices, shaking Ron from his thoughts.

"Yeah, yeah, believe that when I see it. Where is everyone?" The usually buzzing office was empty, except for Mark.

"You wait. They will! Clive and Dennis are on a murder. Graeme, Frank and Si are following up some muggings and a possible rape."

"Liverpool hasn't got a hope! Don't you have any work then?"

"We will, we will, you wait! Yes, plenty but most requires me here." Ron frowned at Mark who, in his opinion, epitomised the laziness some officers afforded the job; just enough not to get the sack but not enough to impress. "Anyway, you got the result on that bird found outside the Liver building?"

Ron sat down, his slicked-back hair emphasizing his large angular nose. "Yeah, it's a strange one."

Mark became more interested.

"She was frozen. *Still* is frozen in places. Do we know who she is yet?"

"Ah," Mark leapt up and marched a file over to Ron triumphantly, much to Ron's inward disgust. "Susan Jones aged thirty-four, worked for Gardener's Soft Drinks in Grimsby, disappeared in November '62 after a meeting with a Mr ..." he thumbed through the notes, "... Talbot, a twenty something sales guy. Her purse was handed in about an hour ago someone found it a couple of hundred yards from her body. Had been emptied."

"Did you say '62?" Ron became animated.

"Yes."

"So where has she been for the last year or so?" Mark shrugged his shoulders, shutting the file. "Well, maybe we'd better go and see this Mr Talbot. I take it foul play was not suspected at the time of her disappearance?"

"No. Although he admitted being out to dinner with her; eye witness accounts confirmed his story and that she was alive when they left the restaurant car park in their own cars."

"Clever, very clever eh?"

"Seems so."

"You got an address?" Ron asked taking the file from Mark.

Mark was an easy kind of guy although lazy and Ron did find himself begrudgingly drawn to him. If only he made more an effort, Ron couldn't understand how someone could be so easy-going about whether a case got solved or not.

"Witnesses even say he hung around for five minutes or so, writing notes, or something. Her MG Midget was discovered about two miles from home, engine still running. Spotted by patrol car."

Chapter 34

1962 March

Medical School Days
The Red Lion

"So the theory is everything can be frozen, but what are the consequences of being frozen?" Sam looked at the others in turn.

It was Roger who was first to speak: "You also have to consider what is the best temperature to freeze to?"

"Why? Frozen is frozen." Sam asked.

Margaret replied, "Because there can still be some degeneration, decay at molecular or protein level even at frozen temperature, and whilst frozen temperature might slow that down, we need to find a temperature that suspends that degeneration or decay, essentially stopping aging"

"How cold?" Sarah asked.

"I suppose we have to consider the possibility of using liquid helium or liquid nitrogen," Mike fidgeted uneasily as the noise grew in the bar.

"What's the difference?" Sarah looked disinterested.

"Liquid nitrogen is minus 196 degrees C, and liquid helium minus 270 degrees C"

"That's pretty cold, Mike. What about the water in the human body? Won't that be damaging to the cells?"

"Yes, Sam. Another consideration would also be that you will get separation of human salts, proteins et cetera that could be toxic to cell structure and therefore destroy any chance of survival upon thawing."

"Okay, but upon thawing there could be some kind of cleansing, such as the kidneys do now Roger?"

Margaret picked up, "Theoretically, yes, but irrevocable damage could be caused killing the cells."

"So," Mike looked up at the ceiling, "a preservative, maybe an propylene glycol, or an ethylene glycol."

"Possibly, or glycerol with DMSO." Margaret offered.

"But how would you get it into the body, and even if you did it would not reach every cell in order to protect it? Let's face it, if you perfuse through an artery it will reach most organs and limbs but not every cell." Sam looked for acknowledgement.

"Replace the blood with DMSO," Sam looked questioningly at Sarah. "Dimtheyl Sulfoxide," she clarified.

"Nice Sarah," Roger complimented, "that would help absorption into the body."

"I went to the British Library and read a book: 'Mechanics of freezing in Living Cells and Tissues' by H T Meryman; there are some interesting answers in it. I have ordered a copy. When I get it, it may well be worth all of us having a look."

"Is it recent Margaret?"

"1957 so not too long, Sam."

Roger suddenly saw the clock on the wall. "Bugger, I'll be late. Got to go." He grabbed his bag and left, returning a second later, "The brain may be too complex to freeze in the body so that may require special attention. Possibly, in the future, everything else can be replaced, but the brain contains our personalities. Damn, I need to go. Bye."

"Bye, Ro… I suppose that does lead us onto another side to this, and that is who would want to be suspended and wake up in … I don't know one hundred, two hundred years time. Maybe even more."

"I would, Sarah."

"Why, Mike? I don't think I would, you wouldn't know anyone. "

"It's an adventure, Sam, that's why." Mike sat back.

"Kind of like travelling to the far reaches of the galaxy, never to return to Earth in your normal lifetime if you travelled under suspended animation." Margaret intimated.

"The possibilities really are endless. Anyone want another drink?" Sam asked.

Chapter 35

1962 November
Northampton
Dinner with Susan Jones

"Well, thank you for dinner Sam. Glad we could wrap things up." Susan said, her cheerful words slurred slightly from copious wine at dinner. "I'll get my secretary to forward a letter confirming our conversation and our first call-off from the contract, pronto, in the morning."

"You're welcome. Glad we could help. I'll make sure the first shipment is ready to go. Do you want me to arrange a taxi for you?"

"No, it's okay my car's just over there." Susan pointed to a pristine red MG Midget sports car that Sam could only dream about owning.

"Nice car." Sam thought about the Ford Consul, which sufficed, although his mind raced to his dream car, an Aston Martin Italian styled DB4 – maybe one day, if he worked hard.

"Thank you. One of the rewards for working hard." She turned to face Sam, letting the warm smile show. "I'm quite sure you'll succeed. You have a good manner, makes it a pleasure to do business. Don't lose it, Sam, it's worth its weight in gold. Believe me, it's been a struggle being a woman in a man's world, but there is a lot to be said for respect and manners." She placed her left hand on Sam's right arm then shook his hand firmly. "It's been a pleasure to have met you, Sam. See you in three months to review everything."

"Yes," Sam beamed, pleased with himself; his first big contract. After walking Susan to her car, he sat in his, the adrenaline coursing through him, excited at the prospect of announcing a deal for fourteen full containers of orange concentrate to his boss. It was ten o'clock as he watched Susan pull out of the car park. "One day that Aston Martin will be mine."

-

Back in his hotel room, Sam telephoned Margaret, leaving it to ring and ring – just like before he'd gone out to dinner. It worried him a little, although he knew she could get immersed in her work if she felt she was onto something and he was away on business. Maybe she had gone out with colleagues straight from work. He started writing his notes from the dinner meeting before going to bed, although his mind was racing as the commission rang up in bright gaudy neon inside his head. His first big deal agreed. Just needing the final sign off from his boss. Sighing, he sat up too restless to let sleep take him.

Switching the light on he stared briefly at the smoke stained ceiling, churning over the good news. Still restless, he grabbed a book entitled 'Application of the Altmann Freezing-Drying Technique to Plant Cytology' By T. H. Goodspeed, from his suitcase. He'd come across it in a bookshop.

Dropping out of medical school was just a dull fact now; the failing grades, a stark reminder that a keen interest or fascination with a subject did not always secure the acquisition of an ambition. It didn't dampen his fascination with the human body and the one area of interest the group now shared. Their side project was evolving, mainly in discussion form; methodology concerning the re-animation after cryopreservation if they could succeed in actual freezing someone. Two sides to the same issue. This book was deep reading and slow going but was one of the newest books he had come across. The subject was huge covering many different fields of science, chemistry, biology, physics; literature was scarce on the specific subject of freezing someone to date; reserved for speculation in the type of science fiction stories in comic books.

Chapter 36

1962 June
Medical School Days
The Red Lion

"Hi guys, sorry I'm late." Sam strolled up to the table where Roger and Sarah sat. "Bit empty in here tonight. Where's Mike?"

"He sa…" Sarah didn't get a chance to answer.

"Where's Margaret, she said she'd be here by now?" Sam carried on.

"Don't know, she said she had something to do but would be along later." Sarah answered.

Roger added, "and, Mike, we don't know. I seem to recall him mentioning something about his stepdad but not sure exactly."

"Probably getting earache from him, you'd think he'd be pleased to have a doctor in the family. All he seems to want is for him to take over the business. Spare car parts I ask you. He'll never do it. Anyway, let me get a drink." Sam dashed off.

"… carotid might be better." Roger was saying.

"What we discussing?" Sam sat down placing two drinks on the table prompting curious looks from the others. "Sarah said Margaret will be here, later so … doesn't matter."

"If we are to perfuse cryoprotectant of sorts into the human body what would be the best artery to use? I said the femoral artery because I think it may be easiest to administer and repair." Sarah looked to Sam.

"And I say the carotid as it is closer to the pump, the heart, and also the brain, probably the two most important organs you need if you are going freeze someone quickly. You have to consider the fact that we are talking about dead people, and the quicker you perfuse the cryoprotectant, the better the chances. We have to work on logic that science will have found ways in the future to replace limbs, organs, possibly re-growing them …" Roger stopped as Sam interrupted.

"Wow, that really *is* science fiction; regenerating organs. And if they can, then surely the heart will be replaceable, so really it is just the brain; that's what holds our personality and knowledge."

"No, Sam, it is not just science fiction." Margaret strolled up looking stern.

"Hi, Margaret. I got you a drink."

"Thanks hun, I need it." She took a long drink. "Regeneration of cells, including organs, is something that is being researched now. We know cells regenerate and bacteria can replicate, so why can we not do it with organs at some point in the future?"

"True," Roger agreed, "I suppose it is whether we are looking at space travel as the need for suspended animation, or for time travel. If space travel, then we need to preserve life for the journey, literally just suspending it. If for time travel, we can discount the need to worry about organs, to a degree, if we hypothesise science will solve the conundrum of replacing organs, limbs and whatever else in the future; then, I guess people will want a whole host of improvements when they are brought back to life."

"I thought we were discussing which artery to use?"

"We are, Sarah. Also, as part of that we need to realise what is the most important organ and therefore the least replaceable, and that is the brain, so the carotid artery would be the best to use." Roger concluded smugly.

Sam nodded as he watched all agree. "How about thawing?"

"That in itself has issues ..." Roger continued adjusting his glasses.

Chapter 37

1962 November

Lincolnshire Storage Yard

From the confines of my car I survey the dark yard, which beckons like a welcoming friend; the trepidation and excitement course through my veins like electricity. It's that familiar feeling; the one I thought I had put behind me. It feels good to be set free again. There *is* a reason for this and the deceit only adds to its delectation.

Studying the small yard, I am questioning my criteria. What exactly do I need for my *experiments*? This is the thirteenth one I have viewed at varying locations around the country under the pretence of my job, some rural and some industrial. In the end it is just a gut feel. Following my telephone conversation earlier, a man called Ben Shaker is waiting for me in the neglected portacabin to the left of the entrance.

Inside, a nervous energy somersaults; it is something I haven't felt for nearly six years, something that I thought medicine would quell yet had only subdued below the surface. This feels so different. Having gotten away with two murders in my life, openly, it fills me with confidence as I start this new chapter; although I know this will be different and there is a need to be more creative now. The conversation about researching suspended animation re-ignited a desire within me, despite knowing the risks. There is something about sharing that harks back to my sister and that instant I sent Rex dragging her across the tracks in front of the train. I knew what I was doing; relished the fact that I would be rid of her. After spending so many years as one half, it was nice to be singular. This will be just like the animals that followed Sheila's death; which only intensified that feeling, that lust for seeing life fade, that instant, although ultimately this is about preserving life. That is the juxtaposition; taking life to solve the mystery.

I think back to Gary's accident and wonder if I could've brought him round to my way of thinking. Would I have wanted to? When I *felt* his life fade beneath my hands. It was glorious. I was in control! I could have tried to save him; yet I didn't want to.

I can still see that day in my head, May 1956, as fresh as it was then, that euphoric, almost orgasmic ecstasy coursing through my veins.

Fascinated I stared down at Gary's body; the blood no longer gushing from his wounds, just a slow pulse as every heartbeat forced a little more out, thwump thwump … thwump … … thwump … … … thwump then more slowly. Watching in awe, I drank in every detail.

I remember placing my hands in Gary's blood: remember its warmth. There was so much of it; unlike the animals. Thick and sticky! I was excited by the expression of shock in his eyes as they pleaded with me, why?

I knew the reaction required when the police and ambulance arrived; but, for now I languished in the excitement of watching a friend suffering, confused by the betrayal.

As the final breaths came, I placed a finger to Gary's lips.

"Thank you."

I am still smiling as I remember my acting when the man turned up.

"What you doing? You shouldn't be playing there. It's dangerous."

"Yes, it is," I whispered, before the tears and the hysteria came flooding out in a big act.

"It was an acc…ide…nt." I sobbed frantically.

"Oh god!" was the stunned reaction from the man as his saw Gary's body.

The warmth of the memory fades as the cold of tonight bites in.

"Damn the heating, it has never worked properly, bloody thing, even before it was stolen!" A cover story – I thought best to have one; it now has false plates.

I check my disguise in the mirror; the flat-cap is pulled low shadowing my eyes, a scarf covers the lower part of my face. Everything I can wear to distort my build I have done. Whilst I know he doesn't know me, I do not want him to get a good look either. I've been practising an accent, one that struck me as easy, and I repeat key words to keep it fresh in my mind. A name – that was easy!

Time to start.

★ ★ ★ ★

I exit the portacabin as the Burgundy Zephyr lumbers into the yard and stand sentry-like to my kingdom, the headlights illuminating it. It is late, even for me and my shady deals, which I normally conduct during the day as it looks less conspicuous – after all, this site of eight units are in a residential area. The guy was persistent, and I am always happy to oblige as it shows their weakness.

I eye the man as he hesitates before getting out of the car.

"We got a right one here." I remark to myself. "What cock and bull am I gonna get?"

"You, Ben Shaker?" He says as he gets out.

"Yep. You must be, Sam Smith?" I reply, noting something seems misplaced about the accent.

"I'm sorry about the late hour, it was the only time I could get free."

"Sure it is. The unit's this way." I indicate with a sideways tilt of the head before leading Sam over to the far corner of the yard. I can't help think about the accent, smiling. They are funny things – accents – difficult to maintain unless well rehearsed; normally once engaged in conversation the person usually forgot to keep it up, a certain word, or phrase tripping them up. I make it my job to look for information that could prove useful. Once I know the area where the person has originated from, I make enquiries with various contacts, looking for suitable blackmailing information, which normally comes to light; even the 'holier than thou' person has secrets.

Pulling a bunch of keys from my three-quarter-length leather jacket, I continue. "It's got power, like you wanted. I'll include that." Springing the heavy-duty padlock, I pull back the doors opening up the vast, dark space beyond. "Here," I flick a torch on and accidentally, on purpose, shine it into Sam's face; he grabs it from me angrily – I let him, as I smile inside.

"Sorry, mate." I flick the switch for the double fluorescent tubes, waiting for them to blink into life.

I can see this Sam mentally planning the layout; he wants it!

★ ★ ★ ★

I walk into the unit. I can see myself here. Everything has a place. The space is perfect, solidly built, dry, electricity, easy to make more secure as there are very few windows.

Almost as if my thoughts had been heard, Ben leans into conspiratorially. "It's not got many windows and this yard is very private. You won't be disturbed; even the law don't come in here. I make sure of that. Hence the price."

I play it innocently. "Not fussed about the police, I have nothing to hide." I lie. "I do like it, it will work for what I have in mind. I'll take it. I'll be arranging some deliveries soon, won't be a problem will it?" I almost scold myself as, lost in the fervour of the moment, I let the accent drop.

* * * *

I knew it! I'll note that.

"Whatever. I can arrange for it to be open, just call this number and let the man know the time and date." I hand Sam a piece of paper. What are you trying to hide, my friend? I'll find it, don't you worry about that. All my tenants are in too deep, and they'll be my eyes and ears. In fact, you could say this is my most profitable yard – maybe *enterprising* would be a better term.

I watch Sam pocket the paper and walk stiffly back to his car. Something about his walk is not right. I note the car registration for the file that I'll start when back in my home office.

* * * *

There is work to be done and definitely new locks to keep out prying eyes and what windows there are will need boarding up. Ben Shaker, you are my only concern. I feel you could be trouble if I am not careful, but my gut feeling is that this is the right place.

Chapter 38

2002 July

"I think there is someone you need to see."

Before Sam had time to answer Sam found himself standing in the middle of a country lane. Two cars, an MG Midget and a burgundy Zephyr, were just pulling up on the side of the road, their headlights the only illumination in an otherwise pitch-black night.

Geoff's voice broke his thoughts, "Do you recognise her?"

"What? I don't understand …" But Sam didn't finish as he saw the door to the spitfire open and a tall, well-dressed woman in her forties get out. She was a little wobbly, teetering on four-inch heels. The Zephyr had stopped behind her and the driver was getting out, a flat cap pulled low over the eyes and a long bulky raincoat hanging down to the stylish Frye boots.

Recognition flashed across Sam's mind. "Susan Jones. My god!"

"You do remember?" Geoff's voice returned.

The woman stopped and looked around as though she had heard something, her warm breath rising into the cold night air. Instantly, she became wary as the figure in the raincoat strolled purposefully towards her, hands hidden in the deep pockets.

"Why did you flash me?" Susan slurred but the man didn't speak just pointed to the rear of the Spitfire, Susan turned to look. "What? I can't see anything?"

The man withdrew a gloved hand holding a folded handkerchief and, as Susan turned her back to the shadowy figure, he took quick long strides to reach her. She found herself knocked off balance as the figure reached round, covering her mouth and nose with the handkerchief. "What the … help!" Her muffled words fell silent as shock was followed by disorientation, the sweet scent mixed with alcohol creating a delirium in which her mind and body swam as she swung wildly to fight free, her normal strength failing quickly falling limp in the figure's arms, before being dragged to the boot of the Zephyr.

Sam stared on in disbelief as more memories came flooding back – how he had been questioned about her disappearance; their dinner meeting earlier that evening; how his boss had had to step in to secure the deal that he and Susan had discussed; the questioning by the police, twice, as every time the investigation led back to him as the last person to see her alive.

"So that's what happened to her!" He paused. "Why am I seeing this?" Sam asked. Then, as the Zephyr pulled through him, an acid-like burning seeped into every fibre of his dead body, paralyzing him as a phantom glow rose up from the boot and encompassed him. Sam cried out in agony. Then all fell silent as a calm took over.

He was back in the BMW racing along the M1, Geoff at the wheel, Sinatra crooning away, carefree. He was at peace, he didn't understand why.

Geoff spoke again.

"Did you feel the burn a soul makes in another?"

"Wha…aaaarrrgh!" Every sinuous morsel of dead flesh ignited with pain, the pupils of his eyes like scalding water, every single hair on his arms and legs like a million electric shocks, his toe-nails burning like molten lava, then a coldness wrapped its cloak around him and he started to shiver.

"You need to know, Sam." was all Geoff said.

But Susan was 35

Chapter 39

1962 November
Lincolnshire Storage Yard

After many stolen days and a multitude of deliveries, I have the lab exactly as I want. I have lost track of the cost; an inheritance giving me the means. I'd paid a couple of out of town guys to give the unit a makeover before the equipment arrived; they have done a good job. The place looks sparkling. The walls were cleaned to within an inch of their life then whitewashed; the floor washed and painted with a deep thick red floor paint; the windows covered with three-quarter inch plyboard – screwed and glued into place, secure; the plain corrugated asbestos roof has been hidden by an insulated ceiling underneath. Three low level second-hand open bookcases will be my storage, an old solid wardrobe converted into a secured closed cupboard to house the chemicals and solutions that I will start with. I feel it is a comfortable place to carry out my work even if it did take nearly three nights to set it up and iron out any issues.

Tonight it was so pleasing to arrive and confirm the freezers, looking like giant stainless steel capsules, are working as planned and keeping constant temperature. Resources are limited and I will need to use smaller caskets for organs as I cannot have large deliveries of liquid nitrogen turning up – the group discussed that this was the obvious choice for freezing as absolute zero is where the metabolism stops, life is suspended.

I have already set in motion valid excuses for getting away on a regular basis, something that will not arise suspicion as home life falls into place; my job providing more opportunities to travel, to conceal my secret. It is almost too easy.

Sometimes, I feel like two people, or at least two personalities: inside, the cold uncaring individual I hide from everyone; outside, I convey a warmer side. Can I ever really love someone the way everyone talks? I doubt it, but I put on a good show when needed. It is tiresome; this time alone is my Avalon.

Taking a victim will not be easy, animals were easy; but people!

I enjoy the warmth from the wood burner that sits in the far corner, beyond the car – which I bring in too, as I contemplate this. It is not the only source of heating, but the best when not using flammable chemicals. I can also burn evidence!

My toppest purchase is a ceramic slab bought from a closing hospital; it will serve as the metaphorical table of enlightenment – easy to clean, it will double up as my desk. A metal trolley in the corner awaits its final dressing – the tools – my present to myself; a velvet roll tied neatly by two blue ribbons containing the shimmering shiny surfaces of scalpels, saws, clamps, and other tools. It was an expensive purchase, but worth it. I even managed to get three extra lab coats when I got them for the group – no one has noticed; now they sit neatly folded awaiting use.

It is tantalising to think that soon I will start my work. I am tingling with anticipation as I stare around admiringly at my lab, the sweet hum of the two freezers, the empty Dewar vacuum flasks merely awaiting their contents, the notebooks ready for my results.

That first experiment beckons like sweet honey. There will be no turning back. Sheila and Gary I had gotten away with: there was no comeback from either. If I get caught now, there will be, without a doubt. It is eclipsed by the immortality of my name in the history books of science; the breakthrough! They just won't know how some of the results were procured.

How do I choose victims? Who to choose? Who deserves the prestige in helping me make history? When and where? A conundrum I have puzzled for the last few months as I watch people walking on the street, or playing in the park, innocent people all good prospects; they call to me, 'Me, me, me', I struggle to hold back sometimes as I see opportunities opening up all around me. There are almost too many questions to fathom.

I'd spent hours racking my brain who to start with. There didn't seem to be any criteria that were particularly useful; then it presented itself like a shining halo. Just something about the situation drew me to it, and to her, maybe it was the intensity of her eyes, her friendliness, plus her slight inebriation made her an easy target. I didn't know if I would carry it out at first; my well thought out plan almost superfluous as I followed her for miles, her MG Midget snaking across the road in places. Finally we hit a stretch of country lane. Almost instinctively I flashed my headlights, I prickled with a heady mix of nerves and excitement. My heart pounded. I flashed her again. She slowed to a stop. I couldn't believe it. Adrenalin was coursing through me at a rate of knots, my palms felt sweaty inside my leather gloves.

I watched her get out; I leant across and soaked a clean hanky with chloroform. Words were a jumble in my mind as I opened my car door; it had all seemed so clear a few moments earlier.

The cold night air calmed me.

She asked me something but the blood was pumping so fast in my ears I did not hear, just merely pointed to the rear of her car.

The woman staggered drunkenly to the back of the car.

In a few long strides I'd closed the gap. She was taller than me in her four-inch-heals, and quite broad shouldered. I reached round placing the handkerchief over her mouth and nose; she struggled, swinging wildly but I was too strong for her as she slowly succumbed. Adrenalin pumped so fast around my body I was almost shaking. Dragging her to the boot I carefully placed her in it, tying her hands and feet, placing a gag in her mouth. I left the chloroform hanky in the boot. Slamming it shut, a palpable tension sent me on a high. I'd done it. I'd actually done it!

The drive back seemed to pass in a dream, a daze of delirium.
I had no qualms, no guilt, just like before, as I pulled into my lab.

'My lab' I like the sound of that. Closing the doors is the opening to a secret world, my secret world! My rules. My ideas. Finally all the pieces roll into place.

Opening the boot I view my prize, she looks so peaceful. I am surprised how difficult she is to move. I'd not really moved an unconscious body by myself before, it is awkward, I break a sweat. Finally, with considerable effort I get her out of the boot and carry her to the ceramic slab, thankfully she is only unconscious as I need her alive. I inject her with a small dose of Ketamene to make sure she stays that way; then carefully strip her. She's had children. The clothes definitely made the woman, as she looks older now, plainer.
I want her heart, liver, and a kidney.

Tenderly I get the velvet roll of surgical tools out, lining them up on the metal trolley, savouring every moment as I admire them. With a fresh crisp lab coat on, I revel in the moment. I don't even notice the coldness. The first incision calls to me, entices me on; I can't resist any longer.

I slice through the skin with my C10 scalpel, exposing the breast-plate, then saw through that with my shiny bone-saw. There, in all its glory, I see the heart beating away; blood is everywhere, there is so much. Working on cadavers never really prepares you for it and I have no-one else to use suction to keep it away. For a moment I lose myself in its own life, its warmth. I'd seen hearts before, working hearts, yet there was something magical about tonight. My first solo! And, despite the fact that blood is flowing over the ceramic slab and dripping onto the floor where I had poured sawdust in anticipation, I am focussed on my mission. I place my hands around it, feeling its beats as they get weaker due to blood loss. I grab my scalpel, clamps and sponges. My crisp, white lab coat is saturated and my clothes underneath feel so too, good job I have a change. A butcher's apron! That's what I need.

Working quickly, I cut arteries and watch as the heart finally stops. There it is, that orgasmic feeling inside me. I savour it. It is a high that is better than sex.

Methodically, I harvest the organs I want, placing them in the Dewar flasks after perfusing them with a mixture of Dimethyl Sulfoxide (DMSO) and propylene before suspending in liquid nitrogen; sourced from a contact of the caretaker at med school, he wanted to make a bit of extra money.

I place her body in one of the freezers, adding the dewar flasks and a small amount of liquid nitrogen, to help the cooling; I know it is not enough to freeze a whole body but at this stage it is just about getting the temperature of the freezer down in order to maintain the canisters and their precious experiments. There is also a ventilation hose that I connect that will send the resulting carbon dioxide out into the night air. It would be so nice to place a whole body in liquid nitrogen. Patience. The body, I just need stored frozen at below zero degrees at this stage; my feeling that if I return the body now, it will arouse suspicion too early. I need to put time and distance between collection and disposal. I need to be clever. Locking the freezer with a padlock I add her initials and date on the side in chalk before starting the clear up, sweeping the sawdust up for burning, then gathering water from a standpipe in the yard. The blood takes longer than I imagined; the mess is worse than I had thought.

My clothes underneath the lab coat are indeed soaked with blood. I need to burn them all.

I start to make my notes:

Susan Jones
November '62
Heart, Liver, Kidney

History has shown that freezing worked. In 1799, near the delta of the Lena River the remains of a Woolley Mammoth were discovered by Ossip Schumachov proving the preservation by freezing alone is possible, but not how to retrieve life from the frozen state.

Cell structure is the biggest obstacle; all the medical references speak about ice crystals forming, the sharp edges piercing cell membranes, meaning any chance of returning life to the human form is impossible.

This journey could uncover the secret to eternal life, the secret we need to be able to explore the outer reaches of space, as space travel becomes likely. What would the future hold if you could suspend your own life, wake up centuries from now? 'The Time Machine' was a fascinating film but the reality of travelling through time in minutes is so off the spectrum! The only time travel will be from being able to suspend life indefinitely just like in R Ettinger's 'The Penultimate Trump'.

I place Susan's and my clothes – after changing – in the fire: the last piece of evidence. I spend the next couple of hours fearing being caught for my stupidity as the burning fibres produce an acrid smell. I will have to find another way to dispose of them.

Finally, time to leave. There is a red sky dawning; it is nearly seven o'clock. I have places to be, a life to lead. I place the notebook majestically back in the converted wardrobe. It is done! Started!

Chapter 40

1963 December

Sam & Margaret's First Flat

"Steak and Kidney pie, my favourite." Sam inhaled the wonderful aroma sitting down at the dinner table still revelling in their first home together. It may be rented but life was falling into place. Whilst leaving med school had been painful to accept, he no longer felt the defeat that it once was. He loved his new job: the travel, the rewards – especially as it had allowed them to rent this flat whilst Margaret finished med school, although her MOD job was taking up a lot of her time.

"I know." Margaret said with a sarcastic smile. "You have a lot of favourites!"

"Only when cooked by you."

"Exactly. You used to cook for me, whatever happened to that, eh?" Margaret countered.

He had to admit that, they had slipped into a stereotypical pattern of husband and wife, although they weren't married – and that was something he wanted to remedy. Now looking at Margaret, he felt she had more to say.

"You're right."

"As usual."

"Yes, yes, okay. I'm sorry, I suppose I have neglected my fair share a little. It is just work has been so ..."

"And what about my studies, and my part time job with the courses they want me to attend?"

Sam placed his knife and fork on the side of the plate.

"Sorry."

"I know, and I do understand about your ..." The doorbell chimed. Margaret looked at her watch. "Who can that be?"

"I suppose we'll never know unless we answer it." Sam got up and smiled at Margaret. "We should get married."

The doorbell chimed again.

"How romantic," Margaret admonished with a wink.

"You're not romantic. You've told me a hundred times."

The bell chimed yet again.

"I think you'd better get that."

As he walked away, "Well?" There was no reply.

Opening the front door Sam saw two gentlemen dressed in raincoats. One wore a green patterned trilby.

"Mr Talbot? Mr Samuel Talbot?" Sam took a step back as they produced warrant cards, fear flashing through him. "Detective Chief Inspector Chappell and this is Detective Harris. Do you mind if we ask you a few questions?" Sam stood open mouthed. "Sir?"

"Yes, yes. I mean no, no, I don't. Come in." He finally replied, racking his brains for why the police would be here. "Can I get you a tea, or something?"

"Thank you, that would be nice." Chappell replied. And then added dryly. "The drive from Liverpool has been quite long one."

"Liverpool!" Sam looked for clarification; none was forthcoming.

Sam led them into the lounge before going back into the dining room.

"It's the police, Margaret."

She looked up at him, panic flashing in her eyes. "What do they want? Mike's okay isn't he?"

"I don't know. Can you put my dinner in the oven and make some tea?" Sam left without waiting for an answer.

"So, Detectives. How can I help you?" Sam sat uneasily in the Guy Roger's armchair, whilst the detectives occupied the same designer's settee.

"Nice furniture," Harris said, impressed.

"Thanks, we've only just bought it, delivered last week," he nervously tried to sound unstressed.

"Expensive." Chappell commented making Sam feel uncomfortable.

"Yes, yes it was." Sam fidgeted. "What can I do...?"

"Mr Talbot," Chappell became serious. "We need you to tell us exactly what you know about Susan Jones."

Sam reeled back as the name struck a memory of the dinner meeting, and it came flooding back. The look was clearly noted by the detectives.

"Mr Talbot. Susan Jones?"

Sam stammered, "Well, mmm, she is, was a business acquaintance, she disappeared, what, over a year ago now, I think."

"After a dinner meeting with yourself?"

"Yes, yes, that's it really. I went back to my hotel and then..."

"She was murdered." Chappell stated with a hint of menace.

Shock ran across Sam's face. "Murdered?"

Margaret waltzed into the room with a tray. "Here we go. The kettle had not long boiled. Just leave it to stand for a few minutes. I didn't know how you take it so there is milk, sugar, and a few biscuits." She said breezily, eyeing the two men inquisitively.

"Thank you, Mrs ...?" Harris questioned.

"Margaret. You're welcome. If there is nothing else?" Margaret hovered. But there was no reply, so she left.

"Yes, murdered, Mr Talbot." Harris poured the tea and added three sugars to his cup before stirring vigorously.

"But, I thought she disappeared." The two men eyed each other.

"Where were you on the seventeenth and eighteenth November last?"

Sam's mind rolled back, it was only a few weeks ago. "What days of the week?" he asked innocently.

"It was a Thursday and Friday." Margaret marched into the room carrying a diary, to the surprise of the detectives. "You were away on business Sam, we were both away, I had my placement at The Royal Edinburgh Hospital that week."

Sam look confused. "I guess so." He shrugged.

"Do you know where you were?" Harris stood up to look at the diary, supping his tea. Sam felt the pressure rising.

"What is this concerning?" Margaret asked, innocently.

"Susan Jones, Mrs Talbot."

"The woman who has been on the news who disappeared in '62, wasn't it?" Margaret queried.

"Yes," Chappell responded frowning. "She has turned up, outside the Liver Building on the morning of the eighteenth November."

"Oh!"

"She's dead, Mrs Talbot."

Margaret looked nonplussed. "What's this got to do with Sam?"

"He was the last person to see her alive and we are just making enquiries."

"So?" Margaret said, sternly. "It does not mean he killed her," Sam shot a glance at Margaret, "and she disappeared over a year ago, correct?"

Harris spoke before Chappell could answer. "Correct. And, no, but we just want to find out as much information as possible. Put together a picture. She'd been frozen, Mrs Talbot. The pathologist has said that some organs and tissue samples were taken."

Margaret and Sam shared a look of shock. Margaret regained her composure quickly.

"It's not Mrs Talbot; we're not married. I still don't see what that has to do with Sam."

"We are just trying to eliminate persons of interest from our investigation." Chappell continued with just a hint of annoyance, which was not lost on Sam who was taken aback by Margaret's abrasiveness.

"I'm sorry, but I don't know anything else. We met up about six-thirty and I think we left the restaurant about ten." Sam explained, innocently.

"Business or pleasure?" Mark threw in, seemingly trying to unsettle Sam.

"Purely business." Sam felt himself redden. "We concluded a contract for fruit juice. It proved quite inconvenient that she disappeared. I nearly didn't get the business we'd agreed."

"Oh, well that's important then. Not that someone lost their life."

"I didn't mean it like that."

"No, of course not, Sir." Chappell pursed his lips as if a sour taste lingered in his mouth.

Chappell and Harris looked at each other.

"Thank you for the tea." Chappell smiled without any hint of meaning it. "We won't keep you any longer. Don't want you to miss Coronation Street. We know where you are if we need to talk again." The insinuation in Chappell's voice clear. "If you do think of anything gives us a call." He placed a card on the table.

"Yes, sure." Sam replied timidly.

* * * *

"They were lying. That's for sure." Harris said, once they were back in the car.

"Something is definitely amiss. But we have nothing we can use for leverage at this stage."

"I wouldn't mind making something up." Harris added, sarcastically.

Chappell turned the ignition aggressively. "That's probably what holds you back getting promotion, you make it known that your morals are, shall we say less than straight."

"Just a joke, I would never."

"You've said it too much about too many cases."

"How many times have I been right though?"

"Doesn't matter, it doesn't sit well with top brass, and they have final say on promotions."

Harris let it go and settled in for the long ride back to Liverpool.

Chapter 41

1963 November

Medical School Days

"Right, ladies and gentleman, today – as part of the new curriculums – and as something that is looking more and more likely to progress to becoming standard, once the issue of rejection has been dealt with, I thought we'd try a transplant. As some of you may have read, Dr Thomas Starzl performed a liver transplant this year in America. Whilst this is still in its infancy, I can see there is a great future for this kind of surgery, as kidney transplants are already being attempted, although not successfully, unless you count, Richard Herrick, who died this year. But some say I am full of shit, behind my back." Dr Grace paused to allow the gathered intellects to have a giggle at his expense. "Yes, I'm a doctor and I know things." Again, another murmur. "So, working in your pairs on your cadaver, I want you to perform a liver transplant with the pair next to you. I want you to assess some of the issues and complications and I will be expecting a joint paper assessing the procedure. I will be assessing your practical work personally. This type of procedure might not come round in my tenure, but I am sure it will in yours, so you can call this a fortuitous lesson and you can thank me at my funeral. Now get on."

"He's feeling toppest this morning, obviously just had sex. Oh my God, I'm turning into Roger, using words like 'toppest'! Help me!" Mike's flippant remark caused Roger to frown. "He is happy; he is not normally this happy. And I'm using your words. I don't know what is worse."

"Mike, it may surprise you to know but some people actually get high on the thought of progress, they do not need physical exertion to gain euphoric, intense pleasure."

"I think you need to work on your pillow talk. Hope you and Tony are going to be ready for our liver, we'll have this baby whipped out in a second, Margaret."

Margaret glanced over as Tony readied their cadaver. Mike was expertly making his first incision on the heavily operated-on cadaver.

"Children, please." Dr Grace admonished.

Margaret watched Mike, admiring his skills. He was good, almost as if he had been born with it. Turning back to her cadaver, Tony was working his way through the procedure, his large hands clumsily fumbling about.

"Here, let me! I think an 11 scalpel will be better, it's more accurate." Methodically and together they worked through the procedure. "We know some of the issues are nicking a vein or artery – easy and obviously a big no-no."

Tony continued. "Then there is blood pressure, and possible heart failure. Anaesthesia."

"Blood units would be needed. How about rejection?"

" Richard Herrick is the only real success to date and that was due to his twin being the donor."

"I suppose another issue is having a donor handy who is a tissue match, which Mr Herrick did. Is there a way round that?"

"Watch the artery, Margaret."

"Ain't you done yet?" Mike chipped in.

"It's not a race you know."

"I know, I could quite happily spend hours with my hands inside a body." Mike glanced back at the cadaver. "Well a live one at least; dead ones just don't do it for me. There is something so nice about feeling the body functioning whilst your hands are in it."

"I worry about you, Mike." Roger added.

"I'm with you on that," Tony agreed. "You do realise we need to be in and out as soon as, so they have a chance of survival and it's not a plaything for you to enjoy yourself."

"Guys, you have to have some pleasures."

Chapter 42

1963 November
Lincolnshire Storage Yard

Ben was viewing Sam's unit from his locked portacabin, as was his protocol with new tenants. It had been a year since this strange guy had taken the unit and still he had not been able to gain any knowledge about him. He didn't really care what he was up to; he just liked to have something he could use – blackmail! He'd spent many nights sleeping in his office over the years and got used to his little camp bed, it was almost home, taking him back to a happier time in his childhood; fishing with his father, before seeing him gunned down in an act of betrayal – his father had been a light-weight-heavy, dealing with small-time criminals until double crossed, leaving Ben the man of the family – taking control of his father's manor in his late teens. With it came the venom that he had to cut a figure not to cross. He also knew how to play the waiting game; this was the longest he'd ever had to wait, but he was patient. He knew that Sam always came at night; he was not regular either, and that is why it had taken so long.

A primitive yet discreet fishing line had been rigged up so that when the door to Sam's unit was being opened a small bell would ring and wake him up. It had proved effective many times.

He was surprised to see the man drive his car into the unit – what was he trying to conceal? Ben had tried to enter the storage unit through a secret, loose panel he'd prepared before letting it out, but had found it to be blocked and had to give credit to this man, who was cleverer than he had initially thought.

Ben waited.

Chapter 43

2002 July

Sam's mind frantically turned over the image of Susan.

"What has it got to do with me?"

Geoff turned to him, his glaring eyes showing the accusation.

"It wasn't me! You don't think it was me? It wasn't!" He tried to recollect the evening and everything he had subsequently told the police. "I went back to my hotel."

"It is not my job to think, merely to deliver you. I have my instructions and it is important that you feel and see what I show you. Everything. But I will say this, was that your car? Was that your coat? Was that your cap?"

The questions were burning fire etching their doubt in his mind. It could have been his car but the number plate was wrong. His car had been stolen some months before that meeting. He'd had his first sexual encounter with Margaret in the back, the first fumblings of an excited courting couple, exploring boundaries; fond memories.

"I am innocent. I told the police. I can't be accountable for lives I didn't take."

"That is not for me to decide. I am merely carrying out my instructions, following orders. I have earned my place in the afterlife, now you must earn yours and this is the first step."

Chapter 44

1963 April

The Red Lion

Mike sat in the Red Lion staring at his pint, not really taking it in.

"You alright, Mike? You look a bit down in the dumps." Sarah interrupted his thoughts.

"Eh. Yeah, fine." Mike continued staring into nothing.

"Surely it's not that bad?" Sarah sat next to him placing her Vodka and orange on the table.

Mike sighed wearily.

"You know you can talk to me if you want." She paused, "It is unusual for you to be down. You haven't got a problem with a class have you? Or, it's not your foster parents again, trying to diss you for studying medicine?" Sarah smiled but Mike still looked solemn.

"Actually it's a birthday." He finally conceded.

"That's hardly …"

"My sisters."

Sarah frowned, "that's nothing to be sad about. Hold on, you don't have a sister."

"Used to. She's dead. Died when she was younger. We were younger."

Sarah sat open-mouthed at the revelation.

"It doesn't normally affect me but …" he paused, playing with his pint on the table. Sarah sat waiting, a compassion exuding from her eyes. "It's just that a cadaver on the slab reminded me of her, the eyes looked so much like hers it was frightening. I don't recall ever being knocked for six like that." A minute went by with only the hubbub of the bar noise filling the space.

Sarah looked uneasy, not used to seeing Mike vulnerable.

"Was this an adopted sister, or real? How old was she?"

"Fourteen."

"That explains a lot about you, Mike." Sam chimed cheerfully dancing up to the table "What do you want to drink?"

Sarah shot a cursory glance at Sam whilst Mike switched mood, instantly gulping the remainder of his drink: the facade was up.

"A pint, please, mate." A smile plastered across his face, although it didn't quite illuminate his eyes completely.

"Sarah?"

"Vodka and orange." She spat out, leaving Sam looking flabbergasted.

"What have I done?" He looked at each in turn.

There was a pause.

"Just get the drinks in. Is Margaret coming along?" Sarah added, testily.

"No, well, a lot later she's been away for a few days and has got an errand to run."

Sam left them to it.

"You okay, Mike?" Sarah asked, the compassion back in her voice

"Yeah, fine thanks. Just thirsty, where's my drink."

Chapter 45

1964 January
Liverpool

A new day dawned on the now familiar beat; Susan Jones still remained foremost in William's mind as he approached the Liver building with trepidation; he kept hoping that he would find a clue that had been missed by the team of experts who'd combed the area.

Nothing.

Like a ritual, he vowed to do his best. That would not be today, as the heavens had opened and the rain was like stair-rods with a chill wind driving it into every fibre.

He'd started to see familiar people on his round: the postman delivering first class, and the milkman busy depositing the breakfast pints. He lamented these short two line casual conversations and especially the one that had led to his first arrest.

"Morning, Stan, enjoy St Ives?"

"William, yes, the kids loved it! We've already booked for next year."

Then both briskly carrying on their business before Stan stopped again.

"Oh, William, I was down Station Crescent yesterday morning and there is something dodgy going on at number sixteen. They were unloading a van, and well, it looked like some knocked off gear to be honest. Probably nothing, but what with those shop break-ins recently and it was five in the morning. And I overhead mention about the job."

"I'll check it out later, maybe speak with a few of the neighbours. Thank you."

It was nice having the eyes and ears.

Later that day, he had gone down, spoken with a few neighbours; there definitely had been something suspicious going on and, within a few days, enough evidence had been gathered to search the place and true to the information; stolen goods had been recovered with three arrests made.

It had proved invaluable and had settled William's mind, giving him the resolve that he still wanted to do this job. There was good that he could do. It gave him the determination to speak to CID about Susan Jones as well, and soon. He had put it off despite his good intentions and because Christmas had got in the way but he knew it was a pathetic excuse and one for which he felt some guilt. Susan Jones' family didn't have her for Christmas – the juxtaposition was that he desperately wanted to see his own family, sister, mother and father back in Hertfordshire – feel their warmth encompass him. Next week was the earliest he could go back, as he'd had to work through the Christmas and New Year period. However he would call into CID later today.

Christmas day, walking the beat, had been an interesting affair. People in festive mood, he'd been handed cups of tea and mince pies, underlying the fact there was more good in the world. His own Christmas dinner had been prepared by Mrs Mason, who had done a wonderful spread for all her newbies who hadn't gone home due to work.

Chapter 46

1964 March
Liverpool

William hesitated outside CID's door. This was his fifth visit to try and talk to DCI Chappell about Susan Jones. He was always out, apparently! Steeling himself, he entered, met with the usual reproachful glances before being left to hover awkwardly.

"Look, he's not 'ere." DC Wallis finally conceded from behind a pile of paperwork.

William felt himself flush.

"Maybe someone else can help. I just want to find out what's happening with the Susan Jones' case."

"Look, we're all busy and don't have time to deal with the likes of you hounding us just because you discovered the body. Let us do our jobs and maybe, just maybe it will get solved rather than dealing with pesky nuisances. Unless you have some information, in which case our door is always open whilst you share, then bugger off."

A murmur of smirks buzzed the room.

"Oh," was all William could manage before exiting, feeling stupid and embarrassed.

Walking back along the corridor he couldn't help thinking, *'we're all on the same side'* – why did that seem so one sided? Was he, DCI Chappell, ignoring the messages he'd left, or were they not passed on?

Chapter 47

1963 November
Hull
The White Tiger Nightclub.

Although she doesn't know it, Karen Littleton is being watched
from the far corner of the bar area. She is downing shots as if trying
for a new world record and being hit on by a group of horny guys
standing nearby. She is in her twenties and apart from the alcohol,
looks to be healthy.

* * * *

Initial test results on Susan are proving what was already known about
cell structure, and what has been established as a baseline within the
group, although only on cadavers. We have talked about using animals
but Sarah has this incessant predilection that all animals should be
protected: it is so annoying, as it would make progress so much easier.
The closest we have come to getting away with it was road kill, but
even then Sarah disliked it.

I thought this club would be a good place to pick someone up and
lose my face in the crowd, no need to hide in this environment. So far
it is proving unsuccessful as everyone seems to be in a group, except
this one woman who is like a honey pot for the men who seem intent
on an easy lay and she is going along with it.

I may have to abandon tonight, which would totally ruin my plans.
Wait a minute, where are you off to?

* * * *

Karen stumbles towards the toilets, which are hidden in a dark alcove
near the entrance to the club.

* * * *

I think it is time I save her from the wolves. I drink up the last dregs
of my drink and give it a couple of seconds until she is out of sight
of the men, then follow casually. The club is thumping enough not to
notice me. I'll wait for her to come out, get chatting and see if I can
persuade her to come with me.

Damn! I've lost her, somewhere in the crowds! No ... there she is! She seems to be growing more and more unsteady on her feet, lurching precariously one step after the next, using the wall for support. I check to see that none of the horny guys are approaching and that they can't see us. They can't.

"Are you alright?" I almost shout to be heard, holding out my hand to steady her. She seems to go off balance, heading towards a table. I think she says 'Thank you,' but the music is too loud. I am beginning to wonder whether this was a good idea, as I see eyes looking in our direction and feel exposed. My gut feeling is saying go, but I want this next experiment, I need this next experiment, tonight. It is all planned, timeframe et cetera. As she regains her composure, I call it time, feeling anger at the wasted evening but survival as commonsense kicks in. I turn to walk away in disgust with the failed plan and suddenly find myself being pushed to the ground. Panic spreads through me like wild fire. A throng of people offer me a helping hand and as I get to my feet, I see a woman is still on the floor. The one I was after.

There are too many people talking and the music is thumping I cannot understand anything anyone is saying. I straighten myself whilst the woman is helped up. She is talking to me, it looks like an apology but I can't hear her. The crowd disperses and we are left to ourselves. She *is* apologising, her hand on my shoulder and I find myself guiding her closer to the door. She is complicit. In no time we are outside and I am surprised.

She stumbles again and I catch her, her face is next to mine, her perfume is almost overpowering.

"You're nice, much more my type! I wouldn't tell them that they had no chance, free drinks you see. Are you going to take me home?" she asks as coyly as her drunkenness allows.

She is coming on to me! I am taken aback. She kisses my cheek and I almost let go of her but just manage to stay focussed. Walking her to my car, I get the keys out to open the door, she plants a smacker on my lips. I freeze.

Finally, I push her back. She looks disappointed and suddenly fear shoots through me. I think she is going to walk away so quickly I add.

"Shall we go back to my place?" I draw her into me, playing along. If it gets the result I need and gets her into my car without a scene, why not?

She is running her fingers through my hair. Then, impulsively, she stops and turns. A second later the contents of her stomach splatter over the pavement. She heaves again and I support her. A few minutes pass before she is finished. Opening the door, I guide her into the passenger seat.

"Thank you. I'm sorry. You're lovely."

Closing the door, I look around the car park. There are a few people meandering around, however no one is paying us any close attention. By the time I am in the drivers' seat, she is asleep.

-

In my lab I sedate her properly, although she probably wouldn't have woken up anyway, as she slept for the whole two hour journey back! Stripping her, I take a little more time; she has stirred something in me, something I didn't know existed and I am surprised by it. It feels almost voyeuristic now. Gary's memory snaps to mind, a connection, then anger springs back as his betrayal returns.

Suddenly I am back in control and begin perfusing a twenty percent solution of Dimethyl Sulfoxide mixed with an ethanol cryopreservative in to her heart which I have hooked up to a machine to pump the mixture through the valves and arteries, knowing that ethanol freezes at minus one hundred and fourteen degrees Celsius. I am not worried about the toxicity at this stage; I am trying to find a way to get to minus one hundred and ninety-six degrees – cryostasis – without formation of ice crystals. Placing the dewar flasks inside the freezer and replenishing every few weeks means they are capable of maintaining that temperature with the help of the liquid nitrogen. I am hoping the ethanol-based cryopreservative will allow the organ to freeze without damage. I make my notes:

Karen Littleton
March '64
Heart
Ethanol based mixture with 20 % DMSO

Following on from Susan Jones' heart thawing I tried two weeks ago – which
failed due to ice cyrstal damage, I have used an ethanol based mixture with
the DMSO in the hope that it preserves the cell structure upon thawing, due
to its different freezing temperature – I am not totally convinced – so am

*expecting a failure, as well as the toxicity issue with such a high level of
ethanol. Yet that is what these experiments are for.*

*There is a new book due out this year, and I have ordered a copy, it is called
'The Prospect of Immortality' by Robert Ettinger. He is creating quite a buzz
in America. I hope it will shed some light; in fact there is a lot of talk about
cryonics in America.*

After an hour, I place Karen's (according to her driving licence) body
carefully in her temporary tomb, marking her initials in chalk on the
side with the date; letters and numbers that will not mean anything
to anyone else.

Karen's possessions I pile into a bag; I have found a lake where I can
dispose of them. It is a few miles away, but I can do it before dawn
breaks. That will give me enough time to get to York for my seminar.

As I reverse out of the unit, I sense I am being watched and sit in the
car for a minute before getting out to lock up. It is only then I notice
the fishing wire glinting in what is left of the moon. I follow it with
my eyes: it goes to the portacabin.

I chide myself for not being more careful, for allowing myself to be
become complacent. There is nothing I can do, so reluctantly I lock
up and go.

* * * *

Ben had been viewing Sam from his portacabin since his arrival at
just after three am; the fishing line had been as effective as always, but
there was not much to see and, as Sam always wore the same outfit
when he turned up – although his hair did look longer this time, like
one of those new hippie styles that had crossed over from the US.
Maybe he was producing drugs. Interesting!

Chapter 48

1964 March

Mike's Lab

"I told you, with a little bit of elbow grease it would be alright." Mike announced satisfied at their hard work. "It's better than where we were and my stepdad said we can stay here indefinitely."

"Well, it is certainly bigger." Sarah praised.

"No need to get personal." Mike batted back lasciviously.

Margaret responded. "Give it a rest for once in your life. The world does not revolve around your cock."

"I don't …"

"Yeah, alright, Mike, let's just get the rest of equipment set up now. At least it's starting to look like a lab rather than that garden shed we were in." Sam cut in. They had worked tirelessly for three days getting the new unit ready in a disused barn on Mike's stepdad's grounds; there was only a peppercorn rent to pay.

"I think we should put the freezer here." Roger indicated a corner.

"And when is that arriving?" Mike surveyed the room.

"Tuesday, next week. I managed to find one second hand via a contact at the hospital. It has been modified to our specification." Roger boomed pompously.

"Ask and you shall receive." Sam responded, "nice boots, by the way, Mike."

"It's like listening to the three musketeers, Sarah. They've only ordered a piece of equipment." Margaret's cutting remark only made Sam smile, whilst Mike tried to look offended.

"We've toiled like there's no tomorrow to acquiesce to your whims and that is the gratitude. Thanks, Sam, had them a while, just never worn them much." Mike stared admiringly at his feet. "Saw them in a sale and, I can't believe I admitting this, always fancied a pair after seeing Roger wearing them."

"My Roger the trend setter." Sarah looked at Mike's Frye Boots.

"Let's just finish up so we can get on with what we are actually trying to do here and research suspended animation."

"Good point, Margaret." Roger agreed.

Chapter 49

1964 September
Liverpool CID

"Happy birthday, Ron." Ron looked up sharply from the paperwork he was reading.

"What?" he said aggressively.

"Happy ... Birth...day. That's all. It is today, isn't it?" Mark said sitting at his desk. Frank and Si looked up from their work.

"Don't want to know, and don't particularly care!"

"Why don't you like celebrating your birthday?" Mark grimaced. He knew Ron hated birthdays and loved to torment him in a once yearly ritual, in fact he made a particular note in his diary so he didn't forget.

"Fuck off and die, okay."

"Seriously though why don't ..." But before Mark could finish Ron had exploded from his desk.

"Because I don't fucking like to, okay?" Frank and Si kept their heads down unsuccessfully trying to hide their smirks, obviously enjoying Ron's show. Ron grabbed Mark by the scruff of his shirt and was inches away from his face. "Every fucking year without fail you ask me the same fucking question and it is really getting on my tits."

Mark had never got this reaction before and shocked him. "Look, I'm sorry, I didn't realise it was such a big deal."

"What, every fucking year?" Ron broke into a smile. "Got ya, dickhead."

Frank and Si smiled.

"Nice one, Ron." Frank stated.

Mark realised he'd been set up, "So you do ..."

"No, I fucking don't, but I thought I'd get you back for keep bloody reminding me. Now can we get on with some work? I am your superior officer!"

Mark straightened himself up. "I suppose." He said, looking

embarrassed that the tables had been turned. "What we working on?"

"That Susan Jones case. Still no leads, nothing, and we need something. I've got brass breathing down my neck and I need to give'm something."

"Nothing in the gazette for other regions?" Mark settled back in his chair putting his feet up on his desk.

"Had a look about a week ago but nothing so far. Missing persons … well, I have got a couple of officers sifting through those, though the pile is about this high." Ron indicated a height, level with his desk."

"Oh."

"Exactly. Oh, and to cap it off, bloody PC wotsit's-face who discovered the body …"

"Travis." Mark added.

"Yeah, that's him, keeps coming round wanting to know what we know. Next thing he'll be wanting a promotion to be a detective so he can ride my arse even more."

"Well, it is a lovely arse, Ron."

"Faggot. I've heard about you."

"Yeah, but don't tell the wife eh! Be a big disappointment to the family."

"Thought you already were." The friendly banter was interrupted as the phone burst into life.

"Hello, DCI Chappell."

Mark picked up a file from his desk and started to flick through it.

"Right … I see." Chappell chewed on a pen as his eyebrows knitted into a frown, Mark noticed the curious tone. "And you say that was in January? Interesting. Thanks." He replaced the receiver. "Well, blow me."

"Thanks, but I'm not really a faggot, just a vicious rumour spread by Frank over there."

"I'm only reporting what I heard." Frank answered without taking his eyes off the file he was reading.

"Are you sure? Look at your clothes." Chappell's face dropped in disgust. "Oh no,"

"What?" Mark turned around to see what Ron was looking at.

"Bloody copper, Tavistock."

"Tavistock? Oh, Travis."

Chappell sat bolt upright at his desk so he was closer to Mark and then quietened to a whisper. "That was Nottingham CID, they had a body dump similar to the one we are looking at, in January this year. Outside Fenton ..."

PC Travis approached Chappell's desk. "Excuse me, I'm looking for Detective Ron Chappell?"

Mark interjected. "Someone steal your bike, sonny?"

"No." Travis responded seriously. "I was hoping for an update on Susan Jones ..." Travis gulped, the image still fresh in his mind, haunting his dreams and whenever he closed his eyes.

"Look sonny, we understand your concern but it's a CID case now. I'm sure you will find out in the full course of time, when and if we find anything out. The usual channels and all." Ron hated being hassled by anyone and this PC was relentless, every few weeks, and what could be worse than a wet behind the ears 'Beat Pete'.

Travis stood, unsure of what to do next, hoping for an end to his nightmares. Si was watching curiously obviously enjoying Travis' discomfort.

"Look, how long have you been out of Peels?" Chappell finally relented feeling a morsel of compassion for the dejected officer. 'Peels' was how they affectionately referred to Peel House, where training started for young coppers.

"About eight months all told." Travis stood nervously.

Mark stood up, clearly seeing the fear in Travis's eyes. "What's your name?"

"PC Travis."

Mark raised his eyebrows to Ron, "No, your proper name."

"Oh," Travis blushed. "William, William Travis."

Mark placed a friendly arm around William's shoulder. "Look, it doesn't get any easier, so maybe you ought to consider a change of career. There's many a crime which goes unsolved. I remember being fresh out of Peels hoping to be the white knight to every victim." Ron shot a puzzled grin at Mark who winked conspiratorially. "But sometimes you gotta let go. Move on."

Travis looked at Mark and then at Ron before turning to leave, which was when Ron saw what Mark had stuck to Travis's back, a piece of paper which read 'Beat Pete's are faggots'.

Ron sighed, shaking his head as Mark stared after him, Si laughing as Frank tried to keep a straight face whilst talking with a contact on the phone.

"Oi, Travis," Ron finally chipped in.

Travis turned and looked curiously at Ron. "You really wanna help?"

"If I can."

Ron got up and walked over to him, placing his hand on Travis's back. Mark looked on as Ron pulled off the paper.

"I'll have a word with your Relief Inspector and see if we can't second you for a bit of over-time. There's some research you can help us with. We need all the men we can get."

Mark gawked at Ron quizzically.

"I don't follow." William said.

"Look another body was discovered in January this year, a Karen Littleton, similarities to the Susan Jones. DI Smith in Nottingham said their case went cold but it may tie in with our case. I'm going over later today, so in the meantime maybe you could start looking for other similar cases in back issues of the Gazette. See if there are any cases maybe we've missed, because we weren't looking for 'em."

Travis couldn't smile wide enough. "Sure, yes."

"If you find anything, report back to me, okay?"

"Absolutely." Travis looked almost jubilant as he left CID.

"You're cruel." Mark laughed. "Bloody back issues of the gazette?"

"Do you wanna do it? He's keen; let's use it until we know what we have. I need to go to Nottingham. I'll see you later."

"Okay ."

Chapter 50

2002 July

"Were there others?" Sam reluctantly asked in disbelief.

Geoff started whistling the theme from 'A fist full of dollars', one of Sam's favourite films, starring his all time hero, Clint Eastwood. But as much as the memory was a cool breeze, he repeated his question with a hint of fury.

"Were there others?"

Geoff stopped abruptly and everything outside the car froze.

"Others?" Geoff toyed with him. "Oh victims," conspiratorially Geoff considered the question. "That's a good question."

Sam gulped. "But it's not me. Why am I seeing this? Why am I on this journey?"

"I don't know." Geoff admitted solemnly. "I am not privy to all information yet, but I am finding this all rather fascinating. How one of my students spent their life. The mind is a miraculous thing, don't you think? Isn't that what I always used to say in Maths?"

Sam stared at the frozen world outside, the frozen speeding cars looking as though they had been painted in a blur of colour.

"Yes, I think so," was his faint reply before adding more thoughtfully, "It doesn't make sense." Regaining his composure. "I talked to the police. I am innocent."

"You think so. Did my lessons mean so little to you? I thought you were a good pupil of mine, good grades, did the homework, answered questions correctly ... most of the time. Yet, you don't remember my good advice, and profound statements of fact. Was I wasting my time? Innocence can mean different things to different people. Innocent people have died challenging the truth, one persons version of truth anyway. It can be so subjective. How well does one knows one's self?"

"I enjoyed my time at school, mostly." Sam said, unbelievingly, more concerned by what he'd seen. "I know myself bloody well enough to know I didn't commit a murder, anyone would know if they had committed murder, it is hardly something you could hide from yourself. That I do know. So why am I seeing this?"

"Murder! That implies singular, I think we still have a way to go yet. Good, I'm glad you enjoyed school. Anyway, I cannot answer your questions, only show you what I am shown, when I am shown it."

The car suddenly lurched back to full speed as the dulcet tones of Frank Sinatra crooning away 'Accidents will happen' filled the car.

"Peter Hittles is next."

Chapter 51

1964 October
Leicester

The Spread Eagle.

"Charlie, can I buy you another drink? Bill, get Charlie here another drink on me." Peter slurred, as he stumbled towards the bar, downing the dregs of his pint.

"Nah, it's alright mate, got to get home to the missus, been giving me earache a lot lately. Now she's expecting."

"Let's wet the babes head then." Charlie is already heading for a door beyond the pool table. "Ah come on. I hate to drink alone. Pint and a chaser, Bill." Peter commanded dragging Charlie back.

Bill stood behind the bar, polishing glasses, sighing: he'd wanted an early night for a change.

* * * *

I eye the door to the pub, tired of waiting – it is in a busy side street, with a small car park and no lighting. It was a fluke finding it. I want a male candidate, two females were fine for starters but a male is needed to baseline the sexes. Susan Jones and Karen Littleton have both been returned to their families so I have vacancies. I feel an overwhelming urgency to fill them, to carry on again, soon. I am strong for my size and shape, people under estimate me, but I know a man would be so much easier to overpower when drunk, so a pub seems an ideal place to look, and with people coming and going, no one would notice someone helping another into a car. I've had two failed attempts so far this evening; sheer stubbornness keeps me trying, although I do feel conspicuous sitting in the car with my flat cap and raincoat on.

The car – I think I need to dispose of. This is the third time, so a change may be best; although the false number plates do conceal its true identity, aided by the fact that it is stored in a locked garage when not used: I catch the bus to its location, followed by a short walk. I can't help but smile. I was clever when I was younger as well – no one ever knew it was me killing people's beloved pets.

Looking at my watch, I consider abandoning tonight.

"Sod it! Time to go."

Fuming I ram the car into gear. Suddenly I spot a character being ejected from within, almost unceremoniously thrown to the ground.

★ ★ ★ ★

"I think you've had enough Peter. I have a bed and a wife waiting for me." Bill chimed angrily. "Charlie, make sure he gets home okay."

"I'm not his keeper," Charlie admonishes. "Anyway, I need a piss."

"I can find my own home way." Peter thinks about what he'd said; it doesn't sound right, he can't fathom why. Turning he trips over a barstool and falls clumsily into a table, sending empty glasses crashing to the floor.

"That's it Peter, you've been here since lunchtime. I know you're a regular but you're costing me in broken glasses." Bill strode purposefully to the open flap at the end of the bar.

Peter recovered looking around, dazed.

Noticing that Peter looked as though he was going to vomit Bill grabbed his arm. "Right, that's it. Out. Go on. Go. Charlie can see to you outside when he gets back." Bill guided the unsteady Peter to the door ramming him through it, knowing Peter wouldn't feel a thing: he never did, and he never remembered how he got the bruises either. Bill is temporarily blinded by bright car lights.

"Goodnight." Bill exclaims, not waiting to see whether Peter falls over or not.

Peter staggered sideways. He hadn't brought a coat with him and it took a few seconds for him to realise that it was raining.

A car pulls up to him, the window wound down.

★ ★ ★ ★

"Can I offer you a lift mate?" I offer politely.

Peter's eyes swim round in his head as he tries to focus, his addled brain trying to compute the hidden face. "Do know you ... I ... do know you?" The sound cumbersome. He looks as though he's had skin full.

"I'll ..." Peter hiccups and, on cue, the rain gets harder.

"Come on, you can't walk home in this. Please get in. I'll give you a lift."

Peter appears to think about it for a while longer.

I start to get the handkerchief ready with the chloroform, the fumes quickly filling the car. Frantically I open the driver's window for fresh air (this could be an awful place to be caught) feeling more anxious as the stand-off continues, I consider leaving.

"Okay." Peter finally shrugs. "But let's go to a club first. We can get hammered some more." He fumbles with the passenger door of the Zephyr, missing the handle as he tries to grab it, almost falling over again. After fighting with his balance he manages to stabilize himself. Opening the door he falls into the seat.

"Dry yourself with this." Peter turns lazily in time to see the handkerchief being applied to his face. Too drunk to fight he succumbs within seconds.

I gulp a big lung full of fresh air, as my head starts to swim, then ram the car into first gear and pull away letting the night air rush through the open window.

* * * *

"Bill, where's Peter?" Charlie calls, still doing his flies up.

"I shoved him outside to sober up. Look at the mess he made."

"Oh." Charlie replies nonchalantly. "Night."

"Yeah, good riddance." Bill says, kneeling down on the floor, picking up the broken glass. "Why do I bother eh?"

Charlie barges through the door and watches as red taillights shine dimly from farther along the road . Looking round, he can't see Peter, so shrugs and walks home.

Chapter 52

1964 October
Lincolnshire
Storage Yard

My note taking is therapeutic. It orders my ideas and theories. Being in my lab, especially when I am just checking up on things, allows me time to research, using some of the organs I have retrieved. The stove in the corner is perfect for providing respite from the cold. I feel at ease here; this is my world, and my world only.

'The Prospect of Immortality' by Robert Ettinger is interesting. Whilst it divests itself of the pros and cons for suspended animation, with some resounding discussions on religious as well as practical implications, it also gives an indication to the serious nature of how the subject is being dealt with in America – far more openly than I can find in Britain. There are meetings taking place; some scientists, physicists and biologists all discussing the topic. I'm in the wrong country!

Glycerol solution as a preservative seems to be the way forward according to Ettinger's book, but another point that was made is that there is still no way to flush the preservative out after thawing or during thawing, as the heart is the pump and, if that is frozen, then it won't work. I think this needs to be a group discussion; see what ideas float.

Peter Hittles is now on ice. I have taken the liver and the lungs and I am trying a formulation, GD2 (Glycerol & DMSO) on these before placing in the dewars for storage. This is painstakingly slow; however, I can hardly line up the bodies and organs. I have considered reverting to animals as I can conduct whole body experiments but there are already records of animals being frozen and returned; why re-interpret those. It is human beings that are the crux to this. Why can't we experiment on the criminals, put them to good use?

Looking at my watch I mentally calculate the time it will take me to travel back to the garage, get the bus, pick up my normal car and then back to my routine. I smile as I think of the luck in finding it: I'd driven into a garage block to turn round after taking a wrong turn, and there, on one of the doors, was a notice: 'Available to rent, ring 8658, Alf'. Away from prying eyes and cash in hand – it was meant to be!

Whilst the freezers work well and keep constant temperature, the dewars are perfect for organs, the vacuum means the liquid nitrogen maintains temperature for weeks, especially as they are stored in the freezer with the body, albeit with a ventilation pipe to the outside allowing the vapour to disperse safely. I find it frustrating having one empty – it is a waste. Why did I end Karen Littleton early? Just a feeling a gut feeling, that left me with nothing ongoing. A couple of months to do some research and plan my next move.

Chapter 53

2002 July

Incredulously Sam watched the disappearance of Peter Hittles conclude in front of him remembering vividly the conversations in the office about the disappearance at the time, as colleagues knew him. He'd worked for a transport company that was about to sign a deal for dedicated deliveries to a customer.

He ran through the images he'd been shown so far: his burgundy Zephyr that had been stolen; there was a dent in the bonnet which he'd tried to repair and had failed and was now rusting. Susan Jones's disappearance; and Peter Hittles. He didn't do these, did he? He couldn't have, could he? Why be shown things that you didn't do. Had he really blocked them out. No! he can't have done. There is no way he wouldn't have any recollection, especially now, being dead, there would be no point denying it.

"I really don't understand."

"Frankly," Geoff stated plainly, "neither do I. It's a shame sometimes that I am not given the whole story at once instead of being drip fed. I would so much like to punish some even more." He stared at Sam malevolently. "However, it is not for me to judge. There is more for you to see."

Sighing Sam let his head sink down. "How much more? I think I feel sick."

"No, that is the souls of the dead." Geoff spoke quietly. "Now we must go on. Remember how it feels to carry those souls, feel their torture."

"What about Margaret?"

Geoff turned to Sam, ignoring the road ahead. "What about her?"

Sam's jaw bounced up and down as if on elastic. All he could say was "I love her so much."

"Ah, love: an invisible force that binds people together, a simple truth that exists in our hearts. True love that is."

"How is she? Will I get to see her?"

"Apparently so. She is an intrinsic part of this."

"What do you mean?"

"She is on the list, and as such is intrinsic to this journey."

"I didn't do these crimes and I don't know why you are showing me them." Sam added almost petulantly.

"Denial is normally the sign of guilt."

"Rubbish! It's the bloody sign that I am innocent." Sam felt his temper rising.

"Then why get so upset, if you are innocent ..."

"If you are being accused of something you didn't do, wouldn't you get upset? I am not some bloody Jekyll and Hyde character you know."

"Frankly, I do not. Lives people lead have many different twists and turns. History is littered with people who existed, detached from reality, living duplicitous lives, convinced in their own minds they have nothing to do with the other; like two brothers who exist in one body but do not know of the others life."

"Mental illness is never something I got a chance to study at med school." Sam conceded exacerbated; searching his own mind for answers, a dim recognition, anything that would justify what he was seeing.

Geoff ignored him. "Never had cars like this in my day," as if on a Sunday drive, "quiet and smooth, and comfortable. You have it too easy."

Sam's eyes widened in terror as the rear of a lorry loomed up ahead. Millisecond by millisecond it got closer and closer. Inches away, Geoff swerved to the inside, glancing at Sam – the look of horror on his face.

"You thought I was going to hit it?" He asked rhetorically. "I wonder if that's what the victims felt. That kind of terror."

The car was doing one hundred and forty ... fifty ... sixty mph and had flown past a second lorry in a blur, they glided effortlessly up to a car to their left in the middle lane. Geoff pulled in behind, gaining ground in seconds.

"Nooooo." Sam finally managed to shout.

The BMW hit the back of the Mondeo. To Sam's surprise they oozed through it and the BMW faded from view again.

Chapter 54

1964 October
Mike's Lab

"Evening, Sammy, my boy." Mike chimed cheerfully.

"Hello," he replied suspiciously, feeling perturbed by the glee.

"What? Can't I be happy and enthusiastic?"

"After last month, no, I didn't think you could. The others not here yet?" Sam hung his jacket up and put on a lab coat.

"There was nothing wrong with me last month. Also, I finished reading that Ettinger guys book Saturday night and it started me thinking ..."

"Interesting, wasn't it?" Sam asked

"Totally! Except for the religious rubbish. Unimportant." Mike looked at Sam as if waiting for his confirmation.

"I suppose; it depends on your stand point. I thought it was a well rounded book."

"Anyway, what I was thinking is that it is all very well freezing someone and expecting science to resolve the thawing issues at some distant point in the future, but that is where we should be directing our research now. They seem to have the freezing sorted, kind of. The damage seems to occur on the thawing stage."

"We discussed this last month, didn't we?"

"No."

"I'm sure we did."

"Defo' not."

"You sure?"

"Yes, last month we thawed and dissected the liver that Margaret had brought in the previous month."

Sam stared at him "That was the month before mate."

"No, it wasn't, we hadn't met for a month and it was our first time back together." Mike countered.

"Oh, yeah. Work has been stressing me out a lot recently. Can't believe

I've forgotten! I enjoy these sessions so much." Sam sighed wearily.

The door opened and in walked Sarah and Roger.

"Evening." Sarah looked at Sam her eyes widening with concern. "Is everything alright?" Panic shone in her eyes. "Margaret's okay isn't she?" Delay in Sam answering seemed to worry her even more. "Please say nothing's happened to her ... Sam?"

"What? No, no, she's fine, she's away on one of those training courses that she attends every now and then."

"Thank God for that."

"It appears I don't recall last months' session. I knew work had been busy and stressful but ..."

"Don't worry about it mate. It happens to us all at times." Mike patted Sam on the shoulder.

"Yes, the brain is a fascinating organ." Roger's boyish enthusiasm buoyed over. "It would be really good to do some research on a live specimen. There are some new organisations where neuroscience is really making leaps and bounds trying to understand how stress affects the brain. It would be great to directly work on a subject. I have got a friend ..."

"I'm sure it's nothing that needs you looking at my brain, thank you." Sam responded. Roger stood, mouth agape. "Let you mess around in my head, I don't think so!"

"It's not good when he gets into your head," Sarah smiled flirtingly at Roger. "Even worse when he gets inside your knickers. Oops! I didn't mean to say that out loud."

"Too late," Mike spoke mockingly, "and more information than I want to process at this time. Urgh! Now I can't get the thought of Roger and Sarah talking dirty out of my head."

"Thanks, Mike. Not an image I really wanted either."

"Shall we get on?" Mike implored eagerly.

It was Sam's turn to try and be humorous. "With what?"

"I was thinking we should work on cell structure breakdown during thawing, as this seems to be a bigger issue than the actual freezing, and one point in particular: how do you flush the preservative out of the body?" Roger enthused as Sam looked at Mike and then turned backed to Roger. "What?"

"Nothing. Good idea."

Chapter 55

1964 October

Nottingham

CID

"Hi, I am looking for DI Smith." The desk sergeant looked at Chappell cautiously.

"Who can I say it is?"

"DCI Chappell."

Ron was eventually buzzed through and directed to where he could find Smith, a rotund man with scraggly beard, his suit crumpled and food stains on one of the lapels.

"DI Smith?" Chappell enquired.

"What?" was the short, stark reply without the man looking up from the bacon roll he looked like he was about to inhale in one bite!

"DCI Chappell from Liverpool, you rang me about ..."

"Oh yeah. It's here somewhere." Smith spoke, chewing the mammoth chunk of roll like some great big washing machine swilling around the clothes vigorously. Ketchup started to ooze out of one side of his open mouth; a repulsive sight. He ate with a loud sucking noise, every chew making Chappell feel nothing but loathing for the man's manners. "Here you go," practically throwing a large yellow file at him. "It's a copy, take it. Remember, mi casa su casa." Smith took a swig of coffee and swallowed like a wallowing hippo about to disappear under the water.

"Mi casa, su casa?" Chappell repeated trying to think what he meant.

Smith took another huge bite of his roll, continuing to chew noisily, "Yeah, you scratch my back and I'll scratch yours ... if you get any leads ... and I'll keep an ear to the ground"

"But it doesn't ..."

"Look, sorry it's short and sweet but it has been a rough forty-eight hours. We've got a nasty gang on our patch that seem to like using good honest people like punching bags and target practise and I haven't had much sleep."

"... mean that, it means my home is your home." He finished under his breath, disappointed that he was not going to be able to ask any questions. Then adding more forcefully after feeling he had just wasted the best part of two hours driving. "So you have no other information to give me, just the file?"

"It's all in there. Pathology, photos, the lot." Smith leaned forward preparing to take another gigantic bite of his roll. Chappell turned and left.

Back in his car he let the engine idle as he turned the heater to full. It had already cooled down considerably in the twenty minutes he'd been inside, most of which had been spent waiting. He flicked through the file. The pathologist stated that the heart was missing; only a significant amount of putrefaction had occurred; and a good deal of the expected body fluids were missing. Toxicology showed high amounts of alcohol present, along with some other toxins as yet unidentified. The putrid state of the remains made the cause of death hard to determine, except for the missing heart, but there were no physical injuries to note: what was left of the organs were too decayed to pinpoint anything else. There were signs of frostbite, as if being frozen at some stage. He'd concluded that the alcohol level was toxic and death would have been imminent.

"Are you connected to Susan Jones, or are you just a coincidence?"

He threw the report on the passenger seat and headed back to Liverpool, computing the possibilities. What was the relevance of freezing? He knew the department workload was already heavy, but he was going to need more resources before upscaling to an incident room; confirming first that they were connected. He would let Travis use his dedication to help with some of the donkeywork.

On the way back, he pulled in for a coffee at a greasy spoon and started to sieve through the plain envelope of black and white photographs showing the victim wrapped in the blanket. Even after all the time he had spent as a detective, it still didn't prepare him for the grizzly sight and he swallowed hard as a bitter taste soured his coffee.

Chapter 56

2002 July

Harriet shivered as the BMW merged with the unmarked police car; Sam and Geoff were now sitting in the back seat.

"You alright?" Stephen asked.

"It's just turned really cold in here, turn the heating up. It's like someone opened a window."

"Yeah," Stephen said, thinking about it. "Look, there it is. Silver Mercedes."

Harriet spotted the car her colleague was looking at.

"Sierra-Mike-Charlie to control, we have suspect vehicle in sight, joining Papa-Tango in position behind to control traffic. You all right, Harriet? You look spooked."

"Yeah, yeah fine," but she couldn't help thinking she had seen a blue BMW speeding up behind her; yet, now there was nothing there. "Been a long shift that's all; be glad when it's over."

Playing on her mind was that they had been called to what appeared to be a broken down car but was in fact a body dump gone wrong; it brought back memories of her own mother, Lucy Davis, whose own body had been dumped after being missing for two years. She had been two when her mum was reported missing; her dad had never hidden the fact that her mother was not coming back and, when she turned sixteen, he told her the awful truth of why. It's what made her determined to go into the police force: it had been an aim of hers to find the killer responsible. She had even spoken with DCI William Travis, who also had not closed his personal case file on her mum or on the other unexplained body dumps.

Geoff accelerated and the BMW shot out of the police car.

"That was the daughter of one of the victims. She still believes she can catch the killer."

"Can she?" Sam asked absent-mindedly.

Geoff shot a quizzical glance in response and ignored the question. "How sad, after twenty-five years, still believing a killer can be brought to justice."

"Is it? Justice is justice." Sam turned to look back at the police car now parked on the hard shoulder. Harriet's face was hardened; big beautiful eyes like globes; neatly tied back auburn hair that he could picture as a long fiery mane when released. The only obvious blemish to a perfect face was a crooked front tooth that overlapped its twin. It gave her face character.

"Can I see Margaret? Or Mike?" It was said with the affection that he knew Harriet must feel for her lost mother. He didn't feel it was going to accomplish anything, but he loved them both and their memories were like a sharp knife that cut loose the pain of the soul he had just felt. They meant the world to him for different reasons. There was no one from his childhood; it was as if life had started at medical school. He could barely remember his senior school's best friend – it made him feel even sadder.

"This is not a request show. You have a path to follow."

Sam frowned in consternation; Geoff ignored it. "Anyway, you might not want to see them after this journey. Many a person has not, you know. Opinions change."

"You must be off your trolley. Of course I want to see them. I can't think of any reason on Earth why I wouldn't."

Geoff brushed the comment away like an annoying fly and the car filled with Frank.

Chapter 57

1964 November
Liverpool
CID

Travis had spent nearly forty hours over the last three weeks trawling through back issues of Police Gazettes, and there was nothing that looked remotely like Susan Jones's case. Years' worth of issues; yet he had enjoyed it, being involved in some way, doing something. Now, reluctantly, he knew he had to report his findings to Chappell. In the empty CID room, he couldn't help himself wallow in its atmosphere; there was a tingling that precipitated in the air. Closing his eyes, he let it soak into him; then he studied the desks and tried to imagine working at them, finger on the pulse. Suddenly, his eyes spied Susan Jones's file on a desk. Like a naughty child drawn to sweets, he eased over and started peaking inside when he found a second file – unidentified female. He started comparing the two files, instantly becoming engrossed in the grotesque pictures that his mind now managed to see as not real, distancing himself from the living person they used to be – enough to be pragmatic but not totally detached – in order to analyse them more fully; although he held Susan Jones' image as a mental carrot to drive him on.

"Hello, 'ello, 'ello, what do we have 'ere then?" Mark smiled as he strolled into the CID room, making Travis jump, almost pushing the files off the desk. "If Ron catches you, you'll be for the knackers yard."

"Sorry, I was just ..." Travis was stopped in his tracks as Ron burst through the doors.

"Too late," Harris chimed joyfully.

"What's this then? Dreams of grandeur, eh son?" Chappell sounded gruff but smiled amiably at Mark.

"I'm sorry, it was just that ..."

"Thought you'd see what it was like to be CID? Well in that case," Travis straightened the file on Chappell's desk. "Maybe you ought to tell me what you think then, show us your mettle." Ron sank into his chair almost angrily, whilst inside admiring the PC's keenness. It was something not very often seen, especially after a few years on CID, watching convicts get let off because of clever barristers – it usually had the effect of dampening the work ethic. After a couple more years on the beat, he would be what this department needed, fresh blood, enthusiasm, energy; but good grounding couldn't be ignored – it helped build up contacts.

Mark's jaw almost fell to the ground, and Travis looked just as shocked.

"So tell me, what are your theories so far?" Ron appeared intrigued.

Travis stood, nonplussed, not believing his ears, then started slowly surmising his own theories, Ron nodding in agreement, seemingly impressed. Travis flicked through the file, quickly glancing over the information, filtering his own theories, mentally adjusting possible angles of investigation, thinking quickly on his feet.

"... freezing is interesting. Why? Two sets of samples taken at different times with Susan Jones – before or immediately upon death and then weeks, possibly months – difficult to conclude on body two. It would indicate some kind of measuring, maybe trying to get a baseline, but to what ends? From what the pathologist reports say, and comparing," he flicked between photos, "the manner of cuts ... they look professional, purposeful." He flicked back and forth, a few more times: "Yes, definitely made by the same person; I'd surmise, although the second body is more decomposed. Surgical. Maybe a medical background. Could be a doctor that has been struck off," then adding, "... or maybe from another field like veterinary. But to what purpose? Why would you store someone for any period of time, frozen? Most killers would not take the risk of holding onto the victim for fear of being caught. If indeed both were taken by the same person; as that is not confirmed. What could be considered more grizzly is that the victims were most likely alive when the first samples were taken, these would have been painful – unless sedated?" William gulped at the gruesome thought. "The pathologist has noted the way one specimen showed signs of healing, if only the initial stages, a matter of hours, maybe? Toxicology results are considerably different, Susan Jones show residual alcohol yet this second body shows high levels, off the scale. Fatal levels." He flipped through some more pages. "Murderers might take tokens, something that is easy to hide, but a whole body! I would say necrophilia, but no signs of sexual abuse after death. Unlikely to be a botched black market operation."

"Why?" Chappell threw in, smiling.

"Because ... if someone died under the knife in a back street, they would dispose of the body straight away, plus in Susan Jones case there would be medical records of an illness that she was being treated for and ..." Travis scanned some notes. "... nothing has been found to indicate she was. I would have to surmise the second body would be the same."

Chappell seemed quietly impressed whilst Harris clearly seethed.

"Not bad, not bad. You'll go far. What do you propose for the next course of action?"

Travis stood nervously, his mind churning over thoughts ten to the dozen. "The gazette shows no other victims of similar nature. I suppose missing persons might be the next place to look. It's intriguing to think that, maybe, these people have been part of some kind of experiment, but what? Where did they work? It wasn't a cover for something was it?"

"Five minutes and he is into conspiracy theory area." Mark jibed.

"Interesting." Chappell concurred.

"We've done missing persons and are just awaiting confirmation of our second body, which we believe is Karen Littleton." Harris interjected sharply re-affirming his own position in CID, obviously not enjoying the same enthusiasm that Chappell did for this trumped up PC.

"Oh, how about hospitals and morgues." Travis realised his error as soon as he said it.

"We would be notified if there were suspicious bodies turning up." Chappell acknowledged.

"The precision with which the samples were taken." Travis repeated, trying to follow his own thought process. "Maybe we could look at medical students who didn't finish courses, or showed skewed tendencies towards this kind of thing."

"Mmm, anything else?" Chappell asked.

William stood dumbfounded, impatiently trying to think of something intelligent to add. In the end he added with a sudden explosion of confidence. "Get you a coffee?" It was said with a half-smile.

Ron laughed heartily, "I like your thinking, black, two sugars." He looked around the room. "There's a desk and phone you can use there. The extra help is always useful. Ring round medical and veterinary institutions, ask for a list of all students that were narcissistic and maybe got thrown out. We'll see if we can't get a connection between the two bodies. I hope not, otherwise we could have a serial. "

"You'll be applying for a job here full time soon," Mark joked, annoyed.

"It has always been in the back of my mind, for later in my career." William tried to sound mature yet it sounded school-boyish.

"White three sugars for me," Mark added as Travis left the room to make coffee. "What was that about?"

"Look, do you want to do all the donkey-work? Do you know how many medical institutions there are to go through? We have two murder cases in two counties." His eyes dared Mark to question the strength of his case. "Hopefully, they are not connected; if they are, this could be big."

"True."

"I'll ring his Sergeant."

Chapter 58

1965 March
Lincolnshire
Storage Yard

It is late and there is something strange about the yard tonight. It looks deserted, yet somehow too quiet. I can't see anything out of place, although there are many hiding places. It has been nearly two weeks since my last visit. It has proven difficult to find a valid excuse for being away again so soon, but I had to, as I have finally received some information from Dr Howery about cryopreserving the liver and heart. I couldn't believe it when I saw his airmail envelope at the PO Box number I use. He has even offered me the opportunity to travel to New York to meet him and discuss further, along with a couple of other people who are currently looking at suspended animation – Curtis Henderson and Saul Kent. It is too good an opportunity to miss. How to achieve it though? The excitement was tantalizing as I made my way here tonight, making me almost forget to change cars. I still want to get rid of the Zephyr, or am I just being paranoid – do I need to? I have been careful, I believe.

I pull my notebook from the shelf:

I still have Susan Jones' liver and heart in liquid nitrogen, as I want to look at the thawing process. I have been thinking about microwave diathermy as a possible solution, and whilst I have not got the equipment – yet, I am going try a slow heating process to raise the temperature slowly, using a glycerol solution with DMSO, the same as the preservative used when freezing. My theory is that the combination of the two different temperature liquids will work together as thawing occurs, limiting the formation of ice crystals.

Our group research is not going very far using road kill animals. I am not surprised; they just won't allow the boundaries to be pushed. I wonder whether they really are as keen to solve this as I am. Just like when I was younger, I am happy to continue on my own.

* * * *

Ben pulls up outside his portacabin, annoyed that he'd had to come in this late tonight; the card game he was due to attend was a big one and he felt lucky. However, one of his henchmen had been arrested and there was a piece of evidence he needed to dispose off quickly, just in case he talked. Of course the man knew he'd be dead if he did; sometimes that didn't stop the weaker ones, and Gareth was one of those – so his gut feeling told him.

"It seems it is my lucky night after all. My mysterious, evasive tenant is in. What are you up to?" As he saw a slither of light under one door.

For a moment he sits, sorely tempted to call in. First, however, he needs to burn the evidence.

* * * *

I hear a car pull up and peer out through a spy hole I have concealed. It is Shaker, I have been very lucky thus far, and our paths have not crossed, although I feel him watching me sometimes. Something inside tells me tonight will be different. I am only halfway through tonight's exercise and I do not want to give up. Fingers crossed, he'll just go away and maybe hasn't realised I am in tonight.

* * * *

A satisfactory smile oozes across Ben's face as he watches the papers burn to ash.

"Now, my friend, I think it is time you and me had a little chat."

A few moments later he is pounding on the door of his mysterious friend.

"Open up, I know you're in there."

* * * *

Fear strikes through me as the pounding continues on the door. I sit silently, contemplating my next move. He can probably see the light through the crack underneath the doors.

"Open up, I know you're in there … Sam."

Silence reins for a few seconds; I can feel my heart pumping madly.

"Come on, Sam, I only want a chat." More silence. "If that is even your name. Which I doubt."

I look at my scalpels then grab the chloroform bottle from the cupboard. I have an empty freezer. I need fresh samples. Maybe this is the way it should play out.

"Coming," I call out, remembering the accent just in time.

I pull the scarf up and the flat cap down as I head to the door. Inside, I know this is too close to home, however my hands are tied – I can't let him go if he comes in.

Slowly, I unlock the door, breathing heavily.

* * * *

"Finally!" Ben mutters under his breath reaching for the door to prevent his access being denied. "What the fuck!" He spins round as three cars scream into the yard. "Fuck it!' as he hears the bolt slide home again.

He stares as uniformed police and plain-clothes detectives swarm around the yard.

"Ben Shaker?"

"Yeah, who wants to know?"

"Detective Copeland. We need to have a little chat?"

"Think yourself lucky tonight, Sam, but next time, me and you need to have a little chat," Ben whispers to the door.

* * * *

It takes minutes for my breathing to calm down. Any second I am expecting the police to knock on the door. The game would be up if they came inside.

I wait, nervous energy stopping me from working, my brain trying to come up with a host of excuses, but nothing sounds credible.

I sit nervously anticipating another knock, studying my lab, and for the first time considering the foolhardiness of this project. Yet an hour later the cars leave and although I continue to wait, expecting Ben to return his attention to me, I feel more relaxed again, about what I am doing.

After a while I peak through my spy hole; the yard is clear.

I abandon tonight. Annoyed.

Chapter 59

1965 March
Wisbech
Sam & Margaret's Home

"Sam? Sam?" Margaret nudged Sam's shoulder gently, as he slept on the settee.

"Huh, what?"

"Your dinner's ready. Sorry I was late back. I got held up at work, had to finish a report."

Sam rubbed his eyes. "Two long days of meetings and driving, and still the bloody deals haven't been sealed."

"You shouldn't push yourself so hard, it'll do you no good you know." Margaret rubbed his shoulder affectionately; she had never seen him this tired.

"I know but Garlan Foods keep stalling." Standing up, he stretched. "I don't know what the problem is. I have reworked the figures again and …" he yawned. "… again. Anyway, what was the report you've been working on?"

Sam followed Margaret into the dining room where bubble and squeak with two fried eggs sat waiting. Seeing Sam's eyes, "Do you want a coffee?"

"Yes, please dear. Don't know why I'm so tired, must be all that driving. I don't know how you're going to fit in those seminars when the children arrive." Sam placed a mouthful of food in his mouth and the egg yolk dribbled down his chin.

"Children!" Margaret stated trying to hide her despair at the idea, "I've got a child here," she wiped his chin with a tea towel. "What do I need with more kids?"

"We always said we'd have kids, didn't we?"

Margaret thought back to a one-way conversation. They'd only been dating six months, it was hardly a marriage basis – she did know that she loved him; it had surprised her how much she could. The years rolled on and, although her mind never changed, she felt the pressure for starting a family growing. It frustrated her, despite every conversation resulting in her same answer. It was simple; she didn't want kids. She liked their life. So many women her age had two children and were balancing their needs with running a house, which made her shiver. That was their life. Nothing else. Would she feel different if she became pregnant? She wasn't sure, although most of her felt she wouldn't. She was twenty-four and they had their whole lives ahead of them; her career was going well, her bosses were very pleased with her.

"*You* always said we'd have kids. I was never entirely sure." The statement was met with instant disdain.

"Then why did we get married?" Sam enquired, placing his knife and fork down.

It almost threw Margaret, marriage then kids – why was it expected?

"Because we love each other?" Margaret answered almost sarcastically. "That's why I got married. How about you?"

"I thought, once we had a home, we'd start a family – you know, have a couple of kids."

Margaret tensed inside – the same argument, without fail. It was as though Sam blanked it out, as he expressed his shock in almost the exact same words. She got up and walked to him.

"Look, I love you very much, and right now we both have a lot going on. I love my career. It's exciting. I am not saying never, but just not this minute." Was that the right thing to say … maybe she needed to be forthright with him, instead of just delaying? She loved him so much and she couldn't ever let him go; it was a foreign feeling for her. "We can wait a while you know?"

"All our friends have got kids: Terry and Suzi, Dave and Tina. Roger and Sarah are trying."

Margaret interrupted, trying to remain calm. "Yes, and I am very happy for them, but it doesn't mean that we have to have them, not yet anyway. I want to spend time with my husband." She kissed him flirtingly on the neck. "Act like reckless teenagers for a while longer. Why rush into things?" Margaret stroked his chest then pulled him out of his chair so she could hold him tight; her buxom chest that he loved pushed tight against him. Undoing her top few buttons, she watched his eyes divert to her cleavage.

Sam felt the strength in his wife's grip and it turned him on. It always had. In bed, she was the dominant one, and he loved it. She started to undo his shirt, touching his smooth chest tenderly. He reciprocated by kissing her neck.

She let him, knowing now that she had distracted him from the subject of children. Then as he reached her breasts, she pushed him away playfully.

"Looks like you don't need that coffee after all. Now finish your dinner; we can continue this later." She pushed him back into his seat.

"You tease!"

"Yes. And you love it, so don't come on all hurt and disappointed."

"You know me too well."

"Yes, I do, so watch it." Margaret walked into the kitchen. She did love him with all her heart; kids were one subject that raised her heckles. She'd had siblings and hated sharing things, just like Sam in fact. Another ungainly commonality they shared was that both had lost siblings before their sixteenth birthdays. They shared so many similarities. They were like two halves of one person.

As the ten o'clock news came on, they were dozing on the settee, their naked bodies intertwined under a blanket, picking up where they had left off following dinner.

Suddenly the reporter's voice took Sam's concentration away from Margaret.

"The putrefying remains of an unidentified woman have been found outside Lenton Lodge, a gatehouse to Wollaton Hall. Early reports are not clear about the identity of the person, but an unofficial source has stated that the remains were wrapped in a tarpaulin which, at first, was thought to have been dumped about two days ago; a passerby believing it to be a fly-tipper. However, on closer inspection, a decaying corpse was discovered hidden inside. Police have no leads and are asking for anyone who knows anything to contact their local station."

"What is the world coming to?" Sam asked nonchalantly.

"Good job you're here, I obviously need your protection from all the sick deviants in the world."

"I'm your knight in shining armour hey, Guinevere?"

"Oh, Lancelot, show me your lance and then take me to your tower and ravish me."

"Your wish is my command."

Chapter 60

2002 July

"I don't get it! I am innocent. Why punish me?" Sam fumed as he felt the residue of the souls burning inside.

"I don't know, Sam. It is not my choosing. I simply follow instructions. Are you sure you had nothing to do with it, even in a small way?"

"No! I bloody didn't." Then thinking about his answer, clarified, "Yes, I am sure I had nothing to do with it."

The car dissolved around him and he found himself in a country lane. A large house towered over the trees, trying to hide the four decaying turrets shooting into the night sky. Large wooden gates stood like decadent timbers protecting the entrance to the drive and gardens beyond. A small gatehouse sat, decaying; a fading sentry on duty.

Sam looked up at the monument.

"What am I doing here?" He turned to look at Geoff, who was nowhere to be seen.

"Look and see," a cold voice in the night called.

A dim recollection started to manifest in Sam's mind. "I have been here before. This is ... mmm, I can't remember. Yes, yes I can." The dark disguised it, but the memory started to become clearer – days out with their son. "No, it wasn't here. Nearby," he snapped his fingers. "Yes. Wollaton Hall. This is one of the gatehouses. I pulled up here thinking this was the entrance but it wasn't, it was further along."

Sam's recollections were broken by the sound of a car engine, and tyres on the wet road. Two headlight beams broke the night, blinding him temporarily. The gravel crunched as the car pulled off the road in front of the gatehouse. Sam watched, bewildered, as the driver got out of the car – the burgundy Zephyr – a flat cap pulled low over the face, a long raincoat done up and a brown scarf worn like a bandit wears a neckerchief. The scarf certainly looked familiar as he noticed a red heart visible on one corner hanging over the shoulder – although Roger had a similar one and sometimes they'd pick up the wrong ones – fashion was a great equaliser.

"It's not Roger, is it?" Sam called out. There was no answer. "It couldn't be, could it? There's something familiar about him."

A tarpaulin was heaved out of the boot.

Sam's attention was drawn to the car. It was the car he'd bought when he was eighteen, second hand from his Uncle John; although the number plate was wrong – but he recognised it by the distinctive mud-flaps he'd added, plus the fancy hubcaps and the scratch where he had scraped a fence post on their honeymoon in Skegness.

"I don't get it." He consoled himself, hoping Geoff would clarify.

There was only silence.

The tarpaulin was unceremoniously dumped at the side of the gravel drive and a note left attached to it. The figure cut a confident stride back to the car.

"Stop!" Sam commanded as he stood in front of the car, pleading with the driver; yet the driver got in and pulled away without hesitation, driving straight through him.

"Who are you?" He found himself alone on the dark road, the moon above playing peekaboo behind forming rain clouds. "Where are you?"

Night instantly turned to day, changing the ghostly relic of a decaying house into a fading monument surrounded by early morning mist. A dog barked and Sam turned sharply to his left to see a mature man walking towards him, a shotgun, broken, under one arm. A Black Labrador bounded and bounced along in front, sniffing the long grass at the side of the road. The gentleman puffed away on a pipe, enjoying the freshness of the morning.

Sam looked once again at the body, noting the driving licence left under a fold of tarpaulin, Karen Littleton. A sudden gust of wind ripped it cruelly away, sending it fluttering off into the air and the trees behind.

Another dog came bounding into view, a grey Labrador, younger than the first, its tongue lolling from its open mouth as the warm air rushed out, forming white mist clouds. It stopped and sniffed at the air, before bounding full pelt towards the tarpaulin, its tail wagging wildly, like a whip, and barking excitedly at its find.

"Boycie what you got there?" Boycie tried to bark and tug at the tarpaulin to uncover the prize inside. "Boycie, leave it. It's just a piece of rubbish." The man looked around for the black dog, who'd disappeared from view.

"Soot, come here girl." A head bobbed up from the long grass before running towards her master with an arthritic stride. Boycie sniffed at his mother then returned his attention to the tarpaulin. "Boycie, leave it I said." The man went to grab Boycie ... and saw a bone protruding from the tarpaulin.

The pipe fell from his mouth, "Mary, mother of God."

Reeling backwards, bile rose inside as he tugged back a flap of the tarpaulin, hoping to find nothing more than an animal carcass carelessly discarded. His years in the army meant he knew what he was witnessing, something worse.

Sam watched in horror.

Pain filtered into his body like razor cuts, hundreds and thousands of them, all at once. The scene faded; and he was back in his car, Geoff at the wheel.

His eyes as wide as saucers staring at the road ahead, screaming in pain until his brain hurt.

"It is important you remember how that pain feels."

"Why?" he screamed. "It's not ..."

"Just remember."

Chapter 61

1965 April
Liverpool
Incident Room

The room was bustling as Ron entered, closely followed by Mark who, for once, looked interested. Travis sat awkwardly to one side, biting his bottom lip. For all his wanting to be involved, now he felt out on a limb, almost embarrassed by his keenness. He felt colleague's piercing glances; in his mind he could hear the cattle calling that might follow on the sly.

There was little he could do as the room was called to order.

"We have two murders. Whilst I know that is not strictly classed as a serial, it could be the start and I want to end the bugger's reign before it starts. It is possibly that we have missed something, as he doesn't seem to like an area, but travels around so we can't pin him down, yet. Four locations so far! We have the first victim, Susan Jones, thirty-eight, disappeared from Northampton after a business dinner in November '62 – her MG sports car was found abandoned, the engine still running, just off the A45. She was head of purchasing for Jinx Foods. Karen Littleton, twenty-seven, disappeared after visiting the White Tiger nightclub in Hull in March '64; her body turned up outside a gatehouse to Wollaton Hall, Nottingham in January '64. She worked as an insurance clerk for Brent Foster Insurance Brokers. Initial preliminary checks do not reveal anything in common. They do not appear to be connected but, judging by the heinous state they were found, and by the fact they had been frozen, I would say it is the same killer, or killers." Ron paused.

"At this stage, it is about information gathering; which is why you are all here. Whilst my department will conduct interviews etc, there is a lot of …" he stressed the next word, "donkeywork, that needs to be done. I want every constabulary in the country contacted to see if there are other cases that may have been missed, or not reported in the Gazette for whatever reason. Nottingham, Northampton and Hull are already conducting separate investigations and will report directly to me with any findings. Whilst both victims have been female, this may not be the case for all, so keep an open mind. Any information is to be filtered through PC Travis, who I am seconding." There was an audible murmur that appeared to get Ron's back up and he scowled at the gathered officers, many of whom were more senior to William. "This is purely about the fact that Travis has been involved from the start and has a good understanding of what we are looking for. He'll report directly to myself, or DS Mark Harris.

"The person, or persons, we are looking for seem to enjoy taking samples or organs. According to the pathologist, medical knowledge is probable; incisions showed precision and we know Susan was alive when her organs were harvested. We believe Karen would have been as well, although the high level of alcohol would have meant – not for long. The only lead we have is a Sam Talbot – he was the last person to see Susan Jones alive. As of yet, we do not have a connection to Karen Littleton. But maybe, with the increased workforce, we can uncover something before it escalates. I hope I am wrong that this is a serial but, if not, time is of the essence. There could already be another victim out there. Possibly alive … maybe dead, we don't know. Let's nip this in the bud before it escalates. And no one talks to the press. Not yet, but we may use them later.

"I'll leave a couple of files in here for reference; familiarise yourselves. Thank you."

Ron promptly left, with Mark keeping pace. Travis sat awkwardly, feeling scathing eyes staring at him as the noise started to build before the room slowly emptied. Sergeant Broomfield stopped by him.

"I don't know what you did, but you have certainly managed to put a few noses out of joint with your colleagues. Don't cut yourself off, sonny; you will need them at some point." He marched off, leaving William wondering what the hell he had to do to make the right start, as everything seemed to be stacking against him.

Chapter 62

1965 June

Wisbech

"What the hell?"

Sam shot bolt upright. The front door knocker was banged heartily again.

"It can't be Mike. It's a bit bloody early."

"Tell him to go away," Margaret said, wearily.

"Why so bloody early? Footie doesn't start 'til two-thirty." Sam trudged down the stairs. "Alright, alright."

* * * *

Outside, Mike was beaming like a Cheshire cat and hopping about like an excited child with a birthday present. As Sam opened the door, Mike held up his hands showing off the LP he had.

"The US version of The Rolling Stones first album. It was released a month after the UK version!" Mike's excitement was exploding like a party popper.

* * * *

"So, we've got it too." Sam announced, tiredly, allowing Mike into the house. "You're a bit early, Footie's hours away."

"I couldn't wait. This group are just brilliant. There is a different song on it too – instead of 'Mona', it's got 'Not Fade Away', a cover of the Buddy Holly song. It's amazing! It's better than the original. You gotta hear it."

Before Sam could stop him, Mike had bounded into the lounge to the phonogram sideboard which stood proudly along one wall.

"Afternoo... no, it's morning, Mike," Margaret said pointedly, as she sashayed into the lounge in her dressing gown.

"Sorry about that, but just thought Sam needs to hear this." Mike was just lining the needle up on the requisite track. The vinyl crackled and spat before the first refrains of 'Not Fade Away' burst into the room.

The three stood as the track blasted out, Mike's hand resting on the volume knob as he slowly cranked it up until Margaret strode over to turn it down.

"Yes, I think the whole street can hear it now as well," she shouted.

"What?" Mike replied playfully.

"I said 'I think the whole stree...'" Margaret started to repeat, before smiling and slapping Mike on the arm in mock admonishment and turning the volume down. "Do you want a coffee?"

"Yeah, that'd be great."

"It's not bad, but I still like 'Mona'. I didn't particularly like the original, but that's just me." Sam looked at his watch. "Anyway, I thought you said you had that job this week, sort of 'Top Secret' project that might help us in our research."

"Yeah, I was meant to, but I changed my mind. It can wait. It's not like we are making massive progress is it? Anyway I'm going to America next week. There is a Doctor Howery, or something, that I want to speak to. He says he is fencing a lot of questions about Cryonics." Mike sat down on the settee as the record carried on playing in the background. He spied a book on the table 'Ice Crystals in the Blood' by Prof Simon J. Malley. Picking it up, he flicked through the pages.

"You read the chapter where he freezes the rat and then thaws it out?"

"Not yet. I think Margaret has though." On cue, Margaret walked into the lounge with three mugs. "Haven't you?"

"Haven't I what?" Margaret enquired.

"Read the chapter where he freezes a rat?" Mike added enthusiastically, holding up the book.

"Yes. But he doesn't really offer us any new insight."

"Wouldn't it be great if you could actually try it on a human?" Mike reflected.

"Yeah," Sam offered in mock consent. "However, I think that's illegal though," adding sarcastically, "I believe they call it ... murder. Yes, definitely somewhere that seems to ring a bell?"

"I'd get that seen to, if I were you." Sam frowned. "The ringing." Mike advised. "But don't all the best breakthroughs come from working outside the rules of convention?"

"Is there something you want to tell us, Mike?" Margaret sat in one of the armchairs and sipped her coffee.

"No, well …" Mike paused, biting his bottom lip. Sam could see he wanted to say something, but then thought better of it. "If only, eh? We should be allowed to experiment on the old you know?"

"I'm sure they'd be more than happy to oblige!" Sam responded in jest.

"They've lived their life. Think what they would be giving to medical science!" Mike continued.

"Yes, and some people do donate their bodies to science … after they're dead! I still don't understand why you didn't take up that research role at Cambridge. You've got an inquisitive mind," Margaret said, curiously.

"You have to answer to other people; their rules, their ways. Would rather work for myself, or us, on that side of things."

"You work for your stepdad, remember?" Margaret chimed.

"Let's just say he lets me get on with things, my way."

"Are you sure you don't want to tell us anything?" Margaret enquired.

"Like what?" Mike replied innocently.

"How about the women that have disappeared, eh? Not been involved have you?"

Mike laughed, with Sam and Margaret joining in.

"Can I borrow your car tomorrow?" Mike interjected. "I have some stuff I need to move and mines off the road."

Sam sipped his coffee, "My precious Triumph, my baby?"

"Oh, come on! I'll be nice to it."

"Okay."

"I suppose you'll both want breakfast?" Margaret didn't wait for a response.

Chapter 63

1965 September
Lincolnshire
Storage Yard

The storage yard is quiet as I arrive. It is eleven pm. I am still wary of
Ben's prying eyes and keep expecting him to 'make a point' of being
here when I arrive, although I am unpredictable, so that must help
my situation.

Closing the doors to my lab, there is something different about it,
a feeling, but I can't put my finger on it. Alert and uneasy, I quickly
lock the doors and switch on the light. The fluorescent tubes flick
into life. Everything looks fine. Nothing unwarranted appears out of
place. Both freezing cabinets are still locked securely; the locks as I
remember, initials of the occupants chalked onto the side, PH & AJ.
There is a faint odour forming in the air and fear shoots through me.
I hasten over to the freezer units, only to discover that the one marked
AJ is not humming. I fumble with the keys to unlock the padlock;
lifting the lid a fly buzzes past me before the putrid odour of decaying
flesh almost starts me gagging.

"Damn it!" Then horror hits me as I realise the venting pipe for
the liquid nitrogen would have allowed the odour to seep out, maybe
alerting a neighbour to the grizzly secret. Panic sends my heart racing
and I stop to listen to the outside world. There is nothing. No noise
of anyone coming to get me. Just the quietness of the night. Luck?
Maybe! I am still puzzled why the freezer stopped working in the first
instance; I've used some of the best equipment I could obtain, some
of which came from America.

So what has caused the issue?

I am about to take off the panel housing the motor when I notice
mouse droppings; finally I see a dead mouse. Then I see the gnawed
through cable. Of all the things I had not accounted for, this was
one of them. I can repair it; that is not the issue. However, I had not
planned Arthur's return for tonight and this scuppers the research

session I was so looking forward to, before being due in Manchester tomorrow. I do not have time for this! What option do I have? None! Seething, I grab some bleach and lemon oil from the wardrobe, which has morphed into my supply cupboard. I place drops of it on the floor by the door, I don't want the stench – that is starting to fill the unit – to escape until I am ready; it starts to bite back against the smell of decay.

Arthur's skeleton is covered in molten flesh as putrefaction has started. Grabbing a tarpaulin, one of a few I have for this, I lay it on the floor. I have a leather butchers apron, which I wear over my gown. As I lift his body out, it feels horribly slimy and as though it will fall apart any second; like a loose bags of bones. There is a pool of bodily fluids in the freezer, the three dewar flasks sit as if wading in the remains; I almost gag at the stench; even formaldehyde is better than this. I lift the dewar flasks out, unstoppering them; the liquid nitrogen, just needs topping up but otherwise the organs look fine. I scoop as much as I can into a couple of buckets I have, adding copious amounts of bleach followed by more drops of lemon oil, I will dilute with water once outside. The fumes of bleach hit the back of my throat and I have a coughing fit; the fumes almost burning my eyes.

The only place I can dispose of the fluid is down the drain in the street. Filling a third bucket with water, I dilute the liquid remains as much as possible. I don't want to lead anyone to this site. I have no other option, though. Hesitantly, I look out of the unit door, concerned that my predator 'Shaker' maybe watching. I wait tentatively. Almost fifteen minutes pass before I dare to venture into the street, eyeing every conceivable hiding place on my way, expecting Ben, my worst nightmare, to suddenly appear.

By my third trip, I am feeling a little easier until a dog scampers up, sniffing at my ankles and the drain. Panic prickles me and I search the street for the walker. At first I can't see anyone and relax, believing it may have strayed from a garden somewhere, then an old guy appears from behind a tree, pipe in hand.

"Oi, Jack, where are you?" He calls unconcerned by the early hour. Jack yaps and, in the glow of a nearby street lamp, I can see the tiny dog is a Jack Russell. Trouble thinking up a name! The man calls again, but still Jack hovers near me, his nose more interested in what I have to offer.

"Go on," I say quietly. The man calls again, louder this time. I hear a window open.

"Will you shut up! Some of us are trying to sleep."

The window slams shut and the old man shouts more angrily at the dog.

"Come here, Jack."

Anxiety tells every part of my body to head back in, out of sight, but a small part re-assures me to act as if it is the most normal thing in the world – pouring human fluid remains down a drain in the street at a stupid time of night. I still have at least a couple more buckets to dispose of.

Finally, the dog reluctantly runs back to his master and I scurry back inside to wait until I feel safe enough to continue. It gives me time to think of where to dump Arthur's body.

I make a note in my book:

AJ – failed due to mechanical malfunction, nothing useful gained. Frozen organs are fine.

I look back to the page where I noted my taking him. It has been less than three months. It is too soon and I cannot get someone else … not just yet. Discretion is the better part of valour.

Finally, I have cleaned and scrubbed the lab; it still smells of bleach and lemon but I need to go. I am late already. I speed out of the yard, my mind somersaulting. I need to be in Manchester by eleven and know I am not going to make it.

Racing down the country lane, a sharp corner catches me unaware. The early morning darkness conceals a man walking in the road – I clip him with my car as I swerve too late.

"Shit!" I shout. I hit the brakes and the car skids to a halt. Adrenalin is coursing through me at a hundred miles and hour. "What do I do?"

I reach over to the glove box, and pull the chloroform out. My mind is racing, trying to battle against the panic that is starting to manifest itself as daylight beckons.

Leaving the car, I am look for signs of life, anyone watching. Today is turning into a disaster!

The man is barely conscious, moaning, when I reach him.

"It's alright mate, I am here to help," and with that I place the chloroformed handkerchief over his mouth and nose.

He is heavier than I would have chosen but somehow I manage to bundle him into the car. Fate has a way of delivering people to me.

I am five miles from the unit. Do I go back? I look at my watch. I don't have time. I need to dump Arthur's body whilst I can. Think! Think!

My route to Manchester, Snake Pass – yes, that will be a good place to get rid of my hit and run victim, it will keep the distance to over a hundred miles, possibly confuse the police if he is found, I won't make it easy for him to be seen. Snake Pass is a lovely road that snakes through the Peak district; it is perfect. However, I do want to return Arthur. I shall scout a place en-route, a country pub, maybe? Is the risk too high, this time? My mind is a whirl.

I floor the accelerator, needing to move to get back on schedule. Looking at my watch, my schedule is slipping further.

I am also a little concerned as I cannot change cars, and I need to work that into my return schedule.

Why do I feel the underlying need to return the bodies? If I didn't, it might be easier to hide them, bury them. I reflect to both Shelia and Gary and their farewells – remembering the satisfaction I felt knowing I was the cause of their deaths and seeing the families mourn. It completed the picture. I have to admit, seeing the news reports and discussing the stories fills me with a certain fervour, and an added pleasure. Is it foolhardy?.

An hour passes and I pull into a lay-by on Snake Pass. Dosing my hit and run with a fatal dose of Chloroform, I manoeuvre his body off the side of the lay-by, down the steep bank towards a cropping of trees and brambles. In this light he is out of sight; he may be visible during the day – but I don't care. I need to be out of here!

-

The dawn is a hint over the hills as, half an hour later, I pull into the car park of a pub called 'The Walkers Rest'. I place Arthur's remains behind a bin and leave quickly, his driving licence securely attached.

A few miles on, the adrenalin starts to dissipate and I feel the tension ease. I am still not happy at the events, but I can't change them. I have done what needs to be done. I try to think when I can next get back to the unit.

Chapter 64

1965 November
Wisbech

Sam kissed Margaret goodbye in the doorway with abandon.

"You drive carefully, dear." Margaret pinched his bum; a restless night of passion had reminded them of their first weekend away to Butlins, Skegness, on their own. For one day, they hadn't left the chalet, picnics in bed. Margaret had been so headstrong that it had caught him by surprise; she knew what she wanted to try and he enjoyed letting her guide him.

He smiled, feeling tired, yet so happy. Opening the door to his blue Ford Consul, he realised how old and rusty it was looking. A new car would be next on the agenda. He needed to promote the right image for work. Money was tight with Margaret still attending med school, although her part-time research job at the MOD was bringing some money in. Hopefully, a family would follow in a couple of years; he so wanted to be a father. Life felt pretty good. After failing med school, he now believed life was on its proper course, the right course; obviously med school wasn't for him.

The cold morning had left a thick layer of ice on the windscreen. The slight delay in getting up meant he was now running a few minutes late and the cold morning did not help matters. He had to be in Grimsby by noon for a lunch meeting with a buyer who had been quite sharp on the phone; a delivery of pineapple concentrate had turned up leaking, which, Sam knew, could jeopardise the rest of the thirty-ton contract. Physically, he could do nothing; this was purely a smoothing job.

Starting the car, it turned over first time; it didn't look much yet was reliable, even if the heating was not as effective as it could be. The next ten minutes were spent trying to clear the ice and hoping the inside would demist swiftly so he could get going. A quick glance at his watch signalled his growing impatience.

"Damn!" Even the lingering delight of last night could not ease the tension growing inside.

Finally, he pulled away yawning. At the end of the road, he glanced through the demisted side window, saw nothing and pulled out. The sound of the van horn came too late as it rammed into him. Glass shards attacked him from all directions as side windows and windscreen exploded into a zillion pieces.

Instantly the world around him faded from view.

Part 3

Chapter 65

1965 December

Kings Lynn

Two days later, Sam's bruised eyes tried to open. A nearby nurse saw
and quickly walked over to him.

Sam watched her mouth as his head swam in delirium, a confusion
of thoughts running though his fuzzy mind.

She spoke again.

Sam looked inquisitively at the young nurse, unsure what was
going on.

"What?" Sam answered, his jaw aching.

She indicated to wait as she dashed off, leaving Sam befuddled.

-

A few minutes later she returned with a doctor.

"Hello, Mr Talbot, I'm Doctor Singh. Can you tell me your first
name?"

Sam's mouth opened, then he seemed to hesitate.

Chapter 66

2002 July

"That was a nasty accident." Geoff stated as he and Sam viewed the accident and the mangled mess of the aftermath.

"When did that happen?" Sam asked. Then he remembered – he had been told about it many times over the years, but yet it always disappeared from his memory.

Geoff looked at him curiously. "You don't remember?" Embarrassed, Sam acknowledged solemnly. "What else don't you remember?"

"It was just a bad concussion, that's all."

"But it wasn't, was it?"

They now stood in the hospital ward watching the doctor perform various checks on the Sam lying in bed, Margaret now at his side.

Reluctantly, Sam agreed. "No, I started to lose time," then as an afterthought, "but it has got better over the years."

"So you say. But how do you really know? You don't even recall the accident. Still."

"But I wouldn't commit murder, without knowing it?"

"Why not? That accident was very traumatic but made no lasting imprint. Why would murder be any different?"

Back in the BMW Sam sat, melancholic, stewing over the pictures, fearful that all those missed days really had been more serious that he knew.

After a few miles Geoff asked, "How well do you know Mike and Margaret?"

"What? Very well. That's a pointless question. Margaret and I have been married for over thirty years; and Mike, I've known for even longer. So I would say I know them very well, actually." Sam stated succinctly.

"How well does anyone know anyone really? You have blind faith that neither of them kept secrets from you?"

Exacerbated Sam replied, "Everyone is entitled to secrets, why shouldn't they be? It doesn't mean anything untoward?"

"Maybe you're right." Geoff shot a sideways glance at Sam. "You weren't right very often in class though."

"You had your favourites, as I recall, so it really didn't matter what I did. The more I think about it the more I remember. Alexander Forrester, no, no, no, Alistair Forrester, teachers' pet, always had his hand up your backside!"

"Nothing wrong with being teacher's pet, unless you're jealous?"

Suddenly Sam felt very small again. Teachers had that knack sometimes.

"Not jealous, merely disappointed that some others didn't get the attention that maybe could have made a difference to their lives."

"Made a difference! It wouldn't have made a difference to you. Alistair is now MD for a big multi-national company, travels the globe in luxury that you could only dream of. And yes, he is happy."

"So was I. You are so sure that little bit of extra attention wouldn't have made a difference, are you?" Bitterness present in Sam's words. "That might have been the turning point to me succeeding at med school. Anyway, some of us are not looking for monetary rewards; just a simple existence and a means to enjoy what we have."

"Good."

Sam snapped a puzzled look at Geoff. "What?"

"It seems some of my lessons did sink in then."

"More riddles."

Chapter 67

1966 February
London
Harley Street

Sam grew impatient after being kept waiting twenty minutes to see this doctor – paid for by his employer, their own family doctor. Work had been good to him with time off for hospital, convalescence; how long would they continue to be so? Plus there was the general forgetfulness – some minor errors in costings, contract periods, very small nuisances but they could become more than acceptable – he felt the pressure that they wanted him to move on after the accident, not stay caught up in the aftermath.

Dr Jacobs finally called him in. He was an old guy with broad, dominant nose that was almost swamped by a bushy moustache sitting underneath like a giant furry caterpillar, languishing after being fed. His voice was a dull drone as he advised the results of yet more inconclusive tests.

"What do you mean you can't find anything wrong? I have lost days. I have been doing stuff; then have no memory of the events, conversations, meetings, contracts won. There has to be something wrong." Sam couldn't hide his frustration.

Dr Jacobs stared at Sam. "Mr Talbot, the brain is a fragile organ and you had quite an accident a few months back. A bad concussion. Very lucky, I would say, to have survived. To suffer from lapses is just …" he paused in thought, "… a symptom of the body trying to heal. You need to allow time. I'm sure it will all work out, the x-rays do not show anything untoward."

Even Roger had more to say on the matter, Sam thought, and he hated admitting that. However, Roger was not his doctor and work insisted on getting answers to assess the situation.

"I will report my findings; I've known the family for many years. They are very generous, you've nothing to worry about."

Flabbergasted Sam sighed. "Of …" he let the thought go.

Dr Jacobs tidied Sams' records and knitted his fingers together, "Sam, people would consider themselves lucky in your situation. No broken bones – that is amazing in itself, and I saw the photos of the car. You just need to allow the brain to repair itself, in its own way. You don't get headaches or any other symptoms?"

"No. Forgive me for sounding rude, but I am having problems remembering days at a time, there must be a reason?" Sam re-iterated.

"But no one can find anything physically wrong. All results show everything is normal. I have studied your records very, very carefully." He emphasized.

"So that's it?" The question was met with Dr Jacobs sitting back in his chair and releasing his fingers from the clasp, in a gesture of closure.

* * * *

"What did the Doctor say?" Margaret called from the bedroom.

"Nothing! Absolutely bloody nothing. Can you damn well believe it?" Sam let his briefcase drop to the floor as he took off his jacket.

"That can't be right surely? Roger said that Dr Jacobs is an excellent consultant by all accounts. One of the 'toppest'."

"I felt like I was being stupid for asking for more. The fourth doctor and as far as they can see nothing is wrong. The company's own Harley Street specialist, as long as they don't use it against me."

Margaret appeared at the top of the stairs in her dressing gown, towelling her hair. "So what are you going to do? Hold on, what do you mean 'use against you'?"

"To get rid of me! I've worked bloody hard for them this last year and they have been impressed. What can I do?" Sam stormed into the lounge, switching on the TV to catch the news. Margaret followed a few seconds later. "Learn to live with it I s'ppose. Not much else I can do really, is there? And hope that the company is okay with it. Dr Jacobs said they would be. So far we haven't lost any business over it, but …?" He let his exasperation hang in the air like a bad smell.

"I am sure they are fine with it. As you say, your work is good. Besides they wouldn't pay for you to see someone if they wanted to get rid of you. You are losing days at a time though and that can't be right?"

"Tell me about it!" Sam flumped into the armchair.

* * * *

Margaret hovered in the doorway for a few seconds remembering, only last week, an instance when Sam had been away for work.

He'd arrived home Thursday night, napped in the chair for twenty minutes and then all his memories from Tuesday up to arriving home were gone. He nearly went out again as if it were Tuesday morning, panicking that he was late.

"I'll make you a coffee."

"Make it a strong one. I think I need it."

Chapter 68

1966 February
Southend-on-Sea

The wind is blowing a gale. Waves are crashing onto the promenade. Huge puddles lie hidden in the blackness of night; driving through them, I have to fight the steering wheel. It gives me an ominous feeling about tonight; yet it is too late to turn round. I have been meticulous with my planning, the winter nights give long windows of darkness. I hadn't counted on the weather being quite so brash. I'd scouted this body dump during the summer; the group came down for a couple of days. It seemed perfect when I left the storage yard, it was a good night, but further south the weather has turned nasty.

I had planned to dispose of the body by the sea wall near the pier. Three bodies now in three different locations; it's clever, certainly enough not to give away the location of the lab and to avoid connection with each other, or me. The news reports about the discoveries are not making scorching headlines, which is good.

Halfway along the seafront, I hear a bang and suddenly the car is slewing across the road as I fight to guide it to the kerb, battered by the gale force winds emanating from the maelstrom out to sea.

I clench my hands on the steering wheel. Ominous frustration growing inside as the hand of capture feels within reach.

The wind is so strong I have to fight to open the door and then struggle to get out of the car. The flat cap, I shove into my pocket for fear of losing it. Opening the boot, I realise that Peter's body is on top of the spare, making it a risky operation to change wheels; not that anyone is likely to pass tonight, especially at three a.m. Luck is definitely running ill as I see another set of head lights appear in the distance.

"Don't stop, don't stop!" I will it.

Do I run? For a second I think about it. There is no evidence linking the car to me. I look at my watch contemplating it. There would be no trains and probably no buses for a few hours yet.

I decide against it and try to move Peter Hittles' body enough to get the wheel out. It is like concrete. I'd spent twenty-four hours at the unit, waiting for the body to thaw enough to take the samples I needed and to make notes, the wood burner speeding the job, although I had to leave it off during the day for fear of attracting attention. It was good as it gave me time to do more research and grab a few hours uneasy sleep in the car, unhelped by a sick feeling that has plagued me all day.

At times it was interesting, listening to conversations going on in the yard during the day, like a fly on the wall; supposedly private conversations, ones concerning my unit. It certainly beckons interest, it made me smile; and yet feel wary. Ben and the Mechanic were the only ones still there by seven in the evening but, finally, even they went and I could continue by starting the fire again. It was another few hours before I could remove the organs I wanted: large and small intestine, and the other kidney so I could do a direct comparison with the one I'd taken previously from him. My stomach still aches a little – maybe something I've eaten – maybe that's why I feel so weak today.

As I struggle with Peter's body, I get more breathless and tired. Maybe I will have to leave the car?

"You alright there?" A voice bellows, barely audible above the howl of the wind and rain, which is as sharp as knives on bare cheeks.

Panic sweeps through me, as I turn round.

A rotund looking adolescent with mongoloid features stands nearby – his round eyes full of innocence; he looks strong.

"Can I help, mister?"

I am too stunned to speak.

"You've got a puncture," he says so innocently, it is almost laughable.

"Yes, I know," lamely, I answer. I don't know what to do. Then, before I know it, he has moved beside me.

"I'm as strong as an Ox I am. I can move anything. My mum says I'm like a bulldozer."

He moves in.

"No!" It's too late as I watch in amazement the ease with which he lifts Peter's body out of the way, so effortlessly. It takes me a second to register before flipping into autopilot. It's all I can do to fight the panic growing inside. This bulk of a boy places the body back down and then proceeds to help me, and together, within fifteen minutes the job is done.

In disbelief a feeling of success starts to ebb inside me and I relax.

"I'll lift this whilst you put the tyre back in. It feels like a body? Is someone playing dead?"

A wave of shock sends adrenalin coursing round every muscle and, before I know it, I have the wheel brace raised high above my head and am hammering blows down on the boys head until he falls to the ground.

Frozen to the spot, dread fuelled adrenalin is cascading through me.

Do I leave the body? I can't think straight.

No, I can't. Can I?

Then, with as much effort as I can muster, I drag the boys' limp body onto the back seat, leaving the punctured wheel, it is so much effort, I feel exhausted.

Slamming the boot shut, I race to my door. The car starts first time. I ram the car into gear and flooring the accelerator, almost choking the engine; it bunny hops away.

Gaining speed, I fly past the pier, my original planned site, and carry on. I do not know where I am going, driven on by panic. Then I see a pub in darkness – The Castle; a sign points to a car park behind. I turn round and quickly scan the area. It seems clear.

I don't know how, but Peter's body comes out easier this time and, within seconds, I am racing away, my heart pounding inside my chest, now knowing I need to return to the lab tonight or dump the body somewhere else. If I dump the body tonight, it may be my undoing. No, the lab it is. It feels safer.

I will need to make some telephone calls to re-schedule things and provide excuses.

Within thirty minutes, I am back on the A127, London bound, with Kenneth Horsley's body lying on the back seat, concealed by a throw, looking as though he has fallen uncomfortably asleep.

-

Seven a.m. and I pull into the yard. I am greeted by a smile from the mechanic who keeps an eye on things for Ben Shaker.

"Morning, Sam." The mechanic barks in a friendly, conspiratorial manner, as I get out to open my unit.

I had stopped and put on my scarf and flat cap but still feel the pressure building. Is the game up? Two close calls in one night!

Waving, I acknowledge the deep-set man, with slicked back hair, chewing on a cigarette. The mechanic starts to walk over to me; I can sense him. I will him to stay away but he doesn't.

"Don't normally see you here at this time of day." The mechanic sidles up to me glancing into the car.

"No. No. Had to be somewhere but I forgot something, so had to come back for it." I try to think of something to get the mechanic out of the way.

"Important was it?" The mechanic fished.

"Kind of. Sorry, I really can't talk got some stuff to do before I go again." I open the door, edging the mechanic to the side to avoid his sly glances at my lab.

"Thought you said you forgot something? Didn't say you had stuff to do? Do you need a hand, I'm not very busy right now."

Damn he is quick.

"NO! No, I'm fine. Quicker by myself. Why you in so early, then?" I ask catching myself out. Idiot! Throwing in a conversation opener.

"Habit, you know how it is? Plus it gets me away from the family – peace and quiet like, you know?"

"Look, I really would love to chat but I must get on, I'm running late as it is." I grab the other door and open it.

"Yeah right!" The mechanic slowly eases away making sure he gets a good look at everything before adding as an afterthought. "Seems a bit long winded taking your car in doesn't?" Smiling at my discomfort.

"Things to load, unload, it is just easier."

"I'll give you hand." He steps back towards me.

"No!" I panic. "It's fine, really. But, thanks anyway."

"Yeah! Sure?" The mechanic hovers a few seconds before walking away, adding under his breath, but I hear him. "Whatever you say. Shaker's definitely right about you, something dodgy. Shame he's not coming in this morning."

Locked inside, I let out a long heavy breath. The night could be considered a disaster except for the fact that I had not been caught. A saving grace.

Heaving the dead body off the backseat is difficult as the boy is heavy, thickset. Panic is rife; a body to cut up and administer whilst everyone is on site, I am almost positive that Ben will be called.

Efficiently I set about my tasks, taking what is needed; the clothes will have to be disposed of another time. There is no time to savour the sample taking, not even sure this new experiment would harness anything. The man has been dead for a couple of hours now – cells do not take long to start breaking down following death unless you cool the body, reports suggest lower body temperature has delaying effects. Liver and eyes are the organs of choice this time and also I am not sure any results garnered are going to be of use because of the third copy of chromosome 21, it might distort any results – but maybe that could provide a twist. Maybe that extra gene will be the gene that allows re-animation to occur. Where we have been trying to modify the genes of near perfect DNA, it might be nature that is showing us that her own modifications offer what we are looking for. It's is an interesting theory; and one I will have to expound on with the group.

The colour of the liver has already changed and I wonder of its usefulness. After placing in a container with ice and cryopreservative, I clean up the blood. There will be no disposing of it down the drain today. I freeze it as well in order to stop any flies, or odour, escaping. A stop on the way back home will be needed to make the telephone calls.

Chapter 69

1966 February
Wisbech

"Hi, Honey." There was no answer. "Margaret?" Sam called closing the front door thoroughly exhausted. "Margaret?"

"I'm in the bath."

Slipping his shoes off Sam padded upstairs, undoing his tie.

"You alright?" Sam sat on the edge of the bath.

"Tired. Been an exhausting couple of days. A professor from Japan has been lecturing us on some exciting developments in cell regeneration."

"I know the feeling. Looking forward to a cozy night in with my wife. That sounds interesting." Sam let his hands swim in the foamy water. "Anything that might help us?"

"Not at this stage, but you never know. So what do you have planned for our cozy night in?"

Sam caressed his wife's chest

"Not too tired then?" she added flirtatiously.

"Well, you're such a nic... oh shit, Mike's coming over tonight isn't he?"

Margaret looked curious and then remembered. "No, he cancelled, said he has been held up and can't make it."

"Thank God for that. Not sure I could handle him tonight. Did he say what he was doing?"

"No, all very suspicious. Just said that it may help with our research but wouldn't elaborate. You quite happy fondling my breast?"

"Yes, thank you. He's been like that a lot recently?"

Margaret frowned. "I hadn't really thought, but yes, I suppose he has. What with his trips to America ..."

"We'll have to go one day. I know you've been for your job but it would be nice to have a proper look around. Although you did get a day of sightseeing, didn't you?"

"Yes, yes, it would. A day is not very much in America though; it's a huge place. We haven't been on a proper holiday since … well, we just haven't."

"Maybe we can save up and go next year? Maybe even try and talk to some people at the cryogenics institutes that are cropping up. Do you want a cup of tea?" Sam removed his hand from the water.

"Excuse me! You start something but don't finish!" Margaret admonished, grabbing Sam's wrist and pulling him into the bath sending water and foam cascading over the bathroom floor.

Chapter 70

2002 July

Sam and Geoff were standing outside a plain municipal looking building.

"What are we doing here? What is this place?"

"A place where unmarried mothers go to get rid-of unwanted babies." Geoff sounded upset by it.

"Okay. So what are we doing here?"

"I asked you about secrets that people keep, and how well you knew the people around you."

"So what has this go to do with ...?" Sam stopped as he saw Margaret stepping out through the plain wooden doors. His heart sank. "No!"

"I'm afraid so, Sam. Even I don't enjoy showing you this. An unborn child is a precious gift."

"But why? We wanted to start a family. When was this?"

"Did you? Wasn't that just you?"

Sam let dejection swallow him as the scene faded from view and they returned to the car and the tarmac road stretching out in front.

After a long silence, Sam tried to stifle his emotions. "Why show me that? That's cruel."

"It is on my list, and you said secrets were okay to have. Are they?"

Chapter 71

1966 June

Liverpool
CID

"Good collar, Sir. Heard you got that bastard banged to rights." Mark said as he marched over to Ron's desk.

"Too right, and, what can I say, he resisted arrest. I don't think he'll be getting a hard-on for anything soon. Shame. I'm sure the lags will make their thoughts quite plain once he's inside." The thought of the rapist off the streets filled him with glee.

"Got what he deserved then." The two men smiled at each other. "How was the victim?"

"Shaken, but at least saved from the ordeal, thanks to our nosey neighbour type."

"S'ppose they do have their uses."

"Very rare ..." Ron's phone rang. He wiped his hand over his face to try and shake the tiredness, it had been a long few hours and he did hate dealing with rapists who, with paedophiles, were the lowest of the lows – always making him feel tainted afterwards. It was a feeling that generally took a few beers and a chaser to get rid-of.

"Chappell!" he barked. There was a pause as his chin dropped, a gesture that was not lost on Mark. Ron slammed down the phone hard.

"Mark, Incident room now!"

"What is it?" Mark stood up.

"Another bloody body's turned up, could be connected."

"That makes three then?"

"Yep, we definitely got a serial on our hands. Bloody sick git. Shit, just as I thought they might be coincidences."

"Definitely same M.O.?"

"Oh yes, but this time dumped the body in a place called Southend-on-Sea, somewhere in Essex."

Ron was almost at a run as they left CID to head for the incident room, which had been scaled back but would soon be a hive of activity again.

"So he's moving around the country then? Do we have a name yet?" Mark asked catching up with Ron and falling in step behind.

"Not yet, coroner has the body, no formal ID, but they've been advised to let us know when they do."

"There'll be a media frenzy if this gets out."

"How shall we play it?" Mark almost tripped through the door behind Ron into the incident room, where Travis and two other officers were still working.

"Travis, there's been another body dump. Southend-on-Sea. No formal ID yet, all we know is it is a male this time. Same M.O. apparently. Have you got any new information?"

"Sorry, Sir, nothing. All the names of doctors struck off or left the profession in the last five years have all checked out. Veterinary – we only have three unaccounted for. There is no word from any informants about a suspected illicit operating room or storage place, thus far. Everything is zilch." Ron registered the disappointment in William; he really was doing his best – the hunger showed.

Ron flicked through a file; their only suspect. "And this Talbot guy?"

"All checks out, can't find anything out of the ordinary, and he has absolutely no connection in the slightest to Karen Littleton. Never met her; never been to her place of work; or to anywhere, from what can be fathomed."

"Any leads on where he, they, could be conducting their experiments?"

"Nothing. As I say, everyone's snouts, informants et cetera have been hounded and no one is coming up with anything."

"Jesus, is this person God? Three bodies experimented on and no one knows anything, or sees anything. We need a break. Mark, I think we need to bring in the media, can you set up a news conference. I think I need to go to this Southend place. Travis get me a map."

Before Mark or William had had time to answer he'd left the room.

One Day Later

"Don't look so bloody nervous." Ron said over the noise of the Ford Cortina rattling at fifty miles an hour as they joined the M10 from the M1, heading towards the North Orbital. A cigarette hanging from his mouth spilled ash on his tie; he didn't care.

"But I'm still not quite sure why I'm here."

"Your work's good, thorough, and I must admit, although I thought you were a little green around the gills to start with, I'm impressed. You said you'd like to work in CID one day, well, with the impression you are giving me I may be able to help speed that up. You know this case as well as anyone, probably better." Ron stated nonchalantly as if it had been rehearsed. Then added more sincerely. "And good coppers are hard to find – except myself of course." He waited for even an intimation of a laugh, but it wasn't forthcoming so he continued, "I know it certainly narks a few people, you being involved, but you'll come across prejudice anyway, so may as well get used to it early." Ron became more serious. "But remember, you being on this jolly with me *is* a privilege that usually gets reserved for the Super's son." He laughed. "Seriously, you've shown aptitude, initiative and determination, and I'll be putting a good word in for you with the selection board when you're serious about moving to CID. I can't promise anything and if you get through, you're on your own; it's a once in a career chance, you don't get to go back and try again."

William smiled. "I don't know what to say."

"There ain't nothing to say. You do well on this case, like you have been and that will be good enough for me. Maybe buying me a drink or two wouldn't go amiss." Ron smiled to himself.

"Sure."

"Now, what road we looking for."

Chapter 72

1966 March
Southend-on-Sea
CID

"DCI Chappell and PC Travis here to see DS Kilter."

The desk sergeant sniffed and looked condescendingly at Travis. "Take a seat, I'll get him."

The door to the green painted stonewalled waiting area was almost knocked off its hinges with enthusiasm as a tall skinny man marched through "Chief Inspector Chappell?" The heavy Scottish drawl echoed around the stone walls as he beamed a smile that contained mainly broken teeth.

"That's not local, I'm guessing," Chappell reeled off smiling a greeting.

"Aye, you're not wrong, been down here a wee while though; it's certainly warmer. Well, normally. Married a wee local lassie, now two small bairns to look after, so I guess I'll be staying." Kilter was overly friendly. "Tea, coffee?"

"Be great, thanks," Chappell said, as they followed Kilter to an incident room.

"I understand that this is the third body dump now?"

Chappell saw Travis was about to answer and beat him to it. "That's right, Travis here discovered the first one outside the Liver Building, November '63. Fresh out of Peel's and already discovering dead bodies."

"And accompanying the Chief already! Is he the Super's bairn?" Chappell noted Travis' embarrassment as he interjected.

"I'm not the Super's son. And, I hope I have earned this special privilege as I proved I didn't want to sit around and do nothing. I kept pushing for more information about the victim, and what I could do to help," he said.

Kilter and Chappell shared a knowing look of appreciation for his enthusiasm.

"You'll go far with that attitude," Kilter said.

"Thank you," Travis answered.

They stopped by a door and Kilter stepped closer to Travis. "Don't let no one take that away from you." It bellowed a father's admiration. "In here." Opening the door there were a sea of desks and telephones being manned by half a dozen officers. "Now, since we spoke, we may have a missing person that may or may not be connected with the case, a Kenneth Horsley aged 19, a mongoloid, but nice enough, wouldn't harm a gnat. Apparently has a history of going for late night walks in the rain, and the publican of the Ship remembers seeing a youngish lad around the same time, as he locked up. You said this was the third victim? Have they all been male?"

"No," Travis answered. "Two women were first, a Susan Jones and a Karen Littleton."

"So your guy's not fussy then?"

"No evidence of a sexual nature." Travis looked to Chappell who cocked a warning eye, although deep down enjoying his keenness and aptitude. "Just some surgical type incisions, samples and organs taken before and after."

"Before and after what?" Kilter enquired.

"Being frozen." Chappell added taking back the reins. Travis and I share a theory that there is some kind of research being carried out. So it could be a struck off doctor, lab tech, scientist of some sort. Our team has made exhaustive enquiries countrywide but any leads seem to pan out to nothing."

Kilter pulled some photos from an envelope, "Like these?" handing them to Travis who took them eagerly.

Sifting through he nodded.

"Every major organ sampled according to the pathologist. And a couple of organs taken: both kidneys, thyroid and a lung." Kilter added. "Definitely the same M.O. then?"

"Did your pathologist confirm whether the body had been frozen or not?" Chappell asked taking the photos from Travis and skimming through them as if shuffling a deck of cards.

"Yes, he mentioned some ice crystals still in the tissue, consistent with the body being frozen at some point, as well as frost bite. He was unable to pinpoint the time of death but assumed he had been dead for nearly all of the time he has been missing. Toxicology results show high levels of alcohol; toxic levels. No formal ID yet, so we don't know how long he has been missing. But I have people looking into it."

Three mugs of tea were placed on the table.

"Thanks, Gary." Kilter slurped noisily from the hot brew. "My Chief has obviously asked that I leave it with you as you have an incident room running. I will carry on here with my team to see what we can dig up; also try to connect Kenneth Horsley. I understand different locations are involved?"

"Yes, and we have been unable to pinpoint an area where he is working as there is no pattern; but for the storage and experimenting he must have a lab, a unit, somewhere he is working from, the equipment would not be portable – we don't believe."

"Time frame?"

"So far, over a four year period, approx."

"And only three people."

"That we know of," Travis confirmed.

Chapter 73

1966 April

Mike's Lab

Mike breezed into the lab, tingling with excitement.

"Evening all, come see what goodies daddy has brought you all," looking over at Margaret and Sarah who were deeply involved in something and didn't even acknowledge him. Roger turned around.

"Hi, Mike. What have you got?"

Mike's smile evaporated from the initial pleasure. "Well, just some fresh organs, that's all, not dead ones from cadavers, as such, but ... fresh out of a person, one who died!" He held up two dewar flasks.

Sarah turned round. "Roger, can you pass the ... oh, hi, Mike. Margaret has brought a liver to work on. We were ... what you got?"

"A heart and an eye." He replied, sourly.

"Where did you get them?" Margaret enquired marching over and excitedly taking one of the dewar flasks Mike was carrying.

"Seven-eleven; it's amazing what you can get in America. They sell everything you know, legs, arms, brains."

Margaret opened it, whilst Mike put on his lab coat. "Very droll, Mike. Very droll."

"What's it like in America?" Sarah continued, looking at the slide of a liver sample under the microscope.

"It's big; everything is big, and even more so ... it's huge!" Mike stated emphatically without elaborating, as per usual to tease her, knowing how much she wanted to go there.

"Thanks, that tells me a lot!" Sarah sighed.

"What?" Mike exclaimed innocently. "It's different to here, that's all. What is there to say?"

Sarah tore herself away from the microscope and back to the actual liver she and Margaret had been working on.

"He'll never get it, Sarah." Margaret lifted the heart out of the metal flask and gazed at it in awe.

"Are you alright, Margaret?" Roger asked.

"Mmm, yes, just such an amazing muscle. What it does, how it keeps us working." The others stared at her. "Well, it is. You have to marvel at what nature does so easily. Now all we need to do is replicate that after freezing." She saw the confused looks. "The spark that allows life to perpetuate itself."

"You're beginning to sound like Sam, Margaret!" Mike pulled on some gloves with a smack.

"What are those?" Margaret placed the heart on the bench.

"Latex Surgical gloves – the norm in most operating theatres nationwide. Where is Sam by the way?"

"So you really do go then?" Margaret admonished. "He's away on business."

"Funny business, eh!"

Margaret looked disdainfully at Mike, "Shall we get on?"

Chapter 74

1966 December

Liverpool
Incident Room

"Come on, Travis, get those boxed, ready to be archived."

William watched his staff sergeant exit, leaving him in the now empty incident room, reading the files that he knew by heart. He couldn't believe that, after seven months, there was still nothing to go on. The television coverage had yielded nothing. Police 5 – whilst relatively new, and reaping positives in London – regional versions weren't receiving the same response. They had been only too happy to assist and it had made him laugh seeing how uncomfortable Ron had been in front of the camera; his usually unflappable persona reduced to a pubescent school child floundering in front of the headmaster. Shaw Taylor managed to coax ease into Ron by the end of the section about the serial killer now nicknamed 'The Examiner' by the newspapers.

The body dumped in Southend-on-Sea was Peter Hittles, a forty-three old transport manager for Janice's haulage whose second wife was expecting their first child when he disappeared after leaving the Spread Eagle pub in the Blaby area of Leicester. Last seen getting into a dark Zephyr, the witness thought. That was October '64, and it had been almost twelve months to the day when he'd been dumped in Southend-on-Sea.

Three victims and no new leads. Sam Talbot was the only name that ever came up. But he always had alibis.

"There's something dodgy about you?" William stood up, slowly, reluctantly accepting it was time to move on and knowing tomorrow the overtime would be over and this part of the job, the part that he relished, would be behind him again.

How do detectives just walk away from a case, leaving it unsolved?

Sitting down again, he quickly compiled his own personal file, not that he really needed it – he knew it by heart. Even knowing it would be reviewed only when another body turned up, if it did, felt like a betrayal to Susan Jones and his vow.

Chapter 75

1966 December

Wisbech

"See you later Margaret. Should be back in time for tea on Thursday." Sam pulled the raincoat from under the pile of coats hanging on the newel post.

"Have a good trip. I might be late in Thursday, there is a professor visiting from America who I want to talk to. They have made some good leaps in genetic modification and I want to talk to him about cryonics and what he might know about some of the institutes being setting up over there. You never know, he might have some insights."

"Cool. Have you seen my raincoat?"

Margaret came out of the lounge still in her dressing gown

"What was that?"

"Have you seen my …"

"What, you mean that one you're looking at?"

"Eh? No, it's not mine."

"Sure looks like it."

"No, mine has an ink stain on the inside pocket. This isn't mine. Looks like it but is not."

Margaret looked at her husband. "You sure? I'm sure my lover didn't take the wrong coat." She smiled innocently.

"He must have done. Thank him will you. Nice not to have an ink stain. His loss."

"I will dear. Actually doesn't Mike have a similar one? Maybe you picked up the wrong one there."

"Maybe. Oh well, good job we're the same size and have such good taste."

"And modest too, don't forget that. See you Thursday." She kissed him before closing the door after he left.

Chapter 76

1967 January
Lincolnshire
Storage Yard

With the fire roaring away I settle down for a few hours research on one of my regular check visits. I have taken to checking the yard before driving in, wary of Shaker. I do like these early hours on my own, even if it does tire me for the next few days. I try and keep my work light where possible so I can catch forty winks. I am awaiting the publication of a work conducted by a Japanese scientist, Isamu Suda, who has had some success using glycerol on a cat's brain, frozen then warmed – due out in the publication 'Nature'.

Following on from the group meeting I am trying a couple of tests that were suggested. I do, however, need to be more careful after accidentally swapping raincoats, luckily I had taken my notebook out of the inside pocket. Regardless of how busy I am, I need to make sure I take certain precautions to ensure I do not get caught. The garage is working out nicely, and I am using different means of transportation to get there, so my everyday car does not get spotted regularly. I still have not done anything about the Zephyr; it has proved lucky to date and I am reluctant to lose that, but know I should – it was mentioned on Police 5.

My current two experiments are showing some stability of cells using the glycerol mixtures with additives – SX2 and SX4. Cell and tissue decay still occurs and I feel, in some ways that may be because the freezers are substandard for the job at hand. Liquid nitrogen is without doubt the way to maintain temperature and achieve rapid freezing but it doesn't help that I am not here to administer it regularly and there are temperature fluctuations.

Money is running out, so I am not sure how much longer I can carry on. I may have to try my hand at the horses again; it worked before. I am a little surprised Shaker has not upped the rent – I have been expecting it. He is definitely playing a long game. Has he lost interest?

One can only hope so.

I still find it a little surreal seeing the odd story playing out on the television and knowing. The Moor Murders were convenient to start with as they grabbed the headlines, so no one was interested in the odd missing person that wasn't a teenager. Whilst they have associated the bodies I have disposed of, with each other, they are not absolutely sure. I watched a Detective Chief Inspector Chappell on Police 5 – it was mildly amusing. They don't know where to look and will never find my lab. They call me 'The Examiner', sounds like something from school!

The palpable sense of power is intoxicating, especially when I openly bring organs to the group. It seems so innocent to them; if only they knew! It is mischievous to know what I am doing to them; making them part of these experiments – but it does make me smile inside, appealing to my dry sense of humour. Deceitful, I know! Reminds me of the pets I used to cut up in the neighbourhood. How I used to pick on someone who had annoyed me. I always said I get my own back. And I did! I'd watch them get upset for their lost friend. They never knew.

Kenneth Horsley – I am going to extend for another six months to see if the decay of useable cells flat-lines, slows or increases with time, I think I know the answer but research needs absolutes.

Jemima Hartridge – I am getting no useful results in the ongoing checks; there were signs of a medical operation: appendix. Blood results did not show anything unusual. I will have to locate another body dump. Quite fancy a trip north this time – maybe Northumberland, Kielder can be nice. I will scout a location.

Chapter 77

1967 January
Mike's Lab

"Hi Mike. Where's Roger and Sarah?" Sam hung his coat on the back of the door.

"They're not coming, Sarah's having a difficult time with the pregnancy and needs to rest, Doctors orders."

"Is that Doctor Roger?" Margaret followed Sam in.

Mike swivelled round on his new 'all bells and whistle' stool obviously trying to show-off. "Probably. You know what he's like, wrapping her up in bloody cotton wool. You would think no one ever had a baby before." Mike pulled a lever on his stool and it shot down a few inches. Sam ignored it, knowing Mike loved to show off new gadgets and he wasn't in the mood.

"I'd like to see you have a baby!"

"Women always say that whenever anyone questions how well they handle pregnancy. It's in your genes, and I think you just want us men to feel guilty about it for as long as possible. You have just as much fun getting pregnant as us men."

Sam walked to the far corner of the lab and the new freezing unit they had recently purchased – it had cost a lot of money and been built to their own specifications – as the banter between Margaret and Mike continued. It had been getting more severe recently; he wondered whether it was just down to lack of progress and the fact they were pouring money into what was becoming an bottomless pit, and all, except Mike, did not have an endless supply of money in which to do so.

Freezing seemed to be the easy part, with many people now stored in cryostasis around the world, although some of the fundamental cell damage issues still had not been resolved. They knew frogs – Rana Sylvatica, Pseudacris Triseriata, Hyla Crucifer, Hyla Versicolor, Hyla Chrysoscelis – could survive freezing, and glucose was one of the natural elements that allowed them to do so, and with this fact they were going to focus their research in this area; probably like most of the scientific fraternity. One of the other questions that needed answering was how the frogs managed to kick start their bodies, after freezing? The Frankenstein films had pumped people full of the idea that the body just needed jump starting and, in principle, that was the case; but getting the heart muscle and other organs to kick back into life after being frozen, possibly death, was still a mystery to the world. An electric shock was easy to give and that would work the muscles; yet how do you get the body to sustain that after a long period of being frozen?

Sam grabbed a plastic container that held a specimen of Rana Sylvatica – which they had stored for over a week at minus 196 degrees Celsius in liquid nitrogen, and placed it on the counter. Today they were going to thaw and dissect it, to see if there was any more research they could garner from it. He tried to ignore the heated discussion raging on.

"Mike, you are a narrow minded idiot. It may well be fun getting pregnant, but the body has to go through so many monumental hormonal changes to carry that organism inside. Do you know what …?"

"Organism? That's a bit clinical isn't it?" Sam heard Mike taunt.

"Oh, go to hell, Mike. You're really getting on my nerves."

"I'm entitled to an opinion. Anyway, it seems like I'm the only one doing any work anymore, Sarah and Roger are more interested in being parents. You and Sam seem to have other *more important* things you want to do."

Sam butted in. "Unfortunately we do have to work – unlike you who seem to only go out and buy more gadgets and contraptions to fill the lab up with."

"Yes, my lab as well. Me and my stepfather have come to an arrangement and I stay out of his way."

There was a second's silence.

"Fine." Margaret grabbed her coat. "You obviously don't really need our help."

Sam stood indignantly as Margaret stared at him, her eyebrows furrowed questioningly. Sam was caught between coming and going. Things had stalled, research wise, and this was making everyone fractious. Maybe their dreams of grandeur were just that, and to be resigned to the far echelons of their memories to reflect on in later life when, maybe, someone will actually solve the question of life.

Sam watched Margaret storm out.

"Sorry, Mike. I don't know what's wrong with her recently."

"Ah, don't worry about it, I suppose it was bound to end someday. Maybe she is just worried about you and your fugue states; maybe that's where her research should be focused. Who knows maybe it is, in her spare time?"

"There haven't been many of those recently, thankfully." Sam said taking off his lab coat.

Mike looked astonished. "Sorry, mate, there have been a few according to Margaret."

Dejected, Sam put his coat on. "I'll see you soon, okay?"

"Yeah, sure. I'll carry on. You know where to come when you're ready."

"Cheers."

* * * *

Mike glanced round the empty lab, its silence an unwelcome friend.

"Aw, bollocks," he said after a few minutes and spun round like a top before walking over to where Sam had left the frozen frog.

"Hello, Fred, how you doing? Sorry what was that? Bit cold. Don't worry we'll get that sorted soon, you'll be dead chuffed!" He chortled to himself.

Chapter 78

1967 January

Lincolnshire
Storage Yard

Jemima Hartridge' body dump went well, everything as planned. There is progress with my research, showing that some organs are more easily stored in a state of possible re-use. Ice crystals are easily solved with cooling followed by quick freezing; however, upon thawing at around minus one-hundred and twenty degrees, ice crystals start forming and I have not found a way to bypass this, yet. Glycerol is definitely the key, but it has limits.

I have contacted a Dr Johannsen in New York who is also working on cryonics; but he said that it is the same situation everyone is facing. No one has worked out how to avoid this; although there is a Dr Cornelius Bandet who has intimated he is on the cusp of a breakthrough for thawing, but will not provide any specifics. There are two more cryonics societies, other than New York and Michigan. America seems to be the place to be for innovation; Britain seems unconcerned about being left behind. It seems absurd.

I have noted some researchers becoming more secretive now, whereas before they would share freely in the hope that it would garner an exchange of ideas, helping the process. Changing times. Money and credit are taking over.

Chapter 79

1967 January
Liverpool
CID

"What the bloody hell?"

"What's up Chief?" Mark looked up, stretching his back after a long morning data crunching, following a long night on the piss; all he wanted to do was sleep.

"Bloody Commissioner wants to talk about a case. Gawd knows why, it fizzled out, if there is no evidence or suspects we can pursue, then there is no case. Why do they have to keep wasting my time, I bet it is bloody paper filing idiots. Jesus!!"

"Commissioner coming here? We are honoured. Do we need to get the red carpet out and some nice little cucumber sarnies?"

"It's not bloody royalty."

"Close enough 'innit?" Harris asked watching Ron stare blankly at a pile of files on his desk that just seemed to get higher and higher. "Did they say what case?"

"Yeah. The Examiner case; the one that brought your favourite plod in here."

"Travis' case!" Mark exulted disapprovingly. "What is it with him? All the bloody cases we work our nuts off on and he has one day as plod, and the heavens grace him with every ..."

"Give it a rest. He is coming to see me, your boss, so don't forget it. So what if Travis gets a lucky break, if you can call finding a dead body on your first day, lucky. Maybe he deserves the luck! I have certainly seen a bloodhound in him. He gets things done and is not afraid to make the effort. When he joins this department, and I will certainly make every effort to secure that, he will be an asset."

Mark fumed silently, conjuring thoughts of Travis being fired, and ways to make it just so.

"Anyway, bloody case is suspended, what is there to discuss." Ron stormed out before Mark added anything.

Chapter 80

1967 March

Mike's Lab

"Come on, Roger, you're the brains of the operation. How can we get past the cells destruction caused by freezing?" It sounded more like an accusation from Mike than an exasperated question.

This was only the second time that Sarah and Roger had been along to the lab since their daughter, Rachel, had been born.

"And thawing." Sarah added.

"Exactly." Mike offered in conclusion.

"I may be the brains, but let's face facts. The whole of the science fraternity are trying to answer that question. I am just one man you know?" Roger exhaled loudly pushing his glasses further up the bridge of his long angular nose. "And besides, that's not really the only problem is it? Unless you can re-animate a body after thawing, then cell structure is a pretty pointless subject to be concentrating on."

Sarah sighed, "Yes, and arguing isn't going to resolve anything is it? We are all targeting the same result."

Margaret breezed in clutching a big blue and white textbook.

"You look pleased with yourself?" Mike pushed yet another frog specimen away. "Where's Sam?"

"I am, and he couldn't make it tonight had to go out on a business dinner."

Sarah responded, "Seems to be doing that a lot recently."

"Well, work is work and we're saving. Anyway that's irrelevant. What I have here is I believe the first concise textbook about cryobiology and it has lots of information that might just be relevant to us. I have had a quick glance through and there are some interesting aspects about freeze-drying. Maybe this is the way to go instead of solely freezing, at least with freeze-drying you are not destroying the cell structure just subtracting the water within it ..."

"... And with less, or no water, then no ice crystals!" Roger exclaimed.

"The only problem I see with that is degradation of the tissue. At least with freezing you are maintaining the fabric of the tissue in theory. Drying is a form of mummification." Sarah's brow furrowed seemingly lost in thought.

"I would agree with you. But maybe, just maybe there is a way to combine the two, get the best of both worlds. That way it may eliminate the formation of ice crystals rupturing the cell walls." Margaret looked to Mike.

"How do you make two almost opposing solutions work together? Is it possible to freeze-dry tissue, then cryogenically freeze, followed by thawing and basically add water to rehydrate?"

"Don't know, Sarah, but it's a good point to hypothesize, and you never know where it might lead. There's some research material in America which I'm trying to get hold of, as they have certainly set science talking. There are two cryonics societies, one in New York set up by Curtis Henderson and Saul Kent, and another in Michigan set up by Robert Nelson. Now he is, was, just a television repair man but even he is progressing, and ..."

"How do you get access to all this information?" Mike asked.

"Do you still want to be involved in this, Mike?"

Mike appeared almost stunned by the question.

"Yes, why?"

"I've just felt recently that you're not that bothered by it. I get this information through contacts in my MOD job."

"Oh yes, what is that exactly?" Mike goaded.

"You know I can't tell you that. I have signed the official secrets act."

"But it's alright to share this information, and do they know you take supplies ... for us?"

"What's your problem, Mike? What does it matter to you? I'm trying to help our group with research, which is more than can be said for you recently. Plus you were the one that always seemed to be enamoured with the prospect of seeing your name go down in history once you came on board. You didn't want to know at first." There was silence in the lab.

"I'm sorry," he sighed heavily. "I'm just getting frustrated that's all. We don't seem to be getting anywhere that hasn't already been discovered before, by some other neuroscientist or whatever."

"I understand that, but we have to start somewhere. Sometimes that means back at the beginning re-establishing theories, and trying different variances to get the baselines for ourselves. You know that research, if it is to stand a chance of being authenticated has to be logged and recorded every step of the way," Margaret paused, "and yes, they do know what I take out of the lab every day, supplies and research."

Roger added. "Can't be very top secret work if you can take research out of the lab?"

Margaret frowned. "What is it with everyone and my job? Can't a girl get on? I have agreed to hold secret everything that I do, and certain information that comes into my possession ..."

"Sounds like a spy movie now." Mike interrupted.

"For Christ's sake. If it's not covered under the official secrets act then I can utilise as I see fit. AS FOR MATERIAL, I'm allowed to do research outside of the lab if I deem it necessary, so I just add a little here and there. God, why do I have to explain myself?" Margaret sighed wearily. "Sod, this I'm going home. I've better things to do than explain my life to you lot." She marched out of the lab leaving the three friends looking at each other.

Suddenly Sarah bolted for the door. "I'll see you at home Roger."

"But we are going to ..." Roger started, but the door was already closing.

"I'm sorry, Roger." Mike spoke solemnly "I think she's right you know."

"If you want to give up that's fine but Sarah and I don't. We still feel there is ground to be made, and this is one area where we could place our names in the history of science. Cryonics is going to be the way forward, especially with space travel coming into play. If we could freeze people, suspending their life temporarily, then we could go further than our own universe, to galaxies that have not been discovered yet, and return."

"You sound like an advert for a space program."

"Yes, well, I, we believe that there is a chance, maybe a slim one, but a chance all the same that we could discover the key to solving cryonics and thawing. And maybe it could be used to help people live beyond their ailments, when cures have been found for some of the tragic illnesses that tear lives apart. Who knows, maybe it could help with the regeneration of limbs, and repairing bodies the way we do machines, give everyone a chance at a normal life after the crippling atrocities that are inflicted on our species." Roger finished, holding his glasses in his hand like a pointer, jabbing the air as though he was trying to puncture it.

"Wow!" was all Mike could say, he had forgotten just how passionate Roger could be.

"What?"

Mike blew out a puff of air. "You make me quite horny!" Roger stared at him. "I think I know what Sarah sees in you."

"She fell for my endearing attributes."

"I really don't want to know, Brains. Now, shall we get on?"

Chapter 81

1967 February

The Zephyr choked and spluttered into the car park at Stonehenge, the thick black night was like a vortex of anger; the wind buffeting the car. Huge puddles like mud ponds.

"Come on, come on!"

I risked the mechanic servicing the car last week, as it seemed to be playing up; he said he had fixed it. Well that certainly seems to be the case!

Stonehenge is my only point of reference although there are trees behind; maybe I should have pulled it in there.

What do I do now?

I try the engine again, pumping the pedal for all it's worth. It misfires then appears as though it might spring into life. But no! I let the clutch out with disgust and it kangaroos to a halt.

It is past two in the morning. I can't sit here and I can't call a breakdown service. I feel exhausted and have a busy day ahead. I could walk but which direction? I am miles from anywhere.

Reluctantly, I get out, feeling the force of the rain, remembering what a calm and peaceful night it had been when I had left Lincolnshire; this was my longest planned drop, a scouted place near Okehampton; it was a church this time. Now, that plan was done for.

Kenneth Horsley's body would remain here.

What is it about him? Storms seem to be his power. Jemima had been a lovely body dump, Kielder had little light pollution and the warm barmy night welcomed me to spend a few minutes marvelling at the night sky, it was easy to forget time wondering whether there really was life out there.

I look at the car, disgusted with myself for not changing it sooner. It is cold and I am already soaked within minutes. I'll be lucky if I don't get hypothermia! Indecision racks me at the main road – which way?

Neither direction seems ideal. I go right. Not a single car is on the road and whilst that is a blessing, it is also my curse; although hitchhiking might not be ideal after dumping a car with a body in it! Somehow, I have to get to Exeter, where I can hire a car, until I retrieve my every day one. I feel an illness coming on – probably a good excuse; hold up in a B&B somewhere and do some research.

Trudging along the road is like wading through treacle; tired and hungry, the wind seems stronger than ever.

A haze of headlights begins to lighten the road ahead and I wonder whether I am hallucinating. The coldness has been replaced by heat, or is it numbness? Maybe hypothermia is setting in? Instantly, the roar of an engine shakes me fully awake and a lorry zooms past, scaring me to death. Stopping a little way ahead the passenger door swings open.

"Oi, mate. You alright?" the wind almost carrying the words away.

For a second I am caught between feeling this could be my demise and this being my saviour. I am too cold. Prepared to take a risk. I run as fast as my aching legs will carry me.

"Do you need a lift?" The man shouts as I get near.

"Too right." I shout, launching myself into the cab forcing the driver back over to his seat.

Closing the door is like entering a sanctuary. I shiver as I am finally out of the wind and rain; the warmth struggling back in to my body. I pull the coat collar tighter – the scarf is soaking but I don't want to remove it; I don't want him to see my face. When the car is found they will seek witnesses; anyone seen leaving the scene – and the less he knows the better.

"You must be soaked? Where you going, or better still, what happened? Get chucked out of yer car by yer bird?"

The Birmingham accent I have been developing has become so easy, even my chattering teeth can't break it. "Exeter, but the nearest station would be great, mister. Yeah, something like that."

It is obvious the guy has been lonely and is looking to chat. "You must be soaked through. I have some dry overalls in the back if you want to get changed. You'll catch your death!"

"I'll be fine once the heat kicks in, thank you. I just need to sleep; been walking for hours. " I sneeze.

"That's what happens being out on a night like this." With that the driver turns the heating up to full blast. "This will help dry you out."

"Thank you. You're very kind."

The driver looks like he is about to say something so I shut my eyes hoping to cut dead any conversation. Yet he stills carries on and slowly I get drawn in as he offers tea from a flask he has. I keep my answers brief. Eventually, as the heat returns to my body I fall asleep, not that I remember!

I am jarred awake by the lorry stopping.

"Sorry, mate, this is where I end."

Groggily I stir, immediately taken by a sneezing fit.

"It's not Exeter but there is a train station about a mile up that road. My yard is just up here on the right."

"Thank you." I yawn and jump down, "Appreciate it."

It is only as the lorry drives off I realise I dropped the accent. Too late!

Thankfully it has stopped raining as I head in the direction of the station looking at my watch it is 5.17 am. Two hours later I am on train to Exeter.

Chapter 82

1967 April
Liverpool
CID

"'nother two years of this crap and I'm taking early retirement." Ron slammed the phone down hard, spilling the coffee in his dirty mug that was balanced precariously on some files. "Oh great, can it get any worse today? It's not even nine o'clock." He moved the mug and proceeded to shake the paperwork dry.

"You won't know what to do with yourself." Mark replied, "You'll miss ..."

"I bloody won't. This job is for the likes of the newbies, Travis and the likes." Mark visibly bristled.

"Yeah, s'ppose."

Ron became more intense, "You know we need people like him. Prepared to go that little further, even in their own time."

"Brown nose." Mark muttered yet Ron heard.

"Maybe so. We could do with ten more ..." the phone sprang into life, its ring like an irritating cry. "What?" he shouted down it before listening intently, the colour draining slowly from his face, his eyes widening in surprise.

Ron replaced the receiver and put his head in his hands. Then dialled a number.

"This is DSI Chappell, is PC Travis in today?" Ron waited for the reply. "Good. Is he in the building or out on a beat, I want to second him." Ron saw Mark smirk as he took an ear bashing and shot him a warning glance that he wasn't in the mood. There was finally a pause.

"Good. Tell him to meet me downstairs in ten, plain clothes." Ron slammed the phone down.

Ron saw Mark's grimace and gave him a look daring him to challenge his decision.

Instead Mark got up. "Colin, how you doing with your contact on the burglary?"

Ten minutes later Ron saw William standing outside like an obedient dog enjoying the sunshine.

"Good you're ready, we're off to Wiltshire, hope you don't have plans."

William shrugged bemused stepping into line behind Ron.

"'nother bloody body dump, although this time they've got a car. Back in February it was, but they've only just realised that it might be connected to our case, back in '63."

"But there hasn't been anything since October that year. It was Kenneth Horsley who disappeared around the same time from Southend, although nothing confirmed."

"That's whose body they've got on ice. So it is now."

Chapter 83

1967 April
Wiltshire

The rain had started a few miles out of Liverpool, dogging them all the way to Wiltshire; Andover police station, they were heading to.

"We're going to need a boat if this carries on. God I hate the rain." Ron stated nonchalantly.

Travis nodded his agreement, still a little uneasy and surprised about how much he was being involved in this case, especially for a beat copper.

"Lighten up, this is a privilege. You've got a sharp eye for detail that outstrips any rank in my book."

"Thanks, Sir."

There were a few minutes silence.

"Oh, spit it out, Travis." Ron could see something was on William's mind.

"How long since you were in uniform, Sir?" It was not what Ron was expecting and he frowned.

"A long time. Too long to remember, and I wouldn't want to go back." Suddenly Ron understood where this was coming from. "You getting stick for being here? Being called a brown hound?"

"Did you ever get the opportunity?"

"No, I didn't, but I did witness my super's son get preferential treatment and the ribbing he got for it from people like myself. There's a lot of petty jealousy in the force, prejudice is rife and nepotism can be harmful to morale, and family."

"Strange thing to say, family?"

"Maybe, maybe not."

"I don't get it. Why harmful to the family?"

"From what I have witnessed, normally nepotism demoralises the people around. Seeing someone accelerated through the ranks, with almost utter disregard for those who may have earned it."

"But this isn't nepotism."

"No, it is favouritism and something I normally admonish, and that's what's puts people like Harris' nose out of joint. It's a gut feeling and, in all honesty, not something I have felt about another copper before. Till you! You repeat any of this and I'll have your nuts in a vice so quick you'd wished you'd never set eyes on me."

"I don't really have anyone I could tell it to, except my parents."

"So you really are getting a hard time then?"

"So, so. It's like I have crossed an invisible line. The fact that I want to get on, and am not willing to just sit around and wait makes me ..." William stared out of the side window for a second, "... unpopular to hang around with, so to speak. People are guarded."

"A cruel lesson in life, that. Success breeds contempt in others. You see that in Harris, although I shouldn't say it. He dislikes you because you represent something that he is not. Determined. Don't get me wrong, he is a good copper but he won't push himself. He is not tenacious. Remember what I said about 'family' and the supers' son?"

"Yes."

"Well, he, not Harris, the supers' son got promoted alright, through the ranks, father pulling strings. Unfortunately, nepotism had worked far too well and was his undoing. His son was too honest, determined to make people understand that he could do the job properly. Well, on his way up he found his father had ... shall we say twisted the rules a little for his own benefit, a couple of backhanders with the right blagger, to help his son get the catch. Deals with the wrong people."

"He got sacked?"

"Nicked. By his own son! Red-handed making a deal with lowlife mob to turn the other cheek. Don't get me wrong, sometimes you need to make deals, but this was far from ethical, or even moral."

"What happened?"

"The father was lucky to get early retirement on reduced pension, can't have corruption being publicly known. The son voluntarily stepped down a rank, earned the respect of all those who despised him to start with. Including myself. I never saw it coming. You see, sons become their fathers all the time, stepping straight in to their shoes, fathers expect it, especially in our line of work. He was quite surprised to be arrested by his own son. Tore the family apart as you can imagine."

"Wow."

"The moral of this story. You may find the ribbing and jibes hard to accept sometimes, and the loneliness; but you do a good job, an honest job, you'll earn their respect later. The journey may be lonely, but you'll meet someone who'll support you, then it won't be so bad. Maybe you have girl already?

"No, not yet. Not really given it much thought."

"Ah, this looks like the place." Ron pulled into the driveway of an old stone built country house being utilised as the police station. Ornate chimneys twisted above the roofline like intricate works of art, the grounds still immaculately kept.

"Nice," Travis commented, whistling through his teeth.

Ron thought back to the bleak 1950's block building they had left in Liverpool. "Yeah, certainly a bit different. This body is probably the most excitement they've had for ... for, well, ever."

"Probably not wrong there, Sir."

The car crunched on the gravel as they parked near the portico.

Inside, the grandness of the entrance hall and reception oozed lavishness, both wiped their feet on the large doormat as if entering a palace.

"Different class of criminal 'round here." Chappell chagrined.

"Can I help you gentlemen?" A petite uniformed officer asked from a doorway.

"DCI Chappell, this is Travis," Ron pointed to William who stood agape at the pretty officer. "We're here to see ..." he consulted his notebook but Travis interrupted.

"DI Jempson, please." Ron smiled as Travis stood like a nervous school child.

The pretty officer smiled appreciatively. Her tone became warmer. "I'll see where he is. He is expecting you isn't he?" She looked at Travis but Ron answered.

"Yes, he is. It's about the body at Stonehenge."

"Oh, right, yes, strange one, that. If you take a seat, I'll get him for you." She turned to leave, but about turned again. "Would like a tea or coffee?" her eyes reciprocating William's appreciation as she studied him.

"Yes, but I'd like to take a piss first." The officer's stance stiffened at Ron's coarseness. "I take it you have facilities here for that?"

"Through that door." She pointed to a large oak door that was about four feet wide and eight feet high.

"Thank you. Black, two sugars." Ron marched off.

★ ★ ★ ★

"White coffee with one sugar, please." William, tried not to blush as he beamed an uneasy smile at her.

The officer appeared to wait until Ron had disappeared through the door. "Is he always so gruff?"

"We've just travelled from Liverpool. It was a bad journey and we think the body dump is connected to another case, a serial!" he sounded childishly jubilant.

"Oh, right. I'll get your drinks. I'm PC Benton, by the way." Then, almost as an afterthought, "Fiona Benton."

"I'm William. That's a nasty bruise on your face, been in the wars recently?" He couldn't help himself staring, transfixed by her.

"Rugby. Weekend match, played Somerset's police force's second team; it gets a bit rough. Do you play?"

"Used to, left wing, don't find much time for it these days though."

"You should come down sometime, I'm sure we could always find a match for you to play in." Fiona smiled flirtingly at William then disappeared back behind the door she had appeared from.

★ ★ ★ ★

"Your coffees." Fiona offered as she returned. "DI Jempson will be wi…"

"Morning." came the deep booming voice from the elaborate staircase just beyond the door Chappell had gone through to the toilet. "Do you wanna bring those up? Benton, bring me a black tea." Then directing his conversation at Ron. "Please, this way. It is not often we get a case like this." Ron shared an 'I told you so' glance at William. "In fact it rocks the very foundation of the community when something this blatant and gruesome even gets close. I'm just glad you could get here so swiftly."

"You said you thought it was something to do with a case we had been working on, an old case." Ron and William followed DI Jempson along a short wood panelled corridor to a large spacious office with a leather-topped desk.

Ron rolled his eyes upwards at the regal splendour.

"I did, you're right. Please take a seat. To be honest it was all a bit of a mystery until one of our filing clerks was putting away the file in central records, for 'unsolved's, when she noticed the picture of Kenneth Horsley, the victim, and remembered his disappearance mentioned in the Gazette, hence my call." Jempson put up his hand to stop Ron interrupting. "You see she used to work in Essex, not sure where exactly, yet she was familiar with the missing person case, anyway she pointed it out and, after a little more digging and a conversation with a …" Jempson, fished around on his desk, "… Kilter, DS Kilter, he mentioned that Liverpool CID were running the incident for a serial. Hence my phone-call this morning."

"Good detective work!"

"We try Mr Chappell. Trevor by the way."

"DCI Chappell." Ron prickled much to Trevor's visible surprise. "You said on the phone that a car had been abandoned as well."

"Yes." Trevor became more animated. "A burgundy Ford Zephyr. It had false plates. It had been raining so there were no other tyre tracks to see whether they might have changed vehicles."

"I see. Do you have a photo? Any witness?"

"Yeah, sure." Trevor picked up a file from his desk and handed it to Ron.

The knock on the door was ignored until a squeak drew everyone's attention. "Your tea, Sir."

"Thanks, PC Benton." She hovered a moment longer.

"That'll be all." Trevor admonished.

"Yes, yes." Ron said, grumpily. "Did you run a check on this car from its VIN number? Any witnesses come forward?"

"Of course," Trevor snapped softly, "it is registered to a … ah, here it is, Samuel Jacob Talbot. Here's his address. No witnesses as such; a lorry driver did eventually come forward to say he'd picked up a hitchhiker early hours of the morning, didn't give much of a description though. Although he did say he spoke with a Brummie accent when he picked him up."

"That name rings a bell. Travis? Picked him up?"

"Yes, the guy fell asleep and, after he woke up, the accent had gone."

"Interesting!"

William searched through his own organised file on the case. "Here it is, that's the guy that was interviewed in '63 about Susan Jones's disappearance."

"Is it now? No smoke without fire, me thinks! So that's the second time his name comes into the frame. I think it's time for another visit don't you?"

"Yes, sir." William fidgeted in his chair.

"Thank you, Trevor, you've been most helpful." Ron's manner had lightened somewhat. "Do you mind if I take the file with me?"

"No, no, that's a copy typed up earlier after I telephoned."

"Did your guys find any other evidence in the car?"

"No. But if you would like to take a look for yourselves, be my guest. I thought you might. I know sometimes it can help to build a mental picture of the assailant, give you a feel for them. Well, it helps me, not everyone's the same granted. PC Benton will give you the details of where it's stored."

"Good, thank you." Ron gulped at his coffee and got up. "If we need anything else, I'll get Travis here to give you a call."

"I'm sure PC Benton will be only too happy to help him, if I'm not available. I will give her full authority to co-operate."

"I'm sure Travis will find a reason to call then!" Ron's remark made Travis blush.

"She is quite a catch, I'll give you that." Then added urgently. "To an unmarried man, that is. She's a tough one though, don't let that demure exterior fool you."

"Yes, well, thank you for your help, it really is appreciated." Ron held out his hand, which Trevor grasped firmly.

"Pleasure."

They left Trevor looking out over the large rear gardens of the property.

★ ★ ★ ★

After getting the car location from Fiona they walked to their own car, the rain now a fine irritating mist. "I know you have a keen eye for detail Travis, but try and keep your mind on the job." Adding a teacher's warning. "Don't let a pretty smile beguile you. There is many a pretty criminal who is sassy and knows how to pull the wool over you."

"Understood." He smiled.

Chapter 84

1967 April
Wiltshire

They've done it! They've frozen the first human being, Dr James Bedford, in January this year! Robert Prehoda has the credit of performing it with Robert Nelson co-ordinating whilst Dante Brunol was also in attendance.

Nelson is just a TV repairman!

They injected Dr Bedford with heparin upon his death to prevent coagulation of the blood, using a cardiac and lung ventilation machine to keep the blood oxygenated, maintaining cell structure, then they perfused a preservative solution of DMSO via the carotid artery after initially lowering the body temperature and then subsequently further using dry ice until final transfer into a large vessel for storage using liquid nitrogen at -320 degrees Farhenheit. This is incredible, if a little disappointing. The first success – with a TV repairman at the helm; albeit with a medical team!

Where does this leave me? Us? Freezing is a success; it can no longer be the sole purpose of my research. Re-animation, bringing back to life: that is clearly what needs to be the focus. Or is that going to be performed by a car mechanic?

Also Dr Bedford died of cancer at 73, so surely we will need regeneration, an elixir of youth, plus a cure for cancer. Our goal was to suspend life, looking at space travel, not curing ills, or old age. But they have done the initial part, although they still can't be sure what they have done will work, until you can thaw someone there still remains unanswered questions

Maybe genetics is a way forward?

Chapter 85

1967 April

Cambridge

"Congratulations, on your new house," Sarah slurred. "We're looking to buy, aren't we, Roger?"

"Yes, we've nearly got the deposit," Roger looked almost as pissed as Sarah. "It is really just waiting to see where the job offers come from. Don't want to be too far from where I am working."

"True. Have you had any offers?" Margaret asked.

"You'll probably want to be near family as well." Mike shifted seating position, unfolding himself.

"Where's Sam with our wine? These are all gone." Sarah went to pick up an empty bottle but knocked the three empty bottles of Liebfraumilch over.

"Why near family?" Roger seemed to lose balance and fell sideways.

"Always handy for children, parents as babysitters." Mike saw Sarah and Roger share a look of disdain. "Have I missed something?" Neither answered. "Where's the wine?"

"It's coming, don't panic. Thank you for all helping today. I know we don't have much stuff, but it is so much easier when there are five people, we couldn't really afford to pay for help."

"Always happy to help." Roger answered.

"He is you know, always." Sarah seemed to struggle to stay upright.

"Here, we go." Sam opened another bottle of wine.

Mike grabbed one of the empty bottles and placed it on the floor between them all "Okay, okay, I think the time is right for truth or dare."

"Really, Mike? We're a bit past that, aren't we?" Margaret held her glass out for Sam to refill.

"What is it with you and this bloody game? Can't we just sit around and talk and listen to music." Sarah took a large gulp of wine, spilling some down her chin.

"Come on, it's just a bit of fun that's all." Mike clarified.

Margaret held her glass out for a refill, "Yes, Mike, it was fine at college, a bit of fun, but we are not at college anymore. What is there left to know about each other? I think we have covered everything by now."

Mike noticed Sarah suddenly sit bolt upright. "I know what we don't know about Mike!" She seemed to think about what she had said.

"And what's that?" Sam sat on the arm of the settee.

"What's going on?" Roger interjected, looking rather pale.

"Nothing, Hun, you go to sleep." As if on cue, he leaned against the wall and started to snore loudly.

"Is he going to be alright?" Margaret asked.

"He'll be fine, Margaret. Now, about four years ago, Mike, you mentioned you had a sister to me, I want to know more about her."

Mike's jaw dropped open as he sobered up quickly.

Sam interjected. "Mike hasn't got a sister. What you talking about, Sarah?"

"He did have though. Didn't you?"

Mike's mood darkened.

"I don't want to talk about it." Mike thundered.

"No, no, you wanted to play truth or dare, so let's play." Sarah's slurring was getting worse as she wagged a knowing finger at Mike.

"I can't believe you had a sister and I didn't know. I've known you how long now? Eight, nine years?" Sam said.

"I don't want to talk about it." Mike repeated adamantly.

"You wanted to play ..."

"Go to hell!" Mike fumed, the bitter memory a twisting knife in his heart.

"I'll think we'll leave this game don't you, Sarah?" Margaret got up and stepped over to Sarah, "I think it is time for bed, don't you?"

"NO!" She stated. "I want to play. Mike wanted to play. I want answers."

"You're drunk, you cow." Mike shouted.

Margaret reached down to help Sarah up.

"I'm not drunk. You just don't like it when someone else ..."

"Come on, Sarah, let's get you upstairs." Margaret tried to placate.

"But I want ..."

"... to shag me senseless, Hun. Try my new toys." Margaret offered shutting Sarah up immediately, her brow furrowing.

"Do I?"

"'Cos you do, everyone does you know. Come on."

Margaret helped a puzzled Sarah off the floor.

"What about Roger?" She said as Margaret inched her out the lounge door.

"He's not watching. Just you and me, girl. That'd be too much hot action for him to handle."

Mike stared at the wall seething, the uneasy silence punctuated by Roger's resonant snoring.

"I think Sarah was a bit out of order." Sam said gulping at his wine. "Eugh, this is beginning to taste like gnats piss. Do you want a coffee? I'm going to have one. "

Solemnly Mike responded. "Yeah."

Mike watch Sam leave the lounge, then stared at the snoring figure of Roger before following.

Standing in the doorway to the kitchen. "I'm sorry mate."

"What for?" Sam placed three mugs on the worktop.

"Ruining the evening."

"Ah, I think it was over anyway. I've never seen them so drunk. Do you think they are having problems?"

"I doubt it, we always knew what a knob Roger was; I'm just thinking how much Sarah is becoming like him. It took 'em long enough to get together, they'll be together forever at that rate."

Sam stared at Mike, not realising he was doing it.

"What is it?" Mike asked.

"What? Sorry, oh, no, nothing." Sam turned to get on with the coffee. "Still three sugars."

"Absolutely. You want to know about my sister, don't you?"

After lighting the gas and placing the kettle on the hob he turned to face Mike. "Only if you want to tell. I was just a little surprised that's all. I mean I've been to your family's house, how many times, and never even seen a photo. You've never talked about her."

"That's part of the problem; my mother wouldn't have any photos of her in the house afterwards, said she had been selfish in her actions, and removed them all. When she died I couldn't find any photos of her, it was like she never was."

"Never was what?" Margaret walked in to the kitchen. "Sarah's soundo, thank god."

Mike sighed. "Existed, my sister." He looked pained at the memory. "You don't have to tell us, if you don't ..." Margaret stroked his arm.

"No, I do, really. I was just surprised by Sarah. Is she alright?"

"She'll be fine. I put her in our bed. Our only bed! I think she'll have a sore head and massive hangover tomorrow."

"Her and Rog. I've never known them to get so drunk." Sam leaned back against the sink.

"I think Roger's family were never that enamoured by Sarah becoming Roger's wife and it has been causing trouble between them just recently, especially since the baby was born; they won't go near it." Margaret explained.

Mike mood's was brightening. "I would've expected them to be delighted someone would take him and that he could produce a child."

"It appears they think he deserves better, at least that's what his father believes."

"How have Sarah's family taken to Roger?" Sam asked adding milk to the coffees.

"They're delighted." Margaret said.

"Really? Don't figure." Mike added, curtly.

"So come on, Mike, tell us about this sister?" Sam handed Mike his coffee.

Mike explained what had happened, about her running away and getting caught out by the cold and freezing to death. "... so it's not really a secret, just something I never talk about. I guess Sarah just caught me off guard."

"Just goes to show, even though we've known each other for quite a few years; you never really know someone. I wonder what other secrets we are all keeping from one another?" Margaret sipped her coffee.

"Are they secrets, or just bits of information not yet shared?" Sam added philosophically.

"Now that is a good point, when does it become a secret? My sister wasn't; it was just something I never really discussed with anyone, and after living with my family who never wanted to discuss it, it became natural not to." Mike stared out the window. "I miss her, kind of. I hated having her around as a kid, but as an adult, would we have got on? Who knows?"

Silence settled between the three friends, punctuated only by Roger's snoring resonating from the lounge.

"So, any hidden siblings that either of you haven't told me about?" Mike asked, back to his usual self. "Dish the dirt, come on."

"No. Although I always felt I had a brother. I don't know why, just did." Sam said.

Margaret turned to Sam. "I think that is the drink talking. How could you feel you had a brother but not know? That is just silly."

"I don't know, I just did. Something my parents said once."

"What?" Margaret asked.

"I knew you'd ask that, and I can't recall but it put a doubt into my mind."

"Margaret?" Mike asked.

"Yes, two. But I killed them! They made excellent laboratory rats – conducted experiments on them." Margaret made it sound so ordinary.

Mike and Sam stared at her.

"I'm joking. I'm an only child, remember?" They all smiled and drank their coffees "Of course, I would be after killing them; that was the whole point." She smiled, sinisterly.

"It's alright, Sam, if you go missing, I'll know who to suspect!"

"Thanks, I think."

"Unless … I'm in on it as well! And let's face it we have discussed how useful it would be for our experiments, to have a live human specimen to work on."

"You're right, Mike." Margaret added, conspiratorially.

"I think I am beginning to wonder about my friends."

"And so you should, Sam."

"And on that note I'm going to bed."

"Not in our room, Sarah's in there."

"Great, can't even sleep in my own bed!"

Chapter 86

2002 July

Replaying the images of the victims, Sam defended himself. "I did not do these things!" His emotions as raw as an open wound. "I didn't. I know I didn't." The words a little lacklustre in their delivery. "I cannot be in two places at once."

"Many people do unimaginable things. It all depends where your moral compass lies. There is always a way, people have faked it before."

"I know where mine is. How then? Tell me that." Sam argued defensively.

"Let the journey play out, you may be surprised. As for your moral compass, really?" Geoff continued. "How about the time you put that mouse in Kirsty Thistlewaite's bag?" Sam stared nonplussed at Geoff before a dim recollection started to fuzz into his memory. "You knew she was petrified of mice, yet you still did it."

"But ..." Sam was flabbergasted. "It was just high jinks at school." No one had ever known it was him; in fact Matthew Curson had got the blame and detention.

"To you maybe. Do you know what happened to her?" The question struck a cautious note with Sam, who was now afraid to ask, instead choosing to defend.

"Nothing, I remember seeing her around school." His words faltered slightly as he racked his memory for the truth. It was so long ago and he was only eight at the time. "She was moved to a different class, that's all." He said, more confidently.

"The memory can be a tricky bugger, can't it?" Geoff replied, smugly. "You should know that!"

Sam stared at the motorway and its traffic trying desperately to see the image of Kirsty around school, after that event. The mouse had been a dare set by a mate, Stuart Hartigan.

Frank crooned 'Come fly with me' in the background.

"I never thought I liked Frank Sinatra, but actually he's not bad. I was more a Beatles kind of guy before the Stones or The Who came on the scene. Maybe my appreciation is changing." Geoff started conversationally, before glancing across to see Sam still pondering his foggy memory. "You're not quite sure now, are you?"

"It was nearly fifty years ago."

"How time flies." Geoff paused. "You have no idea the effect it had on her; it shattered her. You recall correctly that she moved to another class, but that was after six months of being off school. Kirsty actually ended up in hospital ..."

"I remember that but ..."

"You were the cause, or rather, your actions were the cause of the anaphylactic shock that she suffered later that day, on her way home. It was lucky a kindly stranger found her and that the attack was mild in comparison to some. But it had a long lasting effect." Geoff turned to Sam and snarled, "and you don't even have the compassion to recall it or feel remorse."

"I ... I ... it was a long time ago. I was a boy. A kid, fooling around."

"Messing with life, messing with other people's lives."

"Woah," Sam called out, finding his confidence. "We all ... well," he changed tack as a cursory glance shot across from Geoff, "... most kids do silly things with little thought or regret, it's not something that they ... we can change. That's how we learn right from wrong. It's easy now to tell me it's wrong and, if I knew then what I know now, I wouldn't have done it, but I didn't. How can I be accountable for the innocent pranks of a child that has long since gone?"

Geoff shrugged his shoulders. "I am not the judge. I am not the one you need to appease."

"So who is? I want to see them. I want to get this sorted. I didn't commit these crimes." Sam demanded, still not comprehending that he was actually dead, yet, having a perfectly normal-ish conversation.

"Getting angry is not going to help."

"I don't recall anything of what you're showing me and I would have thought that somewhere, somehow I would have some dim recollection. Money, clothes, the car. You're implying that I'm like some Jekyll and Hyde character deceiving myself."

"I am not implying anything. I merely have my instructions."

"Which are what?"
Geoff pointed through the windscreen.

Chapter 87

1967 April
Cambridge

Chappell rang the doorbell for a fourth time, lazily taking in the suburban street scene, just like any other and a scene he had once imagined for himself before Alison, his childhood sweetheart, had died from a undiagnosed congenital heart condition. Since then he had never found that same attachment to someone and that in turn had led to odd liaisons yet a fairly lonely life, except for his job. He watched the kids playing on the street, a wistful feeling tugging at his heart and the dreaded loneliness retirement brought closer.

It was turning into a long day, a phone call to the local chief had cleared the visit to this potential suspect, although they had queried the unprecedented journey to interview a suspect rather than just getting local force to do it. But to Chappell, this was getting personal; it pleased Travis, who also had a vested interest, especially since it had allowed loads of extra overtime.

Finally the door opened and Margaret stared curiously at Ron and William.

"Mrs ...?" Ron started with an affable smile.

"Talbot." Margaret finished the question, keeping the door between them as a shield.

Chappell showed his warrant card and a look of panic swept over her face.

"It's alright, Mrs Talbot, we just want to talk to your husband again." Travis announced, chagrined by a look from Chappell.

Relaxing, she added. "He's at work."

After getting directions they left.

"Travis, don't make it too easy for them, you never know when it is just part of an act. You need to let them sweat a little; a little nerves never hurt anyone.

"Sorry."

"Not to worry, you've got a lot to learn that's all." It was the first time Chappell questioned himself on whether it was right to bring Travis rather than Harris, or one of the others.

-

After showing the officers into the boardroom, the receptionist rang Sam's extension to advise him of the visit.

"Who's been a naughty boy, Sam?"

"What?" Sam flirted. "Not yet, but I could always be tempted."

"Well, the police are here for you, so I'm guessing you already have been."

"The police?" He reeled.

"Yes, I've shown them into the boardroom."

"Thanks." Distracted, Sam tried to think of what it could be about. "I'll be down in a minute." He replaced the receiver.

-

Two minutes later he was closing the boardroom door. Chappell stood surveying the busy yard where two forklifts buzzed around like busy bees as they unloaded a forty-foot trailer. Travis sat at the mahogany table reading through his notebook.

"Hello," Sam bristled.

"Samuel Ta...?" Chappell started to ask but then recognised the cool hazel eyes and the slightly lopsided mouth of the man that he and Harris had interviewed in '63, he felt contempt build up inside.

Recollecting the first interview, Sam asked, "This isn't about Susan Jones again is it?" After no immediate response, "Have you found her killer?"

"No. We haven't." Chappell answered sharply turning back to the window. He was sure the man was guilty but they didn't have any hard evidence as such to pin on him, yet.

"Where were you on the night of Thursday 16th February, Mr Talbot?"

It suddenly hit Sam, the implication of the visit. "I was at home." He replied, feebly, knowing the next question, having watched Z Cars avidly.

"Can anyone, other than your wife, confirm that?" Travis asked pointedly, much to the admonishment of Chappell.

Sam looked at Travis, feeling the heat of the projected guilt. "My wife was away that week, attending a conference in Edinburgh. So no, no one can ..."

"You own a Ford Zephyr?" Chappell stated, rather than asked, making Sam feel the extent of the pressure they were trying to exert.

"Do I need a solicitor present for this? And no, no I don't ..."

"Do you feel you need one, Mr Talbot?" Chappell turned back to the room.

"It is starting to feel as though I might, yes."

"Does it?" Chappell was enthused by the reaction; then refused to let him answer it by carrying on with his own line of reasoning. "You have never owned a Burgundy Ford Zephyr?" Chappell fired. "Registration, Travis?"

"Registration NYX 732." Travis added, dutifully.

"That one, well, yes, but ..."

"You just said you never owned a Ford Zephyr?" Chappell stepped towards Sam making him feel giddy.

"No, I thought you meant now." Sam tried to defend but found himself surprised at how easily he was being tied up in knots.

"Now you say you do?" Chappell continued. "Are you going to tell us the truth or should we take you in?" Chappell was barely two feet away. "So do you, or do you not own a burgundy Ford Zephyr?"

"Well, no, not anymore. But I did! That very one. I think. The number sounds familiar." Chappell glanced at Travis.

Travis got up, "Where's that car now?"

"Now?" Sam stammered.

"Yes, now, Mr Talbot, where is the car now?" Chappell inched menacingly closer; it was a tactic he'd successfully used before to catch a guilty burglar.

"I don't know. We don't, I don't own it, anymore. It was stolen by my wife; I mean when my wife was using it. Have you found it then?" Sam caught his breath and took the chance to step away from Chappell.

"When was it stolen?" Travis asked.

Sam sat down in one of the ornate chairs. "About six, seven years ago. No, more like five years ago. I'm not sure."

"Did you report it, and when?" Chappell stood behind Sam.

"Of course I did." Sam tried to keep his voice calm and even.

"That's around the time Susan Jones went missing." Travis added. "Did you hear that, Mr Talbot?"

Sam gulped; he knew where this was leading. Perspiration formed on his brow as he wondered about the Fugue States and having so many holes in his memory.

"Well, Mr Talbot? I asked you a question?" Chappell sat on the table facing Sam, whose eyes showed his confusion.

"I don't remember."

"That's your defence, 'I don't remember'? You'll have to do better than that. Your car, the one you say was stolen has been discovered at Stonehenge on the 16th February." Sam looked up at Ron. "A car you say was stolen."

"It was. Ask my wife, she'll tell you."

"Maybe you're both in this together, one covering for the other." Chappell paused. "It's a bit strange don't you think?" Ron got up and paced the bland boardroom with its dark brown parquet flooring. "That this is the second time we have been led to you?"

Sam stared on disbelievingly.

"Where were you on 23rd September '62."

"I don't know off hand, I would have to look it up."

"A bit convenient." Chappell said, sarcastically.

"It was five years ago, how I am supposed to remember every moment of every day from five years ago?" Sam snapped.

"Bit of a temper you got there, haven't you?" Chappell swelled with pleasure.

"You are accusing me of things that I know nothing about." Sam stood up meeting Chappell inch for inch.

"We haven't accused you of anything, Mr Talbot, we came here to ask you a few questions, which you seem unable to answer," Chappell paused for effect, "sufficiently."

Sam's eyes darted between Chappell and Travis unsure what to do.

"Maybe my neighbours can confirm I was at home, they must have seen me." Sam said, breaking the awkward silence that had settled.

"Maybe?" Chappell paused. "Maybe we'll just check that whilst we're in the area. Enjoy the rest of the day, we'll be in touch." Chappell smarmily smiled before opening the door.

"Not this house. If you're enquiring about five years ago, we've moved since then. This house, where we live, is our first proper home, always rented before that."

"Makes it easier to move around doesn't it!" Chappell eyeballed Sam making him feel as uncomfortable as possible.

"Can you remember the address, or is that something you'll have to look up?"

"No, I can remember that." He scribbled down the address and handed it to Chappell.

"That'll be all for now. We'll be back, I'm sure."

Back in the car, Chappell hesitated before turning the ignition.

"He's guilty, I can smell it." Travis stated.

"I know. I think they are both in on it. Problem is proving it. There's no real evidence. They seem to have been really careful."

"Mmm."

"They'll slip up."

"I hope so. I want to be there when they do." Travis squeezed his notebook tightly.

Chapter 88
2002 July

"I remember that interview, I got called into my managing director's office afterwards. I thought I'd get the sack; he hated unwarranted attention." Geoff carried on looking at the road ahead as the back of a police car on blue lights got closer.

"You almost did."

"What? How …" Sam answered incredulously.

"Mr Mettiken wasn't very amused. He'd been sympathetic to your memory lapses, fugue states, as they didn't appear to really affect your work, odd discrepancies could be covered, but as you say, undue police attention was not something he liked brought to the family firm. You were lucky you had your Sales Director supporting you."

Sam stared at Geoff, the revelation a shock.

Geoff pulled the BMW into the same space as the police car and immediately they became part of it.

"This is more fun than I would ever have thought."

"This is not fun!"

Geoff replied. "Well, it wouldn't be for you. There is Susan Jones to think of," Sam felt the now familiar phosphorescent nagging scratch, a steadily growing toothache. "Karen Littleton," it intensified marginally, "Peter Hittles, Kenneth Horsley," Geoff continued to rattle off names unfazed, "Michael Anderson, Jemima Hartridge, Francis Hall-Smith, Lucy Davis …"

"I didn't kill those people."

"Didn't you? Then why does it hurt when I say their names; it only hurts if their deaths are connected to you. You have to feel their suffering. Endure their agonies." Geoff turned on Sam, hatred for the first time showing in his eyes. "Do you know what they went through? Do you know how they felt? Do you?"

"I don't, as I didn't do it. Why won't you believe me?"

Geoff did not reply and the BMW dissolved until they were sitting in the back of the police car like two thugs being driven to the station. "This is where you belong."

"I'd remember if I had done it, regardless of the fugue states. There'd be evidence. I'd find things that would prick my curiosity, make me wonder."

"Life is so precious. To take it deserves the highest punishment meted out."

"How about all those scientists who use animals for the their experiments, do they have to suffer? Sometimes sacrifices need to be made in order to make discoveries. That's how all breakthroughs have been made throughout history."

"Really?" Geoff questioned. "That's rather a sweeping statement isn't it? There are many breakthroughs the world over where no living organism had to sacrifice its' life. Who made you God to choose who should or should not die?"

Sam sighed wearily. He always believed he'd led a good life; a few naughty things here and there but nothing too extreme, a little cash in hand, the odd packet of sweets swiftly taken when he was in his teens, normal rebellious stuff.

Chapter 89

1969 January
Mike's Lab

"Oh look, it's the Three Stooges from that film ..." Roger started entering Mike's lab with Sarah following behind.

"The Tooth Will Out; where they become dentists." Sarah finished, looking abashed. "Oh my God, I'm, turning into Roger!"

Mike turned round. "How can you have a brain like yours and love the Stooges." Roger rolled his eyes.

"Hi, Sarah, it's been ages since we've seen you. I think we need to start worrying about you." Margaret said turning round, then looking back at Sam and Mike to see what she meant. "I suppose we do in our lab coats. How are you? Not long to go now, is it?"

"No, about four weeks. Had to get out of the house, I was going stir crazy."

"Hold on, which one are you implying I am?" Margaret wandered over to Sarah, and felt her bump which was now quite large, larger than the first time she was pregnant. "Surprised you can find anything to fit. Rather you than me."

"Nothing! That's what I can find. That's why I am wearing these bloody maternity tents. I can't wait to get my figure back, although I do now seem to have decent tits." Mike obliged with a lascivious ogle. "Speaking of which, and this pregnancy is really screwing with my head, I am starting to agree with Roger more as well. You do look like the three Stooges, except your chest, of course." Margaret nodded in agreement. "It's like that party you went to in medical school when you went as triplets. Can you get me a drink, Rog?" Sarah looked exhausted which only compounded Margaret's thoughts about pregnancy and children, that she didn't want one, ever.

"Yes, dear. What are you working on?" Roger asked.

"Oh gawd. I'd forgotten about that party." Margaret announced. Then a memory struck. "That's the one where you didn't dress up and we thought you and Roger had swapped places."

"Yes, well, let's forget about that, shall we?"

Margaret let it go seeing Sarah's unease.

"Where's Rachel?"

"With Roger's parents, they seemed to have warmed to her now and I needed a break; it's hard enough getting a good night's sleep without looking after a two year old as well."

Sam turned away from the worktop. "Well, Roger, I am glad you asked that. We are trying establish what it is that allows this frog, now dead of course, to freeze and thaw without a problem."

"Now that is a good question." Roger answered.

"And you'd think, with all the brain power in this room, that should be easy." Mike stated.

"Maybe, but we girls are going outside, so that's seventy-five percent down." Sarah said with a smile.

"No, it just allows us to make more progress now without endless hours of fruitless discussion." Mike retorted.

"Touché." Margaret said as they left the room. "On form tonight."

* * * *

As the girls left, Sam, Mike and Roger turned to the frog, laying cut and pinned on the worktop.

"Any ideas, Roger?" Mike asked.

"Have we had the chemical analysis back from the lab yet?" Roger picked up a pair of tweezers and starting poking around the frogs' organs.

Mike responded. "Not yet, so other than glycerol we don't know if other chemicals are at work."

"We should have asked Margaret to do it at work, it would have been quicker?"

"I asked, Roger, she said she couldn't risk it. They were being particularly penny pinching at the moment on small things, like tests. Forgetting that it is a part of her job. Bloody politics sometimes." Sam said.

"We could really do with opening up live frogs and freezing them to see what happens." Mike said gruesomely.

"My Sarah would never forgive you for doing that to a live animal." Roger sated stoically. "You're lucky she doesn't mind you using this dead specimen."

"How does she expect us to progress if we can't break a few eggs?" Mike said, mockingly. "How could we be expected to make progress when restricted to ethics? Progress comes from experiments; without them you just stand still."

"Hey, I just had a thought." Sam said, excitedly.

"Stand clear, everyone, it could be dangerous." Mike joked.

"Haha, very funny. We are looking at ways to prevent ice crystals right. How about if we turn it on its head, and look at making cell structure stronger, so it lessens the damage caused, or eradicates it."

"So instead of working on the almost impossible task of preventing ice crystal formation upon thawing, we simply switch to the other impossible task of genetics? Well thanks Mr Einstein, that is really helpful. Unless you have an idea how to do that?"

Sam flushed a little. "No, Mike. It was just a suggestion."

"He could have a point though." Roger expounded.

"Oh God, look what you've done."

"No, Mike. Listen, Sam might have a point. Maybe we need to deal with the two problems concurrently. If the cell structure is more flexible and stronger, when we find a way to limit ice crystal build up ..."

"When?" Mike interrupted.

"... listen for a second. When we find away to limit ice crystal build up, if the cell wall structure is stronger and more flexible when we reach the first part of our goal. Then it is just the spark of life and re-igniting that."

"Sounds so simple, Roger!"

"I know it will take a lot of work, Mike, but it's a theory that might be worth looking into. In fact, I know a doctor who is researching genetics and genes, I will have a word with him and see what information he can offer."

"Well, it's a plan. I still prefer my live frog one better."

"I seriously worry about your macabre side," Sam said. "How far would you push it? How far is enough?"

"Wouldn't you like to know?" Mike's eyes widened as he smiled broadly, leaving the implication adrift in the air.

"No, I don't think I do."

"I'm with you on that, Sam." Roger concurred.

Chapter 90

1969 July
Liverpool
CID

William arrived early for work, a routine he'd instigated after promotion to detective constable a few months before. CID was usually empty; it was a time he enjoyed. The silence before a maddening buzz; conversations and angry shouts as another criminal gets away, or breaking news of yet another merciless crime. It composed his thoughts, organised his workload and allowed a little reflection on Ron Chappell's retirement, which had been a boisterous affair, hangover a plenty. Ron had been popular with everyone, firm but fair. William couldn't help be overwhelmed by the fact that, without Ron on his case, promotion through the ranks would have been slower. A few out of joint noses at the time were now a distant memory for most, except Mark Harris, who still bore a grudge.

William sat at his desk, looking at the file that Ron had handed to him personally, the serial that had kicked so hard when he had started. Ron's words had been '*Only you will make sure this doesn't get forgotten. Do me proud and bring the bastard in. Let me know.*' Other files had been allocated randomly. The new DCI, Patrick O'Neil, was a bruiser of a character and William wasn't sure he was going to like the new regime. Patrick had transferred from Manchester about a year ago and had a rep that preceded him. He got the results everyone wanted, even though it was rumoured to be with an occasional blind eye turned here and there for slight indiscretions he considered a necessary evil.

Flicking through the file, William felt subdued by the fact there had been no new leads: it was good news but also bad news. Only Samuel Talbot, although there were question marks about his wife too, remained on the list, and it rubbed Travis. Taking a leaf out of O'Neil's book, surprising himself, he had booked a couple of day's annual leave to do a little recon work on Samuel. It was a little bit below proper procedure although, O'Neil seemed openly to encourage that kind of free thinking, even if publicly condoning it.

What was it that O'Neil had said "To break eggs you need to break eggs, it's that simple. They break the rules, I don't see why we can't flex them a little to gain a foothold before stepping onto more solid ground."

Well, that is what he would do.

Chapter 91

1969 July
Mike's Lab

"Where's Mike?" Sam asked closing the lab door.

Both Roger and Margaret turned round and started to answer in unison.

"He had …"

Margaret continued. "… to go away on business, so he said. He was being quite secretive about it, don't know why; he's not normally. All very suspicious! How are you? Busy day?"

"Yes, got some contracts for raspberry, blackcurrant and strawberry, so another good bonus again this year so we can get that new carpet."

Margaret stepped over to Sam and gave him a big hug and kiss. "Well done you."

"Do you have to?" Roger said appalled at the open display of affection.

"Jealous?" Sam defended.

"No, I just don't think there is a need for that kind of thing in front of others. It should be kept behind closed doors."

"He's such a romantic."

Sam smiled at Margaret; Roger had already turned back to the microscope.

"So what are you up to?" Sam asked putting on his lab coat.

"If you recall, my friend has given me access to some research …"

"Of course I bloody recall, I have not totally lost it." As soon as Sam spoke, he realised Roger was not referring to his memory lapses and he had misunderstood the inflection. "Sorry. Carry on." Roger looked blankly at him.

"Oh, no. Anyway …" he shook his head continuing, "… as I said, my friend has given me access to some of his research. I haven't completely explained what we are doing, yet he was happy to share, as long it is reciprocated, as it will help him speed along." Roger lifted up a collection of glass files each with a different label XZR 1 through to XZR 9.

"Interesting. What do they do?"

"Cell regeneration." Margaret added excitedly. "We've been doing a similar thing at work."

"Are you allowed to say that? You signed the official secrets act, remember?" Sam teased playfully.

Roger continued, "And cell strengthening. They have had some success on mice and rats. The intention was to make them resistant to cancer cells, but it hasn't yielded the success they thought it would; didn't even delay the cancer cell attacks. Thought it might be useful for us."

"Cool," Sam said.

"The hope being that, by using this during freezing and with a cryopreservative, it will help the cell be more resilient to damage, and who knows maybe even go some way to help counter any ailments, or the aging process, if that's at all possible."

"So they come out younger than when they died. Cool," Sam jested. "I sounded like Mike then didn't I?"

"Yes, Hun, you did." Margaret frowned her admonishment. "One Mike is enough for any lab!"

"What can I do?"

Roger and Margaret looked at each other; they appeared to have it all covered.

Chapter 92

1970 March
Lincolnshire
Storage Yard

How can a television repairman make more progress than me? Lack of progress is so frustrating! Ice crystals! Bloody ice crystals are the issue upon thawing! I have tried various systems for thawing, including a crude wiring system inserted in organs, but it just cooks them. Organs and tissue react in different ways so it is not a 'one size fits all' scenario. Neither I, nor the group, are any nearer solving the problem. Whilst they don't know about my experiments, I do pass on some results and information in the hope that they may shed new light.

I am managing to avoid detection and capture. Will my luck prevail?

I have thought about stopping ... but feel there is much to be gained if I persist. I don't feel guilty about the sacrifices; why should I? Everyone deserves their opportunity to shine, some in ways different to what they had in mind. A lifetime of imprisonment does churn my stomach, so being careful is uppermost, although my only concern on that point is our Mr Shaker. His initial probes into what I am doing here proved unsuccessful and I thought he had let it drop after all these years. However, recently I have noticed something different about the building, but can't quite pinpoint it.

I can hear him outside now. I thought we had settled into a nice routine of leaving each other alone; obviously not the case.

I open the lid to freezer marked LD.

I think it is time you were returned to your family Lucy Davis. Closure, and a grave your daughter can visit when she's older. She looked so sad on the news.

Gazing at the marbled face, I touch the frosted eyebrows, the open eyes staring up, wide with surprise. A crooked tooth protrudes from the thin lips; just like your daughter, I think.

Flicking off the switch, the crackle of the freezer ceases and my routine starts.

The hours drift by and I flick through the notebooks of results and information, looking for a new direction to focus as Lucy's body slowly thaws. I have amassed quite a collection of reference material, but still nothing resembling a breakthrough.

Turning to look at Lucy Davis, I reflect on the reanimation part of this equation and a theory that had been developed by a Dr Francoire Coit in 1763 after a patient had slipped into an icy lake and been frozen so quickly that Dr Coit felt he could do something to save the them by injecting fresh blood into the body. The notes were a bit fuzzy, and a lot was hearsay. Some rumours say the patient, Heloise San Girard, a twenty-three old maid had died, others said 'she had been replaced by her evil twin sister'; a theory I stumbled on after reading an old book with the translated title 'The Lake Woman of Ice', with the foreword referencing the Heloise's case. After some more extensive research, and many hours of trawling through unheard of books and diaries held in the deepest darkest vaults of various book depositaries around the country, including the British Library, it had led me to investigating the possibility of charging and heating – electrically – the blood whilst circulating through a machine; dialysis effectively.

The only stumbling block would be keeping the arteries and veins flowing whilst freezing the body.

Chapter 93

1970 March
Southport

"Happy first Anniversary, Fiona." William handed Fiona a small blue velvet box to go along with the bouquet of daisies she'd received earlier. "I love you with all my heart."

Fiona beamed as she opened the small box knowing it was jewellery, excited to find out what. Inside were two delicate silver earrings with small pinkish stones set neatly in them.

"They're beautiful."

"Just like you."

"Are you trying to get into my underwear, Mr Travis? I could arrest you for improper behaviour to a lady, you know."

"Lady? I was going more for your handcuffs actually."

"Kinky, eh. I never knew that about you. And yes, I am a lady." Fiona added with demure innocence.

"Really!" William countered playfully. "So that second weekend that I spent with you when you handcuffed me to the bed, that wasn't you?"

Replying in her best American southern accent. "Why sir, I do believe you have the wrong person. I am a lady who values her chastity."

William raised an eyebrow questioningly. "Damn, she was good. You mean I married the wrong person? Don't suppose you have her contact details do you? I'd like to go back and try her again."

"Oh, would you now? And how about a divorce as well, eh? Do you want that too, Mr Travis?" She placed her hands on her hips.

"No, not really but it seems I married the wrong person, I must have been drugged."

"I'll give you drugged. You obviously tried my wild identical twin sister – the one that you have never met, or have never seen together with me at the same time."

William swept Fiona into his arms, sliding his hands down to her firm backside.

"Maybe we could see if we can find her again?"

"Are you flirting with me inappropriately?"

William kissed her neck whilst she tilted her head back in subjugation. "Trying to seduce my gorgeous wife actually."

"Don't you want your dinner? Made it specially." She breathed deeply as she felt the first stirrings inside tingle.

William retracted. "I thought you were dinner."

"Carry on like that and I'll eat you alive."

"What a way to go? I can just imagine the investigation. How did your husband die, Mrs Travis? Oh by the way you seem to have a little blood dripping from your lips?"

"I confess, I confess. He seduced me, and I found him irresistible. I gobbled him all up." Fiona licked her lips coyly. "I say." She continued. "Is that something I might enjoy playing with, that thing you're thrusting against me?"

"Guilty your honour." William continued kissing her neck and Fiona ground her hips into Williams groin.

"I'll get your present." Fiona walked over to the sideboard where she'd hidden it two days before leaving William floundering. As she clumsily pulled it out, a file spilled onto the floor.

It was his copy of 'The Medical Examiner' murder file, which included highlights of all the victims to date, including, Susan Jones, Karen Littleton, Peter Hittles, Kenneth Horsley and Michael Anderson with various notes. Picking them up, she looked forlornly at them, seeing the notes William had made on the inside about each victim, married, family and dates; Susan had been married for seventeen years and left behind two children.

"What you looking at?" William crept up behind her. "Oh." He took it from her.

"It must be so hard for them and their families, and here we are celebrating. Life is too cruel. And not knowing where she had been for two years?"

"Yes. One day they will, one day. It's the one thing about our job I would like to change, the misery. If I could go back and magically change it, swap the places of the criminals and the victim, right the wrongs so to speak; but let's not think about it today. This is our day."

William wrapped his arms around her.

"Happy anniversary." She handed him an oblong parcel and replaced the file.

Tearing the paper off, it was a beautifully decorated pencil case with the words 'With my love always. F xx' inlaid on the lid.

"For your paint brushes and palette knives."

"Thank you."

Chapter 94

1970 March
Derby
Kedleston Hall

My nerves have finally stopped jitterbugging as I settle in for the drive to Kedleston Hall. The Grey Rover 110 P4 is more comfortable than the Zephyr; again, the false plates withhold its true identity and, now out of the yard, I feel more relaxed. I can't believe I fell asleep, only to be woken up by the sound of banging from the mechanic; good job they were in early. My only problem is, I will no longer be under the cover of darkness when dropping Lucy's body off and I can't wait around another twelve hours. In fact, the early morning sun can just be seen lighting the horizon.

I'd removed the heart and the brain; I have a theory about cooling the organs first to help prevent ice crystals forming. I want to try it out, before taking it to the group. It means going back today, a risk I'll have to take.

* * * *

Ben watched Sam pull out of the yard waving to him.

"'Ere Bob, give us a hand." Ben said throwing the remains of his Marlboro on the ground.

"Wha' is it Shaker? I got that job you want done." Bob walked back to the Ford Consul that Ben had requested an urgent switch job on – for a friend of a friend – leaving Ben watching the mysterious Sam pull out of the yard.

"Just come here will ya. I want to check out our friend over there. I fixed the padlock so it wouldn't lock properly once it had been opened, and I wanna see what he's been doing for the last few years."

Bob knew better than to argue.

"Now, you keep an eye out whilst I check him out."

Ben slipped the lock easily and crept inside with an air of confidence.

* * * *

Kedleston Hall, loomed up, the fancy brick built entrance with the deserted gatehouse that sat deteriorating behind. I'd scouted the site a few weeks before, like all dumpsites, determined to put distance between pick up and drop off, so that no one could be clever and narrow down my location.

Pulling in behind the gatehouse, out of sight of the road, I lift Lucy's thawed remains from the boot; the stench of bodily fluids making me want to wretch. The road has got busier but I feel fairly safe as I am out of sight, if a little on edge; yet I still wait until I hear silence.

"Time your family had you back, Lucy Davis. Your contribution to medical science is essential."

Chapter 95

2002 July

"I have never owned a Grey Rover so that proves it is not me, you are wrong."

"You plead innocence like you're raising the stakes in a poker game. Everyone's guilty." Geoff replied. "Something inside made me do it."

"Mike owned a grey Rover, I'm sure he did."

"And you never borrowed it!"

"Occasionally, there was more room in it with the seats down, than mine. Anyway, it got stolen."

"Ah, that favourite one."

"I …" Sam knew it was useless to argue further. Everything about the figure was familiar as if watching a film; the walk, the clothes, the stature, yet he couldn't place it; the disguise concealing the person's identity.

The Rover revved up and reversed through the gates where Geoff and Sam were standing.

Sam replayed every thought he'd ever had; how can one person live two lives, without raising any question from those close to him, unexplained scratches, receipts, money missing from bank accounts, Margaret and he had a joint account, both their salaries went into it every week, that's how they managed their financial affairs, as well as a post office account they used for saving, when they could.

"Do I have a twin brother? Is this where this is leading? Someone that I didn't know about?" He queried almost jovially.

Geoff turned to him. "There is a theory that everyone has a dark side to their nature, every single human being." He let it settle in the air. "The question is really – how can one release that, fully? – Most of us have a line in the sand for what we know is wrong and right, guilt reprimands us for the bad things we do but, what if you have discovered how to throw away that guilt, hide it, hide it so far inside, like it was a different personality inhabiting the same body? Now that would be a breakthrough."

"I asked whether I had a twin. You imply I am my own twin."

Geoff didn't answer as time spun round and a Ford Escort police car pulled up near the entrance, a uniformed woman in her late twenties hesitantly got out, a small posy of daffodils in her hand. She walked towards the gatehouse, her ponytail bobbing behind like a great fiery mane. Kneeling at the front door she placed the flowers affectionately.

* * * *

"We still haven't found the *bastard* who did this to you Mum. But I will, I swear I will. One day. You can count on it." The morning air had a luscious mist to it and Harriet's breath slowly dispersed like a rain cloud being heated by the sun.

"Morning, Miss Harriet. How are we?"

"Fine thanks, George. Well, as fine as you can ever be on such an anniversary. Still bites me so deep inside. The fact that it took its toll on my dad hurts even more."

"That was a dark day for us here too miss. So sad." George acknowledged.

Twenty-three years had passed and, once Harriet had graduated from Hendon with a posting nearby, she had visited on every anniversary. It was a pain she needed to refresh to keep the memory alive, to keep forcing herself to carry on looking. In some ways it would have been easier to let go; death happens and you can do nothing about it – you need to move on – that was what she told victim's families sympathetically. Don't let it destroy you; one of her own contradictions. There was a knot inside her, a knot that reminded her that she never got the chance to really know her mother. She kept the newspaper articles in a scrapbook, one page left blank and she was saving that for 'The End'; for the headline, 'Killer Caught'.

She knew that, as the years went on, it was getting less and less likely. Yet sheer bloody-minded hope would not oust itself. When she gave birth to her own daughter it managed to buoy that hope, refresh the search, and that is what had made her get in contact with Detective Chief Inspector Travis, who shared her desire to seek a successful conclusion. Alas, he had got no further progress to report and shared her frustration, even looking pained at seeing the daughter of one of the victims, another relation in a long list of families torn apart by it.

"I knew you'd be here this morning Miss Harriet, and I have some sad news." He hesitated, "The master has decided to renovate this gatehouse and turn it into a home. These are modern times Miss and the family needs to make the estate pay." Harriet stood up and raised her hand to stop George.

"I understand." She fought the tears. "They can't leave such a lovely building to deteriorate like this, it needs life. I hope whoever is lucky enough to live here will be happy." She paused. "I will stop calling by."

"I'm sorry Miss ..."

"No, it's quite alright." Harriet knew the day might come when she would have to find peace another way, but she still felt the bite of tears close by.

Harriet placed a reassuring hand on his arm and backed solemnly away to her car.

* * * *

"Death affects so many, for so long." Geoff spoke, poignantly before continuing, not hiding the malice and contempt, "And so someone needs to suffer. Balance the books."

Chapter 96

1970 March

Cambridge

"Hi Hun, How was your day?" Margaret called closing the front door to the stiff westerly breeze that had sent icy shivers deep into her bones. Her latest course had kept her away for three days and, much to Sam's displeasure, she relished the freedom, the chance to be part of something developing.

"Sam, you there?" With no response she started to wonder where he could have got to; his car was outside. Poking her head into the lounge confirmed that she had heard the television – which was broadcasting the news. She bristled with concern.

"Sam? Sam?" She wandered into their small kitchen. A cup of coffee sat cold on the counter, some papers to one side. A little panicky, she headed upstairs, a new speed in her steps.

"Sam! Sam?"

The bedrooms were empty, but the bathroom door was closed, when usually left ajar. She knocked gently.

"Sam, you in there? Come on, this isn't funny anymore. Sam?" Panic seeped in.

After a few seconds she opened it, empty. Margaret checked the house again, and the garden; Sam was nowhere to be seen, even double-checking it was his car outside on the road: it was. Maybe he had nipped out to the shops to get some groceries, although there was only one shop that opened late and that was a drive away.

By ten o'clock, she had rung their friends and still there was no sign of him. It was too early to call the police, and it was the third time he had vanished in the last year; she could normally recognise the signs when an episode was coming on: there was a sort of vague mistiness in his eyes, like his brain was starting to fog over and his second personality was taking possession. He had turned up safely before and she had to resign herself, uneasily, that he would do again.

The longest had been three days, and then he'd just been away on business, but couldn't remember any of it. He had even rung home and spoken to her as if nothing was wrong. Her only option was to ring work in the morning and see if he had any meetings planned that he'd forgotten to tell her about. They usually knew. That wouldn't explain the car though.

Two days later Sam arrived home about eight o'clock.

"Hi, Margaret, sorry I'm late I got held up in a meeting."

Margaret came to the lounge door with a face like thunder.

"No, you haven't!"

Sam stood aghast with his coat half on, half off. "Er, yes I have."

"Your car's been outside for the last two days and your work know nothing about any meetings for yesterday and today." She stood waiting for an explanation.

"I have been away on business."

"Funny business, you mean?" Anger exploding inside her, surprising her; she had never been a jealous person.

Sam continued taking off his coat. "No, proper business, like I always do."

"That's funny, work said you rang in and were taking a couple of days off." Margaret's stare penetrated him to the soul. "And why did you not take the car?"

Sam's lower jaw bounced up and down as though on elastic as he fought to work out what was going on? He had been away on business; he knew he had. Hadn't he?

"I had a meeting with Jack Forster at three-thirty today in Knightsbridge, look." Sam opened his briefcase to retrieve his notepad. "He placed an order for two containers of lemon." He thrust the pad toward her and reluctantly she took it. Clearly written in his neat handwriting were his notes.

"Sam, that was Wednesday, see?" she pointed to the date which he'd also written, as was usual.

"Yes, which is what it is today? Here is the train ticket." He tried to curb the sarcasm in his voice.

"Sam, it's Friday." Margaret lost her fight as she read more of the notes. "And this doesn't mention lemon, it says strawberry, redcurrant, blackcurrant. And what about your car?"

"I caught a taxi to the station. I told you."

"No, Sam, you didn't."

The argument evaporated from Sam. Snatching the pad he read it, dismay spelt out on his face like an unwelcome visitor. He flicked impatiently through the pages; three or four pages of notes following his meeting with Jack on Wednesday. He rocked back on his heels as he temporarily lost his balance with shock.

"I ... I don't recall." He slid down the wall as the overwhelming emotion of losing control washed over him. "Margaret, I don't understand, I don't bloody understand what is going on?"

Margaret knelt down to console him. She really felt sorry for him. One question that really nagged was 'why ask work for two days off – would she ever find out?

Part of her was curious whether he did have another woman, maybe another life. She'd read articles in Woman's Own about married men who had two families and divided their time between them without either family knowing. They certainly led independent lives; he did want a family but she loved her career. She had witnessed many friends settling down with families only for their lives to become mundane and child orientated. She loved Sam with all her heart and would never give him up.

She pulled him up into a hug, holding him tightly as he seemed to fight an inner battle; in part it was for her benefit. They'd never been overly romantic to each other but, on the occasion it had shone through, they both liked it – little and often they had concluded whenever the matter had cropped up. It usually did when discussing Sarah and Roger, as Roger was big on romantic gestures – but not public displays of affection, as Sarah did complain about it sometimes.

"Give it time. The brain is a complex organism. I was speaking to Gerald at work and he says that sometimes the brain will just click back into place." It sounded hollow even to her. "I'll make you a coffee."

"I'm sorry, it's just ... I don't know, not knowing I guess. I have notes of meetings, orders." He looked at the pad. "How can I not know where I have been for two days?"

"Maybe we should talk with Roger again; it is his speciality after all. Maybe things have advanced since last time. It has been a couple of years."

Sam pulled away from Margaret dejectedly then collected his briefcase from the floor. "It's pointless. And why did I ask for two days off work eh?" he solemnly trudged into the lounge, plonking himself down on the chair in front of the TV.

The news blasted out another missing person, a teenage man, Brent Johnson.

Margaret watched him from the doorway.

* * * *

Still confused by his own request for two days off, Sam decided to sort through his briefcase as he sat on the bed even though he was tired and needed to sleep. He anxious to know where two days had gone. Margaret was brushing her teeth.

"What's this?" Sam asked aloud to himself.

"Sorry, Sam," Margaret appeared at the bedroom door.

"These notes," he starting scanning them. "I don't ... there in my writing."

Margaret peered over Sam's shoulder

"It looks like research. I don't recall doing this." He flicked through the pages frantically, his mind in turmoil, as he read the content.

"That's interesting." Margaret opined.

"What is?"

"That bit, there, about the profusion process. Where were these?"

"Hidden at the back behind my notes on crop seasons." Staring obliquely at them, "Where did I make these?"

Margaret placed a hand on his shoulder. "It will come to you."

Eventually Margaret, convinced him to try and sleep, yet as he lay in bed, he stared up at the darkness, questioning his own sanity.

Part 4

Chapter 97

1970 March
Southport

William slept fitfully. It was the same dream that had recurred intermittently over the years; it had been a while, but now it was back. Susan Jones' body, her frosted brown eyes staring up at him, pleading to be set free, pleading to be allowed to pass on. Then he sees a reflection in a shop window opposite the Liver building – an impossibility as there are no shop windows opposite it but, in the dream, there is and he is an old man. What's left of his hair is grey and silvery. He has a stoop and walks with a cane. A blizzard blows, the cold biting painfully into his face and fingers. He can't see, as the ice blinds him.

Within the clouds there is laughter, mocking laughter. A thunderous voice calls to him, taunts him 'you couldn't catch me. You couldn't catch me. I'm free'. More mocking laughter!

The snowstorm vanishes and all that is left is William staring at the body of Susan Jones, her daughter and son kneeling in front of her, her husband standing upright like a sentry.

"How could you let him get away with it? You had him in your grasp? Why did you not put him away?" Susan says.

William tries to speak, to say he is sorry, but the words are lost.

Suddenly he is aware of someone else standing nearby, a faceless entity, witnessing the occasion, sneering at him.

"You were so close William, so close. But you didn't look hard enough. Didn't see what was in front of your eyes? What is it you were meant to see? What didn't I tell you? What clue did you miss?" The figure turns to look at Susan; the family have gone now. "She was my first, but not my last. Hahaha."

"You bastard!" William shouts with all his might. But life is failing him; he is old and his strength weakening. William strikes out at the figure and falls to the ground.

"William, William. What's wrong?" A familiar voice calls and for a few seconds he is caught between realms.

"William?" Fiona asked more gently, nudging his arm.

Suddenly, aware of his true surroundings.

"What ... sorry? It's that dream again. I didn't mean to wake you." He sat up staring at her, but almost looking through her as a theory solidified.

"It's okay. Maybe you should talk to someone."

"NO!" William announced in anger before relenting. "I'm sorry, it's just ... I think I am being told something ..." suddenly an epiphany hit him. Something in the dream, a second face. It's always been there; he sees it as he falls, just before he wakes up. William closed his eyes.

"What is it? What is it I'm missing? Come on."

Fiona looked at her husband placing a consoling hand on his hand.

"Oh my, God. Why didn't I see it? It makes sense."

"What does?" Fiona yawned.

"There's two of them, twins! He must have a brother. It's the only possibility, there has to be two. That's why we can't pin anything on him: they're living a life of one. Two people, two places, at the same time. It's a fantastic cover."

"If it was, surely you would know? You did a family check."

"Yes, but it makes sense – how he can be in two places at once."

"How about his friends, one of them could be helping him?"

"We checked them all out, all had alibis. But a twin could live under the radar, if they worked it right."

"I don't know. It seems a bit farfetched. Have you looked at the register of births where he was born?"

"No, not yet."

"Look, sleep now. You can follow it up in the morning."

Yet William was itching to investigate further. He would go in early. Looking at his watch, it read 2.54; it was too early.

He was not sure he could sleep now, the idea of a twin rocking around his head like a jiving teenager.

Chapter 98

1970 April
Liverpool
Incident Room

The incident room was buzzing with trepidation. A new name had been added to 'The Examiner' serial. Lucy Davis disappeared in August '68 from Wallingford after a night out with the girls, leaving behind a six-year-old daughter. The husband had originally been arrested in connection with her disappearance, only released after no hard evidence could be found. It had always been a turbulent relationship. She'd finally turned up outside Keldeston Hall, Derby in March this year. The tally was now five. O'Neill was running the show, but it felt better for Travis this time round as he was a part of CID, although he still recalled Ron insisting he step up and be liaison despite being so green.

O'Neill marched in, DS Hamilton following.

"Right, you know why we are here. I know some of you are familiar with this case. I want him caught. This slimy bugger has been getting away with it for far too long. I want everyone tapping their snouts for info. Turn over every stone. We are going to the press and TV and taking this nationwide, as it appears he doesn't have any boundaries. This guy is storing the victims for up to two years, so he has premises. The only problem is it could be anywhere! So far we have Derby, Nottingham, Liverpool, Bristol, Hull, Southend, Northampton and now Oxford. Talk about a needle in ten haystacks.

We have no definite theories except he has a medical background or training. Everything else is guesswork; there are no age specifics, jobs, types etc. I am looking for insight. I am looking for anything. If you have a theory I wanna hear it, we need to narrow the field, this guy is operating like a ghost." O'Neill sighed.

"Myself and DS Hamilton will be heading up the team. DC Travis will run the room and co-ordinate with us. The only real suspect from last time was a Samuel Talbot. He is our first port of call. See if we can't tie him up to Wallingford at the time of the disappearance. Now go out there and dig up what you can."

The scraping of chairs was followed by a hum of discussions. O'Neill turned to Travis.

"I want you to look in to this Talbot guy again, deeper than before – bank accounts, phones etc." He turned to leave then stopped. "Re-check Siblings et cetera, although I note the record states none; how about foster kids, adopted kids, half brother, bastard children – I don't care, just find them. There is a note about dead siblings – what's that about?"

"I found a birth certificate and the GRO number shown, indexes a page in the register and on that page it shows one child being born, Samuel Jacob Talbot. However, when I delved further, and looked on subsequent pages of the register I found two others – a girl and a boy – born to parents of the same name, at the same time. It could be coincidence but I am trying to track down further information. A bit of hunch."

"I like hunches, go with it."

Chapter 99

1970 March

Lincolnshire
Storage Yard

I stop for a late breakfast on the way back, still a little uneasy about the change to my plans but excuses are in place, a colleague is covering for me. An ominous feeling rests on my shoulders going back to the yard. I suppose I am procrastinating by having a breakfast. I do need to tidy and prepare for the next one and, with some favourable results from preservative SGX14, I want to do a whole body transfusion then freeze. This will mean the person being alive at the time of transfusion.

* * * *

Ben was intrigued searching Sam's lab; its jars of chemicals and canisters labelled with letters and numbers. He toyed with the array of utensils – scalpels, saws and other interesting looking devices – all neatly laid out on the metal trolley next to the ceramic slab.

"Mmmm, there is a dark side to you."

He walked over to the two metal containers near the wall, farthest away; one was pleasantly humming away, the initials JH769 and '-36' chalked on it. Opening the silent freezer it looked ordinary, no tell tale signs of use. More curious than ever he smashed the lock on the second one with a hammer he got from Bob who still wanted nothing to do with it.

Ben was neither surprised, nor taken aback to see the face of man staring back at him. The coldness was intense and, even before he could touch the body, his fingers felt the intense burning as a mist started to escape. He let the lid drop.

"What the fuck?" He studied his burnt fingers. "Looks like you and I need to have a little chat.

Ben looked at his watch wondering how long it would before the mysterious Sam returned. With some errands to run he couldn't wait around any longer, so left instructions with Bob to keep an eye out for

Sam, and not, under any circumstances, to let him leave, if he knew what was good for him.

* * * *

I pull back into the yard at about 6pm, deciding it best to delay my return; it is dark again. An uneasy apprehension settles as I open my unit. Looking around, it is only a minute before I see the broken padlock on the freezing unit. My heart beats at a hundred miles per hour; my brain says 'go' but my feet seem welded to the floor and I jump as a hand lands on my shoulder.

"I think you and I should have a little chat, don't you?"

I don't say anything; fear driving a spike right through me.

"Shall we?" Ben casually walks inside my lab and I follow, leaving the car outside.

I don't know what to say and watch as Ben switches the light on and walks over to the ceramic slab like it is his own and I am the guest.

"What do you want?"

He doesn't answer for a few seconds.

"What I always get – dedication when I ask for it."

I want to gain some confidence and ground but cannot fathom how. "For what?"

"Why don't you take off that scarf and hat and show me who you really are. That Birmingham accent holds no sway with me." I flatly refuse. "You don't have a choice!"

Still refusing to acquiesce, "What do you want from me?" Anger bubbles inside. If I can't subdue Shaker, then I may have to leave the unit and never return, as he won't let it lie – not now. My work unfinished!

"Take off that scarf and hat?" Ben shouts angrily and for the first time I fear my life is in danger. Slowly, reluctantly, I submit.

"Well, I never suspected that!" There is a standoff, as if I am meant to be pleased that I have surprised him. "It's a first for me, but good luck to you. Now, your secret is safe with me if you do something for me. Ring this number in a couple of days, I have a job coming up that can utilise your services, whatever they are." He scans the lab then scrawls a number down on a piece of paper before leaving.

Ben leaves me sweating nervously. I try to think of a way out but nothing comes – except his body in the empty freezer. Would he tell the mechanic though?

Chapter 100

1970 April
Cumbria
A1

William sat in his car observing Sam Talbot; the small normal looking character who was the top of the suspect list. William had cleared it with O'Neill; a little recon work, hoping to confirm the twin theory.

The first two recon exercises had proved fruitless – one of which had been off his own bat a year before. O'Neill had insisted he take a colleague but William had argued, convincingly, that he could get closer on his own. After an elaborate phone call to Sam's work, William had travelled the A1, knowing the first meeting place that Sam was due to go be.

Delving into his life had only proved how dull Sam's life really was. The only tumultuous episodes were his parents dying and the car accident he was involved in '65; everything else was humdrum, and too perfect; a perfect cover. He'd also looked into the friends: Michael Raymond Thompson born in '40 – adopted, the biological parents were unnamed – there was also a sister who had died, Sheila Harriet. Sam's wife, Margaret – nee Reynolds, had proved harder to track down, at first, but eventually he discovered she had a sister and two brothers, and a good job at the MOD; she worked hard. Roger Archibald Smith, married to Sarah Jennifer; he was studying to be a professor of neurology, they had two kids, Rachel and Oliver, Sarah had given up medicine to be a full time mother.

William knew an illicit conversation with Sam might garner more information, suspects could be more open when they thought they were talking to a like minded friend. Checking his appearance once more in the mirror, he was convinced he looked sufficiently different from the previous meeting a couple of years ago, now with his moustache and longer hair. Something that amazed him as a police officer was how people remember differently the attributes of a person; you can end up with totally opposing descriptions of a suspect, even height and build could be described so differently – it made their job harder sometimes.

William made a dash through the drizzle towards the transport café where Sam was seated inside.

The café was busy and William held back outside the door, ignoring the strange glances he received, until he could see there were no more tables available: he needed an excuse to sit down at the same table. It was filling fast and soon his chance came. He strode in shaking the rain from his coat pretending to look around. Sam had taken a window seat and had his back to William.

Briskly William walked over.

"Excuse me, do you mind if I sit here?" William pointed to the vacant seat opposite. "Bit busy in here today."

Sam looked around. "No, no, course not."

"Thank you." He sat down throwing his damp paper on the seat next to him. "Names Leonard, people call me Len or Lennie." William said, affably.

"Sam."

"Awful weather today. Never seen the roads so wet."

"No. It is pretty bad." Sam continued to stare out of the window.

William tried a different tack. "I'm sorry. I jabber away like an idiot sometimes, whilst some people just like to be left in peace and quiet, to let life pass them by. I'll keep quiet." He made a grab for his paper.

"No, no, sorry, it's just been a bad morning so far. Got a puncture which made me late for a meeting, then the meeting went from bad to worse." Sam sighed looking at William, showing the glimmer of a friendly smile. "You look familiar, have we met?"

William gulped and jokingly added. "Doubt it. Probably got one of those faces."

"Yeah, probably."

William relaxed. "I know the feeling. I'm a salesman for a medical supply company, sometimes it is the loneliest job on the planet." The cover story had been a last minute detail.

"'ere's your tea and full English, love." A waitress plonked the plate of grease down heavily, along with a mug of tea, in front of Sam.

"Can I have the same please?" William ordered, pleasantly.

"Coming up." She replied before adding loudly as she walked away. "Full and a mug Ron, table nine."

William continued. "What do you do? If you don't mind me asking."

"Food ingredients to the food manufacturing industry." Sam dunked a bit of fried bread in one of his two runny eggs.

"Really, what sort of thing?"

"Juice concentrates, spices, herbs, that sort of thing."

"Tough business?"

"Can be. Life and death for some." then brightening, "Medical you said?"

"Yes, medical supplies, scalpels, gowns and the like, surgical instruments, you know, right up to x-ray equipment, theatre supplies, et cetera."

"I certainly do. I used to go to medical school." Sam brightened. "I was studying to become a doctor, but just didn't make the grades."

"Really?"

"Yes, loved the idea of it at the time, although I'm not sure about the hours and the pressure; this job can be bad enough. Still it was not meant to be."

"True. What field would you have followed?"

"I don't really know. There are so many new ones opening up. Heart surgery seems favourite to me." Sam squeezed some brown sauce on his breakfast. "The thought of holding the key to life, that must be amazing."

"It must have been hard to leave that behind?"

"Yes, but if you can't hack it, then you can't hack it. I still have friends who are in medicine; it is not the same, but I get to indulge myself occasionally."

William's ears pricked up, although he hid his pleasure. "Really, how so?"

"Oh, just talking and that, my friends share some of the new developments with me."

"I thought for a moment you were going to say you assisted in operations." William chuckled to himself.

"If only! That would be nice, but far from ethical, legal or moral. I doubt my friends would allow it, even if I wanted to. They are not that way inclined."

"I'm sure there are people that do though. Must be mad."

"Yes, definitely mad to do it. I know black market operations happen though, so I've heard, I suppose they're probably performed by people like myself, who never qualified, but in their twisted sense of morality deem the only difference is a piece of paper to say so."

"I s'ppose it must tempting though! If you were desperate for that career, but just don't make the grade." The waitress plonked William's breakfast in front of him, it looked as awful as Sam's, but he smiled; it was all part of gaining trust. "Thanks."

"Maybe, bit risky though without having the back up of a full team. Certainly not something I would undertake. Anyway, I wouldn't have the time, this jobs keeps me on the road enough as it is."

"I know the feeling." William replied dipping a piece of sausage in his egg. "Do you cover the country, or do you have designated regions."

"Wherever the customers happen to be, I'll go gladly." Sam smiled.

"Too true, too true. Plays havoc with family life, being away from the kids."

"You have kids?" Sam mopped some egg residue up with a piece of buttered bread.

"Two," William lied. "Both boys, six and four, right little terrors when I'm not around."

"Bet the missus loves you then." Sam scoffed.

"She loved me when she married me, not sure now as I'm not there much. Although saying that, she probably enjoys having the bed to herself." William chimed cheerfully.

Sam looked at his watch. "Oh shit, going to be late again if I'm not careful. You can never get ahead once you fall behind, can you?" He gulped at his tea. "Nice talking to you Len."

"Likewise, hope the day improves. See you." William watched Sam pay and leave before pushing his plate away. Full English was not really his style; a bowl of porridge any day, yet he knew that sometimes replicating someone's tastes and preferences gave you an 'in'.

After paying the bill he left knowing he'd catch Sam up on the road. He was sure he could engineer another meeting, travelling salesmen doing the rounds, there was bound to be familiar faces that cropped up irregularly.

Chapter 101

1970 May
Cambridge

Margaret was in the kitchen preparing a casserole when she heard the door close. "Hi honey, I'm in the kitchen." She glanced at the clock. "You're early." There was no answer. "Sam?" She stopped cutting a carrot, and wiping her hands on a tea towel walked into the hall to see Sam standing with a confused look on his face. She recognised the familiar sight of him questioning his sanity.

"Sam, you okay?"

He shook his head as if that would clear the fog. "How long have I been gone this time?"

She sighed, "You've been on business for four days." Margaret took his briefcase from him, placing it on the floor before taking his hands in hers. "Look, don't fret; nothing bad has ever happened. Even in that two days you lost earlier this year." She frowned. "Do you remember your trip?"

"Trip?"

"Come on, sit down," she led him into the lounge, "I'll pour you a glass of wine. You were going up north, Yorkshire, said you had a few customers to see." She took his raincoat and eased him into the armchair. It was almost like having a child for a few hours as he tried to piece together some kind of thread.

"Where's my briefcase?" Sam searched the floor frantically worried.

"It's by the front door." Sam went to get up. "Sit. I'll get it."

Margaret let Sam spend the next two hours reading notes from meetings he had no recollection off. The writing, his own; eight pages of notes from four days, he kept flicking from page to page.

It amazed her to think a brain could function like that, switch off yet keep working and not realise.

She'd spoken to him at least twice, he'd sounded normal, but what was normal.

"Come on, dinner's ready." Sam looked at Margaret.

"Why don't you worry?" Sam asked sitting down at the table.

"Sorry?" She replied placing two hot plates of sausage casserole on the table.

"You never seem worried by the times I lose."

She placed a caring hand in his. "But you are never gone, you just don't remember."

"Doesn't that worry you?"

"Why should it, you're just the same, it's only your memory that's affected."

Sam sat looking at his dinner solemnly.

"What about when we have a family?" He asked, pushing the food around the plate.

Margaret hated the thought of children; she loved the practising, the excitement, the feeling of two people so caught up in passion and lust, and love; she didn't want that to end. With a child, she believed it would. She had friends who were now mothers and they did nothing but complain about how tired they were, how unsexy they felt, how their appetite for sex had dwindled. She didn't want to grow old, she didn't want to have that motherly figure; she loved her full buxom build.

Finally she answered compassionately. "Look, we'll cross that bridge when we get to it. Let's just enjoy now." She scooped another forkful of casserole into her mouth watching Sam as he continued to push his food around the plate.

"Look, if you're not hungry I'll put that in the hot cupboard for a while. I've never seen you so melancholy."

Sam pierced a piece of potato. "I'm sorry, I'm not hungry." He placed the fork on the plate.

"That's okay. You sit down and watch television for a while." She watched him as he got up and sit in his armchair, a look of hopelessness in his eyes. Trying to break his mood she continued. "By the way, that course I did was really interesting." Margaret said without a hint of malice.

"See, I don't even remember what my wife is doing. What sort of life is this, when stupid things like that I can't ... no, it's not stupid, it's just." Sam sighed, looking weary, "I'm going to bed." He kissed Margaret on her head. "I'm sorry. I do want to know about your course, can you tell me tomorrow?"

"Sure. You go to bed. I'll join you later. You'll like this one it was about genetics." Sam smiled not really listening.

Chapter 102

2002 July

"It's enlightening, this journey." Geoff said, with a narcissistic smile. "It's amazing how one thing affects so many lives. One act causes such a cataclysmic change."

"You're a bloody maths teacher, not sodding English!" Sam fumed wanting to hit out. He felt the burning souls of murdered victims lingering like severe acid heartburn yet encompassing his whole body, their cries floating around him.

Geoff noted Sam staring into oblivion. "You were like that in my class. In fact you did that a lot. I remember us teachers discussing you, deciding you'd never get anywhere. A perpetual dreamer."

"Shut UP! I made it to medical school didn't I." Sam snapped.

"A raw nerve, eh? And, for the record, you failed at that too."

"What?"

"Medical school, you failed it."

Sam scowled at Geoff who ignored it. "How many more?" Sam asked.

"Don't concern yourself, there's a few more yet, including Mr Shaker."

"But why is it no one ever caught me? How can I be so devious, yet know so little about what's going on?"

Shrugging, Geoff replied. "One of life's mysteries I suppose. Maybe that will become clear."

"So why didn't Ben Shaker grass me up? Surely I wouldn't have been conveniently suffering a fugue state every time he wanted me to perform some heinous crime?"

"Maybe he had a gift; a gift for knowing – some people do."

"Rubbish!"

Chapter 103

1970 June
Lincolnshire
Storage Yard

I sit in my lab, considering what it is Shaker has in mind for me, after our phone call. Whatever it was he had planned, it was put back a couple of months and I had to keep ringing, just in case. It gave me more time to think though. I need to be rid of him. Unlike with Gary – whom I think I loved, looking back on it – whom I wanted to be a partner, I don't want one now.

An angry knock at the door signals the next step. I know what I am going to do and it is set firmly in my mind, I've even left a freezer empty. I am taking a risk so close to my lab, yet feel there is little option.

A further knock rattles my patience and slowly I unlock the door, to see an annoyed Ben.

"Don't keep me waiting like that again. I knock, you answer. Got it?"

I nod my acquiescence and turn to go back inside.

"Where do you think you're going? Follow me."

A dowsed handkerchief of chloroform is in my pocket ready, I also have a hypodermic of Ketamine but Ben marches away too quickly. I follow him to his car, parked in the deserted yard. As he puts the key in the boot lock, I reach round his scrawny frame, anger fuelling me. Instantly Ben fights back trying to shake me free, I get an elbow in my ribs, yet I hold on tight; I have to hold tight. I can't let this go, not now, I've committed myself to this action; it is do or die. I am strong for my build, yet find it difficult to hold the handkerchief over his mouth and nose as we rock backwards towards the wall of the mechanics unit, where he slams me into it, knocking the wind out of me. I've seen wild animals as angry as Shaker, he is strong belying his size. He breaks free, with fists flying towards me at such speed and ferocity I only just manage to twist away, receiving only glancing blows. I fear for my life. I'd hoped to subdue him quickly; that is not going to be the case. The chloroform has some effect but he is fighting it. I run into my lab where he follows.

"What the fuck. Think you can get the better of Shaker do you? You'll pay dearly for this." He marches towards me, and I grab a piece of wood I'd prepared as a back-up. He produces a knife. I really do feel my chances are slim. "Come on you piece of shit, if you think you are hard enough."

It becomes like a dance, each step cautiously countering the other, waiting for the inevitable pounce. I am frantically trying to work out a ploy for disarming him when he lunges unexpectedly, I fall backwards trying to avoid it, hitting the ceramic slab and dropping the wood. Instinctively I grab whatever I can find and throw it at him. It is the chloroform bottle. He swings at it with the knife and it shatters sending its contents over him. There is a second's pause before he lunges again; this time he seems to be disorientated as he suddenly succumbs to the fumes. I pace about waiting for him to fall, hoping he will, he is still fighting its effects. He lunges once more, this time however, it is like his body can't co-ordinate its attack. I manage to land the needle in his neck forcing the Ketamine into him. He throws me off and I skid across the floor. Turning on me he is ready to strike, yet he stops as his eyes fog up, before he stumbles to his knees and collapses face down on the floor.

I lay dumfounded on the floor, letting it all sink in. I know the Ketamine will keep him sedated for an hour or two if it doesn't kill him. I have to dump his car away from the yard, make it look as though he was never here. I lock up, find the keys still in the boot lock and drive it out of the yard parking it several streets away.

Now there is only Ben Shaker to put on ice.

Chapter 104

2002 July

The storage unit materialised around Sam, Ben had the knife raised high as a bottle was thrown. It was cut down mid-air.

Sam stared opened mouthed at the scene played out in front of him. No disguise, the truth without a doubt staring back at him.

"Well, there you go. Now you know."

"But ... but ... I." Sam choked on the words.

"It's just like modern day CCTV. It's quite good this." Geoff jollied.

Sam swung wildly at Geoff. He'd hated him as a teacher and now he hated him even more. As each ferocious swipe passed through Geoff he became more angry and frustrated.

"Come now, Sam, we're not real, remember, we're dead and I am just your journeyman. You still have more souls to collect first, you must see them all."

"I ... I can't. Why? I know the truth."

"Call it your preparation."

Sam turned once more to the view the scene. A burning, searing pain engulfed him as Ben's soul joined the swathe of souls he carried

They were back in the BMW Sam still reeling.

Chapter 105

1970 June
Lincolnshire
Storage Yard

How long it will take for someone to report Ben Shaker's disappearance is anybody's guess. I don't know anything about him; whether he is married, has a family, or living parents. I can only surmise that he has no family because of the hours he keeps; yet it is not a foregone conclusion. One concern is whether the police will search the units trying to find a trace of him; I know he is only probably on their radar because of his reputation, which I have heard through overheard discussions round the yard, yet disappearing in unexplained circumstances might prick their curiosity, even though, they probably won't be too disappointed. For an instant I consider whether it is advisable to pack up and leave, abandoning the unit; there are no records in my name to trace it back, rent is paid in cash, false name – it would mean disposing of the bodies, possibly, or I could leave them on ice. What a fitting end to Shaker's existence, dead and locked up in his own yard! But, it would be a shame to end my research early, even if progress is slow. I battle my own duplicitous determination.

In all my time here, the mechanic was his closest ally. The others, from the overheard conversations, had managed to keep him at arm's length, just doing enough.

Maybe I should just lay low for a while? Buy some local papers. Fear shoots through me as I consider who might take over the yard? It could be worse!

There are too many questions to answer tonight and I can't change anything. What is done is done and I have to see how it plays out. If the police find my unit, then I will know; it will probably be in the press. I'll pack a few of my precious things into the car, just in case I can never return.

Chapter 106

1970 June
Lincolnshire

24 Hours Later

Joseph Smalley sat in the Police interview room, the green walls and cold appearance almost made him feel warm, considering he had just spent nearly twelve hours locked in the boot of a car. After coming round, he had called out until a member of the public had finally notified the police, who broke him out.

Joseph, although badly beaten, refused to go to hospital instead pleading to go home but the police wouldn't let it go, especially after an observant copper had realised whose car it was, the notorious Benjamin 'Savage' Shaker. This was their opportunity to apply some pressure, maybe get some evidence against Shaker, something that always remained elusive; a chance to finally put him behind bars. He'd always remained one step ahead and there was a feeling a copper was on the payroll; now though, they thought the tables had turned.

Joseph was left to ponder his story of events, which had been vague, whilst detectives checked out the lock up yard owned by Ben Shaker, only a few streets away from where Ben's car had been found.

* * * *

The Brown Ford Cortina eased into the yard. The mechanic was the first to look up from the hood of an Austin Princess Vanden Plas he was working on. He recognised one of the detectives from a previous visit, a Detective Jack Spilner, a tall wiry man with thinning hair and a hideously scarred cheek. As he got out of the car, Spilner scratched his left ear, where a piece had been bitten off by an armed bank robber four years previously. The mechanic returned focus back to the engine, but it didn't stop Spilner and his colleague Detective Smyth from walking over.

"I'm looking for Benjamin Shaker." Spilner asked curtly. The mechanic pretended he hadn't heard.

Spilner paused only for a second before placing a firm hand on the mechanics shoulder. "I said I am looking ..."

"Yeah, yeah, I heard." He straightened up facing Spilner and Smyth.

"Well?" Spilner asked, quite happy for a bit of resistance, an excuse to use his brand of gentle persuasion.

"Well what?"

Spilner observed Smyth heading towards the grubby desk, where a large thick brown envelope sat; it looked like it could hold dodgy MOT certificates – he'd seen similar before.

"Maybe I should just search this desk. Everything's in plain view." Smyth remarked conspiratorially.

The Mechanic relented nervously. "Look, I ain't see him. He was meant to be 'ere 'bout eight this morning, but ain't showed up."

Smyth lifted the envelope feeling the contents. "What this then?"

"Just some 'ccounts stuff."

"Legit business eh? Novelty." Spilner smiled at Smyth. "Do you know where we might find Mr Shaker?"

"I don't, 'e only ever meets me here."

"When did you last see him?" Smyth asked, now standing next to his partner still with the brown envelope in his hands.

"Yesterday afternoon 'bout three, said he ..." Spilner enjoyed watching people squirm. "...'ad to go 'n visit someone near Boston. Didn't elaborate, never does."

Spilner stared at the mechanic for a few more seconds.

"Tell him, when he turns up, we want a word with him. It won't take long but the results might last a life time." He smiled at his own joke before walking out into the yard.

"What do you reckon Pete?"

"He's telling the truth. Shaker's got a rep' for turning up when he says." Smyth threw the envelope back at the mechanic.

"A con with dedication to time keeping eh?"

"It's a job, regular hours an all." They both smiled as they headed to the next unit, then the next getting similar responses. There was only one unit where they got no response, so, they returned to the mechanics unit.

"He ain't there. He ain't hardly every there, comes in at night mainly when he does turn up, which ain't often." The mechanic offered.

Spilner turned towards him. "Being co-operative now eh?"

"No, just you're wasting your time, you won't get a response."

"Him and Shaker tight?" Smyth asked.

The mechanic scoffed. "Nah."

"So he might have it in for Shaker then." Spilner picked up the thread of thought.

"Now that is funny, I don't know anyone who don't." Smyth and Spilner shared a look, "But you need balls to go up against Shaker and I ain't come across no one who would."

"Who rents it?" Smyth pointed to the unit.

"Sam Smith."

"That don't sound very legit." Spilner countered. The mechanic just shrugged.

"We'll be back, don't mention anything to Mr Smith."

With that they left.

Chapter 107

1970 December
Liverpool
CID

It was getting late and CID was deserted. The Examiner case had gone cold and been scaled back, yet again, still no usable information from the mammoth media sorté; resources were tight and every police force in the country had been involved. Hundreds of missing persons who could be potentials were looked into. Whilst it had led to the discovery of couple of runaways and a murderer on the run, they were not connected to this case. There was no new lead to who the killer was or where he was based. Anything they did uncover always meandered back, in some shape or form to Sam Talbot who conveniently had alibis in place for some: the surveillance work Travis had done did not uncover anything untoward either. Sam had been interviewed twice and now top brass had warned them off unless they had something concrete. His theory about a twin thus far proved fruitless. All the friends and wife had checked out.

However, William sat ignoring the flickering fluorescent tube as he focussed on a letter that had arrived a couple of days ago, whilst he hadn't been in. It was in connection to his enquiry regarding the birth certificate, to prove his twin theory. He sat dumfounded, re-reading the letter, which enclosed copies of three birth certificates – it wasn't twins. It was triplets! A sister and a brother. Triplets not twins! He couldn't believe it. A line of thinking that had jarred his dreams so emphatically. Maybe Sam was innocent? Maybe it was the perfect crime, just the wrong siblings.

During the war, records had been sent anywhere they were thought to be safe from the Luftwaffe and not all had been returned, some had even been lost in the bombing raids; these particular ones had ended up in Haringay. The siblings' birth certificates, registered a day later than Sam's, was for a Nicholas and an Emily Talbot; it opened up endless possibilities, one of those was whether Margaret was the sister as opposed to wife; in which case her complete history had been fabricated. A perfect disguise, it's happened before. He would need to check?

Why the day's difference though?

The letter also detailed a list of possible names for attending midwives. It was a short list; there was only one that was still alive and she lived near Aviemore, a place called Kincraig. It was unlikely she'd remember anything, but every lead needed to be followed up.

He would speak with O'Neill when he got in, but a trip to Aviemore was in the offing.

Chapter 108

1970 December
Kincraig
Near Aviemore

"Thank you for agreeing to see me, Mrs Faulkner." William took the proffered cup of tea.

"Katherine, please call me Katherine. I don't get many visitors these days. Albert and I thought it was beautiful spot to retire. The highlands are lovely in the summer. Shame he didn't get to enjoy it very long. Passed away not long after we bought this place, nearly seven year ago."

William let her talk, gaining her confidence. He wanted this case closed and Susan Jones' memory laid to rest. "And you never thought of moving nearer to the main town to be closer to your friends?" William glanced out of the window. It truly was a wonderful view, he could see the pull of it; Fiona would love it here too.

"I did at first, yet as time went on I found the thought too stressful. There is a regular bus service that goes along the lane." William could see the pain as she looked forlornly out of the window. "I'm sorry, dear, listening to me rattle on. You don't want an old lady to drone on about how lonely she is. Now what is it that I can do for you? You said something about my midwifery days. Oh, I can tell you some stories that would make your hair curl." She smiled and the years drifted away.

William smiled appreciatively.

"There was one particular family I am concerned with. I have been doing some research into the family of a suspect for a cold case. The family name was Talbot, and she would have given birth on the 16th May 1942. I found a birth certificate for a Samuel Jacob Talbot, yet no time detailed on it – which I understand is normal for multiple births. The GRO index shows a Nicholas Andrew and Emily Sheila Talbot, also born on the same day, with times noted on their certificates, and the same mother and father's names. I suppose I am looking for confirmation, that it isn't a pure fluke to have a set of twins and another baby born in the same hospital to parents with the same names. The records are unclear, and I need to be sure."

"It was a terrible time, dear, with the air raids. Most expectant mothers had been evacuated to the country, but there were a few dissident ones, who wouldn't go."

"Yes, I suppose. Do you know, remember, whether Nicholas and Emily survived? I can't find any record of them after their birth. No death certificates. Maybe they were adopted, if the family didn't have much money – keep the first born? I have checked the censuses of the time and Nicholas and Emily are not shown to be with the family I am looking into." This case was certainly turning up some anomalies.

Katherine stared at him for a few seconds as if expecting him to carry on. William wondered whether she would even remember as the seconds drifted on without even a murmur. He carried on.

"I am trying to understand where they are now, so I can investigate further whether they are related." He felt weary feeling this thread of hope, he wanted so badly to be true, start to unravel.

Katherine had sounded so lucid on the phone now he wondered whether she was fraying at the seams.

"You were saying May 1942?"

"Yes, 16th May. The Talbots. Harry and Ethel."

"I don't recall the names, but it was a long time ago dear and I was a mere slip of a thing. Would have given you a run for your money I can tell you."

William smiled, as she appeared to be flirting.

"Were there any unusual circumstances at the time that would have meant separating one sibling from the others? "

"They may have been different families," Katherine reflected, "I remember once, when I was new to the profession and two babies were mixed up because of that very thing, Smith, was the family name, two sets of John and Jane, both gave birth to boys, both Derek. What are the chances?" She glanced out of the window wistfully. "Once we sorted it out, we did have a laugh about it.

"It was the war you know dear. Maybe it was that awful year the Luftwaffe's bomb's nearly destroyed the hospital. That was before they evacuated pregnant mothers out of London."

"Bombed?"

"Yes. Before the evacuation, in the early years we never believed the Nazi's could reach us, but they did. They were troubled times and I don't remember that family themselves." Katherine started to look pained by the memory and William placed a hand on hers for comfort. The she added. "Giving birth is not an exact science. It is possible that if an air-raid occurred during labour then the babies that were born were moved somewhere safe and registered straight away, we used to have a registrar visit the hospital. Labour can take hours, although normally one baby will follow another unless there are complications. Maybe one died at birth, although that would be noted on the birth certificate along with a time."

He was still no further on.

"Did the mother pass away during child birth?" Katherine added.

"I don't believe so, or at least I have found no record of it."

"I remember one time, we had a mother who was in labour for over forty-eight hours. Two children, neither wanted to come out ..."

William let her ramble on as the conversation started to go round in a circle, feeling sorry for her, knowing he would dread this kind of loneliness happening for Fiona.

Sitting in the car, he let out an audible long sigh, he was no nearer to a clear answer. Records were vague, the war may have destroyed the very ones he needed.

Chapter 109

1971 February

Cambridge

Margaret just made it to the loo. The morning sickness was excruciating, she couldn't believe she'd fallen pregnant, let alone not noticed for the first four months. She had gained a little weight and felt a little more tired than usual, but the morning sickness had come late. From her friends who'd had children, she knew it should be up to twelve weeks, not after sixteen! A couple of visits to the doctor had confirmed the pregnancy, although she'd expected to be told she had cancer of the stomach; that would have accounted for some of her symptoms. But pregnant! Sam had been over the moon, not in the least upset that all the precautions they'd been taking had failed. He was going to be a father, a smile had radiated from him ever since he'd known. Whereas Margaret had accepted it with disdain, seeing her life's work collapsing around her, everything falling to the wayside as the thing growing inside sucked all the energy from her.

Would that thought ever change?

Her own parents showed very little love. Kids were an inconvenience. She remembered being left to her own devices most days, brothers and sisters were the only companions. Her mother had ruled the house with a dominant hand. You did chores as soon as old enough and that allowed her mother to go out during the days – no one ever knew where; it was never discussed. Her father never questioned her and rarely showed affection; it was a passionless marriage. It was surprising they'd ever managed to have kids, it certainly didn't lead to a close bond between siblings; in fact Margaret didn't even know where they were, or what they were doing – except the one who was dead. There had been four: two brothers, two sisters. It was a strange childhood. It became stranger after the death of her sister, even more distant, like everyone was wary of each other, when the opposite would have been expected.

Margaret believed the parenting gene was not in her and didn't even consider that she could change it, or want to change it. To be an individual was what she aspired to. In part, she was scared what effect this child would have on her. Would she ever feel the motherly bond or always feel resentment for the thing inside her?

At work, she'd had to fight tooth and nail to keep her position open. In the end, they had conceded that it would take longer to bring a replacement up to speed on her projects. She hated this male dominated world sometimes.

Resting at the top of the stairs, she wondered whether she would make it into work today. If she didn't, it only added fuel to the fire of sexism in the workplace. Gulping at the water beside her, she entertained ways to end this pregnancy. The world spun round her in a daze.

Before she had acknowledged the idea, she was tumbling down the stairs.

In a crumpled heap at the bottom, she smiled to herself. Not remembering consciously that she had made the decision to do it. She lay quite still for a minute or two, hoping, expectant at feeling the loss of the child inside. Seeing blood on her hands, instant euphoria circulated until she saw the cut on her leg, the broken glass on the stairs, and another cut on her arm. The final condemnation was her unborn child moving inside her. This baby was going to be tough. She looked at the top of the stairs again, but her attention was snapped away by the front door opening.

"Margaret, are you okay?"

"Yes, yes, I just tripped, it was silly really." She started to straighten herself up.

"How's the baby? Is the baby okay?" There it was, the bloody baby! A big exclamation mark in her life! "Here, let me help you up. Maybe we ought to take you to the hospital?" Sam's panicked voice filled the hall.

"No!" Margaret answered sharply, before adjusting her response. "It was only a little trip, I'll be fine."

"But the blood?" Sam asked, seeing it for the first time.

"The glass I was holding broke; I'm fine, honest. Anyway what are doing home?" Margaret eased herself up, mentally feeling the parts of her that felt tender.

"Oh, I bloody forgot my briefcase. I got all the way to work before I realised. Looks like it was a good job I did! I'll call in and stay home, I can make some calls from here."

"No! No, Sam, go. I'm fine." Margaret did not want to be mothered; neither of them liked it, and they both had been respectful of that, until now it seemed.

"But you've had a bad fall."

"No. I have had *a* fall – that is all. I am fine." She saw Sam was about to mention the baby again. "And the baby is fine. I should know. It is inside me." She stated bitterly.

"Alright, alright!" Sam reluctantly led her into the lounge. "Look, I'll make you a cup of tea, and clear up before I go back to work." He put up a hand to stop Margaret arguing.

"Fine, but I have to get ready myself shortly." She sighed hiding the pain from what felt like a bruise forming on her hip.

He looked miffed at the thought of her going to work, but let it go.

Chapter 110

1971 March
Liverpool
CID

"How are you getting on with following up on the triplets? Can we bring Sam and his wife in for further questioning?"

William looked up from his scribbled notes, which he had been studying for the last hour after being asked about it yesterday. CID had been so manic from a major rape case and a murder case on the go; this was kind of a sideline for the moment unless he could break it open again. Soon it would end up going to Ghost squad, for review in a few years, if another body didn't turn up.

"Struggling in all honesty. The siblings seem to have disappeared off the radar. I cannot locate death certificates for either of them."

"The parents?" O'Neill perched on the edge of Sam's desk after nodding to Harris, Jeffries and Lowell as they entered discussing last nights footie.

"I've traced the father to Ripon, Yorkshire; died 17th January '58. The wife Ethel lived in a home in Bournemouth until her death on 5th March '69, suffered dementia."

"Not ones for stopping in one place are they?"

"No, and that is what is making so hard. I'll keep at it."

"Do, but it has to take a backseat for the moment, orders from above."

William knew it was becoming one of those cases that always got pushed back – disappointingly unsurprising.

Chapter III

1971 September
Liverpool
CID

William stared at the stack of reports compiled by PCs from around the country, it was an enigma as they searched for Nicholas and Emily Talbot; death certificates for everyone with the same name – not one corresponded with the age of the siblings. That gave the impression that they would still be alive, and with that, marriage certificates had been searched, council records and anyone with the slightest similarity had been checked. Adoption records. Months of work which had returned zilch!

"Damn the bloody war!"

"I think a lot of people would agree with that sentiment. What's the problem?" DC Tanner asked.

"This bloody serial, every avenue or lead just pulls a dead end. How?"

"Some people are just lucky."

"Even if your death certificate is destroyed, there must be records somewhere, surely."

"Needle in a haystack eh?"

"I can't believe this guy is just going to get away with it."

"They'll turn up, you've just got to persevere."

"Eight years it's been."

Tanner started to walk away, then stopped. "Have you tried church records?"

"Church records?"

"If the siblings died, whether at child birth or not, they should be buried somewhere, church or local parish records for the cemeteries. Problem is there are a lot more churches than records offices, and don't forget crematoriums!"

William shook his head and ran his hands down his face.

"Thanks, I think. I'll try it. They would have central records somewhere?"

"Maybe."

Chapter 112

1972 February
Liverpool
The Wirral

"Ron would be glad he missed this one. He hated murders, especially if it was women, children and men." DI Harris scoffed as he and Travis got out of the car.

"Yeah, I … hold on, that's just about everyone."

"Not blaggers, prossies, rapists and robbers. According to him they weren't human, so they were justified."

"I can see his point." Travis conceded. There was a part of him that wanted to let the scum of the earth kill themselves, although his conscience didn't work that way; everyone was dealt with utmost diligence. "What we got anyway?"

"A body dump, I told you in the car. What's wrong with you today … PC Benton expecting today?"

William hated the way Harris always referred to his wife as PC Benton, her name was Fiona Travis and she no longer worked for the force. After their initial meeting in Wiltshire they had kept in contact; eventually she had transferred to Liverpool and they had got engaged before marrying six months later. Two years later she became pregnant with their first child, Jack. Now expecting their second, William was hoping for a girl this time. Harris had always been sarcastic whenever she appeared in their open plan office, ridiculing William for having such an attentive and attractive partner.

"My wife's name's Fiona." His exasperated tone confirmed the reaction Harris had hoped to get. "But you know that. It's no wonder you missed your promotion last year. It must really bug you, that I didn't."

"Yeah, yeah whatever, let's just deal with the case."

Showing their warrant cards to the copper standing at the edge of the crime scene, an abandoned grand Georgian villa, he waved them through. The body had been discovered by some kids who were trespassing in the decaying building. Luckily they thought it more important to report it rather than worry about their minor offence, for which they had duly been told off for and sent home with a clip round the ear. The discovery was probably enough to deter them from trespassing in the future.

Directed to a room upstairs they found a laboratory Sergeant working the body of a naked female, whose features were showing the early signs of putrefaction; the smell only a faint odour. The cold had aided the preservation.

"Alright, what can you tell us so far, man?" Harris asked not disguising a condescending tone that he had. William raised his eyebrows but said nothing.

The figure wearing a protective white coverall looked their way, pulled back the surgeon's mask to reveal a woman's face.

"Firstly, that you can't tell the difference between a male and female Harris, and secondly, nothing yet. All the usual means to indicate a T.O.D have been inconclusive. When she is taken back to the morgue, I should know more. What we do know is her name, Jemima Hartridge aged thirty-seven, disappeared in Oxford, July of '69, mother of two boys."

"Wow, Janice, you've done your homework." Harris stated sarcastically.

"It's easy when you find the driving licence. You know, I like to gain as much info as possible, it makes my job a little easier, makes it more meaningful when I know their life."

"Whatever." Harris replied, "It's another body, another crime on just another day."

William and Janice shared a knowing look, wondering when the rot had really set in.

"You need to find a new profession." Travis added, with the slightest hint of seriousness in the otherwise half-hearted remark. Stepping closer to the body, "Any guess at the cause of death yet Janice?" William enquired.

"Too difficult to tell at this stage. But …" William looked on, knowing Janice's thoroughness. "… I am guessing, if you look past the delayed decay, she has been somewhere cold."

"Well it is February, you know. Winter!" Harris was ignored.

"How so?" William stepped towards the body mindful of where he was treading.

"There is some residual frost bite on the extremities."

William furrowed his brow as he studied the body closer.

"You alright?" Janice responded.

"Just a thought, really. Are there any signs of samples being taken, organs missing?"

She lifted a corner of the tarp the body had been wrapped up in. "There was some; initial conclusion – a surgeon, maybe a botched black market op. I saw one similar last year. Although they didn't leave any ID."

The colour drained from William's face.

"You alright?" Janice offered.

"His fine, just expecting his second child, that's all, and wondering what kind of a world to expect." Harris lamented.

"Give it a rest." Janice snapped.

William ignored him. "The only case I know that has that M.O. is the serial that has been unsolved from when I started on the force in '63; has a body count of five – maybe this is six. But the dumpsite is wrong. They've always been in public places, or places where someone was due to pass within hours. Unless we've missed some!" The thought turned him colder than he already was.

"Well ..." Janice started to say.

"When you get the body back, I'll bring the files down; then maybe you can check?"

"You think it ..."

"It could be, but something is off." William eyed the scene carefully.

Harris interjected. "Forget it, it won't get you anywhere. Everyone has a case that you just can't solve and then you start to see similar cases as part of it; it's not, leave it alone."

"Is that what you do?" William turned on Harris, "Is that what these glib remarks are about? You're happy just to let things run and run. If they don't get solved, it doesn't matter. They'll be someone else's problem eventually."

"Easy tiger, you'll end up with an ulcer, like Ron?"

"At least he actually cared."

Janice was staring at the two men, seeming to enjoy the little drama.

"I care. I just know when not to take it personally, 'Golden Boy'."

"That really gets you, doesn't it? That I was promoted above you and quickly, with initial help from Ron, and you being his sidekick and all."

"Oh god, give it a rest. Your arsehole must be so tight that you'd shit a diamond."

"Leave him be." Janice said. "Take a look at this."

Both men turned to face Janice. Harris walked off, leaving Travis to see what she'd found.

"What is it?" William enquired, squinting at a tiny tear of cloth, caught on a nail protruding from the floor.

"My guess," said Janice picking it up with a pair of tweezers and placing in an evidence bag, "is a piece of raincoat, judging by colour and look."

William smiled broadly, "Finally, a physical piece of evidence!"

"Yes, but it may not be the murderer's; this place gets all sorts of tramps and the like."

"But it fits the vague description of the only person that was seen near the car around the time of the body drop at Stonehenge." He recalled an interview with a lorry driver. "The car belonged to one person, *Sam Talbot.*"

"Did you memorise the case files, or what?"

"Natural gift, fortunately, or unfortunately, depending on your take of things." He replied smiling. "Now all I need to do is find Mr Talbot and the coat this comes from and BAM, we got him, at last."

Chapter 113

1973 April
Liverpool
CID

"Well, that's it. Again!" William threw a file across the now empty incident room.

O'Neill looked at him. "Don't take it personally. We don't have the resources and, if there is no new evidence, we can't hound the same person. Sam Talbot's alibis checked out and you couldn't find the coat. It can't be him. TV and papers have not revealed anything new, we are stuck."

"It bloody well is him! It has to be. The bastard!" William shouted to no one in particular, almost at the point of tears. He thumped a desk as hard as he could. It caught the attention of two PCs walking past the open door.

O'Neill sympathised and understood.

"Look, take the rest of the day, no, the rest of the week off. Spend it with that lovely wife of yours and the kids."

William slumped down at the desk kicking the chair.

"Don't get mad."

"But he keeps taking more, subjecting them to god knows what, before sending them back to their families. What sicko does that? And keeps on doing it? Ten bloody years and we have nothing, absolutely nothing! No trace of the siblings; like they have disappeared off the face of the earth. The wife and friends check out. What are we FUCKING missing?" William exploded.

"Like I said, take the rest of the week, spend it with your family. It does you no good getting wound up by it. He'll slip up, they always do. Eventually." O'Neill left the incident room, leaving William seething.

Chapter 114

1974 March

Cambridge

"He's asleep. At last!" Sam took a sip from his wine, that sat on the end table, before flumping next to Margaret on the settee.

"Took you long enough, you need more practice. He does love his nursery rhymes though." Margaret unfurled her legs to welcome Sam into an embrace.

"Yes, I had to read 'The House that Jack Built' three times. Thought I was never going to get packed." Sam leaned into Margaret to kiss her but she suddenly slid herself more upright.

"Packed?!"

"Yes, I'm away for the next four days, remember?" Margaret frowned at Sam "The annual contract meetings in Yorkshire that Marcello wants me to look after, not lo… I told you about them." Sam stared at Margaret in consternation as she pursed her lips.

"No, Sam! I have a course this week. We agreed. We decided you would look after Edward; you said you would work from home. My job is just as important as yours, you know!"

"Margaret, without these contracts I could lose my job; these are our big yearly ones. Marcello, gave me these. I can't let him down. These make up half our annual turnover."

"What about my job? Is that not important?"

Sam leaned back against the arm of the settee, giving them both space. "Yes, you know it is, but it is just a course. Can't you do it another time?"

"You bastard! Is that what you really think of my job?" Margaret stood up, grabbing her wine and taking a large gulp.

"No. But you don't have deadlines … as such. If we don't win these contracts Marcello will go ape and it will affect annual sales. After all my fugue states, he was nervous about giving me these, I had to almost beg for the opportunity; kind of a last chance to prove I can still cope."

"No! You promised! You're the one that wanted children, yet it is me that is staying home all the time to look after him. I wanted a career. You know I wanted a career. I have been stuck at home looking after him, now he is at nursery school, it is your bloody turn; and you are not skipping out of it." Margaret stormed out of the lounge, stomping up the stairs. Sam sighed wearily, completely flummoxed. He knew Margaret was immoveable once she had decided something, and for the next hour, as the TV played images in front of him he tried to conjure a solution – or at best an excuse to give Marcello without risking his job; knowing he could not cancel.

Suddenly he jumped off the settee, heading to the telephone table that nestled in the cubbyhole under the stairs. Margaret still hadn't come down since she'd stormed off. The line was answered on the seventh ring.

"Hello."

"Michael, how are you?" Sam joyfully asked.

"What you after?"

"As his Godfather, could you look after Edward for a few days? Margaret and I have double booked and we are desperate? She won't cancel either and I have some contract meetings that I can't miss."

"Can't. Off to America, again, I'm afraid."

"Business or pleasure?" Sam felt a little envy creep in. He loved being a father, even if there were limitations, and now, inconveniences.

"Sorry, Mate, both, and I can't cancel. Try Roger and Sarah."

"Yeah, thanks, I will. Enjoy the States." He sourly responded.

"I will."

* * * *

Roger came out of the downstairs toilet as the phone rang.

"Smith household."

"Roger, it's Sam. I'm in a bit of a hole and was hoping you and Sarah could help us out and take Edward for a few days, 'til Friday evening. I've got to go away for some important meetings, and Margaret has got a course to attend ..."

"Is that the genetics course in Cardiff?"

"To be honest, I can't remember, although Cardiff rings a bell, so probably."

"I'm away, but I'm sure Sarah won't mind. It will be nice for Rachel and Oliver; Rachel loves playing dress-up with Edward. Do you want her to pick him up from nursery tomorrow or will you drop him off?"

Would she mind picking him up from nursery school, that'd be great? If she's okay with that? We'll pack some things ready."

"It'll be fine, what's one more, eh?"

"Thank you. You're a life safer. I'll let Margaret know."

"I'll tell, Sarah." Roger put the phone down.

"Tell me what?" Sarah said, as she descended the stairs.

"Margaret and Sam need someone to look after Edward for a few days. They've double booked themselves." He tutted. "I said you'd be fine with that."

"Did you? Why? Do I not get asked?" She stopped on the stairs frowning at Roger.

"Well, you've got the kids anyway, what's one more and Edward's no trouble, is he?"

"How about asking me first before agreeing to something. I have a life too you know?"

"Would you have said no?"

"No. That is not the point! You can be so bloody thoughtless at times, Roger. It would be nice if you were here to help out more."

"Some of us have already got a lot on our plate, just keeping this place going."

Sarah descended the stairs like a ferocious animal, the slap catching Roger unaware, sending his glasses flying across the hall, shaking loose one lens – which skated across the parquet floor.

Chapter 115

1977 November

Devon

Paignton

A familiar street scene came into view and Sam felt buoyed by it. "I know this place. Yes, this is … Margaret … and I came here for holidays out of season, we liked it, as it was quiet. We brought our son before …"

"… he died." Geoff finished. "It's also the place where the police nearly caught the serial killer."

Sam finished. "They arrested me."

"How did your son die? How old was he?"

"Five, nearly six." He let his mind wander to the joy he'd felt when he became a father, mantled with the privilege of helping him through life as best he could. "I still don't know how he got out that night. I had a last minute meeting that I couldn't miss."

"A case of work coming first." Geoff admonished.

"Money was tight, I had no choice."

"There is always a choice."

"The landladies were watching Edward; they enjoyed seeing him. This was our third year staying with them. We sometimes left him with them when we wanted a quiet night out. Are they …?"

"You were his parent, not them. They're dead, Edith died in '87 whilst Greta survived until '99. What do you care? The amount of anger you vented on them that night, and afterwards."

"I had just lost my son. They were meant to be looking after him."

"Were they? I thought it was Margaret that was meant to be looking after your son. She is, was, his mother?"

"She popped out to buy a bottle of wine for us to share when I arrived. It's what we liked to do on our first night."

"So what happened?"

Sam looked at Geoff condescendingly. "You know what happened. Why ask me?"

* * * *

Standing in Edith and Greta's lounge, the TV was on. Coronation Street was just ending and the two ladies were snoring in unison. Edward wandered round from behind the back of the settee, where a makeshift bed had been laid out on the floor. His favourite teddy hung in his hand like a best friend. He stood, looking at the two ladies with utmost concentration on his face; his brow furrowed, holding himself, wearing his green and white striped pyjamas.

"Toilet."

He got no response. "Toilet." He danced from one foot to the other. Desperately he toyed with what to do, staring at the lounge door then back at the two sleeping ladies. After much deliberating, he walked to the door that separated their private apartment from the rest of the guesthouse and, after a struggle, pulled the handle down. The door opened inwards and he had to fight to get it open whilst still trying to hold his pee in. In the hall, he turned to face the front door, confused. Then, turning, he looked up at the ominous staircase that rose like an intimidating giant into the darkness above. It scared him. Feeling safer he stepped towards the front door. It was not dead-bolted and, with a little struggle and a lot of effort, he managed to open it. Staring out at the dark street, biting his bottom lip nervously, he hugged his teddy for comfort; still holding himself tightly. He could feel the cold night and thought about going back for his coat. His need to pee seemed more important than the cold. He spied a light on in a house opposite; the front door was slightly ajar. He would ask there.

With no shoes on his feet, the stones steps to the pavement were freezing.

* * * *

"Edward no!" Sam called instinctively.

"He can't hear you, this is the past, remember?" Geoff stated.

* * * *

Edward walked straight across the road in front of a racing Triumph Dolomite. The squeal of tyres stabbed the silent night, shaking Edith and Greta from their snooze. It took a few seconds for them to grasp their bearings. Then they saw the open lounge door and, checking behind the settee, were horrified to find Edward missing. They strode from the lounge as a slow, terrifying realisation dawned on them when they saw the open front door. At the front doorstep, they saw a bedraggled figure getting out of a car embedded in a dwarf garden wall opposite.

★ ★ ★ ★

Sam watched as the driver swerved, but not in time to miss Edward, who was running towards the house with the open door. The world spun around as Sam saw the driver stumble out of the vehicle and attend to Edward. Anger flexed inside him.

★ ★ ★ ★

Suddenly, people started to appear at their front doors looking on. The driver hugged Edward's small body and cried out, "No, please no." But it was too late. Edward was dead. At that instant there were two choices; to stay and face the music or run – and run now before the police arrived. As people crowded round, the driver stood up, holding the boy, pleading.

"I didn't see him."

One of the ladies, who had rushed out of her house when she'd heard a noise, took the boy and laid him back down. Then, she knelt down and checked for a pulse.

"I've called an ambulance," another woman wearing a red and blue pinny stated.

"It's too late, he's dead. I ..."

Another woman standing nearby added. "It was an accident! The police will see that. He shouldn't have been out at this time of night. What parent allows their child on the streets? Should be safely tucked up in bed. Come here and sit down, you're in shock."

"No! I mean no. I'll be fine." The driver stood, stunned, appearing unable to comprehend what had happened.

The crowd grew quickly as the minutes passed, people chatting away, sharing experiences of people racing their cars along this road; a sense of animosity growing in the crowd, as the innocent child lay on the ground, covered by a coat, carefully placed. The figure edged backwards, wary of the uneasiness growing in the crowd and, before long, disappearing into the darkness as the arriving ambulance took everyone attention.

★ ★ ★ ★

Stumbling away, the figure appeared overtaken by grief. "I'm so sorry."

★ ★ ★ ★

By the time the police arrived, the driver was out of sight and when quizzed, all Jo-public could do was look around incensed that the person could wander off after killing a small boy. They'd been so taken by the child that no one had really paid attention to the guilty party.

"So, who was driving the car?" A policeman asked the sea of faces, who glanced around at each other.

"It was a man, he was standing here … a second ago, I swear." A young mother, holding her own child, tightly, retorted.

"Yes, but did anyone see where he went?" a tall burly policeman wearing round wire-framed glasses quizzed.

The crowd shook their heads. The policeman found it difficult to believe; he would have expected them to have lynched the man, not let him walk away.

"It doesn't matter." He shouted over the hubbub, "We'll find him, after all he can't have got far without his car." He started to search the Triumph, but it was clear of documentation.

* * * *

Edith and Greta were inconsolable as they watched from the other side of the road. When the ambulance arrived, they'd made their way over, arm in arm; each other's support.

"I'm afraid, he didn't make it." was the confirmation the ladies did not want to hear. A couple of the women, mothers themselves, tried to console the ladies as they became the centre of attention, blubbering incoherently at the death of a precious one.

* * * *

Margaret walked forlornly up the road, her mind lost in thought, a bottle of red wine in one hand and a carrier bag with other goodies, in the other. As she viewed the scene in front of her the bottle fell from her hand, smashing on the pavement, sending cheap Rioja cascading like a torrent over the curb, as she stood glued to the spot. Tears started to fall as she saw Edith and Greta being consoled.

She couldn't move, she felt numb.

Margaret caught Edith's eye and the old lady walked towards her, her eyes pleading. "We're so sorry. We don't know what happened. One minute he …"

"Edward," Margaret said, the name a faint whisper.

She rushed up to the ambulance man, but his solemn face said it all. She fought with him to hold her child. The motherly bond stronger than she could ever have thought possible, something she thought would be alien to her, but had come so naturally although she'd fought it, changing her life; in fact, it made her more determined to carry on as before.

The burly policeman tried to get some information from her, but the emotion wouldn't stop coming, the tears rolling incessantly.

Suddenly, a car's headlights shone like searchlights on the crowd, making people turn.

* * * *

Sam drove towards the guesthouse, although he couldn't remember any of the journey; in fact he struggled to recollect the whole day. He hated the way the fugue states stole whole periods of time from him; he'd always found notes to back up any meetings, yet it still scared him. Pulling up, he saw the crowd of people first, then the ambulance, then Edith and Greta – crying. A prickle of fear ran though him. He pulled up short of the crowd and slowly got out. He saw the car in the wall and relaxed, then saw Margaret in the back of the ambulance. Fear gripped him like a vice and he ran to her.

"Margaret, what's happened? Margaret?" Tears were streaming down her cheeks. He pulled her into his arms audibly wincing in pain as she hugged him tight for comfort.

Broken briefly from her despair she pushed him slightly away and looked at her husband, "Are you okay?"

"Yes, I think I must have fallen over and bruised or cracked a rib, but I don't recall how or when." He answered distractedly. "What's going on?"

"Edward's de…" The words faltered and she buried her head in Sam's neck. As he looked to Edith and Greta they bowed their heads ashamedly.

"No, no, he can't be. No, no, please tell me no." He looked to the ground where a body lay respectfully covered. "No!"

Chapter 116

1977 November
Devon
Paignton

Numbly, he let go of Margaret and walked over to where Edward's body lay. Staring disbelievingly at it. "It can't be," he mumbled.

He turned and stared at the crowd of people consoling Edith and Greta, tears streaming down their cheeks as they comforted each other. As if his brain was trying to protect him from the cascade of emotion inside, he tried to reconcile his memory of the drive. Then reality struck.

He gently pulled the coat off Edward to look at his son. Tears started to fall. "No, no, no ..." The heaving sobs instantly quietening the crowd.

He looked up at the sea of faces waiting for an explanation. Then he saw that the passenger door of the car was open and, on the passenger seat, he inexplicably recognised a blue paint stain.

"That's my car!"

Someone in the crowd overheard.

"Hey, it's his car. The driver's here! You deserve to be hanged!" The angry man's shout turned the crowd into a hungry mob.

"Oi, the driver's here." Another boisterous voice called to the burly copper standing nearby. Sam felt two strong hands grab him.

"What are you ...?" He answered surprised at being manhandled so indignantly. "It's my ... stop it, let go of me." However his cries were lost in the haze of irate voices.

Another policemen, who had been questioning people, tried to step in; yet it was too late to stop the first punch landing on Sam's face. The policeman called for order but struggled to be heard over the mêlée of furious rants, as blows rained down on Sam.

Margaret sprang from the ambulance. "Leave my husband, he's innocent!"

Another officer joined the fight to protect Sam, who was now in the foetal position on the ground, hands covering his head.

The burly policeman finally managed to breakthrough, wielding his truncheon as a warning to anyone who tried to fight him. Sam relaxed as the blows slowly diminished, unable to decide what hurt more as every bruise started to yield its pain.

"Thank you …" he tried to say but his jaw hurt and his voice so quiet the policeman didn't hear it. Then shock registered again as he found himself being hauled up roughly and handcuffs slapped on his wrists. "Arghh …!" He screamed in pain as his ribs smarted.

"I think you'd better come with us." The burly officer said.

"What the hell are you doing?" Sam tried to plead as he was frog-marched to an awaiting police car; yet his face was already swelling up, blood seeped from a couple of cuts. "Let me go. Let me …"

Margaret caught up with them. "Where are you taking my husband?" She grabbed the arm of the officer, who was about to swing out to protect himself, when he stopped just in time, realising who it was.

"Miss, you heard the people. I thought you would be pleased that we are arresting …"

"He's just arrived. They're mistaken. It is not him."

For an instant the officer appeared to take her pleas on board and look set to relent. But then, seeing the angry mob, changed his mind to a different tack. "Well, in that case he'll be able to corroborate his story down at the station." Sensing her next argument. "We'll get him some medical attention there."

Margaret stood, stunned as the officer forced him into the back of the squad car. Sam turned to Margaret, his nose bleeding, a cut above his right eye and his clothes dirty and torn. He wanted to take her up in his arms and console her for the loss of their child. He couldn't believe that it was their old car that had killed their son. A feeling that God was against them drove a stake through his heart.

* * * *

"I remember that." Sam said to Geoff as they watched the police car pull away.

"They also found a coat and hat just like the ones that you own, dumped near the scene, in an alley."

Sam replied, "I know, they kept me in for two days. They wouldn't believe me. I wasn't allowed to speak to Margaret. She needed me.

She moved our belongings out of the guesthouse, not able to face Edith and Greta. It was just too painful. Eventually, they had to let me go. All the evidence backed up my story. Luckily, they rang my office and my customer confirmed where I had been before the accident. They had to let me go.

Then another officer came and asked me questions a few days later, no, it was a detective ..." Sam paused trying to pull the name from a memory he had, "William, Patri... Paul. Oh, bloody hell what was his bloody name? Trampton, no Davis ... no,no Tra, Travers, Travis!" he concluded resolutely. "Yes, William! William Travis. Yes, Detective Travis. How could I forget? He'd been following this serial killer case for a few years, and nearly all the evidence, in some form or other kept pointing back to me – and now I know why."

The road Geoff and Sam were standing on disappeared and they found themselves in a small but quaint bedroom, adorned with pine furniture. Margaret sat on the well-worn bed, her eyes still raw from crying, Sam stood looking forlornly out of the window.

* * * *

"Mike rang earlier asked us if we want to join him later today. Roger and Sarah should arrive this afternoon, after his conference." Sam's words weren't buoyed with any enthusiasm. His world numb, conversation wasn't something he could properly comprehend.

"Oh. I don't think I can face them with their kids." Margaret answered, solemnly.

"We can stay ..." Sam broke down in tears for the second time that morning as more memories of Edward flooded back, and the plans they'd had for the week with, Mike, Roger and Sarah and their kids. It was meant to be a chance to kick back and enjoy a week of family fun. Mike had strangely wanted to tag along, and they hadn't thought it a bad idea. He liked the kids, enjoyed playing with them.

A knock at the door broke the melancholy. Sam despondently opened it, his ribs still hurting. One was cracked, and the bruising on his face had started to darken – it now looked as though it had been used as a football. He desperately tried to recall what had happened. How can you fall over and not remember? Slowly, he opened the door, not really wanting to see anyone.

Before he had time to offer any greeting a disgruntled voice addressed him.

"Samuel Talbot. I think you know who I am?"

Sam looked wearily at the man before him, no semblance of recognition. "No."

"Oh, come on Sam, this is the third time that evidence has led to you. You don't recognise your old friend, Detective Inspector Travis." Travis' sarcasm was lost on Sam, as his dejected expression didn't falter. "Doesn't even take the trouble to commit my face to memory, yet I still remember my first day on the job. But you don't care, do you?"

Margaret appeared at the door, her raw eyes showing disdain for the man she recognised. "How can we help you?" She offered sternly.

"We have a few questions for your husband Mrs Talbot. Please accept my condolences for your loss, I realise it is a hard time but this is important." His voice was flat with a hint of sympathy when addressing Margaret.

"When will you leave my husband alone? How can you even believe he had anything to do with the death of his own ..." Sam pulled her into his shoulder and grimaced as pain ricocheted around his body.

"Can't this wait?" His words were emotionless.

Travis focussed back onto Sam. "Actually, no it can't. We have what appears to be a serial killer on the loose for nigh-on fourteen years and the only leads we ever get lead straight back to you, Mr Talbot. I find that rather strange, don't you?" Travis let the question settle. "Now are you going to come peacefully?" The menace was veritable.

Sam wanted to fight; however, he found the resilience to acquiesce pushing Margaret gently away.

"I won't be long, dear. Okay?"

Margaret's answer was a reluctant nod.

Chapter 117

1977 December

Lincolnshire

Storage Yard

Paignton: A disaster. Edward is dead. I killed him. It was an accident, pure and simple. It is strange, a bit like that feeling when I set Sheila on her path with the train. A numbness.

It had been so well thought out, there is a gay club I'd heard about, I thought it would provide an excellent opportunity. I already had the excuse of a day's business already in the mix; that gave me a clear twenty-four hour window to get back here, deposit the body and return – everyone none the wiser. I'd checked the club out early, just to be sure, as it had been a while since I was last there. Someone must have spiked my drink. When I left, I felt peculiar. I didn't see Edward; he should not have been out on the road.

I think I was too dumbounded when I saw who it was. I nearly didn't leave as the crowd gathered. Then it was like fate was helping me. As the crowd grew and I found myself outside of it. I ran, dumped the coat, hat and scarf. It was a big risk and one I will not take again; it was too close for comfort.

As for tonight, all I can do is check on Andrew Smith-Jones, who will not be getting a companion for a while.

Chapter 118

1977 November

Devon

Sam sat in the cold interrogation room. Travis had read him his rights and then promptly left him to stew whilst he and his partner, Detective Hampton, went and grabbed a coffee.

* * * *

"Do you remember this interview room?" Geoff asked as he and Sam watched the grey figure of his past self contemplate his future. "You kept thinking you were going mad."

"It's not really surprising is it? All the blank parts of my memory were like someone ripping the pages out of my life, and I couldn't remember any of the crimes. I started to believe I'd done it. I think I even believed I'd killed my son! A part of me wondered, hoped they could provide me with solid proof so not even I could question it. If they'd had CCTV in those days, like now, then that would have been a blessing in disguise, unequivocal evidence staring me straight in the face of what I did during my blackout phases."

"They did have evidence though, didn't they?"

"Yes, but it was still circumstantial and they knew it."

"You do remember this interview though, don't you?" Sam looked quizzically at Geoff then turned to look at his younger self, desolate and frightened.

* * * *

The door burst open and Travis and his partner walked in, Sam didn't even look at them.

"Mr Talbot, Sam, what are we going to do, eh?" The question was sardonic. "We're looking forward to finally wrapping this case up and unravelling what is really going on. Of course, it would be easy if you just came clean."

Sam locked eyes with Travis. "If you have proof then please just show it. My son is dead and I need to be with my wife. His mother."

Sam sat sternly. "This is the third time …"

"Oh, you do remember then?" Travis spat the words out with bitter sarcasm.

"You think I don't want to remember. You think it doesn't tear me up inside, being accused of things I know nothing about?" Just as his anger reached a crescendo, "You think I would want to kill my own son?" Sam leaned over the table eye to eye with Travis, tears streaking his cheeks.

Travis kept eye contact, not wavering. "I think you are a very clever man. Fourteen years, ten victims – that we know of – unceremoniously dumped anytime between six months to two years after they disappeared." Travis relished the inexorable pleasure as he sensed the finale coming.

"So you say." Sam sank back into his chair. "I know it wasn't me."

Travis felt anger start to wile its way into him; he fought against it as hard as he could as the image of Susan Jones flashed up in his mind. "Mr Talbot, this case has haunted me since the day I started the job, the very day! Do you know what sort of a scar it leaves on a fresh mind? No, you probably don't. Probably don't care, that is something I have learnt over the years, your sort never do." Travis folded his arms, all too aware that he wanted to punch the guy sitting opposite; he had to fight it. "But, do you know what? We've got you this time!" Sam's eyes widened. "We've, I've taken quite an interest in your life, Mr Talbot, as more bodies have turned up, innocent victims." Venom started to creep back into Travis's voice. "And there are anomalies that you may think are coincidences, but that I know are the truth."

"Then please, just tell me, or let me go. I need to be with my wife. We've just lost our son to some person who you are letting escape. And, while we're at it," Travis sat back in his chair knowing the evidence he was getting ready to bring in any second, "you let the driver escape and arrested me instead. I arrived after the incident, too late to do anything. MY son is dead! DEAD!" Sam's eyes told the story of an angry father.

"Yes, and it must be hurting you like crazy." Travis paused for the slightest moment. "Knowing that you did it?"

Sam seethed. "Just get on with it."

"Detective Hampton, please."

The next minute appeared to last for an hour as Hampton left room, leaving Travis and Sam staring at each other like two cats getting ready to pounce. Hampton returned with a clear plastic bag.

Sam looked on horrified.

Travis noticed the look. "So, you do recognise them, then?" Travis took the plastic bag from Hampton and placed it on the table between Sam and himself.

* * * *

Disbelievingly, Sam grabbed the bag containing a raincoat, scarf and flat cap; they looked familiar. He pawed the bag as his mind cogitated the implications. Had he really done it? How? Had he killed his son? If so, how on earth could he blank that information out? Each thought spun at a million miles an hour, as he tried to decipher what was real and what was – maybe – a fabrication his mind was creating. Had he run over his son then run away and got in another car, all so innocently? He needed to look at his notes, his diary to confirm he was where he said he was at the time he said he was there. But they had confirmed it all. Every time he'd been questioned the alibis tallied. How can this be?

Travis stared at Sam, a look of triumph on his face.

Torment started to rage in Sam's eyes. He didn't want to believe it, but the raincoat and flat cap were definitely his, although he had not worn the flat cap for years. But the coat! He turned it over; there was the ink stain, just visible on the inner tartan lining, from a fountain pen; he remembered how lucky it had been that it hadn't soaked through to the outside.

"No, no, no ..." Sam heard himself saying calmly, but the words were an angry protest as he screwed up the coat in his hands.

"Now, Sam, something is not right." Travis continued.

"You're bloody telling me. I'm innocent." Sam almost faltered unconvincingly.

"I don't believe you're operating by yourself. There's no way you can be in two places at once." Sam looked up, still holding the coat. "So the simple question is, who is your accomplice, or accomplices?"

"What? I ..."

"Don't want to snitch on them?" Travis mocked. "Maybe it is your wife, or your friend Michael." Sam stared questioningly at Travis. "Don't worry, we are checking them out, again. Maybe it is your twin brother, or sister. I have still not been able to trace what happened to them. Vanished off the face of the planet. It's all a bit strange. But, from what I've gathered, your whole family is. Your father was a bit a troublemaker, wasn't he? Liked a drink, liked to throw a punch here and there. Although he was not a clever man, not keen on family either, from what I have gathered about him."

Sam let go of the bag and crumpled back into the chair. "What are you talking about?"

Hampton interjected, his high-pitched voice not having any force with it. "You don't even remember your brother and sister, you were one of three, Mr Talbot."

Suddenly, a faint memory fired a shot in his head; something that was buried very deeply as it had never been spoken about but, suddenly, as Travis had mentioned it, it came screaming back from the dead. "My sister died immediately after birth. I don't recall a brother being mentioned."

Travis was quick to jump. "So you do have a sister. First you say you don't; then you say you do. What else are you not telling us, Mr Talbot? Eh, Sam? You act innocent, but you are not."

Sam started to rub his hands together nervously; the loss of his son, the loss of a sister he'd never even known. A brother? He was sure he didn't recall a brother being mentioned; his parents didn't really talk about his sister, why would they talk about a brother?

"You look guilty." Hampton continued playfully.

"I don't know what is going on but I am innocent."

"How can you be? This is your coat, and your cap – Yes? At the scene you confessed that it was your car."

"It was, yes, my friend Mike sold it for me, he can tell you."

"Sounds like you're reaching for the truth, Sam. Maybe you need some time to get your story straight."

"I didn't do anything. Nothing."

"I am not sure the victims would have so little to say if they could talk. If they could, it would be so simple. What did it feel like, experimenting on them, whilst they were alive? Taking their organs? What exactly, were you researching?"

Sams eyes widened in horror as his mind raced to Mike's lab, which was all he could think of. "What … we …?" His jaw bounced up and down as he searched frantically for an answer that didn't make things worse.

Hampton leaned forward. "It may be best just to confess. The courts will go easy on you, maybe do a deal." He pushed a pad towards Sam who looked up questioningly. "Just write it all down. In your own words."

After what felt like minutes of silence, "We were …" Sam stopped. It sounded bad in his head. They had done everything above board, the cadavers, organs, everything. "I think I need to speak to a solicitor."

Travis breathed in heavily and got up.

"Fine. Let's get his wife in for some questioning." Sam's eye's followed them and the evidence to the door. "Stick him in a cell for few hours. Maybe that will loosen his tongue – a taste of what is to come."

The door slammed shut, leaving Sam floundering in a cold sweat.

* * * *

"Well?" Geoff said with an air of satisfaction. "Do you remember your friends all being interviewed?"

"Of course I remember, it was so bloody embarrassing. I wanted to bury my son, but they charged me. They knew they didn't have a case – it was all circumstantial. But they let me stew inside for a few weeks. It was the hardest time of my life. A horrible place. Interviews with barristers and doctors, lots of doctors, psychiatrists as well." Sam paused before solemnly continuing. "Margaret came to visit, I saw the pain etched on her face. I wasn't even allowed to bury my own son."

Sam looked at the sad figure of his younger self, reliving the feeling of desolation that racked him that day.

Geoff broke Sam's reverie. "The supportive wife eh?"

"They kept asking me about my brother. I didn't know anything about a brother. I'd forgotten about my sister. They showed me the birth certificates. There was nothing in my parents' stuff; my mother's letters didn't mention it. I did remember, as a child, pretending I had a brother but always put it down to the usual childish games."

"I can tell you, you did."

Chapter 119

1977 November

Liverpool
CID

William sat at his desk, a jumble of thoughts whizzing through his head. He needed to bolster the case against Sam Talbot. It was so thin; a coat and cap would not please CPS, even if Sam admitted to owning them. Some leniency had been given in allowing him to be held on remand, due to the nature of the case and pressure from the top brass and public. Susan Jones and Peter Hittles were the only two victims that they could clearly place as seeing Sam on the day of their disappearance; and they had the manslaughter of Edward Talbot, his son, and the car. Whilst William loved the idea of finally having someone for the murders; a little boy's death, however ironic – did not rest easy on his shoulders. Margaret Talbot was due in later for an interview, so he started to prepare with his first coffee, a nectar from the Gods, as he organised his day mentally. Not that the day would stay as planned, hence these reposes, allowing him to prepare; putting aside anything that was going on at home: kids, money worries, etc. It was almost a meditation that set the mood, keeping him even throughout the day, something he had learned to do not long after starting in '63, much to the mockery of colleagues who often saw him sitting quietly in a corner, sometimes with his eyes closed. They couldn't argue with the results; he very rarely lost his rag with the scumbags that they had to deal with, or turn back to drink like when he'd first struggled to cope with Susan Jones.

* * * *

William sat down stiffly opposite Margaret.

"Thank you for coming in."

"I didn't exactly get a choice, did I? And Liverpool is a long way."

"No, and yes, but if it helps your husband ..."

"When are you going to stop harassing me and my husband? We have a funeral to arrange." Margaret sat with her hands clasped on the table.

William sat stony-faced, with detective Hampton next to him.

"Never, if he is found guilty so you may as well get used to it." William was almost stunned by his own coldness. "We don't believe your husband is acting on his own, hence our search this morning."

"Fine! You won't find anything. My husband is innocent."

"We'll see. Now I do have some questions about you that I want answered."

"That's nice for you. You're the detective, detect."

"That's just it, we can't find out too much about you, Mrs Talbot. Contrary to my earlier findings. I find that strange. It is like you never existed. We have your driving licence details and tax records but there is little before that on public record."

Margaret looked at the wall behind William.

"So?"

William tensed.

"Are you purposefully being difficult?"

"You ask me a sensible question and something relevant and I will answer it."

"Do you want to be arrested for obstruction?" Margaret stared at William. William expected Margaret to be helpful; after all her husband was on remand for murder. "Mrs Talbot, if you and your husband are innocent, then answering a few questions might just resolve his current predicament quickly."

"A person is entitled to privacy. Anything on public record is there for the reading. I know my husband is innocent just as I know you do not have a case against him. I work for the MOD, detective, I have spoken with a lawyer and I know my rights. So, unless you have something more substantial, then let me go. If you think the government haven't done their background checks on me, then you'd be very much mistaken."

"Mrs Talbot, where were you on the night of 18th November 1965?"

"Is this what you are going to do, throw dates at me?"

"I have asked you a question, I expect an answer."

"I'm sure you do. However, as I have said, I work for the MOD and I am quite sure they will not appreciate me disclosing confidential information, as I have signed the official secrets act, so unless you have something concrete that does not involve me disclosing national secrets then may I go?"

"Not yet." William got up trying to disguise his annoyance. "I'll be back in a minute."

* * * *

"She's right." O'Neill conceded. "You'll get a brick wall if she signed the official secrets act, unless you have concrete proof that she has done wrong, then they'll throw her to the wolves and absolve themselves of any wrongdoing."

Exasperated, William left O'Neill's office, slumping back to his desk. He'd expected support and hated being told she was right. All he could hope for was that something turned up at the house search. Oh, well, he still had Michael to go, and he would be being picked up about now. The warrant had included his family home as well as his flat.

He rang down to Hampton and asked him to let Margaret leave, there was nothing more he could do, for now.

Michael was another interesting one; he and his sister, were adopted at birth, no biological parents known and the birth certificate was missing from the adoption records; mislaid. That would be one of the questions for later.

The phone broke his silence.

"CID. Travis."

"I hear congratulations are in order." The voice sounded familiar but it took a few seconds to register.

"Ron?" Travis queried.

"Absolutely. Thought I'd just congratulate you. Saw it in the morning papers. Although your name is not mentioned I am guessing it was you?"

"Not strictly speaking. But I am following it through in conjunction with CPS. I didn't know we had advised the press yet. We still have the house searches to do plus we think he is working in conjunction with friends, or maybe a twin."

"Good, keep at it; usually after long enough something comes out of the woodwork. I hear you're doing well. That keen mind of yours getting a few backs up according to Harris." Ron let it settle before continuing. "But, whilst he was a great drinking associate, he was always a jealous bastard and too lazy to makes waves in the right direction. I explained that to 'im once. Waste of breath. Of course I give full credit for your abilities to me." Ron laughed heartily and

William couldn't help but smile, he liked Ron. "Anyway good collar, I'm glad you can finally put that one to bed."

"Thanks. How's retirement treating you?"

"Great. If you like gardening and watching TV! I've taken a consultation job instead, far more interesting. Anyway best go. Keep up the good work."

"Thanks ..." But Ron had already hung up.

Suddenly the CID room door kicked open and in walked Harris and Williams ensconced in a heated debate about last nights' top of the pops.

"Golden boy here already." Harris chipped in, the usual sarcasm present.

"Give it a rest Harris. So what if he got a blagger, good for him. Well done on that catch." Williams countered.

"It wasn't really my catch, just hope CPS can run with it."

Williams threw his bag down at his desk. "It's been a long time coming and it's going to be through your evidence that he gets sent down. Accept the credit if I were you."

"Cheers." Travis responded.

"Arsewipe." Harris muttered.

Both Travis and Williams ignored him.

Chapter 120

1977 November

Liverpool
CID

"Mr Thompson, I hope you are going to be more co-operative than Mrs Talbot?"

"Depends. I don't appreciate having my flat turned over, or my parents' place."

"Needs must."

"Well, if it gets Sam out quicker, then maybe it was worth it." Mike surveyed the room. "Not what I expected."

William sat down. "Mr Thompson, what can you tell me about Samuel Talbot and his wife?"

Mike appeared surprised by the question. "Is that what I am here for, so you can get the low down on their marriage. Look, he didn't do the crimes that you are holding him for and I think it is particularly bad taste splashing his picture across the tabloids when he is innocent, it is hardly going to help his case is it?"

William breathed in. It had irked him that it had been released to the press, as the case was thin and, if it fell apart, it could be embarrassing and detrimental to his career; everyone remembers the ones that get away. True, it could open things up, but he wanted to get more facts first, be sure that CPS would get what the prosecution needed. If there was more than one murderer, then Sam could get away with it. Mike came across as a spoilt brat.

"Quite, then maybe you can help us help clear him." This was the tack he would play. "Firstly, I understand the Triumph Dolomite is, or was, his car and that you sold it on the Talbot's behalf approximately fourteen months ago."

"You want to talk to me about cars? I know my dad's firm is in car parts but really. My friend is being accused of murder."

"Yes, Mr Thompson, really I need to know who you sold the car to, as it is still showing as registered to Mr Sam Talbot."

Mike looked blank. "I don't know, some guy paid cash, picked it up when I wasn't there."

William really didn't like Michael. "Do you normally not pay attention to details when you're helping out a friend. How could they pay cash if you weren't there?"

"They dropped it off at the reception of my stepdad's firm, she gave him the keys. I'm a busy person; I try not to take life too seriously. It's too short; most people are honest enough, I thought the guy would do what he said and send the reg. document in, never heard anything so didn't give it a thought."

William paused. He was not in a rush, if this guy wanted to waste time, then fine.

"How long have you known Sam and Margaret?"

"Since med school."

"What do you know about their histories, prior to that?"

Mike shrugged. "Only what they tell me."

"You never asked?"

"I'm not nosy, if people want to tell me then fine but if they don't, it doesn't matter. He is my best mate, I like their company and that is all that matters."

"I see." William couldn't help thinking this guy was a waste of space, no wonder he didn't become a doctor – too much hard work. "Mr Thompson, can you please advise me why a guy who sells car parts for a living would order these?"

William pulled some sheets of paper from a folder, invoices for scalpels, liquid nitrogen and various other chemical and medical supplies.

"A hobby. Kind of." Mike answered, almost wearily.

"A hobby. Please describe this hobby." William leaned back expecting a colourful story.

"It's kind of our secret, a research project that five of us are doing, working towards a breakthrough in medical science. I have got a lab ..." William's ears were pinned back as he tried to hide his surprise at the revelation, "... on my stepdad's grounds, in one of the outbuildings. We meet up occasionally and try and solve the mystery of eternal life."

William's train of thought raced away; this was an admission.

"What kind of experiments?" DC Hampton asked.

"Mainly on dead animals, road kill, as Sarah won't let us touch live ones. Shame really, because we could really make some progress."

"Human organs?" William interjected casually, not sure what the answer would be.

"On the odd occasion, I kept in contact with someone at the college." "It's all above board, I got all the permissions and authorisations to handle human body parts and the like as a research facility."

"I think we will need to see those."

"Yeah, no problem."

"And Sam and Margaret were part of this?" DC Hampton interjected.

"Yes, we all chipped in, including Sarah and Roger."

There was a pause whilst William considered what to do next, glancing at DC Hampton. This could be the centre of operation, or at least close to it. Was Mike being overly open to avert the eye?

"Tell me, Mr Thompson, I understand you are adopted." Mike frowned, then nodded. "Did you ever look for your biological parents?"

"Frankly, no. They didn't want to know me or my sister, so I didn't want to know them." It was the first time Mike had shown any seriousness.

"That was your sister, Sheila, right? Not even curious if you had more brothers or sisters?"

"Sam and Margaret are the only family I need, they are as close to a brother and sister that I need. And yes, her name was Sheila."

William really wasn't sure what to make of Michael. "Can you wait here a minute, I just need to check something."

"Yeah, it's not like I have to be anywhere. Could I have a coffee? Will I be able to take Sam back with me?"

"Hampton can you arrange a coffee?" William left and hurried upstairs.

* * * *

"Yes, Travis." DCI O'Neill called from behind a mountain of paperwork.

"I've got a new lead. Michael Thompson, supposedly Sam Talbot's best friend, downstairs and his has just admitted they have got a lab set up on his stepfather's property, an outbuilding where they conduct experiments on body parts."

O'Neill almost dropped the mug he was sipping from. "And you think it may be where the bodies have been stored and operated on."

"Something is off. It is too easy. He is being too open, almost trying to throw us off. Yet he stills comes across as genuine though, which he either is, or is a bloody good actor." William paused as he tried to construct his thoughts.

"Spit it out."

"I think it might be a red herring but, if we don't check it out, CPS and the chief will have a field day if we miss something."

"Do you think he is playing us?"

"Maybe. Something is definitely screwy."

O'Neill nibbled at his mug. "Get the address and notify local to go in and seal it off. Take Hampton and go have a look around. And get a dog team lined up, and get something of the victims to see if they can't gee things up a little. I'll get that warrant extended."

* * * *

"Sorry to keep you waiting Mr Thompson."

"Not a problem."

Nothing seemed to faze the man and that rubbed William a little.

"We're going to need to take a closer look at your lab." William was hoping for a reaction.

"If you must. The animals were road kill though, we didn't kidnap them." Michael laughed.

William felt strangely uneasy. It was too easy.

Chapter 121

2002 July

"So that's how they found out about the lab. It never even occurred to me. He never said."

"You knew he had been interviewed though?"

"Yes, I just assumed they found it through investigating me."

"As persecuted as you thought you were, the police did actually follow other lines of enquiry; you weren't ever their only suspect. You were however, the only one that crossed paths with a few of the victims, which is why you tended to be top of the list. At times they had nearly two hundred officers all over the country working on this case."

"I just thought …"

"It's all about you?" Geoff asked snidely as the visiting room of the remand centre came into view. "Just like when Margaret came to visit whilst you were being held."

Chapter 122

1977 December
Remand Centre

"... innocent. Why are they still holding me Margaret? I didn't do these things. You know I could never hurt anyone." Sam pleaded.

Margaret took in the visitor room, a cold soulless void where lives seemed to be held in limbo. The last couple of weeks had been telling on her, her normally rosy features had lost their vibrancy, replaced with a battleship grey. Her eyes had a dullness to them that was enough to quell even the heartiest of laughs, as if hiding a truth.

This was her third visit, and she was finding it more and more uncomfortable in the surroundings. Edward's funeral was coming up and making the arrangements was hard alone; she wanted to put it off but it needed to be done. Sarah had helped where she could.

"You haven't even asked me about the funeral arrangements?" Margaret finally said. She had hardly spoken since arriving.

Sam sighed, his head and shoulders visibly sinking. "I'm sorry, I've been trying to get out of here but, because of the nature of the case, the courts have enacted special sanctions to hold me without further charge ..."

Margaret wasn't interested in his excuses. Sam reached across to hold her hand, which she instantly retracted, immediately regretting the gesture; however, she was unable to force herself to accept the offering. She was suffering a mixture of emotions she'd never expected to feel.

Stalemate reigned, as silence consumed them both.

Chapter 123

1977 December

Mike's Lab

Margaret sat next to Sarah, her mood sombre.

"Well, it's been a while since we've all been here." Sarah said, breaking the silence. They'd arrived to do some research in the hope of taking away the melancholy Sam's arrest was causing, yet no one could be motivated, and they had just sat down making pleasantries until even that had dissolved.

"Surprised they left it in one piece! Bloody dogs everywhere." Mike added

"What? Who?" Sarah looked agitated and clearly uncomfortable.

"The police. Spent two days searching the bloody place. I don't know what they hoped to find. And we're not all here. Are we? Sam? Roger?"

"Oh, you know what I mean."

"You mean what is assumed?"

"What is your bloody problem Mike? Are you being purposefully arrogant? Or is it just natural?" Sarah stormed.

"Actually, I'm pissed off that my best friend is being charged with something he didn't do and your husband, Roger, is more concerned about his bloody career." Mike responded loaded with anger. "Associating with a known murderer was what you said before Margaret turned up."

Sarah went red with rage and embarrassment. It is what she had said. Ever since Sam's arrest Roger had flatly refused to have anything to do with the group and didn't want the kids to see any of them. It had surprised her greatly.

"This isn't helping Margaret," was the only lame retort Sarah could think of.

"Helping! What can we do to help?" Mike offered kicking the bin. "I still can't believe it of him. He hardly has the killing instinct, or the nous to lead a secret double life without any of us knowing, especially

Margaret. Plus, I really believe they think we are all in on it."

Sarah suddenly looked shocked. She was as sharp as a razor at med school, intelligent and smart but, since leaving and having a family, she appeared to have dumbed down.

"Will you two give it a rest, you are doing my head in. Sam is innocent – there is no doubt. That will come out. I know it will. Mike is right about Sam." Margaret paused in thought. "And Roger is wrong and stupid for thinking otherwise, and quite frankly, I'm astonished that he would believe such a thing."

Defensively Sarah rallied. "So am I, Margaret. I know they say you can never really know people but I don't believe that for a second. Anyway you're married to him and I know that it is difficult to hide a double life, like that, from your spouse."

"I would never have accepted you as being naïve, Sarah." Mike blasted. "It's the easiest thing in the world if you really want to."

It was hard to believe that Sarah could get any redder. "No, it's not, Mike. Bloody hell what is wrong with you? You're really becoming a condescending arsehole. Is that what comes of joining the family firm? It's more likely to be you than any one of us; you keep going away on secret little business trips of late." Her tirade paused. "And in the past, actually; a lot in the past when I think about it."

"Great. I came here for a little support and friendship and it seems I have landed slap bang in the middle of the beginning of world war three. What would make you say that Sarah? Why would you even think it?"

Sarah sunk further into her chair. She'd had a turbulent time over the last few months; Roger had been working longer hours and she was getting jealous of his adult interaction. Being a full-time mother was what she wanted, but it lacked the adult conversation she needed. Mothers she met only talked about their kids. She felt insecure. When Roger and her did speak, he chimed on about how easy it must have been to disguise the murders using the 'fugue' excuse. When he had refused to have anything to do with them anymore, it had pushed the wedge between them even further and she wasn't sure what the future held.

"I think it best we all go our separate ways don't you?" Mike continued.

Sarah looked at him in astonishment.

"Oh," Sarah choked.

"Come on, Mike. Let's not …"

"No, Margaret. We're not getting anywhere. We haven't done since day one. No matter how hard we try. It was fun, I s'ppose. Originally. But let's not go down this route, I don't want to lose my friendships because of it."

Sarah gave an almost apologetic look. She understood and felt the same, though she could not bring herself to apologise.

A silence hung in the lab, only broken by the gentle hum and tick of the freezer.

"Say 'hi' to Sam for me please, Margaret, when you see him next. And I'm sorry about Edward, truly I am, I wish I could change that."

"Of course, Sarah."

Margaret stood up and grabbed her coat.

"Don't be strangers, either of you. Please be at the funeral next week. The solicitor has managed to secure time out for Sam so he can now attend, and he'd want to see you there." Margaret looked to Sarah. "Even if Roger won't come?"

"Yes." Sarah said quietly.

"Of course not, not strangers, that is, where else would I get my cooked brekkie before footie on a Saturday?" Mike jovially replied, but it didn't lift the mood.

Margaret left, followed a few seconds later by Sarah.

Chapter 124

1978 January
Remand Centre

Mike sat in the visitor's room waiting for Sam, drumming his fingers on the table. He wasn't even sure Sam would see him after so long, it had been over a month since Sam's arrest and this was the first contact he had tried to make. Guilt racked him; having been friends for years, he had the crazy notion that if he didn't see him, then it wasn't real. It had taken this long to see that wasn't the case.

As the minutes rolled on, he watched the quiet conversations taking place between the families and loved ones and drew the conclusion that some looked as guilty as sin itself, whilst others looked like they would break if you sneezed at them – bad circumstances maybe; a bit like Sam – wrong time, wrong place.

The chair opposite scraped, breaking his reverie and he looked up into the eyes of his friend. For a few seconds he didn't know what to say; which was not like him. Sam looked a shadow of his former self; older and frail with a couple of days' stubble sitting uncomfortably on his chin, his cheekbones more prominent than he could ever remember.

"How are you doing?" he asked lamely as Sam sat down crossing his arms.

"What do you think?" came the curt retort. "Rotting in this stink hole for something I never did. Knowing that most don't believe me, yet I can't seem to be able to convince them of that."

Then, even more lamely, Mike added. "I thought they'd let you out on bail?"

"Is that why you haven't visited?" Sam accused.

Mike swallowed hard, ashamed.

"No. It's just ..." Mike desperately raked his brain for a substantial argument, none yielded. "I'm sorry."

After a long silence Mike continued. "How are you holding up in here?"

The hardness in Sam's eyes relaxed a little.

"I get by … just. " He looked around then lowered his voice. "There is a guard who keeps an eye on me."

"Is it as hard as I've seen on TV?"

"It is not prison, it is just a remand centre. We are kept away from some of the real heavies. You still have to be careful though."

"I was going to bring you some cigarettes."

"I haven't started smoking for something to do."

Mike felt a little foolish. "I just thought you could use it as currency."

"How's Margaret holding up?"

"You know she is as tough as nails. Although I think she is worried about money to finance your defence."

Sam sighed. "That's our savings going up in smoke."

"She must love you, though, as she has the best defence she can get. No expense spared." Mike almost succeeded in sounding buoyant, "and I've chipped in as well."

Sam shook his head. "What is going on? How did I end up in here? I'm innocent." A tear escaped his right eye.

Mike shrugged, not knowing what to say, before adding. "It will all work out. The truth *will* come out." To try and lighten the mood, Mike changed the subject to cover his own awkwardness. "Aerosmith's fifth album came out in December it's really good. Of course, I had to import it from America – we really don't get them over here."

Sam smiled. "I'm so envious of your trips to America, I'd love to go one day. The rate you love some of their music you ought to move there."

"Cheers mate, you trying to get rid of me? I'm one of the few that believe your innocence." It was said with joviality that had the opposite effect. "Sorry, foot in mouth syndrome."

"I know a doctor who can sort that for you!"

They laughed heartily, attracting attention.

"I'll take you one day, to America, when you get out."

"Thanks. I'm not sure I'm getting out anymore."

"What's your brief say?"

"He doesn't believe they've got a strong case, and the only reason CPS are pursuing it, is because of public pressure."

"Then you'll get out. It'll be fine."

"I wish I had your confidence."

Chapter 125

2002 July

"You and Mike were close, weren't you?" Geoff was flicking through the radio stations looking for something more rocking. Suddenly the loud grinding of loud guitars and the thick heavy pounding of a bass drum filled the car. "What the hell is that?"

"I think they call it, thrash metal." Sam answered looking melancholy.

"Rubbish, that's what it is. Where are the Stones? The Who?"

"Bit old hat, although they are still going. And yes, Mike and I were close. Why?"

"Did it never occur to you why he never married?"

"Not at the time."

"He didn't tell you everything though did he?"

"Like what?"

"Him being gay."

"Yes, he did."

"Only recently though, he never mentioned it before did he?"

"No. So what. He took time probably finding himself. Plus, he'd always had lots of girlfriends, although we never met many of them. I also think he liked being single, liked his independence. I think it was a hangover from losing his sister and the way his adoptive parents were with each other."

"He was in love with you."

"I don't think so." Sam denied.

"Why not? How long is this motorway, seems to go on forever?" Geoff found a station playing something rocking, but not too heavy. "Ah, this is better. Who is it?"

"Bon Jovi, I think.

"Why is it so hard to believe? Don't look so astounded by the revelation that Mike loved you."

"I doubt it."

"Unrequited love – it's quite romantic really. The longer you live with something, the harder it can become to admit to it, I guess. Sometimes to love from afar can be better than the reality."

"I don't believe it."

"That's up to you. You still don't believe the images you've seen."

"No, I must say I have my doubts."

Chapter 126

1978 February
Liverpool
CID

William reflected on the news of Sam Talbot's imminent release, feeling sick to the pit of his stomach.

Christmas had been a washout, snow had created chaotic travel conditions and the family day that had been planned got cancelled. New year hadn't been much better when a body was found on New Year's Eve. As it went, it proved an open and shut case and was over in two days. There was a smouldering melancholy in the office, as everyone wanted to roll the clock back.

William was once again boxing up the case that was fast becoming a millstone in his career. Sam Talbot was to walk free after CPS called it a day, due to lack of evidence; the special sanctions to hold Sam for nearly two months had been rescinded and the charges dropped, knowing they'd never secure a conviction based on current evidence alone. They couldn't even prove Sam had been driving the Triumph Dolomite on the night that his son had been killed. Whilst he'd admitted to openly owning the car, a receptionist – as per Michael's statement – confirmed the transaction she'd played her part in. The search of Mr Thompson's lab had turned up nothing, everything was above board, the paperwork was completely in order, even the human organs – which had buoyed the detectives moods briefly – proved to have a traceable and legitimate history: invoices for medical supplies, scalpels all checked out with B Collins, an established medical supply firm. All the right licences were in place to operate the lab, and it had been registered under all their initials, which is why it had not turned up in earlier investigations. Bank accounts all checked out, funds etc. Hundreds and hundreds of hours of police work and not a damn thing out of place!

The case was doomed to haunt him. Worse, there was no rest for the victims. The evidence boxes were their final resting place, metaphorically; at least until another body turned up. TV cops and police shows made it look so easy; one hour and it was solved – even the books he read had a conclusion, this looked as though it never would.

The families appeared in the papers every now and then appealing for information, Susan's father rang him once a year; it was now sixteen years since her disappearance. He sighed wearily. He knew eventually it would get passed to the murder review board – affectionately known as Ghost.

Chapter 127

1978 July
Lincolnshire
Storage Yard

It has been a strenuous few months. I have been careful about coming back and am delaying returning the bodies, or taking any new ones.

Our research group has stalled; hopefully we will get back soon. I feel vindicated that they didn't trace some of the specimens I'd brought; our paperwork appeared satisfactory for them. But where are we? Certain tissues are easily and readily frozen and thawed, in fact it is already being used in modern medicine for blood and semen. However, organs remain a difficult conundrum. The cryopreservatives we, and I, have tried do not help – the organs will not survive the process. I am having limited success with a process I call RA59 – a heating cycle that has shown potential in two organs, thyroid and liver, certainly raising the temperature where ice crystals start to form. I used it in conjunction with an additive of the cryopreservative, KF2R, and it is the closest I have come to a breakthrough. Cell structure damage was lessened and the ice crystals that formed were smaller, although damage was still fatal; cell structure more resilient. This makes me wonder whether the experiments conducted by the group using Roger's friend's gene strengthener XSR1 & XSR2 would work now! Combining it with the heating process could prove to be the small step I have been looking for. I need to try and increase the dose of additive KF2R although, in the theory, it is still toxic at higher levels. If I can balance that out with XSR 1 or 2 – it might work.

Developing the heating system further will cost a lot of money and this may be where I need the group to come in with funding. What will it cost though? I will do some investigating.

Chapter 128

1980 June
Norfolk
Diss

"Hopefully, now we can finally live a normal life." Margaret stated as they opened the door to yet another home, their fifth in two years. Turbulent times had followed his release without charge, with some members of the public not believing his innocence and, upon discovering a home address, made it their duty to make life very unpleasant.

She looked at Sam, who was a shadow of his former self. Work had been supportive and allowed him to take an office based position to avoid any undue biased reaction from customers; it was a disappointing state of affairs that only added to his low self-esteem. He'd started to use his middle name, Jacob, which had made things easier when on the phone; face-to-face meetings he was still wary of. There had been only one member of staff who didn't quite believe in his innocence and refused to have anything to do with him; a short while later they'd left the company.

Margaret turned to Sam as they stood on the doorstep "I hate this as much as you do but, since our home was fired bombed, renting seems the obvious answer – with the added advantage of being able to relocate relatively quickly, if needed. It will be forgotten eventually. You're innocent."

"So why does it feel as though I am guilty? Everyone thinks I am guilty. I can't get away from it." He paused. "How do I know I didn't do it, I don't remember, remember?

"Sam, we've got to stay strong, positive." Margaret looked at Sam's forlorn face. "There is a positive, we get to christen our new bedroom."

Sam seemingly ignored the comment. "Is it worth unpacking." He sighed wearily. Then suddenly anger burst forth. "I am sick of this. I have done nothing wrong. I AM innocent; they found nothing! Why can't people just let me get on with my life." An old couple walking past stared upon hearing Sam's outburst

"It will get easier Sam."

"I hate it. I hate work. What have I done to deserve this, eh?" He jerked his shoulder away from Margaret's hand and stomped inside, leaving her standing on the step of their new – temporary? – home.

"Life can be so cruel," she announced to no one in particular and followed Sam inside, where he was unpacking the kettle.

"Why don't you change jobs? You know, a new company, a new start?"

"Who would employ me? If they don't recognise the face, they'll recognise the name. I'm bloody lucky I've still got my old job. Marcello is a good boss. It's just, I want to be back on the road again, not stuck behind some stupid sodding desk, putting orders through the ledger books like a bloody administrator!"

Margaret looked at her husband trying to find something consoling to say. Sam's eye's had a glazed look about them and a nerve in his cheek spasmed. Margaret knew the sign, it was another fugue state coming on, she had witnessed the signs only a few times over the years.

"Sam, are you alright?" He looked at her, his eyebrows knitted together in a pained expression. "Sam. Sam?"

"What! Yes, of course I'm alright. Where are we?"

"Our new house. We're moving in today."

"That's not for another week."

"No, it's today."

"We were only discussing it last night."

"No, Sam, we were packing what little we have, last night, a week ago."

"No, Mike's coming over tonight."

"That was last week." Wearily Margaret took the kettle from him.

"I suppose you don't remember my course this week either? I know you hate being alone the first week in a new place."

"Course? You're away?"

"Yes, you know, I've got that weeklong conference near York, Beningbrough Hall."

"Great, I don't even remember moving here and we don't even get to spend the first week in this new place together. I hate being alone in a new place, unpacking and sorting everything out."

"I'm sorry, but I can't just cancel work, can I? Anyway, it's important. We have a professor coming and he's got some new information on a project I'm working on."

"What project?"

Margaret turned away from him to unpack some mugs and the teapot. "You know I can't tell you."

"There should never be secrets between a husband and wife."

"Secrets are good, keep things exciting." She sashayed playfully up to him.

They kissed. His mood softened.

"Oh, come on, your work is so much more interesting than mine, it always has been."

"You should have studied harder then. It may have taken you longer but, I'm sure if you had stuck with it, you would have got there in the end."

"I was never clever enough, you know that, even with yours, Roger's and Mike's help I struggled. Now where's the tea or coffee?"

"Why don't you see Mike this week, see if he's got anywhere further with our project, it's been a while since we've got together, that will occupy your time."

"Have we got any milk?"

"Bugger, no. I'll go and get some later. Oh, I'll just have it black for now. Now what was so funny?"

"Can't say, it's top secret. He'd kill me if I said anything."

"Fine, be like that." Margaret went to the window to look at the overgrown garden; it was small, although it could be nice with a bit of work.

"Do you want to know?"

"No, not really. Unlike you, Sam, I'm happy for you to have some secrets, if you want."

"He was saying …"

"No, I don't want to know now."

"Well, I'm telling you anyway."

"Not listening." She put her hands up playfully to her ears although she was interested.

"You sure?"

"Just bloody tell me if you're going to."

"He managed to get a rat electrified, like a puppet. Plugged into the mains like it was some strange toy. He'd implanted these two probes into its dead body, one was in the head and one in the heart, then did something ... I must say, completely lost me. But the end result was the rat walked for about four seconds."

"On its own?"

"Yes. Until it burst into flames. He called it a 'Frankenrat Flambée'. It did fry all the electrics in the lab though."

"We could use someone like him on our team; Trevor – the team captain, as he likes to be known ..." She smiled, insincerely. "... wouldn't know a new idea if it was injected into his brain. Still won't have to deal with him too much longer. His wife's pregnant with their first ..." Margaret broke off as she thought of their late son Edward.

Sam stared at her, before pulling her into his arms.

Chapter 129

1980 June

Lincolnshire
Storage Yard

The storage yard seems to have a new ambience about it with the bad element seemingly gone – probably prison – and, judging by the overheard conversations, the yard is taking on a more respectable note. I pay by cash on time – with the exception of a blip a couple of years ago – and the guy reluctantly accepts that I will not do it any other way. Ironically I almost feel like a villain for not co-operating! He does ask what I do and I fob him off with all manner of lies. The mechanic has finally left as well, free from Shaker, I am not surprised, there is another in his place, he seems all right.

The two freezer units have remained empty for too long. The experiments were proving fruitless, and the potential court case was a little too close for comfort. Maybe I had been foolish to return the bodies instead of just disposing of them. A wake-up call that even I couldn't ignore, despite the lust I still feel for it, the pleasure.

Edward's death is a dark shadow over everything; tainting all the work.

I am not sure what I am going to do now. This lab is under equipped. I have paid up for the year and advised the guy, Harry, that I would not be back for a while.

My meticulously detailed notebooks are full of useful analysis, yet it is like trying to isolate one single grain of brown flour from a bag of white. Results of tissue samples show that cell structure is still the biggest issue before anything else can be addressed, despite the positives that some cryopreservatives have shown. The ice crystal formation can be limited upon freezing – but not upon thawing! This is regardless of whatever cryopreservative is used to replace or add to the blood before freezing; it only changes the temperature at which it happens.

I feel like a demented scientist, flicking from page to page, notebook to notebook, believing there is something that I'm missing.

What is the missing spark that will unravel the mystery?

Flinging the notebooks across the storage space I send a lamp, one that occasionally added more illumination to the workbench, crashing to the floor – the bulb explodes in a dazzling fizz of energy.

* * * *

"What is the point of bringing me back here?" Sam asked Geoff.

"The mad scientist at work." Geoff replied antagonistically.

"Yes, if what you have shown me is the truth, then it is not in dispute."

"I can only show you the truth." Geoff answered, nonchalantly.

Sam asked, "When is this?"

"This is the Wednesday after you moved into your new house."

"Makes sense. What is the point to the exercise? What exactly is going to happen now? "

"To understand. This is your journey?" Geoff scowled. They watched the figure on the ground picking up the now broken lamp.

An intense heat erupted in Sam as he heard the cries of the victims, feeling every bit of their wrath, the pain that their families had felt for their loss.

"Alright, alright, make it stop." Sam screamed, walking towards the figure as the pain he felt grew to an electrifying, scorching torrent. Sam swung at the figure standing by the bench.

* * * *

In the blackness I can sense someone, an ominous presence.

"Am I going mad?"

* * * *

"Please stop it. What do I need to do to make amends?" It was a simple question to Geoff. Sam's emotions were on fire deep down and, in a sudden explosion, he swung his fists at the figure in the unit as if it would stop all of this.

* * * *

I shudder. Something about tonight is creeping me out. This is my lab. I am safe here.

* * * *

"I think it's definitely time to move on." Geoff announced.

* * * *

I walk across and gather up the notebooks, it is time to go, for now.

* * * *

Sam and Geoff watch the figure walk over to where the books had come to rest, carefully picking them up and straightening their pages from where they had creased as they had skidded across the floor.

* * * *

"What am I missing? What's that final key? Maybe I should try one more, just one more before I give up completely."

The power has a pull. I don't want to resist.

* * * *

"NO!" Sam screamed as a thousand torturing thoughts tumbled through timeless memories, constantly rearranging themselves into neat little storyboards. The more he punched at the figure, the more he saw them react painfully to his scorn; dropping the books again as a spasm of pain ricocheted through them, and Sam felt part of a soul flow from him into the figure. It was an awe-inspiring moment and suddenly he stopped, choked by the realisation.

"Now I understand the purpose of my task in showing you these images," Geoff added, smiling.

"Only now?" Sam stammered still reeling from the effect he'd had on the figure. "I don't get it. Surely you knew what you were doing? Knew why you had to show me this?"

"That is not the case, you create my guise then I just do as directed."

"Now what?"

Chapter 130

1982 October
Fakenham
Roger and Sarah's House

"He's gay, he must be."

"I don't think so, Sarah. Anyway, so what if he is? It's none of our business."

"Why doesn't he just come out? It's not like it is a big surprise these days, I mean look at the guy in the charts at the moment singing 'Do you really want to hurt me', he must be gay, if it's a guy, that is. You can be anything you want these days."

"There's still a lot of prejudice though, Sarah."

"We're his friends."

"Why are you so concerned?" Margaret frowned at her

"I'm not. Oh, I don't know. I'm stressed and it takes my mind off the builders starting Monday. I can't say I'm looking forward to it, with the kids running around."

"It will be really beautiful when it is finished." Margaret noted the not so happy look on her face. "That's not the problem is it?"

"I'm fed up. Roger doesn't pay me any attention anymore and he is always away, days at a time."

"What do you expect? He is a professor now, and let's face it, he needs to be to pay for this place."

"It's not what I imagined."

"Probably not, but it is better than a three-bed terraced house, like most."

"But we never see each other." Margaret watched Sarah bite on her bottom lip.

"Some people would call that bliss. And, I seem to remember you used to like Roger being away. Especially before the kids; it allowed us our girlie nights out. I still don't understand the fascination with Mike."

Sighing, Sarah flumped back in the comfy sofa. "I guess I'm jealous of his travels. Even you and Sam travel more than I do. Everyone has such exciting lives. Mine is so boring and mundane."

"Oh dear, you really do have it bad. Why don't you suggest to Roger going away for a few days, do a late booking? I was looking at some in the travel agent's window the other day and there are some good deals. Be ideal for just you two. Surely his, or your parents can look after the kids for a few days."

"His parents still don't like me, so, I don't go there, he just goes with the kids by himself, more days not together."

"It really is bad?"

"You don't think he's having an affair do you?"

"Roger!" Margaret couldn't stifle her laugh. "I'm sorry. No. I don't think he would have an affair. Is that why you think Mike is gay?"

"Yes. No. Oh, I don't know. I don't know anything anymore."

"Right, you and me are going out next weekend. We'll book a hotel, find a club and have a bloody good time. Roger can look after the kids for a night. We'll go to London, see if we can't have a lot of fun."

"Thank you."

"You're welcome. Now, my glass seems to be empty." Margaret downed the last gulp of Liebfraumilch.

Sarah got up. "Do you think he is though? Gay?"

"I've never given it a thought."

Chapter 131

1983 January
Mike's Lab

"What are you doing?" Sam walked over to where Roger was peering through a microscope.

"Ah, Sam, I have been looking at our techniques for freezing following on from some research I was doing."

"Been going solo, eh? Looking for all the kudos." Mike added.

"No, Mike. I just had an idea following on from a discussion I had with a colleague where lower body temperature was proving to have beneficial effects. So I want try something on an organ, to see what impact slow cooling would have before freezing; using Ethylene glycol, DMSO plus a couple of other chemicals. As we have found out, freezing causes structural damage that cannot be repaired …"

"Well, not yet anyway!"

"Will it ever, Sam? And that is kind of my point; we started focussing on the thawing side of the problem for reanimation when, actually we still needed to address the freezing side."

"Where did this liver come from?" Mike was looking at the container it had obviously been transferred in.

"It doesn't matter, I picked it up last night as I wanted to start quickly. It had already been stored in dry ice, and since …"

"You've been here all night?"

"Yes, Mike. What's the problem?"

"Won't Sarah wonder where you are?"

Roger stared at Mike like he was analysing a specimen. "NO! Now can we get back to this? Look, I have compared my initial findings with some previous experiments we'd done, and the structure is intact. Granted I haven't taken it to minus 196 degrees yet, I was just starting to prepare for that when you came in."

"What else is in the cryoproservative?" Sam asked skimming through Roger's extensive notes.

"Formanide plus Polyvinyl pyrrolidone. Something I read about, can't remember where, but I did a bit of research and I think these may help the process. I am also thinking about vitrification because, if we can get it to a glass state, then there would be no ice crystals; therefore, no damage and, in theory, a perfect case of life suspended. However, trying to get a whole body into a glass-like state is problematic to say the least. But just think what could be achieved if we could do it for an organ, like the liver. We really could have a spare parts business – like we do for cars – harvesting organs from accident victims."

"Vitrification." Mike smiled. "I like it."

"Okay, what do we need to do, Einstein?"

Chapter 132

1985 March
Lincolnshire
Storage Yard

I find it difficult to control my excitement and get back here quickly enough. This last two weeks have seemed like a lifetime. I believe I'm firmly onto a breakthrough. The incubator style box with the kidney has worked. In principle, the only issue is, as I correctly foresaw, the toxic nature of KF2R – and this needs further breakdown to see if it can't be made safer. BUT it only becomes toxic upon warming; until that point, the ice crystal stage is bypassed, going straight to liquid. That is when the damage is done! In a frozen state KF2R remains safe, the warming cycle changes the chemical make-up.

Can it be flushed out before damage is done?

My lab is too simple. Funds are short; I use what money I can siphon away discretely, but I can see this is going to cost a lot more than I have. I need to get the group involved – collectively we might be able to solve this.

To think I nearly gave up after Edward. A painful memory; just goes to prove you should never give up on a dream.

Chapter 133

1985 May

Mike's Lab

"It's a sound theory and, with that research stuff you showed us Roger, this really could be the breakthrough we need. I am happy to carry on investing in it." Sam replied.

"Let's not get ahead of ourselves," Roger said. "I am very wary of pouring money in. Maybe we need to look at outside investment. I know …"

"No," resolution showed on Mike's face. "This is our project; outsiders always want to take over."

" I agree, Mike."

"Thanks, Margaret. Do we know how much the new equipment will cost?"

Sarah spoke up. "I don't mind investigating. I have more time on my hands."

"So, in principle everyone is happy to carry on investing?" Roger concluded.

"Yes," they all said unanimously.

"Roger, it is nice to have you on board again, I don't think we would have got this breakthrough without you. I did just say that didn't I?"

"Yes, Mike. You did," Margaret commented.

"Why wouldn't I have been?"

"I think he is referring to the time I was arrested on suspicion of murder," Sam said pointedly.

Roger looked embarrassed. "Yes, well, mmm, I had to do what was best at the time. And …"

"I'm not sure I've ever seen Roger so lost for words." Mike laughed.

"It's alright, Roger. I was angry at the time but I do see where you were coming from, and understand."

Sarah placed a loving hand on Roger's shoulder. "You understand my Roger?"

"Yeah, I did just say that didn't I?"

"You did, hun, you did." Margaret turned to Roger. "I think the fugue states have become more serious. Can you check him out?"

"It's too late for that." Mike smiled.

They all turned to Sarah who was suddenly crying.

"What's wrong, Sarah?" Margaret put her arm around her.

"I don't know, it just reminded me of us being back at med school. Laughing, joking, it seems so long ago. It's nice. I enjoyed med school."

"It had its moments. Glad I'm not there now." Mike spun round on his stool. "Shall we crack on?"

Chapter 134

1986 October
Lincolnshire via Buxton
Storage Yard

I stare at the naked body on the ceramic slab. Sven Lihara's chest is still rising with shallow breaths as his unconscious body beckons me. He was almost my downfall. It nearly all went wrong as his friends spotted me bundling him into my car. They even tried to chase the car and, with the traffic, they almost caught me. I have never felt so out on a limb. My Austin Maxi is not exactly a getaway car and I will definitely have to get rid of it now. I have never been so pumped with adrenalin as when one of his friends miraculously caught up and angrily knocked at the window! It was pure luck the traffic eased and I could pick up speed, although the 1600 engine spluttered and coughed before the power jerked in. Finally some distance opened up and, in the rear view mirror, I could see the man shouting something – in Bulgarian I assumed, judging from Sven's passport. I drove around in circles trying to remember my route. It took twenty minutes and a sign for the A6 before I was heading in the right direction.

I nearly dumped the car and Sven at the earliest chance. CCTV is cropping up everywhere and I have a faint recollection that I saw a few cameras en route. How long would it take for Sven's friends to alert the police? Would a call be put out straight away? Would I be far enough away? The eighties are bringing a more conscious need to plan routes and dump sites. It was certainly my wake-up call tonight.

My hands are still shaking as I start the transfusion of KS9F – D, which should be less toxic. My thoughts are still focussed on what to do with the car? I can't keep it.

-

A few hours later, I am calmer and Sven is in the freezer. I have decided to dump the car; I don't have a choice. If it is spotted on CCTV, then it is only a matter of time before it could be spotted on the road. I think I know a place to make it disappear.

Just as the cover of darkness fades I watch the car disappear below the surface of a lake, easing my mind; although I still have a long walk back to the nearest village, and a bus. I need to make some phone calls.

Chapter 135

2002 July

"Is this all part of the process?" Sam snapped, "tearing my whole life apart. One big lie! So it seems. No, two big lies. This isn't real. It can't be real. It is probably some strange delirium as I lay dying? Made up images."

"You still can't believe this isn't some imagined picture about your life. This isn't 'It's a wonderful life' you know, and you are not James Stewart. Boy, you are not him!"

"No, and I don't think anything of what you're showing me is real, not anymore; it can't be. I won't believe it. I'm back there in the mess of cars, dying, that's all." Sam pointed towards the rear window, although the accident was long out of sight.

Suddenly they were at the scene of the accident: flames sending plumes of thick, black, toxic smoke into the air; traffic behind starting to tail back as far as the eye could see. Sam could see at least four lorries as well as numerous cars and vans through the flames. Fire engines, police and rescue vehicles had arrived at the scene and were busy trying to get as many people to safety as possible. Vehicles on the opposite carriageway were rubbernecking: a macabre curiosity.

"Still believe you're alive?"

Sam didn't answer, intently watching a firemen spray foam onto the source of some flames.

"I might ..." But before Sam could finish Geoff had whisked them to a place nearer Sam's squashed BMW, a crumpled mess under a forty-foot container.

"Your car is there." He pointed to a protruding section of front wing with a wheel, a distorted disc of alloy and rubber.

"The flames haven't reached ..."

"Do you want me to show you inside? It's not a pretty sight."

Sam gulped. "No."

Suddenly a meek cry of help came from within a contorted upturned van; a hand, barely visible, was desperately flailing about through the broken windscreen, the driver clearly trapped. The thick dirty smoke was rapidly advancing towards him, concealing the heat of the fire. Sam looked around at the emergency services. It appeared no one had heard the man's call. He watched as the smoke engulfed the cab, with the exception of a man-shaped outline.

"Surely someone's going to help him? He's alive."

"His time is ... now." Geoff answered, as both watched the silhouetted figure in the smoke became two people, then fade from view. Sensing the next question, Geoff answered, "He will have his own sins to answer for. His own journey awaits; it was how it was with me."

"How did ...?"

"Lung cancer. Painful and very prolonged. My journey was relatively short compared to yours. See, whilst you and most children thought I was some kind of ogre, I actually achieved goodness with my life. You may have been a disappointment, but many of my children did well. Admittedly, they are not well known, but success is not always about financial, or even celebrity status. Sometimes it is just about making a difference."

"I have made a difference." Sam implored.

"Really? Your journey is your journey; the reason for it and what I do is not always clear until the end."

Geoff guided Sam to a car on the periphery of the flames; there were no cries emanating from within, although the flames were advancing.

"There is a child in there." Geoff motioned.

Sam looked into the mangled mess of a car. Inside a woman and man were unconscious, covered in blood; he couldn't tell if they were alive.

"That fireman ..." Geoff pointed, "... he will rescue that child." A fireman nearby was busy pumping foam onto the flames of another vehicle.

"But how will he know?"

"He will be guided; a feeling, an inkling. You know that gut feeling you sometimes get when you know something, you are just not quite sure what." Sam nodded. "Well, watch."

Sure enough, as the fireman circled a section of flames, he noticed the red mangled car.

He shouted something that was inaudible over the roar of the fire, but was understood by another firemen standing nearby. He'd noticed the two occupants. Two other firemen joined him, followed swiftly by a police officer.

"Are they alive?" a fireman called.

"Difficult to tell, John. I'll bring the hose round if you take a look."

There was an anxious minute while the three men grabbed the adult occupants and dragged them to safety some distance away; there wasn't time to be careful about any injuries, if they had any. The fire was the real danger at this stage as the foam struggled against the intense ferocity.

The hose-man visibly relaxed as his colleagues got clear, but then he heard a noise that turned him pale. The roar of the flames was doing its best to drown it out, but it was there. And again!

"Sean, there's a baby in there." John angled the foam as the flames leapt from the car behind onto the bootlid of the car that the man and woman had been travelling in. "Sean, Sean," he shouted.

There was a crash of metal and the side of a lorry nearby moved as the fire stripped it.

In a moment's recklessness, John turned off the hose and ran to the car. He saw the baby locked securely in its baby seat. Not a scratch on it. Without time to relish the amazement of it being unscathed, John reached in. At first, he struggled with the straps. Another sound of grating metal stiffened him. He fumbled some more with the fastening, his gloved hands making it difficult. He threw them off recklessly. Finally, after furiously tugging, the baby came free, screaming as its head hit the back of one of the front seats.

"Sean, I've got ..." John turned in time to see movement and dived clear. The baby flew out of his hands. Sean was quick and throwing himself to the ground caught the baby before it landed ten feet away from where John now lay, pinned by a giant piece of burning lorry.

"Some people are just so unlucky." Geoff stated.

"What do you mean?"

"It's his time."

"Surely not; he has just ..." Geoff raised a hand and silenced Sam.

"It's the way of death."

Sam stood, completely taken back by the act of heroism, without a thought for the consequences. The emotion was like a raw cut, admiration with a hint of envy, not knowing whether he could have done anything like that. Maybe he would; maybe he'd have just stayed on the sidelines, shouting, waiting for someone else to take the plunge. He was just an ordinary guy. Weren't all heroes?

"So what is the point of this journey? Why bother? I can never atone for these crimes."

"Maybe, maybe not." Geoff replied.

"What else can I do? Especially now I'm dead?"

"Who knows what the higher beings have in store for us."

"I ... I don't" Sam felt his world spinning around him, the crash scene gone, a whirling, twisted mirage of faces and images that he didn't understand. Falling. He felt himself falling, falling through his life, the happy days with Margaret, the scientific discussions in the lab with his friends, his friendship with Mike.

Sam hit the ground with such ferocity that the breath was knocked out of him, making him dizzy, as if for an instant alive again.

Geoff stood staring down at him.

Part 5

Chapter 136

1988 November
Manchester
Ghost CID

William stood outside the Manchester Murder Review team's office – known colloquially as Ghost; it heralded back to when he first entered Liverpool CID, hoping for more information on Susan Jones. He felt like that naive officer again; the only difference being the file he carried under his arm, the very one with Susan's names written neatly on the inside cover, at the top of a list of names that had plagued him for twenty-five years.

Hesitating outside the door, he nervously listened to the hustle and bustle inside. This was meant to be a way to carry on working; less stress, supposedly – although, from the sound emanating from inside, it didn't sound like it would be.

"You must be William Travis." The Geordie voice behind broke his reverie. "We don't bite, friendly bunch, we don't allow biting. Neal Shearer, I lead the team."

William turned to see a goliath of a guy. "Good to meet you, finally. We spoke on the phone," he replied, as timidly as he had that day in Liverpool CID. It shook him.

"Bringing your own files as well, I see." Neal led William through the door. "Team, I like to introduce our newbie, DSI William Travis, transferred from Liverpool for a quieter life."

"Not much chance of that here."

"Don't scare him off just yet, eh, Matt! That's DS Matt Spearman, the youngest of our team, but smart. Into all that new computer stuff; can't say I understand it."

"You flatter me, sir."

William studied the room. It was bright with windows that looked over an immaculately kept courtyard garden. At one end of the office were metal racks, some empty, some housing boxes of evidence and files; all behind a wire mesh grill that, whilst open at the present time, looked as though they would be padlocked. There were three four-foot-high maps of England on the wall in different places, with markers placed at various points with strings tied round them; the other end attached to a note or comment. At the top of each was a case reference number and, on a table next to the maps, crime scene photos and piles of files; all three areas looked busy, yet organised.

"Your desk will be that one." Neal pointed to one near Matt. "The work here isn't any different to any other CID, except that these are cold cases; the clock isn't ticking as fast – although, with new forensic techniques, time can be of the essence if we get a lucky break. We've got three cases we're focussing on at the moment, none of which are going anywhere." William noticed Neal looking at him. "Maybe fresh eyes will change that. I checked you out, and I am glad to have you on our team."

"Thank you."

"Matt and the team will bring you up to speed." William turned away then stopped. "We will get to that case," William frowned, before getting Neal's meaning, "just not yet."

William weaved through the desks to his own. It had paperwork all over it.

"Here, let me clear that. I'm Matt, they sometimes call me 'Spearmint' 'cos of the fresh thinking I bring to this place."

"It's a hint, Spearmint." William looked at the female officer who was animating 'bad breath'. "I'm DC Sandra Kempson. Pleased to meet you."

"Ha ha," Matt responded. "If you need anything just let me know. Do you want a coffee first and then I'll bring you up to speed?"

"That'd be great, thanks."

"Follow me, I'll show you where the kitchen is; all mod cons here."

William smiled, there was a pleasant atmosphere in the room, the team outwardly appeared cohesive and good-natured with each other. Maybe this was a good move after all. Less stress – good for his blood pressure.

Chapter 137

1989 March
Mike's Lab

"... so JTF37 doesn't work either. Margaret, I thought, you guys were good!" Roger admonished.

"My team are very good. It wasn't exactly developed for what we are trying to fathom, and no, before you ask, it didn't work for what we intended either." Margaret returned to the formula Roger had written on the blackboard. "This is different from last week. What's changed?"

"Mike, had a theory about ..."

"What did I have theory about?" Margaret turned as Mike entered. "Oh, that, yes well, the less we say about that the better."

"Why? I thought it was a sound ..." Roger defended.

"I spoke with a guy from New York during the week. They tried it, and whilst the additive at first appeared to work, the genetic cell mutations were not pleasant.

"I'll add it to the file then." Margaret grabbed an A4 jumbo file from a shelf, and proceeded notating. " We're gonna need a new shelf at this rate."

"Yeah, this was meant to be a lab not a library." Mike sat down.

"So, where does that leave us?" Roger took some samples out of the freezer.

"Well, I would say that leaves us where we started, no further on. Where are Sarah and Sam?"

"Sarah's looking after the kids, Rachel's been sick." Roger explained.

"And Sam has a meeting in Newport." Margaret advised.

"Maybe we need to go back through our research so far. There must be something we have missed?"

"You're a professor, Roger, I doubt you'd miss anything?" Mike picked up a specimen. "Plus most cryo societies are no further than us, so that doesn't put us in a bad position. I started subscribing to one in America; they issue regular magazines. Why did we think we could solve this?"

"I seem to recall, Mike, it was all of our ideas. Something about our names emblazoned in science books of the future."

"Minor detail, Margaret. It could still happen. And, if you remember, I was reluctant at first."

"Whatever. Not if we don't find some slight breakthrough soon, it won't." Margaret continued to note the formula, the results. Then flicking through previous pages. "Maybe Roger is right about going through past notes."

"Okay, okay, Margaret, I give in, let's do it."

"Mike, this liver sample, what did we use?"

"Why, Roger?"

"Because, I have just sawn a bit off and warmed it and cell structure looks fine."

"That impossible."

"It's happened, so it is not."

Margaret grabbed another file, where they kept notes on all specimens."What's the reference number?"

"LT34/ST."

Margret flicked through the pages, frantically. "It's not detailed."

"What do you mean not detailed?" Margaret saw Mike peering over her shoulder. "ST, that's Sam. He must have noted it somewhere. What did he use?" they stared at each other "Ring him, Margaret!"

Chapter 138

1991 March

Manchester
Ghost CID

"What is that file?"

William looked up as Spearman perched on his desk.

"A reminder."

Spearman looked bemused. "Let's take a look."

"No!" William couldn't believe he'd sounded so possessive. "Sorry, sure; it is just a cold case," he sighed, "something I was hoping to solve before I retired. A blemish on my career."

"I suppose everyone has a case like that, something personal. When is it due for review?"

William fingered the file. "Next year. Will be five years since the last body dump. No new leads, nothing new to go on."

"You really do take it personally," Spearman flicked through the file, "'63? Geez that is a long case." William watched his eyes scan the list of names and dates.

"Yes; my first day on my own beat. What a great start? A bit of a strange serial – it doesn't follow the normal models the profilers use these days."

"Might be dead."

"Might well be. It doesn't help the families though. They don't get any closure."

"True. I think that is what I like about working in this unit; the closure it brings. Modern forensics is helping so much, that we can catch people, especially the one-offs, even unknown serials; we can piece together patterns which we didn't know existed."

"How old are you?" William was surprised by the thoughtfulness of the young man.

"Twenty-nine."

William leaned in to Matt. "If I never get to close this case, would you take it over for me?"

Matt looked surprised and a little daunted. "You'll sort it, you'll see."

"But, if I don't, will you?" William persisted.

There was a moments' hesitation.

"Absolutely."

Chapter 139

1991 May
Lincolnshire
Storage Yard

I've had Sven Lihara on ice for five years. It is the longest I have kept anyone; there was no valid reason to do so, only the fear of getting caught. Police 5 still roll out the images of the car that abducted him and, because of that, I have lost my nerve a little. It is strange because, in some ways, keeping him here is more risky than dumping the body. Without experiments, there seems to be no need to have this place; it is just a drain, not that money is a problem anymore. I have no useful data to take from him. I miss the thrill of feeling life fizzle out, but risks have to be evaluated even for me, a contradiction according to the reports in the news about me: supposition.

What was that LT34/ST? How bloody stupid not to write it down! I can't believe it! We get that close and there is no note of what was used. Retracing steps is a minefield; we might as well start at the beginning.

How do I move forward now?

I spoke with Professor Schaefer of the Massachusetts Cryopreservative trust; they are no closer, in fact they are closing down – too many estates have reneged on payments and, financially, that has left them with crippling debts. Those that have paid are being transferred to New York. The Chatsworth Scandal has meant that there is closer monitoring. He advised that a Dr Yan Ling has come up with a new additive that is proving non-fatal to the organs and body, but it is a closely guarded secret. However, the professor also advised that still no one had been brought back and they still couldn't; so maybe I need to look at the re-animating side, focussing on that conundrum – the spark of life. The Professor also advised that no non-toxic additive solved the ice crystal formation upon thawing.

Twenty-five years and still no further; yet we are seeing kidney, liver, even heart transplants, it is incredible how we move on yet cannot preserve even these organs longer than a few hours at most. Blood &

semen, fine, no problem – we've been able to do that since 1940; but fifty-one years and we have not progressed past that. It's absurd!

It is like being lost in a night of absolute darkness. I still feel the urge to try more experiments, to take another body – I really want to feel that power again. If I do, I will have to dispose of Sven's body, finally. I need to find somewhere CCTV free.

Chapter 140

1991 May
Manchester
Ghost CID

DS Mark Roberts steamed through the door and scanned the office with a palpable sense of urgency; only DS Sandra Kempson, DI Dylan Smith and DC Spearman were in.

"You alright?" DS Kempson said looking up from a file; the others remained engrossed in their own tasks.

"You seen Travis?"

"Not today. He's following up on the Harpington case. I think he went out with Harvey to interview the victim's family; they think they are covering up. Why?"

"You know that call I got this morning. The body dump. The local CID thought we might be interested as it looks like it fits that case that Travis hawks around in that file of his." Roberts took off his coat and sat at his desk as Sandra wandered over. "Missing persons confirmed that the victim disappeared in October '86, Sven Lihara, aged forty-seven. This is the autopsy report, a kidney, spleen, voice box all removed, along with other tissue samples taken. The only difference is, the body was dumped in the New Forest. A couple walking their dog found it."

"Do you reckon he's taunting William?" Sandra shuffled the autopsy photos.

"Maybe, sometimes the 'serials' can get fixated on the investigator. Just seems an extraordinarily long gap of ..." Mark walked over to William's desk and looked at the inside cover of the file where William had handwritten the names and dates of each victim, along with locations taken and where each body had been dumped, "... nearly ten years."

"You better watch out. If Travis catches you looking at that file, he'll go berserk." Spearman stood up, stretching his back and grabbing his coffee mug.

"Yeah, like we all haven't looked. Anyway he'll be out all day by the sound of it."

"Who'll be out all day?" William asked, pushing through the office door.

Mark jumped up. "You might wanna see this. We believe it is connected to your file. Another body dump."

"Where's Copeland?" Sandra replaced the file.

"Booking in Teresa Harpington's father. He confessed. What do you mean connected? Another victim?" William took the report from Mark, eagerly thumbing through it. "Jesus! Where was Sven found?"

"He was placed leaning up against a tree in the New Forest. Forensics are gathering evidence but it is fairly clean and there are no cameras in the vicinity."

"A different place yet again. How can he get away with it so easily? Keep me posted on what forensics find. Sandra, can you get the whereabouts of Sam Talbot for the last forty-eight hours, and don't let him know, otherwise we'll end up with a harassment charge. Any traffic cameras in the area?" William sat down at his desk. "Mark, can you do a record check on any new releases of any convicts who had medical tendencies that have been inside for five years or less. Maybe he's been inside? Maybe Sam is innocent?"

"Why do you have a downer on this Sam bloke?" Spearman enquired.

William visibly sank into his chair. "Because everything keeps coming back to him, or close to him and there's no smoke without fire. I even checked all his friends and family out in my initial investigations. The wife attends lectures and symposiums irregularly to do with her MOD job. I have seen the tickets and spoken personally to people at the venues she attends, and they confirm her presence. Michael, the best friend (adopted, by the way) goes to America on business and pleasure quite regularly; his other friends, Roger and Sarah, are married with the requisite two kids. Roger, or rather Professor Roger Barton, is a highly regarded neurologist." He paused. "I even looked at siblings. A theory I came up with, and he, Sam, was one of three, triplets. His brother is supposedly dead, although I cannot confirm or deny they ever grew up together, or if he died. His sister; court records were sealed and subsequently lost in a fire at a storage unit – don't know why, all a bit strange. Born during the war, their birth certificates were filed separately because of an air raid at the time. I don't have a downer on him, just a gut feeling that I am right and the fact that evidence always comes back to him; even the two cars that we know have been used were owned at some point by him. Coincidence? I don't think so."

Spearman looked to be considering the information. "I watched a program once, where these two guys lived one life in two different parts of the world, posing as the same person." William sat silent. "They used to meet at the airport and hand over anything they'd need on their business trip. This meant that the one that stayed behind had time to kill, so he started another life somewhere else. I think he had a part time job or something."

After a pause, William answered in seriousness, "So you are saying that, although tickets were bought in the correct name and used, it was actually different people using them – so one identity, two different looks. That would possibly mean false passports et cetera."

"Pretty much."

William had to concede, unlikely as it was, it was plausible and could open up the pool of suspects again.

Spearman continued, "it would also explain why Sam Talbot is innocent, and you could never get a strong case against him."

William arched back in his chair. "Well, let's look into it then."

A Day Later

"Sorry, William, it's bad news. Just spoken with the chief and they do not want any of us to go near Sam Talbot, his wife, his friends or family." Neal strolled to William's desk; the rest of the office was empty.

"That's ridiculous!" William exploded. "Matt has come up with a good theory and we need to investigate fully; not all public records go back far enough. We need to look at bank and credit card records ..." He was interrupted.

"I know, but that's the order. They are out of bounds unless you come up with anything conclusive that supports that theory. We need facts. Use what we have."

"But we can't get those facts unless we have access to those records." William thumped his desk in frustration and then coughed heavily, a throaty, phlegmy cough.

"Have you got the results yet?" William shook his head. "I

understand your frustration, but he has been interviewed numerous times and you actually arrested him once. CPS will not go near him unless we have concrete proof. If we go after him or his friends and family, you and I both know how that will look. I am with you and think the theory is sound. Just keep your distance. Run this new body dump like a brand new case; no known suspects and look for clues with an open mind. Obviously, if you find even a loose connection to this Talbot guy, you check it out – from a distance; build the case by the book. Sorry." Neal patted William on the back in consolation then headed back to his own desk.

William spent the next few days making phone call after phone call, trying to find answers and connections to Sam and anyone connected to him: all to no avail.

Sandra came back with only one man who'd recently been released from prison and who had form for abducting and keeping his victim's bodies for a period before dumping, but he had an alibi – being in intensive care after a car accident. And, whilst CCTV was multiplying like horny rabbits, nothing came up for the Ford Sierra seen close by on the morning of the dump – and it wasn't registered to anyone in William's pool of original suspects.

Chapter 141

1991 August

Mike's Lab

"What you got there, Mike?"

"Hi, Sam, Margaret. It's 'Flashpoint' the Stones live album."

"That came out in April, took your time getting it didn't you? I'm kinda moving away from them, I've been listening Tony Bennet, Sammy Davis, they've got nice hooks to them once you really listen."

"Margaret, I think your husband been exchanged."

"It's called mellowing, Mike, it happens. Sometimes it is nice to expand one's tastes."

"Nah."

"It still doesn't explain ..." Sam stopped as Mike flipped the album cover over. Sam could see the signatures. "Really?"

"Yep."

"Did you stalk them, Mike?"

"No, Margaret. My contact in America got it for me."

"Why bring it in here?" Sam took the record and studied the autographs.

"I just collected it from the post office, I wasn't going to leave it in the car; it will buckle in the heat."

"True. Are Roger & Sarah coming tonight? I want to discuss an experiment using a pig's kidney and heart and Roger's input would be good. We've had some success at work with an artificial suspension system that keeps the blood flowing, and the organs working – in good condition, at very cold temperatures without deterioration, as low as minus 86 degrees C. Cell structure remains good: it uses a gel additive for the blood, main ingredient is an extract from the Aloe Vera plant."

"They'll be along later. A plant extract? Interesting. I know it was meant to have medicinal properties, but isn't it toxic taken orally?"

"Conflicting information, Mike. And we have not found anything too major, yet; it is still early stages."

"Last night, Mike," Sam handed the album back to Mike, "we discussed connecting up the kidney and heart and lowering the temperature to see how far we can take it. Margaret has got the formula for the extract and we have everything else here so we can ..."

"So instead of freezing completely, we just store at the lowest possible temperature and then use a ventilator and dialysis machine, and see what affect it has." Mike wiped Sam's fingerprints off of the cover with his lab-coat sleeve.

"Yes. Whilst we know freezing works and creates stasis, this may be a way to suspend and delay. Obviously, we need to set up some control parameters and do some long tests along with concurrently running frozen specimens stored in liquid nitrogen. Still working towards achieving a 'glass' state ideally."

"Cool. By the way I did get your message the other day, thanks and the requisite items are in the fridge. These mobile phone are quite good. I'm quite impressed." Mike took out his Nokia 3310.

"Work is getting me one. I'll never be able switch off." Sam sighed.

"Never mind dear. Shall we get on?"

Chapter 142

1991 September

Manchester
Ghost CID

"You wanted to see me, Neal." William sat down in front of Neal's immaculately kept desk.

"Yes. How is the non-serial serial coming? Any progress?"

William had dreaded this. His head sank. "No, it has gone cold. Nothing at the scene, no trace of the Red Ford Sierra seen in the area, and let's face it, they are not exactly unique. The part plate we were given, B26* **M, we have all but exhausted and there are now only ten unaccounted for, and those ten registered keepers, we can't locate. It could be they were sold, scrapped, or rotting in a field somewhere, even abroad with false names and addresses on the reg docs. They have been highlighted as needing to be traced. So, if a car is stopped, it will flag up."

"Police 5 been helpful?"

"Lots of calls but nothing useful." There was a pregnant pause. "I know. It needs to go in a box."

"Sorry, four months, we can't spare the resources. We know that the first seventy-two hours are crucial, but four months! I think we have to face facts; he is clever, prepared and cunning. Forensics found nothing, CCTV doesn't give us any clear picture of the driver's face then there is little we can do. William, I know it's personal and, if you want to keep at it during your spare time, there is little I will do to stop you. However, the Chief wants to scale back with this one. Finances, the usual restrictions on budgets against results."

"Understood." William stood resignedly.

"One day, one day." Neal added consolingly.

William walked back to his desk, thick with reports and files. Dejectedly, he slumped into his chair and started to pick through the files and reports, not really reading them, just cursory glances.

His mind raced to thoughts of the theories over the years. What was the missing piece? It had to be here, staring at him. Looking at his watch, he saw that it was nearly time to go home. He had been feeling tired recently and knew he should go home, but Fiona was out tonight and the kids were at scouts. He didn't fancy being home alone and decided to study the files he knew by heart one last time.

Chapter 143

1991 October
Lincolnshire
Storage Yard

Am I getting too old for this? People are getting stronger and heavier. Bloody cameras are everywhere! Our group research has stalled again, although I am so close with a cryopreservative; if only I could resolve the toxicity issue. I know, if I bring it to the group, that solution could be investigated, but I am loathed to do so; it is so within my grasp that I want the kudos, and I wouldn't get that if they helped.

It is so frustrating!

Andrew Seargant's picture appeared on Police 5 on Sunday, along with my other experiments going right back to the beginning with Susan Jones. Twenty-eight years! It is a thrill in itself and it started me thinking back fondly to Sheila and Gary, and that imaginary barrier that people live their lives by, yet I crossed it – and what it takes to break through it: courage of one's conviction, a desire to succeed, a belief that you won't get caught. I can't help but smile. Three people that could have easily been the end for me, including Ben Shaker, but still I remain as elusive to the police today as I did then. I can't quite believe they have been so close, yet still seem so far.

I went to America and spoke with the New York institute of cryonics and, to say it was disappointing is an understatement; they are no nearer. How can that be? They have vast sums of money being ploughed into research that should have paid dividends. People are paying handsomely to have their bodies stored: whole estates being indulged.

I divulged some of the information I had, hoping they could shed some light on the toxicity issue. It was an avenue they had not looked at and were interested in; in fact they invited me back longer term to join their team.

It is so tempting, yet it is unpaid, being run like a charity.

Maybe I should? I am not achieving anything here and sooner or later they might catch up with me. This way I would be out of the

country and safe from capture. What does hold me back?
Love! That's what it is. The one thing that holds me back; my one
weakness – something I would never have believed possible for me.

Chapter 144

1992 July
Manchester
Ghost CID

"... so if you have any more questions, then speak to either DSI Travis or myself who will be co-ordinating with drug squad. Be vigilant, and careful; this gang are not scared of taking anyone out." Neal paused. "As we have found out.

"Gary's memorial service will be on Tuesday next week, please show your support to his family. I know this is not normally in our remit but our cold case has stumbled onto something big, national, and they need all the man power they can pull in, so let's all work with it."

William could feel the palpable tension prickle the air as the tricky three weeks trying keep this out of the press was drawing to its conclusion. A cold case like this would have been passed back to the local CID, but the operation involved sixteen CID units around the country, working in conjunction with the drug squad. The gang were responsible for importing ten billion pounds worth of drugs, and the case was on the verge of falling apart. It had already killed one officer and put another undercover officer in jeopardy: she was currently in hiding.

"Dismissed."

William sunk down on the nearest chair as the incident room emptied. This wasn't what he imagined when he joined Ghost: a quieter life. Over the last forty-eight, hours he'd received very little sleep and had missed his son's school play. Fiona understood, and Alex said he did, but at fourteen he wasn't sure. Alex wanted to pursue an acting career and had worked enormously hard on his part, hoping to impress his father. Yet, when the call had come in, William had no choice – his leave for the day had been suspended, like everyone else's, and extra staff had been drafted in. It was the biggest national operation he could remember, and it had been hard getting everyone in position. It was called 'Operation Big Dog' and was due to go down the following morning at 3am.

Pinching the bridge of his nose William closed his eyes to clear his head, trying to steal the sleep his eyes desperately tried to take. The empty room brought a relished calm with it.

Suddenly the door flung open as Officer Chang; a newbie, urgently strolled in.

"Sir?"

William sat upright, taking a deep breath and sighing. "Yes."

"I've been asked to give you this." She handed him a thick, large envelope.

"Thanks. Where is it from?" William took out the contents.

"Came in from Newport this morning, marked urgent, said it was for your eyes only." Chang turned to go.

"Bloody hell! Another one."

Chang stopped and was about to turn as William stormed past her out of the incident room.

At his desk he opened the file he'd brought with him to Ghost; then, with disgust, read the new file, cover to cover, shaking his head as the familiar feeling made him reel.

Grabbing a biro, he added another name to the green file: Andrew Sergeant 55 – Found Newport – Disappeared Aberdeen. Missing fourteen months.

Newport police had exhausted all avenues of investigation, with none panning out to anything useful; not even realising it was part of a serial – only someone in filing making the connection. Forces were just getting too busy and every force used a different system – it was crazy. No wonder solving crimes was hard when it involved different patches. William's name had popped up as someone to be contacted if a connection was made to the yet unsolved case.

Sam never put a foot wrong, never left a shred of new evidence; it was like having a 'get out of jail free' card.

"BASTARD!!" William threw the file across the office, tiredness showing its toll. The rest of the department momentarily stopped and looked in his direction.

Chapter 145

1993 February

Brighton

"Thank you, Roger. It is a lovely surprise."

"It's been a while since we've had a weekend away. I thought it would be nice, just the two of us. I have been so busy and I wanted to spend time with the toppest wife ever."

Sarah, looked questioningly at her husband, he'd been absent a lot over the last few months and sometimes she felt she was not married at all, physically – she'd even suspected an affair.

"I am not allowed to bestow a compliment?"

"It's been a while, that's all. I felt a little cut off from you." Sarah held Roger's arm tighter.

"I know. It's that project I am working on with Professor Davies, it has got huge potential to help with Alzheimer's research. He has this theory, an extension, of sorts, to the amyloid hypothesis postulation that extracellular amyloid beta deposits are the cause. Support for this theory comes from the location of the gene for the amyloid precursor protein on chromosome 21, together with ... what?" Roger stopped looking at his Sarah.

"I just love seeing you so animated and passionate about a subject. It reminds me why I fell in love with you. Something I missed over the last few years; you don't talk about it much at home anymore, and you always used to share – even when I didn't understand."

Silence rested between them.

"I hadn't realised."

"Realised what?"

"That you liked talking about my work. I know you love our cryo project, but I just thought my work bored you."

"You were never bright. I love you – just because I can't expand on your theories. I love the way you light up when you talk about them. I want to be part of that, part of you. I don't just want to be your wife, our kids' mother and general dogs body. I want more, Roger. I need stimulating as well." Sarah frowned at Roger who was smirking. "What?" then she registered what she said. "Well, I do. So how about it?"

"Before or after dinner?"

"After is fine, but during would be nice too." She smiled flirtatiously.

-

Sarah felt relaxed and happy again as they sat at the table in the window of a French, seafront restaurant holding hands; she was running her toes along the back of Roger's calf muscle almost mindlessly.

"...so I said I would do it. Plus it means we get to spend a week in Edinburgh with the children."

"Sounds perfect, Roger. When is ...?" Sarah, caught sight of someone outside the window. "Oh god, that's Mike! What's he doing here? He said he was going to America."

"What? Where?"

"Look." Sarah pointed at two men across the road.

"No, can't be. Probably just someone who looks like..." The two men kissed. "That's definitely not Mike, then."

As the pair parted Sarah stared in disbelief.

"Good likeness though. What are you doing, Sarah?"

Sarah reached for her handbag.

"Ringing Mike." She scrolled through the names on her mobile.
They watched.

In amazement the figure pulled a phone from his pocket."Hi, Sarah. Wha...?"

Sarah hung up, clutching her phone tightly to her chest. Then, without notice, ran outside leaving Roger aghast.

* * * *

"Who was that?"

"My friend, Sarah. She just hung up. Strange." Mike shook his head. "Do you have to go to work? Can't you skive off for the night, Colin?"

"Mike, I have to pay my rent. It is alright ..."

"Mike? Mike?"

Shock registered on Mike's face as he saw Sarah darting across the road dodging traffic.

"So it is you then?" she asked breathlessly.

"What are you doing here?" Mike suddenly felt flustered.

"Are you married? Are you playing games with me?" Colin's anger became obvious.

"No. Hi, Sarah. She's a friend."

Mike watched Colin eye her up and down. "So he does have friends. I was beginning to wonder whether they were just fictitious."

"You're gay." Sarah answered.

"Yeah, he is gay. Oh my god, your friends don't know?"

Mike frowned in consternation.

Colin touched Mike's arm. "Look, I've got to go. Call me later, I think we need to talk." Mike watched Colin walk off.

"What are you doing here?" Mike asked, embarrassed.

"Never mind that. Is this where you have been coming all those years when you say you're in America?"

Mike floundered. "Don't tell the others. Please. Especially Sam."

"Why not? Because you're gay? Or because they'll be pissed that you didn't tell them?

Mike stood silent; it was his worst nightmare. He'd kept his two lives separate. He didn't feel comfortable everyone knowing.

"I ... I just. This is my private life. Aren't I allowed to have one?" he countered, defensively.

"You can do whatever you please. I just thought we were your friends, that's all."

"You are." He pleaded.

Silence fell between them.

Sarah broke it. "Look we are eating over there. I'll call you tomorrow, okay? Maybe we can talk, if you like?" She turned to go, then turned back. "I won't say anything if you really don't want me to, but I don't understand what the big deal is."

"Please, I'm not ready."

She was about to leave then stalled. "How long?" Mike's silence dragged on. "That long. That explains a lot."

Chapter 146

1993 July

Manchester
Ghost CID

William sat with his hands around his mug of coffee, enjoying the tranquillity of the morning, pleased that the previous day, the team had finally closed a twenty-year-old murder with new DNA evidence. It always made him feel euphoric seeing a Ghost case laid out to rest.

He looked forlornly at his now jaded file – his own Ghost case – that still sat like a millstone round his neck.

"Morning, William."

"Morn … ing," the hacking coughing seemed to be getting worse.

"You ought to get that checked out." Neal threw his sandwich box in his desk draw.

"I've … got … an … appointment nex … t week."

"It probably doesn't help with this place being so bloody cold. We'll get the heating fixed one day."

Finally William's cough abated. "Be nice. What case we got next?"

Neal strolled over to the kitchen door, his mug in hand. "You all right?" he indicated to the mug.

"Fine. Still warm." indicating his own mug.

"A serial, six victims between '78 and '87, all boys aged between nine and twelve, all from the Lowestoft area, Suffolk. They were all raped." William shuddered. "Yes, I have to agree, sick git. Anyway, a diary has been turned in with some new information."

Neal disappeared into the kitchen leaving William to his thoughts as he ran a finger over the names of the victims of his own cold case, each one etched into his memory. He thought about all the new techniques being applied to cases, helping to close them, put the ghosts to rest – DNA being one of the best, but even fingerprint technology had moved on.

"I take it," William jumped, having not heard Neal walk over with coffee in hand, "you didn't get any further with your supposed suspect last year, what was his name?"

"Sam Talbot. No. No DNA evidence, well nothing that supported a case I could bring to anyone's attention. He's clever."

"Or just lucky, or, maybe he is innocent."

"No, definitely not that. But a thirty-year lucky streak ... wow! It really has been that long. Susan Jones' face appeared like a fresh memory in his mind; it seems like it was only yesterday." William sat back in his chair sighing. "I wanted to make a difference."

"And you have. Don't ever think you haven't. One case is not a career. Hold everything in perspective and never lose sight of it."

"You got any cases that remain ..."

"Four. I know who did them; could never prove it though. Three of them are dead, now, and I know they died horrible deaths – so they got their just deserts."

"And the other one?"

"She's still walking around."

"A woman. When was this?"

"'81. Poisoned her husband. Now, she was clever. We could not pin anything on her. Meticulous. I know it was her; and she knows I know, and also that I keep a distant eye on any deaths close to her, just in case." Neal smiled and looked wistfully away. "Sometimes that's all we can do."

"But how can I, when I cannot even check bank records?"

"I'm afraid with all the harassment cases, and human rights crap; the criminals know their rights more than ever, so we have to be scrupulously clean. It's an unfair time. I've seen the odd bit of *pressure per se* break a case wide open, but we can't do that anymore. And ..." The door crashed open. "... looks like the troops are arriving with our new, old case."

William watched Neal greet the couriers with the evidence boxes and files.

"If he's been clever, be cleverer!"

William sighed then repeated Neal's quote to himself, "If he's been clever, be cleverer! But how? I've looked at every angle. Maybe it's just not meant to be." He looked at the latest missing persons list that he regularly checked – an endless list of names that got longer and longer every month. It was an arduous task to follow up every one – some people didn't want to be found. Computers and CCTV had at least eased some of the avenues he could check in his spare time; not that there was much of that – and he was constantly tired. Forlornly he got up and joined Neal.

Chapter 147

1993 August

Mike's Lab

"How you doing, Sammy boy?"

"Alright." Sam eyed Mike suspiciously. "You?"

"Absolutely. Back from America in one piece and, I had an enlightening conversation with a professor over there who is working with some students; they think they may be onto something. They have found a cryopreservative that is non-toxic and applied by transfusion after the person is dead by artificially pumping the heart. They have successfully frozen and thawed a rat, and a pig. They were still dead of course, but the tissue samples revealed no further damage other than initial death. The brain is still causing some problems due to its complexity."

"Cool. Sounds interesting."

The door opened and in walked Sarah and Roger. The atmosphere tumbled as Sarah acknowledged Mike coldly, before turning to Sam.

"Hi. How are you? No Margaret tonight?" She said hanging her coat up.

Roger just nodded a greeting.

"She is not feeling well, so I left her in bed. Hope she feels better by Saturday though, as she is heading off to America herself for a few days with a couple of colleagues."

"At least someone gets to go to America?" Sarah seemed to direct the loaded comment at Mike.

"Have I missed something?" Sam became aware of the frost that was settling.

"No, mate. So what shall we try tonight? Any ideas?"

"Besides trying to find out what LT34/ST was?" Roger put his lab-coat on.

"I said, I was sorry, I don't know what happened that day. Can we move on?" Sam looked at each pair of eyes staring at him; Roger's seemed to harbour the most animosity. " We could always get it analysed?"

"Tried that," Roger stated, "and it narrowed it down to over a thousand possibilities."

"Oh!"

Chapter 148

1998 June
Lincolnshire
Storage Yard

The lab seems strangely quiet as if stuck in limbo. More trips to America and still the progress is slow. Dr Sophie Cho said there were some students who thought they had made advances, but the research has proved to be misleading. We had a good chat over dinner and, somehow, that turned into spending the night together. It is strange that I can feel guilt for doing that, yet not for taking a life. It does invigorate me again though.

I am not sure what I should do next. Funds are not enough to expand the thawing system I have in mind – I did think of bringing the group in on it, but something always holds me back – and, I am not even sure whom I could get to fabricate it. I still have not got closer to the cryopreservative theory I had; something still remains elusive.

I need to think about my strategy. I will keep in contact with Sophie though; her domination was a nice change. I almost want to bring her in on my experiments – that would be foolish!

Sarah has started talking about Crimewatch a lot, and the old crimes that get solved with new evidence. It concerns me with so much CCTV being shown from so long ago. I had never realised how abundant it had become, or how much was kept. I can't remember everywhere I have been, places where I may have been susceptible; whilst my disguise has changed over the years, and the cars I use have as well, I do sometimes wonder whether capture is just down the road. Sven was my biggest error of judgement. I think back to Sheila, how easy it was, how open.

Part 6

Chapter 149

2001 June

Lincolnshire
Storage Yard

"So what have you found, Dr Yanovic?" DI Ashworth commanded with an air of fatigue that had increased, almost daily, by the spate of arson attacks which continued unabated; they were no nearer to catching the culprit. Even the CCTV that the yard owner, Harry Tuffnell, had installed did not show anything useful that could be used.

"Not much. Definitely deliberate! Started in the mechanic's lock-up and quickly spread. This place is like a death trap really. Not many units survived, except that one over there." She pointed to one with slightly charred doors. "It did take some damage. Probably have to be pulled down like the rest, start again."

"Who's is it? Do we know? Maybe they saw something."

"The owner's coming in later to survey the damage. Apparently been on holiday, conveniently."

Ashworth wandered over to unit with Dr Yanovic following. "Lucky bastard, at least whatever they got in there has been spared." She tugged absent-mindedly at the door before turning away.

"Maybe. Maybe prime housing land, this. Maybe the owner will decide to ... "a loud snap and creek caught both their attentions, freezing them to their relative spots; before Dr Yanovic dived away dragging Ashworth with her – just in time to see one of the doors break free and fall, stopping short of hitting the ground, as the lower hinge and padlock held it at a precarious angle.

"Thanks." Ashworth said, getting up, bewildered.

"Bit lucky there. Was told it was all safe."

"Don't think that is the case!" Ashworth studied the hanging door and looked beyond.

Dr Yanovic walked back to the mechanic's garage and continued working the origin of the fire, only to be distracted by Ashworth's cry.

"Jesus, what the hell?"

"What is it?" Dr Yanovic rushed over to her, "Wow, smells like decomp!"

"I thought you said no one was injured." Ashworth looked around. "Oi! You two, over here, help get this door down," two coppers standing guard marched over.

"Put these on before you go in." Dr Yanovic offered a pair of shoe-coverings to Ashworth.

Ashworth studied the lab set up; the hairs on the back of her neck standing on end as her internal antennae became attuned to something that sparked suspicion.

"What do you think?" Dr Yanovic followed.

"Not sure. But something is not quite as it seems. Check the wood burner?"

A minute, or two, passed as Dr Yanovic raked through the ashes in the fire carefully, whilst Ashworth studied the two metal freezers.

"I've got remnants of clothing. You got anything?" Dr Yanovic called.

"Not sure what I am looking at but, what do you think?" She was looking at specimen jars on a shelf.

Dr Yanovic arrived at her shoulder, "that's a liver and they're kidneys."

"Human?" Ashworth enquired.

"Looks like it, but will confirm back at the lab."

Turning round to study more of the lab set up, Ashworth saw a broken jar: and the source of the decomp odour. Ashworth turned to see Dr Yanovic studying some notepads, neatly stacked on a shelf.

"I think you need to read this."

Ashworth meandered over. "What you got?"

Dr Yanovic handed her two of the notebooks, which she flicked through, scanning the scribblings, reading some extracts:

1962

It is 3.14am and the lab is complete. It is simple yet adequate for the experiments. I can feel the trepidation and stirrings of excitement. Some things are always best kept to one's self, and I can feel that savouring the moment is something quite exquisite. The selfish side of me wants to push the boundaries for which I know will be limited within the group. There are politics, and morals to adhere to, and to make history, you have to ignore the rules and break the shell of what we use to guide us.

How do I choose an experiment? Should I set criteria? Gary and Sheila were happy 'chances' but that euphoria is too strong to ignore. Now, I may not be so lucky, so I will need to make my luck. Dumping the bodies? How should this be? Should I dispose of them where they will not be found? It is tricky. One of the euphoric moments about Gary and Sheila was the fact that someone knew what happened to them, and I knew they had been returned. It added to the pleasure, like an aftershock.

Returning the bodies is a must! After all, Gary and Sheila both had burials, and it was closure. Gary I loved, as a thirteen year old loves, although I never told him. Maybe because, after I told him about the animals, he betrayed me. Maybe that's why I did what I did, for fear he would tell on me. I thought it was an accident, but maybe it was just how I want it to be remembered. Mmmm??

I have a cover story in place, so my absences are easily explained. It's almost too easy. It was right in front of me.

I really am eager to start, but I have to be back home tomorrow evening. Still, a couple of weeks should see it through. This journal will help focus my thoughts, and avoid letting my guard down like I did with Gary.

1962
Organs used: Pancreas, Liver.
Experiment: Susan Jones

I think it is important she is given her rightful name – after all, this is medical science, and an order needs to remain. I thought, for an instant, I would find it difficult to take the first; but the adrenalin fuelled the urgency. It was a nice quiet country lane, almost too simple. The chloroform worked perfectly, keeping her alive long enough for the journey back. Maybe the first was a little too close to home; but for want of a better choice, and a way to choose, it seemed appropriate.

As I felt her life ebb away, it was an explicit feeling, just as I remembered. The blood over my hands was like nectar filling me with an exuberance I am unable to quantify. It is enough for me to want it more; that instant of passing, like the closing of a book – the breath the pages exhale as the story concludes.

I have placed the organs in canisters of a very rough preservative called EX32. I am planning to leave them for a year to see what the cell degradation is. EX32 was found to be toxic, but I hope it will reveal a baseline I can work from.

I have a limited supply of liquid nitrogen – at the moment enough for the

*canisters; although my source says he can get it readily. I am trying to keep
my distance, but maintain contact. The first freezer is ticking away nicely.
I will monitor the temperature levels over the coming months, although
the insulation I have used is ahead of its time, a nice find through various
contacts.*

Picking up another notebook Ashworth flicked through the pages;
one word jumped off the page and she stopped to read.

*... KIDS! What the hell? The bane of life sometimes. They tie you up, sap
your freedom. This is important work I am doing here. Missing visits has
meant the liquid nitrogen has run low, causing an increase in temperature ...*

"What the hell? This guy has a family!" Ashworth exclaimed almost
frightened by what she was reading.

"What do you think?"

"I think we've stumbled onto something." She flicked through
the pages of both notebooks, hurriedly catching names, in her mind
noting them, Karen Littleton, Lucy Davis, Peter Hittles. The second
notebook gave more names – Kenneth Horsely, Francis Hall-Smith,
Andrew Sergeant.

"Do you want me to extend the crime scene?" Dr Yanovic pulled a
fibre from one of the metal containers.

"No, treat it as an separate crime scene...unless the fire was started
to dispose of this unit to throw us off the scent."

"An ancillary victim?"

"Exactly. Judging by how quickly the fire reportedly spread, it
would be an easy assumption to make: throw forensics off the source
and destroy the evidence they were trying to conceal. I'll call in and
get a check on these names, see if they mean anything; maybe missing
persons, et cetera. You might want to start bagging evidence."

"I'll bring my kit in."

Ashworth called CID. It took only ten minutes before her phone
burst into life.

"Ashworth ... really ..." came the astounded reply. "Thanks." She
cut the call. "Roberta?" Ashworth called, unable to see where she was.

"Here." she called from behind one of the metal freezers. "You'll
never believe this. These freezers are just not like I've seen before."

"I will. I got a hit on those names. A cold case, excuse the pun, that Ghost have in their system. I'm going to talk to them some more. You might want to get a team in here. The fire may well have been a disposal operation, so keep an open mind."

Chapter 150

2001 June
Lincolnshire
Storage Yard

I am dumfounded as I see the yard. It is not the burnt out units that rally my concern, as my unit looks relatively unscathed – although that would've been a blessing. It is the crime scene tape that mortifies me. Is that for the fire, or my unit? I almost pull off the baseball cap, that I wear now – how fads change and I have had to move with the times to avoid standing out in a crowd – I don't like it. It is not about liking, it is about disguising.

Suddenly a car-horn breaks my thoughts and I realise I am still in the middle of the road, after being pole-axed by shock upon arriving. I quickly drive on, raising my hand in apology to the other motorist. I'm shaking, and have to pull over a little way up the street. My mind is racing; my heart is pumping wildly. I can't think straight. It is not just a case of preparing the tears, as in Gary's death, when that man appeared. This is more serious. I try to think – what clues might I have left lying about? Have I got complacent over the years, settled into the feeling of security?

My notebooks, fingerprints, DNA – all those scientific advances that criminologists have made. It could be my demise. Have they gone into the unit? Maybe they haven't?

What should I do?

Not one thought stays long enough to join with any other.

Maybe they are watching the yard?

Damn!

Sharply, I look around, expecting an army of officers to ambush me. When nothing happens, I sit very still; shaking inside.

Distance! I need distance.

I pull away, almost stalling the car in the process. I can't stop shaking; the adrenalin making my heart palpitate. I take deep breaths.

I stop at a park and get out to walk around. I need air. I need to think. What should I do next? When was the fire? Is it a set up? Do the police know who I am? They can't do, otherwise I'd have been arrested by now.

What will I do then?

Lose the car! If the lab is gone then that is it; the game is over – it is too late to start again. There are too many records being kept. Have they discovered my lab? The doors looked secure – didn't they? No, they weren't!

Sitting down on a bench, I view the car in the car park. It needs to be burnt; got rid of along with any DNA it may have. Or, I could just leave it in the garage. The old guy is happy still with the arrangement. I could pay in advance, and then it would sit undiscovered for years; whereas, if I burn it, it will bring attention. Yes, the garage. That would be safer than burning. Nothing in the lab had my name on it. Did it? No. I'm not sure.

It's fine. I'll just put it behind me. I can do that. I *can* do that.

More relaxed, I head back to the garage, preparing to just walk away. In the back of mind hoping it is that easy. I suppose there is no point worrying about something that I can't change. I just need to be prepared to run.

Chapter 151

2001 June
Mike's Lab

"You alright, Roger? You look a bit, distracted." Sam enquired as he sliced a section of liver, before placing it under the microscope. There was no answer. "Is he alright, Sarah?"

"There something nasty going on at work, his whole department is being investigated ..."

"It's not something I want to discuss, or want to be discussed, thank you."

"These are our friends, Roger."

"And, I don't want to discuss it. Is that understood?"

"Well, I do. It has been quite stressful. You talk about moving away, and I don't want to. This is my life too!"

"And I have my career and reputation to think about."

"And I have our family to think about."

Sam looked to Margaret for help at diffusing the charged situation, but she was engrossed in a book about nanotechnology.

"I'm sure it will all blow over, Roger's an upstanding member of the medical profession." Sam placated.

"Mud sticks! Now can we not talk about it, I came here to get away from it. What are the results for that liver, Sam?"

Sam stood silently for a second, feeling the tension from Sarah, who looked as though she wanted to cry. "Using the microwave heater and a warmed solution of the glycerol, there is certainly an improvement in damage limitation. However, I don't see this brings us any closer to having a viable organ that can be used after being stored cryogenically for so long. There are still ..."

Margaret interrupted, "Nanotechnology of the future will solve some cell damage."

"How does that help us now?" Sam asked.

"It doesn't and, to be honest, I am not sure that we can progress much further. I mean, look at what our research has garnered in the last ten years. Not a lot in regards to solving the thawing issue; we still get cell damage. At the moment, that damage cannot be repaired, but Drexler talks about tiny robots – roughly cell size – that will be able to fix the body one cell, one molecule, at a time and, whilst genetics is inching closer to that, we are not there yet."

"So what we've been doing for years is a waste?" Sarah sighed.

"Nothings ever a waste, Sarah. You have to keep pushing, keep trying as you never know where the breakthroughs are going to come." Roger appeared to have lost his anger, "There has to be a way to solve damage due to freezing and thawing. It is like when we first started. We froze everything quickly in liquid nitrogen once the cryoprotectant was perfused. Now, we know that you need to lower the temperature a few degrees first, to about 5 degrees, then lower using dry ice to minus 76 degrees before submersing in liquid nitrogen, therefore avoiding the fissures that occurred due to sudden expansion or contraction of cells."

Sarah looked placated, and less tearful.

"But we have tried so many variants with the glycerol; there can't be anything left to try. And, let's face it, unless we can come up with a non-toxic form of formaldehyde that can suspend animation without freezing, are we ever going to make any progress?" Sam slumped onto a stool.

"Maybe, Sam. But we can't just give up after so long. We know genetics is making some amazing leaps. Some vertebrates can grow new limbs, body parts. Maybe we need to look at combining the two." Roger thumbed through the files sitting on the shelf. "So you're suggesting a regeneration under frozen storage, Sam?"

"Along those lines." Margaret agreed, cutting in.

"But, when frozen you suspend all cellular life, so you won't be able to regenerate, or repair." Sarah added.

"Correct, but if it is in the cryoprotectant, then, as thawing occurs, it can repair so the thawing becomes the healing process."

"Yes, but, Roger, if we have that regeneration potential, why bother with freezing in the first place? Because you'll be able to solve the ailment that caused the death." Sam queried.

"It is just a theory. What if the freezing is part of the cure? We know that cooling a body a few degrees can extend life if you have received life threatening injuries on the battlefield et cetera – but what if the genetic modification works when frozen, just not at such low temperatures. Let's face it, we used liquid nitrogen because, at minus 196 degrees, life is suspended; but, if we just slow it down – enough to allow the genetic modifications to take place – we would also eliminate any ice crystal damage whatsoever because the body would never go through it."

"Definitely interesting." Margaret confirmed.

Sam looked around at their primitive lab. "I'm not sure our lab is up to standard for that kind of work, nor do we have the money I feel that we would need."

Chapter 152

2001 July

Lincolnshire
Grantham

"Thank you for seeing us, Mr Tuffnell. I just have a few questions about the arson attack on your yard a couple of weeks ago."

"Have you bloody got him? Bloody insurance are arguing the toss." Harry sank further into a battered armchair.

"We're not sure but, hopefully, with a little of your help, we may be able to narrow it down."

Ashworth and Collins sat on the settee; it had also seen better days like the white faux fur rug.

"I already told your lot that the CCTV was bloody useless. Waste of money. That yard has got to be my biggest mist..." Suddenly Harry eyed the detectives warily. "I didn't do it. And I never arranged for it to be done. I must be a mug for not. But, I believe in playing above the line. Took me long enough to get rid of a couple of the bad tenants from when I bought it at that bloody auction. Bloody thugs the previous owner had in that place. Just 'cause I got the lot number wrong. Jesus, I have been paying ever since." Harry's rant stopped.

"Quite. I heard the rumour Benjamin Shaker was quite a nasty character as well. You say the tenants before were thugs. Does that go for the one in unit four? The only one left ..."

"... standing. No. Strange, maybe, but quiet, keeps himself to himself. Pays months in advance, cash, always cash. I put it through the books before you think different. Probably the only one I didn't have problems with."

Collins interjected. "Don't suppose you have his contact details do you, in your records?"

Harry sighed wearily. "This is a bloody young man's game." He got up.

"Sir, if I may ask? Did you ever report the problems to the police with the previous tenants?"

"Don't make me laugh. And get me bloody face smashed in? I played the waiting game."

He left the room.

"You gotta have a back bone to get into property. He doesn't seem the type." Collins stated.

"Quite. But, then again, if you bid on the wrong lot, you are asking for trouble to start with. Surprised he didn't sell it."

"Would have made sense." Harry plodded back into the room. "I would'a' done, but I valued my legs. As I say, nasty thugs. Parasites. Gone now, and finally it is starting to make some proper money. Was!"

"Left of their own accord?" Ashworth tried to hide the cynicism.

"Yes, they bloody did. I don't have the stomach for that kind of thing." He handed them an index filing card with a telephone number, name and address.

"That's it?" Ashworth took it.

"I've learned to keep details short, and as I say he was never any trouble, paid in advance. Although, I do recall a time – late seventies, maybe – when things went a bit AWOL. But came good in the end, and has been as good as gold ever since. That's actually when I took more details, just never had call to use them."

Collins took up the reigns "Don't suppose you ever got the guy on CCTV did you? We have some enquiries we'd like him to help us with."

"Do you think he started the fire?" Harry sounded the most positive since they had arrived.

Ashworth continued. "Let's just say it is a line of investigation we would like to follow. As my colleague said do you have any footage of him?"

Harry gazed out of the French doors; the bright sun was trying to shine through, only emphasizing the fact that they needed cleaning. "I doubt it, tend to record over everything. Plus, I wasn't allowed to have CCTV at first, clientele didn't like it!"

"I can imagine." Collins joked.

Suddenly Harry became more animated. "Hold on, I might have some old VHS in the garage. Not always been best at clearing out. That has become the store.".

"Do you mind having a look?" Ashworth asked.

An hour later, after handing him contact details, they were back in the car with a cardboard box full of VHS tapes to view, along with confirmation that Harry would contact them if the owner turned up again.

Chapter 153

2001 July

Mike's Lab

I'm on edge. I have never felt so insecure. My mind is distracted. Every time a door opens, I expect the police to turn up. I am just glad to be here on my own tonight. I do need to ring Harry to find out if the police have been in my unit. There's been nothing reported in the press and that, in some way, soothes me. All I can do for the time being is keep my distance; keep watching the news. If they have, I am sure it would have been released to the press by now. The coup in ending a forty-year spree! My god it has been forty years? There have been so many changes, so much information, so much progress, yet we still can't succeed in thawing a human and restoring them to life. At least it is being taken more seriously now.

With transplants being so common these days, the only real issues are how long an organ remains usable. The major organ of concern from our project's view is the brain – it is the one organ that is essential; it is the one organ than defines our personalities and holds our memories. Some people have only had their heads stored cryonically: because it is cheaper, and also because of the firm belief that science will move on enough to allow regeneration of our bodies; growing new younger, stronger bodies. But we still need the physical brain, as this holds the essence of us – as individuals. I have been reading some articles on hyperthermia therapy; where cooling the body has actual increased the chance of survival in cardiac cases. People have been revived with no brain damage after being submerged in ice-cold water for more than two hours. This proves one thing – that memories are locked in, just a like computer.

Nanotechnology, cell size robots are purported to be the thing that is going help science with re-animation after thawing, ice destroys the synapses and until we can repair them … what was that?

The door suddenly opens. Sarah stands there looking upset. My mind turns over a hundred thoughts and my heart palpitates.

Chapter 154

2001 July
Lincolnshire
CID

"Well?" Ashworth folded her arms.

"Jesus, my eyes ache," Whitley moaned, "but we have some footage. And better news: technical discovered some footage from his last visit about two months ago."

"And?" Ashworth wanted more.

"Alright, I'm getting there. He is driving a Mark II Escort. Harry has confirmed red in colour. I have run the plate and it's fake. Registered to an Orange Skoda and an Angela O'Donnell in Scunthorpe. She still has the car, so I am guessing just a mock-up job."

"Not your average fake plate then?" Ashworth scowled.

"No, and that's what is strange. Fake plates are normally based on a duplicate car, less suspicious. So we must be dealing with a complete idiot." Whitley took a gulp of his cold coffee, hidden amongst the VHS tapes and VCR.

"Is he though? I spoke to Liverpool nick: this guy has been on the loose since '62, when the first person went missing according to them."

"Jeez, forty-odd years. That's some serial. How's he got away with it that long?"

"Good question. I am trying to get an address for the detective who investigated the case, a William Travis, he retired about five years ago due to ill health ..." Ashworth flicked through her notebook "... to see if he can shed some light on it." Ashworth turned to go, stopping to face Whitley again. "Is there any CCTV, or traffic cameras, in the area that can trace that car? We need to see where it goes. I can't believe it has survived unnoticed on the street. It must be parked, or stored, somewhere. If this guy is old school, and stupid, then he probably stores it at home or in a garage near his home. You may need to go cross country."

"Already on it."

Chapter 155

2001 August
Manchester

"Thank you for agreeing to see me." Ashworth sat in one of the two armchairs.

William placed two mugs on the table. "No problem. It is been a while since I have spoken to anyone from the force. In fact I was quite surprised to get the phone call."

Ashworth looked at the now sixty-one year old, frail and aged beyond his years. After she had contacted Ghost she'd been turned onto Liverpool CID and spoken with a couple of colleagues who had worked under DCI Travis. The reports were that he used dedication to hammer a conviction home, his persistence leading to an affectionate nickname of 'Bloodhound Bill'. William let slip at his retirement that he knew about it, much to the embarrassment of his colleagues.

Ashworth felt affection for the guy, for his rep. "How's retirement treating you?"

"Not very well, in all honesty." William's voice was husky with a hint of weakness. The spirit within alive but the shell showed decay. "A few scares here and there. That's your lot, I guess. I've had a good life. Children, so can't complain." came the chipper, false reply.

"Sorry to hear that. I understand you had, have…" Ashworth corrected, "a good record, and were well liked by all accounts. Praise was commending, even heard you had a chance of promotion to the higher echelons."

William smiled. It gave his skin's dull sheen a glimmer of brightness. "Pen pushing is for other people, not me. I like to be in the thick of it. But all things must come to an end. Stress is not good for your health. That's why I moved to ghost."

Ashworth took a sip of coffee. "Sounds like we could do with more of you on the force now. The criminals are getting smarter and budgets smaller. Do more in less time." She couldn't hide the bitterness; she loved her job but it was frustrating. The victims tended to suffer two fold, she'd seen it many times, not only a victim of the crime but when they were put through the ringer by clever barristers. Many suffered emotionally afterwards; a couple she'd heard about had committed suicide. It was a sad state of affairs.

"I'd love to be back on it, the garden can only fill so much time. I never really wanted to do anything else. I don't mind the cricket, when it's on. Although my health hasn't helped – deteriorating this last year."

"Sorry to hear that." Ashworth meant it.

"What can I do for you? You certainly haven't come here to hear me blathering on like an idiot." William smiled and Ashworth reciprocated.

"It's about a cold case. An old case of yours."

For a moment William looked flummoxed before realisation flushed his cheeks a healthy red, his eyes darkening.

"Serial, by any chance '63. Susan Jones being the first." William looked the most alive that Ashworth had seen thus far.

"Sharp as a button! They said you were good, didn't realise how good."

"The body may be shot but the brain is still good." Ashworth smiled. "Well you are either here to tell me you finally got the guy," William paused for a fraction of a second. "Sam Talbot, or there is another victim not on the list."

Ashworth sort of nodded her head. "Kinda. As you know I'm from Lincoln CID and a few weeks ago there was a fire in a small industrial estate hidden away in a residential area. Supposed arson attack; there have been a few in the area. Anyway, and I'm telling you this in strictest confidence, and out of respect." William nodded acceptance, "The only unit not damaged too severely, led to us finding some journals; in which were detailed experiments carried out on the victims from a case your name is linked to. We had some DNA tests done from tissue samples found. They matched a couple of the victims."

William interrupted, a seemingly youthful exuberance bubbling away. "The victims were frozen and samples taken, as if for experiments, we could never understand why, or for what purpose. One theory was a medical fanatic, or whack job, but yet there was always something methodical about them. Every lead dried up. The only time we came close was in '77. Sam Talbot killed his own son, run him over, although we couldn't prove it." William sounded resolute, then mellowed. "Poor kid. Even though we found evidence, circumstantial evidence, we just couldn't tie it up in nice little bows for the prosecution." He sighed wearily, the frustration still visible. "Some people are just so slippery."

"Well, hopefully this is good news then. It sounds as though the guy fits your profile and he has been at this unit since about '62, apparently. The new owner bought the yard in '71 at an auction, bid on the wrong lot." Ashworth smirked. "Couldn't offload it. A certain element wouldn't let him. They've met their demises though. From what records there were, your guy was there and has been there all the time. With the advent of CCTV, we have a car, a Mark II Escort – false plates of course. We're just trying to track it down now. And, we have a rather grainy image." Ashworth held out the photo.

William grabbed his glasses and analysed the picture. "Could be anyone."

"We never found any photos of this Samuel Talbot on file so have nothing to compare it with."

"Like I said could be anyone. I did keep a copy of some bits when I left." He put up a hand before any remark came from Ashworth. "It's the only thing I ever did that was out of context of my clean record. Call it, an old man's determination to find the truth. And it's only photocopies. The originals should all be in the files, including photos." The insinuation was not lost on Ashworth – it shouldn't, but sometimes evidence did go missing.

"Well, then I would say that you were just being careful at your filing." Ashworth smiled as William retrieved the file from a draw.

The file didn't show anything conclusively and except for some different papers Ashworth had it all. Another hour of pleasantries passed, rejuvenating William.

"Thank you for your help, I'll keep you posted. It's the least I can do."

William smiled and shook the offered hand, feeling a sense of belonging again.

William watched from the lounge window as Ashworth pulled away.

"I miss the excitement."

He turned and faced the large art deco mirror over the fireplace and looked at the old man staring back at him: the gaunt features and the thin grey hair. For an instant he saw the young PC from '63 and yearned to be there again. The minutes passed, only broken from his reverie by the front door opening.

"Hi, I'm home."

William turned sharply to see Fiona in the doorway. In his mind, he saw PC Fiona Benton as she appeared that first time he met her, her vibrant eyes and tantalising smile like a youthful elixir. Without a word he swept her into his old arms with as much young lust his old arms would allow.

Chapter 156

2001 October
Lincolnshire
CID

"Ashworth, my office." It was a friendly call from DCI Nadeen Gupta.

"Ma'am." Ashworth replied, taking a large gulp of coffee before grabbing a file, anticipating what it was about.

She closed the door and sat. Nadeen conducted a fairly relaxed office, she found that's how she got the best from her people after witnessing too many grumpy, stressed, gits doing her job and pushing for quick fixes, and not necessarily getting to right result. She had said one day to her team, 'You come in here, you sit, we sit, we chat, we discuss. I may shout, I may get upset, but I will listen. Stand your ground…when it's right to do so.' She was popular, respected; fair.

"The arson case right?" Ashworth held up the file.

"Absolutely. I understand it has tripped into Ghost's shoes." Her voice was flat.

"Kinda. But I have a hunch that it is still connected to the arson. Ghost said they were happy for me to continue, I took the initiative as our cases crossed and have spoken with the officer, now retired, who seems to have had the most to do with the case – been open since '63 unless you count when the victim disappeared, in '62."

"A serial, covering forty years and no one has come close to a suspect?" Nadeen sounded cynical.

"Only one, a Samuel Talbot. Not enough evidence in the end. Was in the press at the time. Went cold after that in '78. An occasional body turned up but no firm new leads or evidence linking this man to them. They were told not to investigate Mr Talbot for fear of harassment charges, unless there was solid evidence. It had appeared on Crimewatch a few years ago but nothing."

"We also have a car, a red, Mark II Escort, false plates et cetera. Have put a broadcast out to other counties, as this guy liked to use the whole country as his playground. The victims picked up and dumped in different places."

Silence consumed the room as Nadeeen considered. "You want to stay on this?"

"Yes, ma'am, at least for a little longer. Have a gut feeling we are close and…"

"… and your gut feelings normally pan out. I know."

Nadeen stood up and looked around the vast undermanned office. There should have been over twenty people; there were only fifteen and they were always under pressure.

"Alright, you can have Whitley, but get Sanjay, Tolga and John to look after the arson side of this. I'll give you a couple of weeks but, if no results, then give it back to Ghost. If anything else serious comes up in the meantime you drop it."

"Understood."

Chapter 157

2002 January

Lincolnshire
CID

"Hey, Tolga. How was Burns night?" Whitley patted him on the back.

"Like you'd never believe." His Scottish accent was back with a vengeance, after only a week back home; the years of living in the south had bled the accent so it was normally a distant relative of its former self.

"Sure your liver will be glad of the rest now?"

"Too true, too true. Is Ashworth in today?"

"Yeah, just got a date with the school about her daughter – been fighting again."

"Aye, kids will be kids. Well I've got to go out myself now. Can you pass this message onto her?" Tolga handed him a piece of paper.

"Sure." He looked at it as he headed to his own desk. "Harry Tuffnell! Harry Tuffnell? That name sounds familiar."

-

An hour later he was sitting down with his green tea when he remembered. "Bloody hell!"

A few colleagues looked round but none made a comment.

Whitley dialled the number for Harry Tuffnell, it was answered on the fifth ring.

"Mr Tuffnell, it's DC Gary Whitley. You asked DS Ashworth to give you a call. She's out at the moment so thought I would give you a ..."

There was no time for pleasantries as Harry interrupted. "That man you asked me about last year, the one who rents the unit, he contacted me last week asking about the unit, understood there'd been a fire and that he was sorry he hadn't been in contact for the last few months – had been travelling. Said he would like to collect his things and settle up if that was possible."

Whitley almost sprang out of his chair. "And? You didn't tell him we were investigating him did you?" Whitley held his breath, the last thing they wanted was this guy to know they were onto him.

"No, I said the unit wasn't damaged; just that I am closing it down – gonna see if I can get planning for houses. He said he would pay back rent and wanted to come and collect his stuff."

"Does he now? That's good. When can you get him there?"

"Sorry?"

"When is the earliest you can arrange to meet him? I can get a team in place later today, or we can do tomorrow."

"Oh."

"Oh?"

"He came last Friday …"

"And you're ringing us now!" He couldn't hide the anger in his voice, although it was lost on Harry.

"Yes, well I thought it was important."

"So why not bloody call beforehand? He is a person of interest we wish to speak to!"

There was silence like it had just dawned. "Oh…yes, I suppose that would have been best." No wonder he'd bought the wrong auction lot Whitley thought. "I do have CCTV footage if that is a help. The guy did turn up, but when he saw the unit, or rather what is left, panicked and drove off without paying."

"I'll call in to pick it up. From your home?"

"Yes, that's fine."

"I'll be over shortly." Whitley slammed the phone down. "Jesus, are people really that stupid?" He grabbed his coat and left.

Chapter 158

2002 January
Lincolnshire

Maybe it was silly to visit the yard, but forty years worth of research, gone! There has been no mention in the news, or local papers, that I could find; plenty about the arson, yes – and wishing to speak to persons of interest. Deep down I needed to be sure. I had to be sure. Now I know.

I'm shaking. There's nothing I can do. Do I need to run? Now would be the time, sell up and go, Spain is nice, warm climate. Maybe further afield; Mexico or Jamaica – that was nice. Harry looked astonished when I just reversed out and left, but seeing the unit, I knew, I knew they know about me, even if not who I am. Can I leave everyone and just go, without a word? It's that, or prison for the rest of my life. Not a choice I relish.

Chapter 159

2002 January
Lincolnshire
CID

"Coleen, I got some CCTV from our friend Harry Tuffnell." Ashworth turned round and pointed to the phone plastered to her ear. "Oops!"

He sat at his desk and inserted the DVD whilst making a phone call to traffic requesting urgent coverage from cameras in the area.

Ashworth joined him a few minutes later. "What's occurring? Is this that case? So that's our guy is it?"

"Yep, and yep. The guy arranged to come and pay the rent due. Just can't believe that numpty didn't call us beforehand. I have asked traffic to see if they can track this car via other cameras on the day, see if we can see where he goes. Could take a while though. It's been five days. We may be lucky if they haven't deleted any footage. I gave them the time so at least it could speed things up."

"Excellent. He didn't hang around after he saw the place."

"Harry had the audacity to ring back to ask us to chase him for the rent which was due."

"Hope you told him 'we would'" The sarcasm was not lost of Whitley who smiled. "If you were using a second car, how far would you travel to store it? Also would you park close to it when changing over cars? That may cause suspicion to the right person."

"Personally, I'd want it close by, but not too close, ten miles perhaps."

"So, ten miles to the unit. How close would you then live to that, presuming you stored it off site from your home?"

Whitley was staring intently at the screen shot he'd made. "That depends on what your time frames are? If there is no need to be that close then what better scenario than living, say, in Scotland, and travelling down every so often. We know it was not a regular journey for him." Suddenly Whitley noticed something. Clicking rewind he played a small section of film, repeatedly. Then added distractedly

"He didn't pay regularly, but would pay for months at a time. It varied. The only time he was ever late was '78 and we know that ties up nicely with what's-his-names arrest. You know it probably was that guy after all, but a botched investigation led to him getting off."

Ashworth noted Whitley's concentration and also started to stare at the screen. "No. I met the lead detective, almost photographic memory, his record is exemplary, there's no way it was botched. There is something weird, or off, for my liking. What are you looking for?"

"See that reflection? Whilst he conceals his face to the camera I wonder if our techies could get an image from that?"

"Worth a try."

Chapter 160

2002 January
Lincolnshire
CID

Two Days Later

"Sarge I got CCTV from the surrounding areas. Looks like the car gets parked down Wentworth Avenue. Unfortunately there are no cameras viewing that road, so it is a bit of punt. But it's a dead end down there; it used to come out onto London Road but the council blocked it off, quite a few years ago. There are now close's, that's all."

Ashworth looked over Whitley's shoulder at an on screen map. "Wentworth leads to these areas," she said pointing at the screen, "and you can access the park from there, which means you can exit … one … two, three, four, bloody hell five places. How about here? Bennington Lane, isn't there a new parade of shops – built a few years ago? Any cameras?"

"Not that I know of but I'll check it out. There are also some shops here, not far from Wentworth …"

"Maybe …"

"On it." Whitley concluded heading for the door, leaving Ashworth studying the map.

"Did the techies manage to isolate that reflection?" Ashworth called across the room.

Whitley was by the door. "No. Too small. How about a woman?"

Ashworth. "Thanks, but I'm not that way inclined." she smiled, a positive feeling starting to course through her veins.

Whitley walked back to Ashworth. "No, not what I meant, there was something bugging me about the image, that's why I wanted the reflection magnified."

"Did we get any DNA hits from the unit other than the victims?"

"I don't think we did. They would've told us if they had. He must have been careful over the years."

"I'll double check."

Next Day

"Local chemist had footage and I have looked through. Luckily it is fairly quiet, I have gone an hour either side, to narrow it down. These are all the cars with male drivers, three hundred and seventy–two. Jeez."

Ashworth patted Whitley on the shoulder in a friendly way. "Good luck. I am sure I have something else to d… wait, we could narrow it down to single occupancy, so just a driver. Did you get local bus CCTV as well? They may have walked out of there and caught a bus. Maybe a train?"

"Bollocks. No wonder this guy never got caught. And not all buses have cameras, yet."

Three Days Later

"Ain't you finished going through that stuff yet?" DC Vince Singh questioned.

Whitley sighed. "Nope, there is still more coming through, plus I am only doing this in between doing that Sheppard case; this is a cold case after all. DCI is giving me ache to pass it back to Ghost."

"So what? It's not as if we don't have that much to do anyway?" Vince was conscientious, but practical, and very methodical.

Whitley rubbed the weariness away from his eyes. "Maybe you're right, it's flogging a dead horse."

"There's no shame in it, you probably did Ghost a favour, they'll take it up in their own time."

As if on cue, DCI Gupta called him into her office.

"What's the position on the cold case? Have you seen DS Ashworth today?" Nadeen was a little short in tone, just biting on cordial.

"She's checking out the burglaries, following up a lead. As for the cold case, I have to confess, bloody freezing." He joked.

"Mmm, you've gotta know when to let go. I think that time is now. I've been generous enough with resources. Send it back to Ghost, let them know what you've achieved and move on."

"Yes, ma'am." Whitley resigned. "Ashworth will be pissed."

"Well, she can carry on in her own time, and you. I can't devote any more resources to it. Your focus is best spent on the cases we got. There was another arson this morning, so I don't think our suspect was involved. Theory was fine, but not now."

Whitley slumped back to his desk, hating the thought of leaving something for someone else to finish, but Nadeen was right – a forty-year serial cold case was not a big concern, unless a new body turned up. He boxed everything up and spent the next two hours writing up his notes before labelling for the internal courier to take it to Ghost's archive.

He did wonder whether it would be another ten years before it was acted upon. Would the killer be dead by the time it was discovered?

Chapter 161

2002 April

Manchester
Ghost CID

DSI Tanya Wells had been in Ghost about six months and, today, was looking at a case that hadn't been due for review for another two years but, late last year, it had crossed with an arson case before being discounted as unrelated. DS Ashworth and DC Whitley had run with it until they were told to leave it. DC Whitley had reached a point when he'd forwarded the files with his copious detailed notes. Because of this, it had been fast tracked for action, but a cold murder/rape case had sprung open with new DNA evidence. That finally wrapped last week, and now her attention was focussed back on this serial.

Scanning through the box, she saw the CCTV footage labelled up and a long list of possibilities, around two to three hundred faces.

"Langston, come in here." Wells called.

"Gov?"

"Got a trawl job. Hundreds of people. We need names, address etc. It's a serial, been unsolved for forty years. An arson last year got tied in because the location could be the centre of where the murders took place. There are no fingerprints or DNA from what the local force are referring to as 'a lab'. There was only ever one suspect, a Samuel Talbot – arrested, charged but released; warned off after that for fear of an harassment case. DCI William Travis was the officer involved with the case at the time, now retired. DS Ashworth spoke to him a few months back and requested he be kept advised of the outcome.

"From what we have here, Ashworth and her colleague, Whitley, found an area where a second car was being used." She glanced through the notes. "Looks like they didn't actually locate the car, just a residential area. There is CCTV footage from around the time and these stills." She pulled a pile of paper out of the box.

"That lot?"

"Yep. Get DC's Roberts and Cooper to help. They think that one of these people could be the killer."

Langston's face looked pained at the mammoth task, but his dedication kicked in.

"This is the person and the car they drove into that area." She pointed to a printed map that had been circled. "They either live in that area, or just use it for storage. House to house did not dig up anything. You're lucky this was just one hour after the car entered."

"Timescale?"

"Just do your best; we'll review in a week, unless you get somewhere sooner."

Chapter 162

2002 May
Fakenham
Roger and Sarah's House

"What do you mean, move? I don't want to move. Especially not to Australia! Our kids are settled, they have friends. Roger – why?"

"That bloody woman who accused me of sexual harassment is making life hell. I'm a bloody professor. They are threatening to take my position away. It is causing a bad reflection on my department." Roger fumed. "Are the kids upstairs?"

"No, they are with your mother. We've got Margaret, Sam and Mike coming over tonight." Sarah poured herself a glass of Jacobs Creeks Red, almost feeling the anger boil when she saw that it was Australian.

"Great!" Roger slammed annoyed.

As if on cue, the doorbell clanged. Neither moved.

"Are you going to get that, Roger?"

Huffing, he walked out the room, leaving Sarah close to tears as she found it hard to believe that he wanted them to move. A colleague of Rogers had offered him a chance to teach in Australia. Australia! Why the hell would they want to go there?

"Hi, Sarah," Sarah turned to see Margaret, "you alright hun?"

"Roger wants us to move to Australia. No, I'm bloody not alright," she stormed into the kitchen as Roger, Sam and Mike entered the lounge.

* * * *

"Something I didn't say." Mike offered looking a little nervous.

"No, something I said." Roger admitted. "That bloody sexual harassment case is ruining everything and I have been offered a chance to teach in Australia for a couple of years … "

"Isn't that almost like admitting guilt – running away?"

Roger stared at Sam. "Actually, no, it's called getting out of the way of the punches when they seem relentless. I'm innocent. Why would I want to go near that narrow minded, troublesome arrogant woman;

she was difficult from the moment she started working there."

"Why did she accuse you?" Mike sat down.

"How the hell do I know? But it is making work so untenable that I needed to do something, and a colleague had an opening, and approached me, so it seemed like a perfect solution."

"Surprised they didn't suspend you on full pay." Mike added.

"They have contemplated it, but they have no one to take over my work load and they believe me."

There was silence.

"Do you want a drink?" Roger sounded calmer now.

"Yes, I need one. Then I need to tell you guys something."

"Oh, yes Mike. What's that then?" Sam kicked off his shoes as he sat down in the armchair.

"I'll wait until the girls join us."

"What was that?" Margaret asked, Sarah following.

"Mike has something to tell us." Sam confirmed.

"About time." Sarah immediately clamped her hand to her mouth, much to the curious glances of Margaret and Sam, and the embarrassment of Mike.

Mike looked hesitant. Gulped and sighed resignedly, "I'm moving in with someone. My partner."

"You haven't got a partner." Sam seemed astounded. "When was this? You've never mentio… "

"I have. He's name Pablo, he's Spanish … "

"So you are gay then? About bloody time you came out. Good for you." Margaret stated.

"What? What!?" Sam glanced around the room.

"Oh, come on, Sam, you're not saying you didn't know?" Margaret asked.

"You all knew?" Mike queried. "Sarah and Roger said they wouldn't say anything."

"They didn't, Mike, but I knew you always fancied Sam, I've seen you looking at him. Oh, come on, Sam, surely?"

Sam sat speechless. "No."

"Well, it looks as though we are going to relocate to Murcia, where his family are. We can get a nice home, and there is work on the vineyard they own. It is lovely there, I actually feel as though I belong. You'll have to visit us once we get settled."

"Blow me, I'm flabbergasted."

"Thank you, but I'm over you now, Sam." Mike mused.

"So all those trips to America, they were ... "

"No, Sam, they were legit, except a few. I'm sorry I lied; sometimes I used to go to Brighton. That's where I met Pablo, a couple of years ... "

Suddenly Sarah started laughing. "I can't ... believe ... you didn't ... oh god, I'm going to pee my pants ... Sam. Your face."

"What? How should I bloody know?"

Chapter 163

2002 June
Manchester
Ghost CID

DS Clive Langston had indentified seventy-seven faces, with names and addresses, so far. All had panned out to nothing. Cars had been easy to eliminate, regulars on the buses – also. Occasional shoppers, and travellers, had proven harder; with no criminal past there was nothing to go on. All identified people had been cross-referenced for alibis at the times of victims' disappearances and body dumps. It had taken weeks. No one matched all of them and there were no obvious connections between the ones that did.

Langston sighed rubbing his eyes.

Whilst CCTV had certainly made its mark, with cameras almost everywhere – including obscure random cameras – which were sometimes the best sources, as the owners rarely deleted stuff (hard-drive capacity now seemingly endless) still nothing panned out to anything tangible.

He looked around the empty office – he liked it quiet. Roberts and Cooper were out chasing a couple of leads. In the meantime another cold case had re-surfaced and they were under pressure to move onto it. Time was running out on this one yet again, unless a solid lead was forthcoming.

"You're here somewhere you git. Now, where are you hiding? No one can be that lucky."

"I was last night," DC Charlie Phillips replied, entering, carrying a black sports bag. "And gee you should have seen the legs on this one. I certainly did some investigating I can tell you. Surprised I got out alive. She works for MOD, there was no secret there though, just pleasure."

"One day you won't. You'll get caught, the way you put it about." Langston replied with a little envy. Charlie always pulled, wherever he went, the women just seemed to fall for him. Langston was in a relationship and happy; they were even discussing kids.

"I want kids, a family, but I just want to feel my way around first. You any nearer with that?" Charlie leaned over to see what Langston was doing

"Two months and nothing. We've nearly exhausted every avenue and the pressure is on to move to the Freedman murder; that has just kicked up a new lead."

"Who you got left?" Then adding after seeing the pile, "Or should I say how many?"

"Thirty-seven I cannot get a name for. The pictures are a little iffy as well. But gotta keep trying."

"How long has Wells given ya?" Charlie sat down at his own desk. He'd only joined a month ago although he'd settled in quickly.

"Another week, then it is back in the box until something else crops up. They may be dead by that time. Another Jack the Ripper mystery."

"Look, I've got an hour or so to spare as I am waiting for the lab to call back, I'll give you hand if you like."

"Be my guest." Langston carried a wad over to Charlie.

Charlie skimmed through the photos as though shuffling a deck of cards. "Eeny meeny miny mo. You'll do."

"Nothing like following a system." Langston mocked, returning to his seat.

"Sometimes random is the best system. I'm sure that was some philosopher's theory."

"Yeah, right."

Roberts and Cooper entered looking decidedly dejected.

"Hey, Clive, where did you say this was?"

"Pointer's Cross, near that council estate, the one that was built in the sixties. Why?"

"It's just … you're looking for this person who dumped a car, sorry, stores a car there?"

"Yes." Langston responded, unsure where this was going.

"Well, has anyone checked out the garages just off Pond Road?"

"Yeah. The guys who were handling this before it came back to us …" Langston started to rifle through the box file that had sat by his desk for the last two months. He made clicking noises with his tongue. "…er…oh…no, would be the answer. They checked out people on the estate, about four hundred."

"Well, if they don't live on the estate, maybe they rent a garage."

"They checked them all out, I'm sure." He started rifling through more papers, "It's here, I'm sure. Yep, here it is." Langston scanned through the stapled sheets of paper. "No, it doesn't seem that they did, actually." He thought about this for a second, a light bulb came on in his head. "And they may have always rented one! There could be records going back to '62. I really hate you." It was said with admiration.

"See, random works."

Minutes later both were making phone calls, trying to establish who owned the various garages that sat in parallel lines just off Pond Road. An hour later and they had printed off a map showing the garages and the streets surrounding them.

"Fifty-six garages," Langston stated, "and they belong to this group of houses." He outlined with his finger on a screen shot of a map.

"And back to the beat work. House to house."

Chapter 164

2002 July
Manchester
Ghost CID

"Ma'am, got a hit." Langston called to DSI Wells from her doorway. She looked up eagerly. "An elderly guy has been renting his garage out for the last forty-odd years. Tenant pays cash every few months; varying length, just like the storage yard where the lab is. He very rarely sees them, just gets an envelope pushed through his letter box every now and again, and then, if he wants to get in contact, he posts one under the garage door. The family only recently found out after the old man died; the sale was progressing nicely until this kicked up. There's an agreement, just no legitimate contact details."

"Name on it?"

"Yeah. Sam Smith, same as the lab."

"S'ppose the name is fake? Don't' s'ppose they've got a description?"

"No, but I did notice one of the neighbours has CCTV." The news was a sweet nectar. "Got a clear image of our serial; we know who it is. Been right under our noses the whole time. Thank God the guy with CCTV was a bit of a nut, and kept all the recordings; he had years' worth. We've got dates and just doing final comparison checks with disappearances and body dumps as far back as you can."

"Good. I'll get a search warrant for the garages. Excellent work."

Langston turned to walk away then stopped. "It was Charlie's hunch."

She looked at him appraisingly. "We are a team, but credit where it's due. Although he has got a bit of a big head, so will let this one go, eh?" She smiled conspiratorially.

"Sure." Langston headed back to his desk.

"Did I get the credit or did you sabotage me?" Charlie chimed.

"Oh, I took the credit myself. Why would I give you the credit?" he said playfully.

"I'm too good for here!"

Chapter 165

2002 August
Chester
William Travis' Home

"How was bridge?" William asked. The once strong voice sounded exhausted. The lung cancer was taking its toll; exacerbated only by the arthritis and weakening heart.

"It was okay. Jan and Maureen won. How you feeling this evening?" Fiona asked, placing her bag by the armchair.

"Stiff, and a little unsettled, I must say. I tried to get out in the garden..."

"Yes, it is was lovely evening."

"Yes. I wanted to sort the beetroot out but I didn't feel as though I had the strength." William coughed a deep chesty, phlegmy, cough that rattled.

"I really don't like the sound of that. I think we ought to get you to the doctor tomorrow. I'll book an emergency appointment."

"Thanks love." For a second he remembered how he felt when he first saw her in her uniform, her lovely bright flirty brown eyes flashing their tempting brilliance at him. As the thought faded, a shudder ran through him and he turned a deathly grey.

"How about I make us a lovely pot of tea before we go to bed?" Fiona had turned to put her bag away when she remembered why she had wanted to get home so sharply. "William, do you remember that case of yours that never got closed."

"The Sam Talbot one?" His frail voice barely made the words and, as Fiona turned back to him, she couldn't hide her concern. William, whilst putting on a brave front, knew he didn't have long left. The last visit to the doctors had confirmed that his heart was failing, outdoing the lung cancer. He had not fully disclosed it to Fiona, not wanting to spoil the time they had left. It was getting harder to hide the fact that he would soon be gone; a welcome relief from the suffering, but sadness at not being with Fiona, his love, his life.

"You don't look well William. I think I might call an ambulance."

"No, please don't make a fuss love. It's nothing, probably just a summer sniff. Just tell me what you were going to say." Fiona looked at him, her face showing she knew it was more serious than William was letting on.

Hesitantly Fiona continued. "Well, you know that accident on the M1 last month that killed fourteen people."

"Yes, I think so." William rasped, coughing again. "The memory is still good, even if everything else is shot."

"Well, we were talking about it at bridge tonight," she continued more cheerfully. "I can't remember why now; it was something Jan said. What was it?" William looked at his wife, knowing it would bug her until she recollected how the conversation had come about. However, at the same time, he felt an importance that he just needed to know the facts. A sixth sense; which had helped many a time on the force.

"Just tell me ..." he spluttered.

"Oh, that was it. One of Jan's cousins died in it, she only found out this week. She showed me an article from the paper. Well ..." Fiona sat on the settee to finish her story, "... as she showed me the list of names, one name shone out: Sam Talbot!" Fiona saw William's eyes widen in horror and surprise. "There was an interview with his twin brother Nigel, or was it Nicholas."

"So he still got away with it." He said dryly. "Nicholas. I could never find out what had happened to him, or the sister." He coughed harder as his chest tightened.

Fiona tensed, seeing William's pain; and the joy she thought the news might bring him drained from her. "Yes. Yes, I suppose he did," and then adding more resolutely, "at least he can settle the score with his maker now." Fiona had found her faith shortly after her fiftieth birthday. It had been like a calling for her and, ever since, she had gone every Sunday and some evenings. William had not shared her love of the church, only embracing Fiona's happiness for it. He doubted that Sam would pay the price for his crimes and it was little consolation that he had died a free man.

"You said there was an interview with the twin brother, Nicholas?"

"Yes. She showed me the article. They'd got separated at birth. He had been called Michael, I think, by his adoptive parents. There was a sister too, but it didn't say what had happened to h… " Fiona trailed off seeing him turn even greyer. "You really don't look well. I think I will call that …" Fiona got up urgently.

"No. Please, don't." William reached out for Fiona's hand, gripping it as tight as he could manage, grimacing at the pain in his arthritic hands. "A cup of tea would be really nice now. You're right; at least he didn't survive. It's over now!"

"I really think an ambu…"

"No!" He said rather more harshly than intended. "Just a cup of your lovely tea and a scone if there is any left."

Reluctantly she concurred and left the lounge; the nine o'clock news was just starting.

"Bye, my sweet. I love you with all my heart." William uttered, reaching for the pad and pen he'd always kept at the side of the armchair, on the largest table of the nest of three they'd bought in an antique shop, some twenty years previously.

On the pad he scratched his spoken words. As a tear left his eye, he felt life drain away painlessly, as though soothed by giving in. The only hurt was the emotional one of leaving his beloved Fiona behind.

-

"Here we go." Fiona breezed into the room a few minutes later, her eyes red from crying. She'd had a feeling that William didn't have long for this world and, when she saw him slumped in the chair, she knew. She placed the tray heavily on the sideboard and rushed to him, knowing there was nothing to be done. Taking his hand in both of hers, she read the shaky writing on the pad as the floodgates opened and the well of her love spilled over.

"Oh, William. What am I going to do without you?"

Chapter 166

2002 August
Mike's Lab

Outside

"That's Mike's lab." Sam stated indignantly as he and Geoff stood, looking on.

Geoff added scornfully, "Yes, I know. It is near the end of your journey now. You have one task left."

"What's that? What good will it do now? I can't exactly go to the police." Sam was infuriated with the betrayal.

"No, you can't, but you don't need to. Look!"

Sam watched as a police car pulled up to the gate of the yard where the lab occupied an outbuilding. Two uniformed and two plain-clothes detectives got out. The older, frail detective looked familiar to Sam and stood with conviction and energy of youth, contrary to how he appeared.

"I know hi…" Sam started.

"Yes, you do. And you should, he interviewed you a few times."

"Travis!" Sam stated aggressively.

Sam jumped as Travis turned and looked straight at him.

"What the hell?"

"Rather appropriate terminology to use, Sam, considering the situation."

"Sam Talbot!" William spoke with disgust.

"How does he know I'm here?"

"You're both dead." Geoff added matter-of-factly.

"You mean I've got put up with that bastard haunting my death as well as my life?" William stepped towards Sam, his fists finally free of their arthritis, clenched and, for a second, they stood in stand-off, before William swung a punch at Sam with youthful exuberance. Sam was too late to duck away as the fist went through him without making any contact, although he flinched in anticipation of it landing. William immediately lost his footing and went tumbling to the ground. "This isn't fair! I worked my ass off in life to look out for decent everyday people. Doing my damnedest to get rid of the rubbish on the streets. Like you!" he scowled at Sam. "And what do I get for it? Eh? To put up with it in my afterlife? I never believed in the afterlife; just thought ... just thought ... it would be ... I don't know, but not this, not with scum like him."

Geoff walked to William. "Things are not always as they seem. You are not destined for here, but this is just a chance for you to find eternal peace. Let's call it the final closing for you, as well as for Sam."

"Wait a minute. If he can see you as I see you, that doesn't make any sense. You said that I, or the person that dies, chooses the form of their journeyman; surely his ..." Sam pointed a disdainful finger at William, "... would be some form from his life, not mine?"

Geoff sighed and both men stared at him, trying to fathom the situation. "I am not all answers to everyone; all I know is that it is important your paths cross this last time. After that I don't know."

"Don't tell me I have to share my time here with him?" William interjected furiously, standing up.

"At the moment, yes. There is resolution. Sam knows it already. And you, William, you need to know in order to find eternal peace."

"Knowing he is dead gives me some peace; but not knowing how he got away with it." Then turning to Sam added. "I hope you died painfully. Excruciating, agonising pain and it took a long..."

"William, I think you need to hold that thought a little longer. Look." Geoff pointed to the lab door, where the two uniformed police officers and a plainclothes female detective were standing, waiting.

* * * *

"Talk about the run around. They'd better be here, if not we'll have to put out a call. I can't believe someone can get away with this for so long."

"Well, Rob, some people are lucky that way, but at least we catch up with them eventually."

The door slowly opened as DSI Wells went to knock harder.

Mike stood at the door, his face pale and drawn.

Chapter 167

2002 August
Mike's Lab

Inside

"A twin brother. I can't believe it. He never mentioned it." Mike flopped down on a stool.

"He had mentioned he felt like he should have had a brother, although he never did anything about it. He turned up at the funeral. They had a sister too, however she died young according to Nicholas." Margaret wiped her eyes as another tear formed.

"That's a bugger isn't it, all that time and, too late. Does he look like him?"

"Not far off. It is uncanny, the resemblance. I miss him, Mike, I never believed I could miss anyone so much." She started to cry.

Mike put his arm around her.

"How are things with you and Pablo?"

"Good. I just had a few things to do back here; some more stuff to pack up ready to take with me. Our new villa will be finished by November – you'll have to come and stay."

Margaret blew her nose. "I'd like that."

"Are you going to stay in contact with Nicholas?"

"I doubt it, there seems little point ... "

Pounding from the outside main door interrupted her.

"That's probably my step-dad. He wants to sell these barns and for us to clear out."

"Had to happen sometime."

There was more pounding and a raised voice.

"All right, all right."

★ ★ ★ ★

"Is Mrs Talbot here?" DSI Wells looked past Mike.

"What's this concerning?" Mike defended the doorway. "She's very upset at the moment. Can't it wait?"

"No, it can't. If she is here, then I suggest you let us in, or we will arrest you for aiding and abetting a murderer."

"What, and what?" Mike recoiled releasing his firm grip on the door. DSI Wells didn't answer, only stared belligerently at him. Mike conceded.

"Thank you."

Inside, Margaret was sitting on a stool, a tissue in her hands, her eyes raw from tears. She looked up at DSI Wells, her eyes seemingly questioning.

"Mrs Talbot?" Margaret nodded, then she saw the two uniformed officers followed by Mike. "Mrs Talbot you are under arrest for the murder of twenty-three people. Anything ... " Wells started to reel off the caution as the two officers handcuffed her.

Mike stammered as shock took hold. Finally he found his voice.

"I don't understand. Why are you arresting Margaret?" Mike protested, stunned; then, realising exactly which murders Wells was referring to, continued, "You tried to pin this onto Sam, her husband. Now you're trying to pin this on Margaret. Sam's been dead a month."

Wells stood eying Mike carefully. "You're not involved as well are you? Is there something we don't know?"

Mike stumbled backwards as the implication hit him.

"Murder? No, and neither is Margaret. Are you Margaret?" His eyes pleaded with Margaret for confirmation of her innocence; yet there was nothing – only a steel grey coldness, which was emphasised by the red rawness. "Margaret?"

Margaret said nothing as she was marched out, leaving Mike still struggling to comprehend what was going on.

"You never really know who your friends are. Don't leave the country; we may want to question you at some point." Wells said before she left.

Mike looked around the empty lab, gripped by a strange numbness before his legs went weak, sending him sinking to the floor in dismay.

* * * *

Sam sank down onto his knees as the final resolution, the final confirmation bit in; his whole life's worth of memories somersaulting in his mind. Recognising her in the lock-up, he had hoped it was a sick joke, a trick of the light. He even wished it *had* been him and not his wife of forty years; it would have explained the fugue states. Deceiving him all that time! How gullible had he been? She had stood by him when he had been accused; protesting his innocence, knowing it to be the truth – because she had been the guilty one.

A sudden thought exploded in Sam's head, a thunderbolt of anger and rage, something that hadn't even occurred to him. "You killed our son!" He ran after the police car as it drove off, the pain of all the victim's souls biting like razor sharp teeth. He wanted to confront her, needed to confront her.

William looked on in astonishment. "I don't understand."

"You were so close to the truth throughout your career but, there was just one piece missing and that was the final one. It was Sam's wife who was the murderer."

"How? Nothing ever came back to her. Ever! I looked into her."

"No, not until a few months ago when there was a fire at a storage yard that she'd used for nearly forty years. Some people are very clever; you have to be to get away with murder for forty years."

William felt deflated; regretting his single mindedness in believing it was Sam all along. Blinkered. "How stupid? All my years on the force; I should have seen it."

"Why? You were only human. You did a lot of good in your life. Let it go."

Chapter 168

2002 August

Lincolnshire
Police Station

A sullen looking Margaret sat resolutely facing the stone wall, her hands resting on the table. A PC stood guarding the door.

Sam watched, looking at her as though she were a stranger. He'd listened to the first interview, which had lasted a few minutes, as she had sat stoically, answering questions without giving anything away.

"You bloody heartless cow!" Sam exploded. "How could you do those things? You're an ... How could I have ever loved you?" Sam couldn't comprehend the real rage he felt in every fibre, every thought and emotion of what he wanted to say. The betrayal. The hurt. Their son. His son! The souls of the victims spiked in him and, finally, with every ounce of strength he could muster, he swung at Margaret.

She smarted, as a sharp searing pain appeared to shoot through her.

The officer guarding the door didn't even flinch, appearing emotionless towards her.

"That's good, Sam." Geoff said, his voice warm, hinting at sympathy, "That's your vocation in this semester of death, to torture her the way she tortured you, by letting you take the blame all the time knowing the truth."

"Shut up!" Sam spat, feeling vengeance rise like a cobra ready to pounce. He swung again, and again, in quick succession, exuberant valiant attempts to do her physical damage; years of love and trust turning to distaste and hatred in an instant.

Margaret flinched, again and again, as each intense static charge of a tethered soul touched her; every sinuous fibre of her being seemingly coming alive with electric shocks. She started to jerk, her eyes darting around the room like crazed bees spinning inside her head. She almost fell off her chair.

The PC guarding her started to take an interest; visibly shivering as the room temperature dropped a few degrees. Coldly he asked, "Are you alright? Do you need to see a doctor?"

Sam stopped swinging at her.

* * * *

Margaret stared coldly at the officer.

"No, I don't ..."

Suddenly the thought of Edward's death – that fateful night – caught her. The mother and son bond had grabbed her, shaken her steadfast career minded attitude. That night had tested any resolve she'd had, forcing her to run when she had wanted to stay.

Part of her despised Sam's mourning for their son, because she would never have felt that way if she'd never got pregnant; a choice that was taken away from her by fate and failure of the contraception. Love for Edward had grown, though, and she'd seen in him a chance to carry on the research when he was old enough, with a little guidance.

It still had not been explained what evidence they had against her, although the questioning had been methodical and laborious like they were fishing, even though they said they knew. She'd remained resolutely silent when arrested, almost accepting her fate with grace.

* * * *

Sam watched his wife, his despised spouse, sitting as if waiting for a meal to be brought in. He had managed to lose some of his anger, although he could feel that more was still to come. He still couldn't quite fathom how he had never known that she had a double life and felt foolish for trusting her so implicitly.

Sam watched William pace the room, his earthly image slowly dissipating yet clinging on as if wanting more. Maybe he wanted to know how, and why?

As if hearing Sam's thoughts Geoff approached William. "The killer has been caught, and your life of servitude has been blessed. You have left a great legacy behind you, one that your grandkids will be proud of for a long time to come, and one that your wife, Fiona, has been proud of her whole life. She has more time on this earth still to go." Then more consolingly, "She will join you ... eventually, and until then you can watch over her."

"But why didn't I ever see it? We were so close. How could we not connect the pieces?" Williams' forehead creased in a frown.

"Because you didn't have all the pieces." Geoff replied, but William was already fading from view.

* * * *

The interview room door opened and in walked a woman, wearing a grey trouser suit and a crisp white blouse. Her deep-set eyes and pinched angular nose gave her face a stern, narrow appearance. She was followed by a sturdy looking man, whose receding hair still showed the odd vibrant flame of red; his stomach oozing over the top of his trousers like surf was up.

The interview started unceremoniously, the tape machine switched on.

"DSI Wells and DC Langston present. Time is now 14:23. Mrs Talbot, is there anything you wish to add to your previous interview? Are you still refusing to have counsel here?"

Margaret sat stock-still. Sam felt the anger boil up again inside.

"Tell them. Tell them everything," he added spitefully, "you heartless bitch!"

The rage was a cataclysm of lava and he reached out to strangle her, to squeeze every morsel of unrepentant stoicism out of her. He couldn't fight his own deafening hatred for her, the woman he had loved all his whole life, a love that had never faltered with an unerring sense of belonging together.

"I make this promise to you, I will do everything in my power to make the rest of your life a misery." His eyes filled with tears as he tried to rein in the choke hold he had on his wife, although he was not actually, physically touching her.

"Mrs Talbot? Mrs Talbot?" DSI Wells looked panicked seeing Margaret convulsing as though an electric current was coursing through her.

Langston ran to the door. "Call an ambulance," he commanded the officer who was standing on duty outside. Footsteps echoed down the corridor.

* * * *

"Mrs Talbot?" Wells was filled with fear. She couldn't have another one die in the station! It was only two years since the last one; it didn't matter that it had been a drug dealer who had swallowed his own stash, whilst unattended, to avoid getting caught – the baggy bursting.

"SAMANTHA!" Wells shouted desperately.

Suddenly Margaret's eyes were sharp as razors. "My name is Margaret." She gargled, but it was only for an instant.

* * * *

Geoff placed a reassuring arm on Sam's shoulder.

"You kill her now and she will not suffer. She will not have to answer to the families. Her time is not now, she must pay and that is your journey to take."

Sam half listened, letting the rage subside slowly, replaced by a sea of tranquillity that nestled like a far off memory of a sun drenched beach where they had once holidayed; the late evening setting sun warming their slightly bronzed skin that glowed a radiant heat and ignited a passion. Recklessly, they'd caressed each other's bodies from the seclusion of their beachfront hut, a romantic reminder of the good times that juxtaposed the revelation Sam had witnessed in his death. The truth that the fugue states had merely played a part of an intricate web of deceit by the one person whom he'd loved wholeheartedly his whole life.

* * * *

Wells looked at Margaret; she saw the cool burning intelligence that rallied underneath the calm exterior. Wells was not afraid of anyone. She was not going to let some trumped up woman get the better of her.

"Cancel the ambulance, David. I think this one is just being feisty. I think we can ..." Suddenly she realised the tape was still running. "Interview suspended 14:54."

Chapter 169

2002 August

Lincolnshire
Police Station

The interview room had been quiet for an hour. The officer was back guarding Margaret. Geoff was striding the room like an expectant father whereas Sam was struggling with regret for attacking his own wife, even though she deserved it ... and more. Geoff consoled him that it all was as it should be.

Wells had insisted that they get Margaret checked out before continuing, delaying their questioning, yet satisfying a need to comply with new strict guidelines regarding prisoners' 'well-being'.

"Interview reconvened at 19:23. Suspect still declines counsel. Samantha, do you want to tell us what you have been up to for the past forty years?"

Margaret sat complacently staring at a point beyond her interrogators.

"My name is Margaret, and not Maggie, or any other derivative. I hate the name Samantha." The venom with which she spoke shook Sam.

"Very well, Margaret." Langston said. "Would you like to tell us what you've been up to ...?"

"Nothing that you would understand." She replied, looking almost demure.

Wells and Langston shared a look of knowing, as the sudden change in personality was something they were used to with criminals, especially when they knew their time was up: the fight wouldn't quite let go and every now and then it would rear its ugly head.

"I see," Wells added with a conciliatory smile. "Well, that's not the case according to the evidence we've found."

"Really? I think you'll find that will be my husband you're after. He died last month, in that accident on the M1. I seem to remember a detective," She paused as if thinking, "Travent, no, Travis, Detective Travis could not find the evidence to convict him then, either. Is this how it is? My husband is dead and you are now going to try and pin the murders on me. You'll be sorely disappointed when I bring an harassment charge against you." Margaret felt sure there was no evidence linking her to the crimes.

* * * *

"You, you ..." Sam lunged at her, immediately passing through her physical body and landing in a heap on the floor. As he did, she briefly convulsed again, her eyes widening instantly in terror. Margaret looked around the room, bemused.

Wells, believing it to be an act, continued. "For the record, Mrs Talbot has exhibited some kind of convulsion, mini fit, similar to earlier. Dr Benzie has checked her out prior to resuming this interview and confirmed nothing is physically wrong. Are you all right Margaret? Are you on any medication? Do you need to see a doctor?"

"No, she doesn't need to see a doctor." Sam shouted angrily punching her again, his mind in turmoil with the deceit: each burning soul of her victims punctuating her body with every punch, feeling every fibre of their pain. She shook violently.

"Feel that." Sam uttered menacingly. "You deserve it. For everything you ever did to those people. And our son!"

"Sssssssaammm." She responded through the intensity of the pain.

Sam pulled back, aghast, looking to Geoff for an answer; he shrugged his shoulders. "It's not my destiny. Things work differently for everyone."

Sam plunged his hand deep inside Margaret. "Can you hear me, Margaret?"

Margaret convulsed with pain as Wells and Langston looked on bewildered, and a little concerned. Suddenly she jolted, kicking the table although it remained firmly bolted to the floor.

"Get that ambulance. I think she is going for insanity. Is that what you are going for, Mrs Talbot?"

"Okay." Langston responded, although transfixed by the strange behaviour.

"Go away, Sam, you're dead." Spittle trickled from the corner of Margaret's lips. She looked a stranger to him.

"Can you feel their pain? The pain of the souls of the people you killed; the pain that I have had to suffer in my death? These should be yours."

"They were a necessary means for our research, the group, we all benefitted." Margaret spluttered out, every part of her jerking ferociously.

Wells looked on, amazed by the sudden admission, checking to see if the tape was still running; it was.

"Our little club was getting nowhere, I just tried that little bit harder. It was needed. Where do you think some of the body parts came from?"

Wells couldn't believe that the confession was so easily forthcoming, after such a denial; it was all they needed. She could see Margaret suffering.

"Margaret!" Wells shouted vying for her attention. "Mrs Talbot, you're not fooling anyone. This insanity will not help you in court." Wells was losing the forcefulness of her voice as Margaret fell off her chair as if having an epileptic fit.

Geoff watched Sam as he prodded Margaret, letting her feel the full force of the souls of the dead, their pain amplified in her living body. Even with the pain, she showed little remorse in her words.

"You said they were old cadavers from your MOD research" Sam responded harshly.

Margaret's eyes were becoming blood shot; her head had already hit the cold, hard concrete floor a couple of times, and there was a spot of blood visible. Sam looked up to see panic on Wells' face as she rushed round and tried to put her hands under Margaret's head to protect it.

"Where's that's ambulance?" She shouted through the open door.

Wells jerked her hands away sharply as a static shock of pain passed to her, visibly frightening her. Losing her footing she stumbled backwards into the wall, coming to rest on her backside, looking on curiously.

"Ambulance is on its…" Langston strode into the room. "What is it?"

"I have no idea, never seen anything like it." She pulled herself up. "I think she's talking to her dead husband!"

Sam relinquished his attack on Margaret as a happy memory prodded him. She stopped jerking.

The cold interview room settled into a sombre calm, all persons – both living and dead – reflecting on what was taking place.

Chapter 170

2002 September

Fakenham
Roger and Sarah's House

"Well, I never saw that coming?" Mike sounded flabbergasted.

"But why?" Sarah enquired, still unsure it was real. Margaret, a murderer? The news was full of it.

"I reckon they were both in on it. There is no way Sam didn't know about it. I suppose those business trips along with Margaret's conferences and courses all helped cover it up." Roger concluded.

"That's a bit harsh." Mike defended.

"No, I don't think it is. What effect will this have on us? My work might get scrutinized even further, on top of that harassment case; this will ruin my reputation. They may try to drag us in to the melée of crap that is going to float around them. Associated with serial killers! How about the body parts she brought in?" Roger looked at each in turn. "We need to seek legal help to avoid being arrested with her."

"Hold on, Roger, these are our friends?" Sarah tried to sound forceful.

"Not mine. If this has repercussions for me, I will not be happy. I have worked bloody hard to get where I am."

"You're an arsehole Roger." Mikes words were meant to be insulting yet, inside he had to concede that being deceived hurt. Was his beloved Sam involved? The two people probably closest to him, his best friends, and they had betrayed him. He couldn't quite believe it, or didn't want to.

Sarah sat confused, looking at both Roger and Mike; indecisive about where her loyalty lay. Margaret had always been there for her. Inside she resolved to go and see Margaret, but then why should she? If it was true!

"I think I'd better go." Mike stood up.

"Yes. Probably best," Roger added coldly.

"Bye, Sarah."

Lost in thought, she took a few seconds before she answered. "Yes. Sorry, I'll see you out."

Roger switched on the TV and left them to it.

"I'm going to see her. Do you want to come?" Mike offered at the door. "I almost want to hear it from the horses' mouth."

Sarah looked daunted and visibly shaken. "I'd like to. Not sure Roger will allow me. This whole thing has made him so angry, and he is right, we might get arrested and then his position at the hospital and on the board will be in jeopardy; he can kiss goodbye to Australia. What about our children?"

Mike sighed. "I do understand, kind of, but I can't leave it like this. They are, were … my best friends. Well, Sam was. I so want to speak to him right now."

They stood looking at each other for a minute.

"I'll let you know when I have arranged it, if you wanna come along, then fine."

She nodded and closed the door as Mike walked away. Turning to face the grand staircase of their Georgian terraced house, she looked up to the ceiling three floors above, as if wanting a sign, a sign that it was all wrong. Emotionally overwhelmed, she felt only hatred for the life she'd chosen; a Doctors' wife, giving up her own career to be manacled to the house, keeping it immaculate to impress guests that Roger loved to entertain. Her life seemed empty. She thought of Margaret, not afraid to pursue something, even it was wrong: it was bittersweet. She thought of Sam and what he would have made of it all. As tears started to well, Amy, her first grandchild, came running down the stairs.

"Nanny, nanny," she sang excitedly.

"Walk! Don't run down the stairs." Motherly instinct kicked in.

* * * *

"Jesus, Sammy, what the hell have you got us into?" Mike asked of the night sky, feeling alone for the first time in a long while. He dialled Pablo's number, but it just rang and rang.

Chapter 171

2002 November
Hospital – Psychiatric Ward

"Is she getting any better?" Wells asked.

"I'm afraid not. The pain appears to be more intense, it's definitely physical," the middle aged doctor looked bemused, "although we cannot find anything wrong with her, physically, that is. It's like someone receiving electric shocks; that is the closest analogy I have. She talks to her late husband you know? That could just be guilt of course." Dr Lolita was looking for confirmation. Wells nodded. "Not all the time, but when she fits – a term I use loosely as I would not classify them as such in the strictest sense. More episodes."

Now the question Wells was dreading the answer to. "Is she going to be able to stand trial?"

Dr Lolita sighed heavily, as if he were a builder appraising a job. "I can only recommend. I will advise the court my findings accordingly." Wells felt her impatience rising. They finally had the serial killer but it was debateable whether she would stand trial for her crimes.

"What will that be?" Wells asked reluctantly, thinking she knew the answer already, although still waiting for this giant of a man to give her a straight answer.

"Well," he took another deep breath placing his long hands in his pockets. "Apart from the obvious eccentric behaviour that she shows, she knows full well what's going on around her. Ask her a question; she will answer without fault or hesitation. A strange case indeed, most fascinating. I only wish I could get to the bottom of it. The shocks that she exhibits have no physical form. Scans, tests, everything we have tried, have all come back negative. I have ruled out epilepsy of any form."

Their attention was taken by a loud shout from Margaret's room.

"Leave me alone! You're dead! Why are you here?"

* * * *

"Because of you. I'm here to make sure you pay. You made me think I was going mad. I will leave when you get what you deserve." Sam's voice was calm now, he had been tempted to pass on all the souls at once, yet Geoff had advised him that maybe he wanted to draw out the punishment; meter out the most justice. Whatever, he needed her to stand trial, so the victims' families could finally have closure. He had refrained during tests, just so she could be declared sane.

"It was all for medical science; you did it yourself."

"I didn't take human life; only cadavers. You use it like a justification."

"There has to be sacrifices, medical research requires sacrifices."

"They were wilful sacrifices. People who donated their bodies to human science, or volunteers for drug test schemes. Not forcibly taken against their will. Taken from their families."

"Not all experiments and answers can be garnered after death; the experiment needs to start during life, at the instant before death occurs. How else can we completely understand what happens: how bodies can be preserved, how to circumvent death, or even illnesses?" Sam didn't take great joy in torturing his wife anymore, just felt compelled to do so; retribution on her victims behalf. The strangest thing was a part of him still loved her, loved deeply the person he had first known, had fallen in love with. He hoped his servitude would be up soon so he could fade into oblivion, putting this weary world fully behind him.

There had been twenty-three victims in total and, with Geoff's teaching, he'd learnt that he could release each soul in part, or in full, slowly or quickly.

* * * *

"See what I mean Detective? Her comments sound like one half of a conversation, a rational conversation, not a psychotic one, or even a drug-induced rant. I'm sure her defence will try to avoid her taking the stand but, in all honesty, I don't see why she shouldn't."

"Thank you, Doctor. You've been very helpful."

Wells left, feeling a little lighter.

Chapter 172

2003 February
Norwich
Court Holding Cells

The trial came quickly. Margaret stood, emotionless in the witness box, answering questions, stoically, as if following instructions. Sam stood to one side, listening, as the answers rolled out, holding back the temptation to inflict pain, knowing the time was getting close when he could close this chapter of his death and move on; his service finished. It couldn't come quickly enough for him; his feelings for her leapt from love to loathing as she uttered each syllable, then back to love as fond memories melded with the hurt.

Press coverage was wide with the gallery bustling with reporters; it fuelled the public contempt for her.

The jury took less than three hours to agree unanimously that the modern science of DNA which they had got from the notebooks, along with video surveillance was damning.

Roger, Mike and Sarah had narrowly avoided any charges as the prosecution declared they had been unwittingly involved, without their knowledge, and they'd co-operated fully with the investigation.

-

Margaret was sentenced to twenty-three life sentences to run concurrently. Standing in her cell, awaiting transfer, Sam let the remnants of the remaining soul's course into her; as the last soul travelled into her he watched the pain intensify to a crescendo knowing that it would never die, would never let up; there was no 'off' switch. A perpetual agony for her to reside in, until her time ended – maybe beyond!

Sam felt a great sadness weigh him down as the end of his journey beckoned; the betrayal brought stinging tears.

The cell and Margaret faded from view and a gradual tranquillity took over before a strange loneliness swamped him. An echo broke his thoughts. It was distant; yet all around him.

"Daddy," the cheerful voice called sweetly.
Sam felt a hand slip into his and he looked down.
"Edward?"

THE END

Palbable sense of
power!

God complex?

Bringing organe to the
group - mike

Toppest - Rodger

didn't have an endless
supply of money escape
mike

Sam always believed
he'd led a good life
p220.

Price

William Wains

Ren

Mark

DSr Chappell (Ron)

Fiona Benza

Harriet Davis

Chapter 37
Sam / Ben Chomer
Yard ~~Northampton~~ Lincs.

Fame plants?

Sam has 1st Car
accident 66 - memory
loss

Mikes lab

Not Roger, he wants to
do it to prolong people
until cures can be
found or surgical advancements
growing limbs